Courting Elizabeth

Renata McMann
&
Summer Hanford

Acknowledgment

With special thanks to our editor, Joanne Girard

Cover by Summer Hanford

By Renata McMann and Summer Hanford
The Second Mrs. Darcy
Georgiana's Folly (The Wickham Coin Book I)
Elizabeth's Plight (The Wickham Coin Book II)
The above two books have been published in a single volume as:
Georgiana's Folly & Elizabeth's Plight: Wickham Coin Series, Volumes I & II
The Scandalous Stepmother
Poor Mr. Darcy
A Death at Rosings
Entanglements of Honor
From Ashes to Heiresses
The above two stories have been published in a single print volume as:
Entanglements of Honor with From Ashes to Heiresses
The Fire at Netherfield Park
Caroline and the Footman
Mr. Collins' Deception
Mary Younge
Lady Catherine Regrets
The above four stories (and two additional stories) are collected in:
Pride and Prejudice Villains Revisited – Redeemed – Reimagined A Collection of Six Short Stories

Books by Renata McMann writing as Teresa McCullough

Enhancer Novels: Stand-alone novels in the same universe
Enhancers Campaign
The First Enhancer
The Pirates of Fainting Goat Island
The Enhancer with Meg Baxter

Bengt/Tian stories:
The Secret of Sanctua A Bengt/Tian novel
Kidnapped by Fae: a Bengt/Tian Short Story

Other stories:
The Slave of Duty with Meg Baxter
Lost Past

Thrice Born Series by Summer Hanford

Thrice Born Novels:
Gift of the Aluien
Hawks of Sorga
Throne of Wheylia
The Plains of Tybrunn
Coming in 2017 - *Shores of K'Orge*

Companion Short Stories:
The Forging of Cadwel
Hawk Trials for Mirimel
The Fall of Larkesong
The Sword of Three

Table of Contents

KENT

Elizabeth woke with her mind full of Mr. Darcy's unexpected proposal.

1

Darcy set aside his pen. He flattened his hand alongside the word-covered sheets resting on the mahogany desk, surprised at the stiffness in his fingers. He, a man often deemed terse, had filled the pages. It seemed, for once, he had much to say.

Was it too much? He looked down at the letter he'd written Elizabeth, his rejoinder to her startling rejection of his proposal. Jumbled candlelight made the words seem almost to move, alive on the page. Now that Darcy had it all down, he was unsure he shouldn't simply burn it.

He'd begun, he knew, in anger. Why shouldn't he have? She'd pricked him, heart and pride, her rejection made all the more painful by its inconceivableness. A woman of her means, rejecting him? It was unprecedented, surely.

He'd never before put forth his heart in such a manner. He wouldn't have done so that afternoon if he'd any inkling she would decline him. Now, he must bear this bitter weight pressing down on his chest. Bear it and give no indication of it, for a man did not reveal such sentiments and a Darcy of Pemberley certainly did not acknowledge how sorely it hurt to be rebuked by such a low person as Miss Elizabeth Bennet.

Darcy leaned back in his chair. So why, then, had he permitted himself to write the letter? He reached for it, thinking to crumple it. He knew the secrets it revealed better belonged to the flames in the hearth than in Elizabeth's hands.

With a sigh, Darcy returned his hand to the desktop, leaving the pages untouched. He wrote to her out of hope, and he couldn't persuade himself to lightly abandon it. A small, lingering sliver of that cursed emotion whispered that if he could set right her misconceptions about him, he could still win her. He knew after her vehement rejection it sullied him to curry her favor, but he couldn't deny himself the painful boon of a second chance.

Yet, the secrets contained within those neat lines weren't his alone, and the emotions portrayed, for all his careful wording, were too raw. Darcy shook his head. He needed to walk, to think. He couldn't deliver the letter now, in the dark of night. He would employ the time he had to decide between delivering it to Elizabeth or to the flames.

Pushing back his chair, he stood. Taking his coat for warmth, not for appearances, as all had retired for the evening, he left his room. He caught a glimpse of a skirt disappearing around the corner ahead but, sparing little thought to whatever servant had been scurrying about, he made his way outside. For long hours, Darcy paced in the moonlit garden, Elizabeth's words and visage his lone companions.

Finally, resolved, Darcy retraced his steps. He would give the letter to Elizabeth. There was no shame in further revealing himself to her. He'd already been laid bare. As for the secrets contained therein, though she'd hurt him, he still deemed her trustworthy. He'd seal the letter tonight, and tomorrow would see it in her hands.

Darcy entered his room and crossed to the desk, but the letter was gone.

***

Elizabeth woke with her mind full of Mr. Darcy's unexpected proposal. She lay abed, unsure what to do. Her eyes traced the sloped ceiling of her guest room in her dear friend Charlotte Collins' new home, a parsonage in Kent. Elizabeth took in the austere curtains muting the morning sun, likely selected not by her hostess but by Lady Catherine, patroness to the parsonage. Trailing her fingers over the tightly woven fabric of the coverlet, Elizabeth frowned.

Somehow, in the wake of Mr. Darcy's words, everything seemed changed. Though nothing was truly different, Elizabeth felt as if something ought to be. To see Mr. Darcy, a man so sure in his ways and so indifferent to her charms, proclaim love for her . . . it seemed to shake the foundation of how the world was ordered.

Knowing she would soon be sought out if she failed to appear, Elizabeth roused herself. With as much normalcy as she could muster, she readied for the day, though Mr. Darcy's words continued to spiral through her thoughts. She was still unable to banish them as she reached the parlor to join her host, hostess, and Maria Lucas for breakfast.

"Elizabeth," Charlotte greeted, smiling. "You are later than usual. I trust you slept well?"

"Tolerably well, thank you." How much easier Charlotte's question than Mr. Darcy's, yet mustering a reply seemed effortful. Elizabeth turned toward the sideboard, hoping the back she presented would discourage further discourse. She reached for a plate, though none of the offerings appealed to her.

"Cousin Elizabeth, I have been informed Mr. Darcy called on you yesterday afternoon." Mr. Collins' whining tone cut through the silence. "I am sure you were honored. You must consider any attention from a relative of Lady Catherine's to be of the best sort and a compliment you can hardly presume yourself worthy of, and of course for Mr. Darcy to pay a call, why, that's nearly as great an honor as if Lady Catherine herself had come. You must tell me how he was, and each word that passed between you. I am sure her ladyship will want a full report of her nephew's doings, so she may properly praise and guide him. Come, select something, for all of it is good, and sit beside me and relate every detail."

"Mr. Collins, she's only just come in. Do recall Elizabeth wasn't feeling quite herself yesterday." Charlotte's tone was one of mild reprimand. "Elizabeth, are you feeling well now?"

Returning her plate to the stack, Elizabeth turned to face them. Mr. and Mrs. Collins appeared composed, but Maria Lucas's wide eyes indicated Elizabeth wasn't projecting the vision of normalcy she wished to. She smoothed her palms along her skirt. "In truth, I'm not feeling quite well."

"We shall go to Lady Catherine, then," Mr. Collins said. "She will know what ails you and what best to do. She is a font of wisdom on all things."

"I should think I might be the best judge of what ails me, sir." Elizabeth worked to contain her ire. "As such, I also feel myself ready to point to a cure, and that treatment is a walk. I shall take it now, finding myself with little appetite."

Charlotte and Maria regarded her with matching eyes and mirrored concern.

"A walk is just the thing for a poor appetite," Mr. Collins said. "Lady Catherine has advised as much on many occasions. I would never presume to speak for her ladyship, but I can put forth that she would approve of your course, cousin."

"Thank you," Elizabeth said, taking his words as a chance to hurry away.

Her host began speaking again, but she lengthened her stride, all but fleeing the parsonage. In truth, she hadn't fabricated. She had little appetite, her stomach twisting along with her thoughts as she replayed Mr. Darcy's hurtful words and her too-angry reply. Along with her appetite had fled her patience and she knew she couldn't endure a meal spent in her cousin's company. Even Charlotte, whose friendship she had long cherished, today seemed but an unwelcome intruder into Elizabeth's turmoil.

As she walked, Elizabeth soon realized her disquiet was as much from the cruel nature of Mr. Darcy's proposal as with herself. She'd permitted her temper to run free, a shameful act under any circumstance, but especially in reaction to Mr. Darcy proffering his heart. Elizabeth did not like to think herself cruel, but she had been. She could defend herself by enumerating the ways her feelings had been attacked, but that wasn't a worthy reason not to have spared his. Men's feelings, so seldom acknowledged or shared, were delicate things. She should have taken more care.

Elizabeth looked about, surveying the bright greens and blues of the world, sunlit and cheerful, in spite of her woes. It was, she admitted, in the nature of an extreme complement that Mr. Darcy had proposed. This was especially in view of how offensive he apparently found her standing and her family. In truth, he'd sounded almost as if he'd rather be forced from England than bind himself to her in any way, yet he'd offered for her all the same. She smiled slightly, beginning to see the amusement in what he'd done. The grand Mr. Darcy of Pemberley had figuratively bent his knee to so much of what he loathed in the world, all for the illusion of love.

For an illusion it must be. Elizabeth could never bring herself to see true love where only one side was engaged. Furthermore, how could it possibly be such a pure emotion as love, when he knew her so little as to think the words he'd used would stir her? Just as with her cousin Mr. Collins, whose proposal she'd rejected politely, Mr. Darcy's proposal had pertained more to himself and his view of the world than to her. As such, she could easily be substituted, his affections directed toward another woman. Hopefully, for Mr. Darcy's sake, one with better connections and more greed, to ensure her acceptance of his offer.

"Miss Bennet," a woman's voice called.

As if the words drew Elizabeth's senses back from her musings, she became aware of the sound of an approaching vehicle and horses. She turned, squinting into the slanting morning light. The air about her teemed with the clicks, chirps and buzzes of nature, and through them approached a low phaeton. It trundled down the wide path at moderate speed, coming ever more near.

To Elizabeth's surprise, it appeared as if Miss Anne de Bourgh, daughter to Lady Catherine and cousin to Mr. Darcy, manned the phaeton and owned the voice. In an additional oddity, Miss de Bourgh wasn't accompanied by her companion, Mrs. Jenkinson. Rather, a young woman in a maid's uniform sat beside her. She was crowded against the side of the carriage, giving Miss de Bourgh's slight frame more than half of the seat.

"Miss Bennet," Miss de Bourgh repeated as she drew the vehicle to a halt beside Elizabeth. "I would like to speak with you. Will you come up and ride with me?"

Elizabeth hesitated. It hardly seemed possible Miss de Bourgh had stumbled upon her accidentally. Elizabeth worried a turn in the phaeton would mean listening to talk of Mr. Darcy, for what other topic did she and Miss de Bourgh hold in common? Elizabeth wasn't sure she wished a conversation about him, whether he'd confided his failure to his cousin or not.

"Please. It's important." Miss de Bourgh's tone was imploring, her narrow face betraying worry.

Elizabeth saw no easy way to put off those words, or that look. "Then I will ride with you."

At a nod from Miss de Bourgh, the maid climbed out, allowing Elizabeth to get in. Miss de Bourgh turned to the maid. "Wait here. Go over in the shade of those trees if you grow too warm. I will return for you."

"Yes, miss," the maid said, heading for the indicated cluster of elms without looking back.

Miss de Bourgh flicked the reins with a more practiced hand than Elizabeth would have credited to her. The team, a matched set of smart looking chestnut mares, stepped out at a slow trot. For a moment, there was only the steady thrum of insects, punctuated by the jangle of tack, the creak of springs and the horses' steady hoof beats.

Miss de Bourgh cast a quick look toward Elizabeth, then cleared her throat. "I'm afraid I must speak to you on a topic that is of a somewhat sensitive nature, Miss Elizabeth."

Elizabeth nodded. "I suspected as much."

"There was an . . . incident, shall we say, last night at Rosings."

"I am sorry to hear that. I hope all is well now?"

"That remains to be seen." Miss de Bourgh pursed her thin lips, her eyes forward. "It seems Darcy was up quite late, writing a letter."

Elizabeth frowned. Mr. Darcy's writing habits were an unexpected topic. "Oh?"

"It also seems Darcy left the letter and took a walk in the gardens. I believe he was gone for some time, though I don't know when he returned. I also surmise the walk was in an effort to settle his thoughts, which seem to have been quite agitated, but I suppose you must guess that."

"Indeed I must not." Now they were coming to topics Elizabeth wished to avoid. "It is not my place to make suppositions on Mr. Darcy's state."

"But it might have been."

Though Miss de Bourgh's statement seemed to confirm she knew of Mr. Darcy's proposal, Elizabeth saw no reason to issue a response to what hadn't been a question.

"While Darcy was out, my mother entered his room." Miss de Bourgh sighed. "She considers it her right, perhaps even a duty, to know what takes place under her roof. She was curious why Darcy was up so late. As she seems to have no compunctions, Mother took Darcy's letter and read it."

Elizabeth couldn't contain a small gasp at that. Even for Lady Catherine, it seemed highhanded. Entering Mr. Darcy's room at all was not in keeping with good behavior, but to take his private correspondence and read it was disreputable.

"The letter put her into such a state, she came with immediacy to my room, insisting I rise from bed to read it."

"And you did so?" Elizabeth knew her voice betrayed her condemnation, but didn't care. The act was deserving of such.

"In my defense, I was roused from sleep, candles lit, and the letter thrust into my hands before I realized whose letter it was or that my mother must have taken it without permission." Miss de Bourgh cast Elizabeth another sideways glance, a wry smile curving her lips. "I will not pretend that I didn't quickly comprehend what my mother had done, or that I suffered much in the way of qualms. The letter was already taken. My mother had read it. I was curious."

"I still fail to see why you wish my conversation, Miss de Bourgh. If you're looking for absolution, I am not the one to seek it from, nor inclined to grant it."

"The letter was to you, Miss Elizabeth. My mother and I both know Darcy proposed to you, and that you refused him, among other things contained therein."

Elizabeth felt her face heat. She was unsure which reigned, anger or mortification. "I see."

"No, you do not, but you soon shall."

Elizabeth shook her head. "You have come to remind me you and Mr. Darcy have an agreement of sorts, to warn me off. You need not fear. I do not believe he shall ask me again, and I remain firm in my intention not to accept."

"No. To remind you of my mother's hopes for us is not why I've come. I'm here to give you Darcy's letter, as he surely intended you to have it when he wrote it."

"You have it?" Elizabeth was further horrified.

Miss de Bourgh nodded. "My mother believes I burned it. Myself between her and my desk, I substituted a letter I'd written with Darcy's. I then proclaimed we didn't have a right to read his and, in a great show, crumpled the pages and threw them on the fire."

"But, then, Mr. Darcy must know his letter was taken." Elizabeth was baffled. "Why would you not simply return his letter, hiding the entire incident? Surely, Mr. Darcy must be angry."

"Quite," Miss de Bourgh said. "He and Mother had a terrible row over it this morning."

"I'm sorry to hear that, but if you are not here to assure yourself I have no intentions toward Mr. Darcy, I am still confused as to why we are speaking of what, to me, seems to be a matter for family, regardless of who Mr. Darcy addressed the letter to." Elizabeth was growing a bit vexed with Miss de Bourgh's meandering line of conversation. She'd sought Elizabeth out, insisted on speaking, and asserted the importance of the matter. Having done such, Miss de Bourgh ought to convey what was in her mind.

"First, I would like you to read the letter." Pulling the horses to a walk, and moving both reins to her left hand, Miss de Bourgh pulled out several folded sheets, offering them to Elizabeth.

Elizabeth eyed them, sure they could contain nothing she wished to know. Did he rail against her? How could he not? With his pride, there was no chance the letter was placating, especially in view of the adamant nature of her refusal. Elizabeth felt her face heat as it occurred to her the letter might contain her ill-chosen words, one of the only signs she believed she'd ever given that her breeding might not be to his standards. Had Miss de Bourgh read that? The pages fluttered in Miss de Bourgh's hand, offering Elizabeth tantalizing glimpses of words. "I cannot accept a stolen letter and I doubt it contains anything I wish to know," she finally said.

Miss de Bourgh pressed the pages on Elizabeth, forcing her to take them or allow them to scatter to the wind. "You are correct in part. The beginning of the letter, you will not care for. The remainder, though, that you will want to read." She readjusted the reins, now that Elizabeth clutched the letter, and flicked them to increase their pace. "Incidentally, I can confirm Darcy's statements about the living Mr. Wickham was supposed to receive. The truth was well known by the man who actually received the living and by the people in the parish."

Elizabeth looked down at the pages, realizing she'd been snared by the mention of Mr. Wickham. She now wished to know what was contained in the letter. Besides, unlike the others who'd read it, she wouldn't be violating Mr. Darcy's trust. She was the intended recipient. Smoothing out the pages on her lap, Elizabeth began to read.

She soon realized Miss de Bourgh was not wrong in saying she wouldn't care for the beginning of the letter. In truth, it angered her. Mr. Darcy condemned Elizabeth's family. He went on to say that his objection to her family's behavior was one of the reasons he'd done his best to separate Elizabeth's sister Jane from the man she loved, Mr. Bingley. Mr. Darcy also stated that he did not think Jane loved Mr. Bingley at all. As if he, of all people, would possess the ability to understand Jane. Elizabeth was incensed by how much Mr. Darcy seemed to think of himself, and how much he took on.

She nearly stopped reading there. The gall of the man. To propose to her in so insulting a way, and then return to his room to write a letter adding further insult and maligning Jane. It was intolerable.

Still, she hadn't reached the part, alluded to by Miss de Bourgh, which pertained to Mr. Wickham. Steeling herself, Elizabeth read on. She'd begun the letter. She may as well witness the extent of his venom. Perhaps it would ease him to learn she had. Certainly, it was going a long way to salve her guilt over her harsh words.

The rest of the letter did not assuage her guilt, however, instead serving to increase it. She read of how Mr. Wickham had accepted three thousand pounds in lieu of the living he was willed. Worse, his tone honest and calm, Mr. Darcy described how Mr. Wickham had attempted to elope with Miss Darcy. Miss Darcy, a girl of only fifteen, had initially agreed to the elopement. Fortunately, when chance brought Mr. Darcy to visit her, she'd changed her mind and Mr. Wickham was sent on his way.

Elizabeth read the letter three times. Each time, the first part went by more fleetingly, having lost its sting. Though it pained her to acknowledge it, a modicum of her outrage was giving way to the nagging knowledge that at least some of his claims against her family held hints of validity.

The remainder of the letter, in opposite effect, grew in proportion. It became more clear with each reading how horribly she'd misjudged both Mr. Wickham and Mr. Darcy. Possessed of the truth, she could clearly see the holes in Mr. Wickham's tales, the gross inconsistencies in both word and behavior. She shook her head at how cleverly he'd misled her, while needing hardly to lie. Were she being frank with herself, Elizabeth could admit her gullibility and behavior concerning Mr. Wickham quite embarrassed her. Where had her mind and manners been?

Finally, Elizabeth folded the letter, tucking it away. She lifted her gaze to study the tree-lined track, her thoughts more turbulent even than when she'd woken that morning. Blinking several times, she looked about, realizing they were somewhere she'd never been before. She glanced back, wondering how far they'd come. Certainly, it would be a long walk back to the parsonage. She'd been so engrossed in Mr. Darcy's letter, she wasn't even sure if they'd taken any turns. "You said I must read the letter first, meaning you didn't ask me to ride with you for that alone."

"No, I didn't." Miss de Bourgh's words were quiet.

"I assume if I don't wish to walk a long distance back, I must listen to what you have to say." Elizabeth supposed it was only reasonable that Lady Catherine's daughter would have inherited some of her autocratic ways.

"I would not be so unreasonable, or, to be honest, so forceful."

Miss de Bourgh's tone was almost wistful, as if she wished she could live up to Elizabeth's accusation. "Do you not want to hear more?"

"You have piqued my interest," Elizabeth responded, for it would be a lie to say she wasn't intrigued. If not to warn her off Darcy or to give her the letter, what was wanted of her?

Miss de Bourgh drew in a long breath, as if to steady herself. "I do not wish to marry Darcy, nor he me. We've made my mother's promise to his mother into a waiting game, always putting the matter off. Unfortunately, Darcy's proposal to you seems to have pressed the issue. After her argument with Darcy this morning, my mother came to me and told me that if Darcy and I refused to marry within a month, she will publicize Georgiana Darcy's near elopement. She was quite gleeful, sure she'd struck on a tactic which would succeed."

Elizabeth stared at Miss de Bourgh in surprise. What sort of women would defame her own niece to force a marriage between unwilling parties?

"You do not know Georgiana, but I do. She is devastatingly shy. She will neither be able to deny the accusation nor carry off an attitude that will make it unimportant."

Elizabeth nodded. A shy young woman would likely possess the exact attitude to make the claims into something much worse than they were. It would affect her ability to find a decent man to marry, and may even entice indecent ones to pay her unwanted attention. In short, the rumor, especially perpetuated by the girl's own aunt, could quite conceivably ruin the rest of Miss Darcy's life.

"What Georgiana did is nothing, by the way." Miss de Bourgh cast Elizabeth a challenging look, as if daring her to refute that. "But with Georgiana's bashfulness and Darcy being so straight laced, they don't see that. Because of her shyness, when she is brought out she will have a terrible enough time as it is, without her error in judgement being public. The scandal would make it much worse." Her expression grew thoughtful. "Georgiana will eventually grow out of it, I believe. I was just as shy until I was in my twenties. Darcy is still a bit shy, but he's greatly improved from how he was."

Miss de Bourgh's claim that Miss Darcy was shy seemed to go against Mr. Wickham's portrayal of her, but could anything Mr. Wickham said be believed? The idea that Mr. Darcy was shy seemed even more foreign. Elizabeth had never considered that. Could that be part of why he was reluctant to dance with anyone not in his own party? Could some of his condescension simply be a cover for what he would likely consider the greater failing?

"You can see my predicament," Miss de Bourgh said. "Much as I love Georgiana, I am not going to marry Darcy."

"Why not?" Elizabeth asked, truly curious. Mr. Darcy had excellent lineage. Even Elizabeth had to admit he was uncommonly handsome of face and possessed a tall, powerful physique. Not to mention, though she supposed Miss de Bourgh didn't need money, Mr. Darcy was reputed to be exceedingly wealthy. She couldn't imagine Miss de Bourgh as the type to hold out for love. Not when so many found it much more practical not to. Truly, there was no reason any woman in England would refuse Mr. Darcy. Well, no woman other than Elizabeth. "Has he wronged you? Unfairly maligned you or those you care for?"

Miss de Bourgh raised her eyebrows. "Of course not. Darcy is unflaggingly fair, honest and well mannered."

Elizabeth detected a trace of reproach in the other woman's tone, but refused to be baited. "Then why do you not wish to marry him?"

"For one thing, he does not wish to marry me. I find that to be a poor basis for a union."

"For another?"

"I don't want to leave Rosings. Darcy will never leave Pemberley. We can't live in both places."

"Rosings is beautiful," Elizabeth said, although she meant the grounds, not the house. "You are certain you can't persuade him to live here?" She held her breath, waiting for Miss de Bourgh to answer. Somehow, it felt wrong to Elizabeth to encourage another woman to seek Mr. Darcy's hand mere hours after he'd proposed to her, even though she'd refused him.

Miss de Bourgh shook her head, freeing Elizabeth to breathe. "To Darcy, nothing can compare to Pemberley." She slowed the horses to a walk again, looking about. "I managed to get a message to him warning him of my mother's threat and asking him to meet me. He doesn't know what I'm planning, just that I have a plan."

"Meet you?"

"Yes." Miss de Bourgh shot her an amused look. "We're nearly there."

They were on their way to meet Mr. Darcy? Elizabeth felt something near panic stir in her. She wasn't ready to face him. Not with all that had passed between them yesterday, and in his letter. Perhaps it wasn't that long of a walk back after all. She looked up, tracking the position of the sun. How long had they been driving? "I don't know what you're planning, or why it must include me. I don't know that I care to be a part of any of this."

"I will explain my plan to both of you together. I only wish to go through it once."

Elizabeth took in the pleading note in Miss de Bourgh's voice and wondered if the meek woman worried she only had the fortitude to argue her scheme once.

"Neither of you will initially care for my idea, but I ask you to hear me out," Miss de Bourgh continued.

Elizabeth swallowed, trying to settle her nerves. Should she jump from the phaeton? Miss de Bourgh wasn't driving that quickly now, but jumping from a moving vehicle to avoid seeing Mr. Darcy seemed overly dramatic. How terrible could it truly be? His anger had obviously cooled by the time he'd finished the letter, and likely remained cooled, so she would not be facing that.

Elizabeth clasped her hands tightly before her, realizing it wasn't him she dreaded so much as confronting her own guilt and embarrassment. She'd behaved wretchedly toward him, and discovered an alarming lack of good judgement in herself regarding Mr. Wickham. She was, in fact, quite mortified.

Still, she reminded herself, there were scores on which she knew she was in the right. Mr. Darcy had belittled and insulted both her and her family. Even if some of what he'd said had merit, it was still rude of him to say it. Worse by far, Jane had loved Mr. Bingley and Mr. Darcy had no right to interfere in that. Holding these thoughts firm, Elizabeth raised her chin as they turned off onto an unused looking track. She was, she assured herself, quite ready to face Mr. Darcy.

2

The overgrown roadway Elizabeth and Miss de Bourgh traveled down curved through the trees. In less time than Elizabeth expected, it spilled them out into a sun-dappled clearing. Mr. Darcy stood with his back to them, presenting broad shoulders encased in an impeccably tailored coat. He was letting his horse, a fine looking roan, graze nearby.

As Miss de Bourgh's phaeton drew to a halt, Mr. Darcy turned. His eyes registered surprise when they alighted on Elizabeth. She could feel her cheeks heat.

"What is Miss Bennet doing here?" Darcy asked his cousin, his tones clipped.

Affronted, Elizabeth hopped down from the phaeton. Her short jump must have reminded him of his manners, as she'd intended, for he hurried forward to help Miss de Bourgh down. Elizabeth smoothed her skirt, tipped up her chin again, and marched around the phaeton to join them.

If anyone should feel uncomfortable, she reminded herself, it should be Mr. Darcy. He was the one who'd spoken so boorishly yesterday, and with such arrogance. To assure herself she was more in the right, Elizabeth resolved to clear her conscience of her transgressions of misjudgment immediately. "Mr. Darcy," she greeted.

"Miss Bennet." His acknowledgement was devoid of emotion. He nodded to his cousin. "Anne."

Elizabeth took another step forward, recapturing his attention. "Mr. Darcy, as I find us together and am apparently able to speak freely on this before Miss de Bourgh, please permit me to apologize for misjudging you, and for being taken in by Mr. Wickham, which must have been . . ." She trailed off, suddenly realizing how upsetting that must have been for Mr. Darcy. He'd loved her, and watched her fall for the charms of a man he knew to be dishonorable, just as his sister had.

"It must have been unpleasant for you to endure," she concluded in a softer tone.

He stared at her for a long moment, his expression closed. "It was." Again, he turned to his cousin. "What have you been telling Miss Bennet?"

"I? Nothing. You have told her many things, however, in your letter."

"My letter? The one your mother took and you burned?"

Miss de Bourgh gave a slight shake of her head. "I did not burn it, Darcy. I kept it. I gave it to Miss Bennet, as you must have intended."

"I see," Mr. Darcy said, at his most stern. "And what, then, is Miss Bennet doing here? Your note said you have a way to spare Georgiana."

Elizabeth cast a glance at Miss de Bourgh but she, who cowed so easily before her mother, seemed unconcerned in the face of Mr. Darcy's ire. "And so I do."

"Well, we are both here now, as you obviously wanted." Mr. Darcy folded his arms across his chest. "What is your plan?"

"The two of you must become engaged."

"No," Elizabeth blurted at the same time as Mr. Darcy said, "What?"

"It's plausible." Miss de Bourgh held up her hands beseechingly. "My mother thinks the letter was destroyed, but there is no reason the two of you couldn't still have met. You would have found it in you to speak what you'd written, Darcy."

"It is not the plausibility of us exchanging words that I refute," Elizabeth said, aghast at Miss de Bourgh's proposition. "It is the notion that Mr. Darcy's words, whether written or spoken, could make me acquiesce to what I have already refused, when neither my mind or heart have changed."

Miss de Bourgh leveled pleading eyes on her. "I read Darcy's letter. With all of your objections to the marriage explained, it is reasonable you would change your mind."

"Not all of her objections," Mr. Darcy said.

Elizabeth looked down, pursing her lips. Miss de Bourgh clearly didn't know everything that had passed between them. What hadn't been addressed in the letter was Elizabeth's criticism of Darcy's manners and her declaration that he was the last man in the world she would marry. She realized she may owe him another apology still, for the vehemence of her rejection. Perhaps she could have mustered greater restraint, though he'd sorely tried her, to be sure.

"All of the objections mentioned in the letter were addressed," Miss de Bourgh said. "My mother knows of no others, nor will she be able to imagine any. She was already amazed you refused, Miss Elizabeth."

Elizabeth shook her head. She had to end this ridiculous scheme. "How can you ask me to pretend to be engaged? My family would expect the marriage to take place in a month or so. What would--"

"Yes, they will want you to wed soon," Miss de Bourgh cut in before Elizabeth could finish. "But you can delay the wedding for two months. That's all I require."

"Your birthday?" Mr. Darcy asked.

"Yes. I'll be twenty-five." Miss de Bourgh's wide eyes pleaded with Elizabeth. "My father's will left Rosings to me, but I have no control over it until I'm twenty-five."

Elizabeth frowned. She didn't consider herself slow witted, but she didn't understand how Miss de Bourgh inheriting Rosings would end the threat Lady Catherine had issued. "How does you inheriting Rosings help Miss Darcy and ensure you needn't marry Mr. Darcy?"

"My mother loves Rosings. I will threaten to cast her out if she doesn't give up on my wedding Darcy and leave Georgiana be."

"Your own mother?" Elizabeth didn't know what to think of these people. As dreadful as Lady Catherine was, she was still Miss de Bourgh's mother. Elizabeth found many faults in her own mother, but she would never pitch her out. She sought Mr. Darcy's reaction, but his face revealed little. "You would cast Lady Catherine from her home?" she asked Miss de Bourgh.

"She wouldn't be without recourse." Miss de Bourgh's tone was painfully beseeching. "My mother has her jointure. She's been living very comfortably at Rosings without spending much of it. She also owns a small estate that neighbors Rosings. No one lives there but the caretaker and a few servants, so she could easily take up residence. When I have control of Rosings, I can threaten not to allow her to live there anymore. She wouldn't be desolate but she would have to pay for her household expenses. Now, she only pays for her maid out of her own money. Mother dislikes spending her own money, and would hate to live anywhere other than Rosings. With the consequence of expulsion hanging over her, she will give up her threats."

"Why not make the threat now?" Elizabeth asked. "Tell her what you will do in two months so there's no reason to put her off?" And leave me out of your schemes, she added silently.

Miss de Bourgh looked at Darcy. She lifted her hands in an imploring gesture, as if she'd already spent her reserve for argument.

"Because Lady Catherine will presume, given two months, she can persuade Anne to do as she wants," Mr. Darcy said, his expression thoughtful.

"Surely you can convince her you are set in your course of action." Elizabeth pressed, even though she wasn't sure herself that Miss de Bourgh could do so. She'd watched the two. Lady Catherine dictated and Miss de Bourgh obeyed.

"She's always bent me to her will in the past," Miss de Bourgh said, wringing her hands. "Shortly before I was to come out, when I was seventeen, I fell ill. I had a fever, my throat was raw, and I was subjected to terrible swelling and sensitivity. After a few weeks, the symptoms disappeared, but I was weak and tired. It took me almost two years to recover my strength. I missed the season when I was seventeen and the following year as well."

She closed her eyes for a moment. When she opened them, Elizabeth could see the pain there. "My father got sick before the season when I was nineteen. He died half a year later. That took care of that season and the mourning took care of the one when I was twenty. It was after his death that the arguing began. Mother became tyrannical, overbearing." She shook her head.

"I wanted to come out when I was twenty-one, but my mother had a different plan. She desired me not to because my younger sister would come out with me if I waited one more year. I did debate it, but eventually Mother wore me down and I agreed. My sister was very shy and I was starting to gain confidence. I decided Mother was right and it would help us both if my sister and I came out together." Miss de Bourgh's expression grew wistful. "My sister got sick and died, costing me another season."

"I'm sorry about your sister," Elizabeth said. She hadn't known Miss de Bourgh had a younger sister, but she could easily imagine how terrible it would be to lose one. They'd always been lucky, she knew, her sisters and her. For many families, death was nearly as common as life.

"It happens," Miss de Bourgh said with a sad little shrug. "I really wanted to come out the following year. We went to London and I got sick. As soon as I was well enough to travel, we were back at Rosings. Although I was well within two weeks, Mother convinced me I was genuinely sick and couldn't stand the London winter. We went to London last year. I had something a bit like a come out. We attended parties and other events for nearly three weeks, but then Mother persuaded me to return to Rosings. I believe she'd meant to permit me a season, but once it became obvious there was a man who was interested in me, Mother exerted her will."

"She is that determined you should wed Mr. Darcy?" Elizabeth asked, though she wasn't surprised that someone who would sacrifice the reputation of their niece would also destroy the happiness of a daughter.

"No, I don't believe so. At first she found the gentleman suitable, but he let it get out that he would make her leave Rosings if he married me." She looked down. "I didn't love him. He was no loss, so I don't regret him."

Elizabeth was suspicious of the return of a wistful note to Miss de Bourgh's tone. She wondered if Miss de Bourgh truly didn't regret the man, or if her mother had convinced her she did not.

"So, you see," Miss de Bourgh said. "She has every reason to believe she can change my mind, and she is correct. I have never won. I can't keep fighting her."

"I still don't see what good any of this will do you, and can imagine a great deal of harm it will do me," Elizabeth said, tamping down the sympathy for Miss de Bourgh that tried to well in her. "You may threaten to cast your mother from Rosings, but the threat will lose its force and she will return to her highhanded ways. You will still need to stand up to her eventually, twenty-five or no."

"No, for it is no idle threat. I will banish her. I'll tell my servants I won't receive her, and let them go if she gets by them. If she chooses to live on her property, I will visit her once a week and if she starts arguing with me, I'll leave. In something so important as what man I shall wed, it will take her weeks to wear me down. I won't give her that and I'll let her know it."

Elizabeth shook her head. Lady Catherine wouldn't relent. "Her ambitions for you and Mr. Darcy and her threat toward Miss Darcy won't disappear simply because she no longer resides in Rosings. From what I've seen of Lady Catherine, she will never give up so long as you and Mr. Darcy both remain unwed. I will not agree to a false engagement and certainly not to a marriage."

Mr. Darcy eyed her for a long moment. Elizabeth felt her face heat. She supposed it was in poor taste to declare she wouldn't wed Mr. Darcy when he hadn't reissued the offer. She wasn't about to let manners hedge her into agreeing to Miss de Bourgh's scheme, though.

"There is another aspect to this," Mr. Darcy said. "Lady Catherine knows a doctor, the one who helped convince Anne that London winters are too harsh for her. Colonel Fitzwilliam and I once overheard her asking the man what steps would be required to declare someone insane and unfit to govern their own property." He cast an assessing glance at his cousin. "Though it troubles me to consider it, I feel your mother has the force of will to persuade this doctor to declare you incompetent, leaving her in charge of both Rosings and your finances."

"That seems farfetched," Elizabeth said, somewhat surprised Mr. Darcy was taking Miss de Bourgh's side. He couldn't possibly wish to embarrass himself by pretending to be engaged to her. He'd hardly been able to bring himself to attempt it in truth, let alone for subterfuge.

"It is, but it is also a possibility," Miss de Bourgh said. "Mother would do anything to keep Rosings." She let out a deep sigh. "I shall never be rid of her."

"You will be if you marry."

Elizabeth and Miss de Bourgh both turned to Mr. Darcy in surprise. Elizabeth wondered if that was his way of proposing to his cousin. Miss de Bourgh must have come to the same conclusion, for she took a step away from him.

"Not me," he said, raising his eyebrows. "Someone else."

Miss de Bourgh shook her head. "I would need to find someone very quickly in order to beat Mother's timeframe and save Georgiana. I've only managed to attract one man in my nearly twenty-five years. I still think putting her off for two months, until I inherit and can credibly threaten her with expulsion, is the only way to save Georgiana's reputation."

"Then Miss Bennet and I must contrive to render me unavailable for two months, as you asked, while you contrive to find a husband. As Miss Bennet said, we cannot remain engaged forever, nor would it help. Lady Catherine would eventually recognize the deception and renew her demands."

"We cannot be engaged at all," Elizabeth declared. She sympathized with Miss de Bourgh, and with Mr. Darcy's sister, but this was asking too much of her. A long, then broken, engagement with Mr. Darcy would destroy Elizabeth's reputation and the effect it would have on her family hardly bore thinking on. "Forgive me, Miss de Bourgh, but I am not willing to go along with this. My father will be unhappy with me if I became engaged to Mr. Darcy and my mother would be devastated when the wedding didn't take place. My reputation would be irrevocably tarnished. I simply must decline."

"No, you must accept." Miss de Bourgh returned to wringing her hands. "I know you do not know me well, or Georgiana at all, but surely you must see the right thing to do is to help us."

"In truth, I don't even concede it will help." Elizabeth was growing cross. For someone who claimed an inability to stand up for herself, Miss de Bourgh was being quite persistent. Of course, it was one thing to plead with Elizabeth, and quite another, she supposed, to bear up under Lady Catherine's constant company, day after day. "If Mr. Darcy asked me to marry him and I said yes, wouldn't Lady Catherine simply reapply her threat of tarnishing Miss Darcy's reputation to force Mr. Darcy to break off our engagement?"

Miss de Bourgh shook her head. Her pleading gaze turned to Mr. Darcy again.

"For all her faults, my aunt believes a man's honor should be on a pedestal," Mr. Darcy said. "She would never ask me to sully myself, or her by association, by backing out of an engagement."

"So instead she will unleash her machinations on me, to force me to break it off?" Elizabeth asked, mild anger sparking in her. She wondered if they would have admitted as much if not pressed.

Mr. Darcy nodded. "She will."

"This plot grows less savory by the moment." Elizabeth pulled back her shoulders, standing firm. "I simply cannot agree."

"Even for five thousand pounds?"

"Five thousand pounds?" Elizabeth repeated as Mr. Darcy's startled, "What?" rang through the clearing.

"The money means nothing to me." There was desperation in Miss de Bourgh's face now. "I inherited forty thousand pounds, which I cannot do anything with, although the income is mine. I spend less than six hundred pounds a year." Spinning, she paced away from them, then back. Words continued to pour from her mouth as her heavy skirt

29

pushed aside the tall grass. "My mother has not allowed me to have any friends. I don't spend too much time with Mrs. Collins, because if I did, my mother would get jealous and keep me away from her. Mrs. Jenkinson is my mother's creature, employed to spy on and curtail me."

Miss de Bourgh was gesturing widely now, more animated than Elizabeth had ever seen her. Unfortunately, it was obvious it was the liveliness of a cornered creature. Elizabeth, whose own mother could be domineering, obsessive and invasive, felt sympathy well in her again. What could she do, though?

"The tenants I talk to treat me with the greatest respect, but that eliminates the possibility of real friendship," Miss de Bourgh railed. "Besides, they are uneducated and have concerns that mean little to me. I've been waiting for my twenty-fifth birthday so I can get out from under my mother's control. I love Georgiana, but I can't let *her* mistake ruin *my* life."

"Surely, Mr. Darcy would stand up to your mother once you wed, freeing you from her. Is marrying him truly so terrible a fate?" Elizabeth posed the question though she knew she'd already asked once, for it offered the most ready solution.

"Yes," Miss de Bourgh cried. "Yes, it is."

Elizabeth caught Mr. Darcy's slight wince and hid a smile. His conceit likely didn't care for the presence of two women who so vehemently wished not to tie themselves to him.

"This will be the most important decision of my life." Miss de Bourgh stopped pacing, coming to a halt before Elizabeth. "I cannot permit my mother to make it for me. I won't bind myself to a man who holds only cousinly affection for me and who will go on living in Pemberley, likely no matter where I choose to live. What life would that be? For once, I shall make my own choice."

For all her fervor, Elizabeth could see Miss de Bourgh was shaking from head to toe. They stood thus for a long moment, Miss de Bourgh beseeching, Elizabeth thinking, until an idea came to her. "May I pose a suggestion?" Elizabeth asked, the words slow as she thought the idea behind them through. "It doesn't need to be an engagement. In fact, if it isn't an engagement, it would be more plausible and give us more time."

"I don't understand," Miss de Bourgh said.

Elizabeth cast a quick glance at Mr. Darcy as she illuminated, finding his expression typically impassive. "Mr. Darcy and I met, as you suggested and as we have. I was made aware of the contents of the letter, also a true statement. I apologized for my misunderstanding."

"Which you already have," Mr. Darcy said with a slight bow to her.

"We reached an agreement. Not to marry, but to get to know each other better," Elizabeth concluded.

"A courtship," Mr. Darcy said.

"No, because that is an agreement that is meaningless," Miss de Bourgh said, sounding almost as if she would cry. "My mother won't respect it. An engagement is the only thing short of marriage that I dare hope will divert her."

"An engagement can be one sided," Mr. Darcy said. An odd look slid across his face, though his futures settled into inscrutability as he turned to Elizabeth. "Miss Bennet, will you do me the great honor of becoming my wife?" He held up a stilling hand, though Elizabeth was too surprised to speak. "You do not need to answer me for two months because you don't know me very well and you will want to know me better. I want you to understand that the offer remains open until you answer, two months from today."

For several seconds Elizabeth was still too astonished to reply. "You are asking me to marry you? I will not destroy my reputation over your family's disagreement." Had she not been adamant? Did he think the offer of five thousand pounds had moved her? Did he think so little of her as that?

"You won't be. I can now honestly say that I have proposed to you and given you two months to answer. All I ask is that you do not refuse me until then."

Elizabeth smiled in relieved understanding. It was more than a courtship, but less than an official engagement. Mr. Darcy's offer was binding on him, but nothing yet bound her. Thus, she could eventually decline in good grace. "It is a good idea, and will permit me to leave as planned, so I do not have to endure Lady Catherine trying to come between us. You don't need me here while awaiting my answer." She looked to Miss de Bourgh, wanting to make sure her next statement was clear, and perhaps to impart some understanding of the mild insult she felt at the offer. "And you do not need to pay me."

Miss de Bourgh's eyes were filled with unshed drops. "No, you can't leave. Please stay. If you and Darcy are not frequently in each other's company, my mother will not believe there is anything to it.

You should accept the money and pretend he is a suitor you are seriously considering. Please."

Elizabeth sighed. Miss de Bourgh looked so frail. Honest within herself, Elizabeth admitted she didn't care much for Lady Catherine, her highhandedness toward everyone including Charlotte, and her nearly complete control of Miss de Bourgh's life. It would be satisfying to help thwart her.

Aside from missing her family, it wasn't as if remaining in Kent would harm Elizabeth in any way. The way Mr. Darcy had proposed made staying reasonable. Elizabeth's reputation would be spared, perhaps even augmented. When word got out that a man like Mr. Darcy wished to wed her, others might follow.

At least, her reputation would be augmented with anyone who wasn't Lady Catherine, Miss Bingley or Mrs. Hurst. Safe enough, for when it was over, the three would forget about her. Then, she would have only her mother to suffer, as Mrs. Bennet would surely be in agonies over Elizabeth's refusal. Still, better to be tormented by her mother for a secretly good deed than to continue to endure her mother's most recent grievance, Elizabeth's refusal to marry Mr. Collins.

"I will stay." Elizabeth watched Miss de Bourgh slump with a relief so strong, it seemed she might faint. "I will even give every impression of welcoming Mr. Darcy's courtship. I will not, however, accept any payment. You must understand my aid can be won, but not bought."

Mr. Darcy had a slight smile on his face as he turned to her. "Perhaps we could leave the issue of the five thousand pounds unresolved? I understand your inclination, Miss Bennet, but it could be that, on occasion, an act of pride is also one of folly. Think of the difference such a sum could make to you, or to your sisters."

Elizabeth frowned. He was correct. The money could offer them greater security in the face of Mr. Collins eventual claim on their home, assuming they didn't all wed.

"Do you have someone whom you could confide in who could give you advice about accepting the money?" Mr. Darcy asked. "You said your father would not be happy with the engagement, but could he counsel you about the money?"

"I will be seeing my uncle sooner, and he could advise me," Elizabeth said, for she still hoped to visit her aunt and uncle in London before returning to Hertfordshire, even if she did remain longer in Kent.

"Talk to him," Mr. Darcy said. "And Anne, you must agree that the offer remains until Miss Elizabeth replies, just as my offer to her does."

"I do," Miss de Bourgh said quickly.

"I believe we are concluded here, then?" Mr. Darcy suggested. "I think it will be for me to ensure enough people know of my proposal that Lady Catherine won't be able to easily set it aside."

Elizabeth tried to contain a grimace. She still didn't care for the idea of the world at large viewing her and Mr. Darcy as more than acquaintances. She said nothing, however, for she'd already agreed.

"Yes, I think we must be done here." At the sound of her voice, they both turned to Miss de Bourgh.

"Anne," Mr. Darcy said. He bowed to his cousin, proffering his hand.

Miss de Bourgh accepted and he led her the few steps to the phaeton, handing her up. Elizabeth hurried around to the other side, not wishing for or needing assistance. She was seated and arranging her skirts by the time Mr. Darcy came to stand beside her, looking up. Though still grudgingly, she couldn't help but find him decidedly handsome.

"Miss Elizabeth," he said with a low bow.

"Mr. Darcy," she acknowledged, nodding.

"I shall see you both soon." He turned away, crossing to retrieve his horse, mounting with an ease that bespoke of practice and strength.

Miss de Bourgh jangled the reins, warning her team their respite was at an end. As she executed a careful turn about the clearing, Mr. Darcy passed them. He didn't look at her again, but Elizabeth caught a slight smile on his face as he rode away.

Once the phaeton was facing the road they'd come in on, they headed back down the lane. Elizabeth soon recalled the maid. She hoped the young woman had anticipated a long wait and wasn't worried at being left for so much time. She also hoped it wouldn't come out that the maid had been left at all, for that would surely tip off Lady Catherine.

"Miss de Bourgh, will the maid who was in your carriage talk to Lady Catherine?" Elizabeth asked.

"She will tell my mother what I ask her to."

"Can you be sure?"

Miss de Bourgh cast Elizabeth a sly smile. "Once or twice a month, I take a supposedly random maid with me on this kind of trip. I usually do it after an argument with my mother. I give the other maids a shilling. This maid is taken less often than any of the others, but only when I want to do something I don't want my mother to hear about. I give her a pound a month for her cooperation. She is saving it for a dowry. Her mother keeps it, so there is no danger of it being discovered."

"A pound a month?" Elizabeth was again surprised by Miss de Bourgh's extravagance. It appeared she was quite willing to spend her money in order to get her way against her mother. "Why, she can't be paid more than ten pounds a year."

"Six, to be precise," Miss de Bourgh replied, guiding the horses down the lane.

There was little additional talk as they continued to where Miss de Bourgh had found Elizabeth. She alighted and the maid took her seat. As they drove off, Elizabeth could see Miss de Bourgh turning toward the young woman, issuing instructions. The maid nodded animatedly.

Elizabeth returned to the Hunsford parsonage with mixed feelings. At first, she worried over having agreed to Miss de Bourgh's fantastic proposal, but she had, and so pressed doubts from her mind as best she could. All that accomplished was to open space for thoughts of the five thousand pounds Miss de Bourgh had offered her.

The idea of not having to worry about poverty if her father died was comforting, but accepting felt wrong to Elizabeth. It seemed almost immoral to receive so much money for agreeing to see more of Mr. Darcy, even given what had recently passed between them. It wasn't as if his company was entirely unpleasant, after all. So long as he managed not to belittle her or her family, she was sure they could put up a front of getting along. Or, at least, she hoped they could.

3

Darcy rode for quite some time after the meeting in the clearing. He knew it was best if no one thought he and Anne were returning together, but was spurred by more than simple caution. He needed solitude to clear his head. As his roan traversed sunny lanes and open meadows, Darcy's mind roamed over Elizabeth.

Somehow, in the wake of her refusal, she was even more lovely than ever. The softening of her tone, when she'd apologized for believing Wickham, had tortured Darcy. At the same time, her continued avowal she would never wed him lashed his already tattered heart and pride. In the wake of these conflicting emotions, he could only regard with shock his agreement to be a part of Anne's scheme. If not for Georgiana . . .

Darcy shook his head. No, he would not lie to himself, at least. In the end, it wasn't consideration of Anne or of Georgiana that drove him to become involved in subterfuge. It was Elizabeth.

He frowned at the blossom bedecked meadow before him. How had he permitted this to happen? He abhorred trickery and stratagems. He was a Darcy. A Darcy stated the truth, gave reasonable orders, and expected the world to adjust accordingly.

Yet, Elizabeth hadn't behaved accordingly. She'd rejected his proposal. He'd told the truth to no avail. He wasn't fool enough to think reasonable orders would work where truth had failed. He wanted her, this slip of a woman who would defy him, decline him, and bristle at Anne's offer of thousands of pounds. More than wanting her, he loved her. He, who'd never felt such a stirring for any other female, was in love with Elizabeth Bennet.

Darcy grimaced at the fickleness of fate. That he should desire a woman who would refuse him was absurd. Over half of his life had been spent evading the clutching creatures.

Now, instead of evading, he was pursuing. He was humbling

himself and offending his sense of honor by engaging in a scheme. He hadn't even argued against it. His mind befuddled by lack of sleep, the emotions spewed forth in his uncharacteristic argument with his aunt, and pining for Elizabeth, he'd readily agreed. He hadn't seen reason or propriety. All he'd seen was a chance to woo the woman he loved.

His only hope, the thing that would mend his honor, was to win her. If he accomplished that, it wouldn't be a scheme he'd embarked on. It would all be the truth. In the strictest sense, it already was. He'd asked Elizabeth to wed him and declined to hear her answer for two months. She, in turn, had agreed to spend more time with him.

Darcy shook his head, turning his roan back toward Rosings. It was a fine line he'd set himself to walk. He hoped his honor could survive the upcoming weeks, for he doubted his sanity, or his heart, would.

As he drew near his aunt's imposing dwelling, Darcy sternly turned his thoughts toward implementing what he'd agreed to. After all, if the thing must be done, it was best done well. To that end, he decided the correct way to handle his aunt was not to permit her to issue her threat to Georgiana before he announced the situation he, Anne and Elizabeth had contrived. He was glad he'd left that morning before Lady Catherine thought of the threat, and that Anne delivered her note to him via his own groom. His second proposal to Elizabeth would seem sincerer if it didn't come in the wake of Lady Catherine's ultimatum.

Upon entering Rosings, he went to find Lady Catherine. She was in her favorite parlor, one where only her chair had any pretense of comfort and the lighting was never sufficient for anyone to read, leaving them at the mercy of her conversation. Deep red fabrics with garish gold tufting abounded, entrenched in dark wood and set on a carpet so deeply woven it seemed to suck at a person's feet, especially if they attempted to leave. His cousin, Colonel Richard Fitzwilliam, was there, as were Anne and her companion, Mrs. Jenkinson. Darcy considered this ideal, for their plan would work better with an audience.

"Darcy, where have you been?" Lady Catherine asked as he entered the room, her tone even more querulous than usual.

"Aunt Catherine," he said, bowing. "Anne, Mrs. Jenkinson, Richard. I've been out riding."

"Wish I'd thought of that," Richard muttered.

"Well, you took your time with it, didn't you?" His aunt glared at him, looking for all the world like the insulted party in their morning's argument, not the offender. "If you felt you had to go out, you should have had the decency to return in a reasonable time."

"I did not return sooner because I required time to organize my thoughts." Darcy caught the flicker of worry on Anne's face and realized she was afraid he'd changed his mind. Annoyance touched him. For all he'd permitted himself to be drawn into her game with her mother against his better judgement, he wasn't low enough to go back on his word. What did she take him for?

"They were in dire need of organizing, to be sure," Lady Catherine said, somehow looking down her nose at him even though he stood while she sat. "I trust you have them in better arrangement now."

He didn't avail himself of a chair, but instead crossed the room to stand before his aunt. "I do. Much better. While I still object to your unreasonable behavior in entering my room and reading a letter I was writing, I am pleased to say some good came of it."

"Aunt Catherine." Richard shook his head, looking disappointed. "That wasn't well done of you. A man's letters are his own business."

Lady Catherine sat straighter in her chair. "What takes place in Rosings is my business."

Richard shook his head again, but turned back to Darcy. "You were saying, Darcy?"

"I was saying that some good came from Aunt Catherine's snooping. While I was out this morning, driven forth by my anger at being misused, I met Miss Bennet. She now has full knowledge of what the letter contained."

Richard frowned, likely wondering what Darcy's letter had to do with Miss Bennet, but he showed no inclination to pry. Lady Catherine opened her mouth to speak.

Darcy didn't let her, pushing ahead. "She apologized for misjudging me and I proposed, telling her she need not give an answer immediately. We agreed to spend two months to get to know each other better. Then she will answer my proposal."

"This is outrageous." Lady Catherine's screeching tone set Darcy's teeth on edge. "You are going to marry Anne."

"I am not. I hope to marry Miss Bennet. I am honor bound to her for two months or until she gives me an answer." Darcy closed his mouth, wishing he hadn't added the qualifier. Lady Catherine would have thought of trying to influence Elizabeth on her own, but that didn't mean he needed to plant the notion.

"I say, Darcy, that was bold of you, proposing to the girl," Richard said. Standing, he crossed and offered his hand. "Good luck with the chase. She's a fine specimen."

"Thank you," Darcy said, returning his cousin's handclasp. His eyes went to Anne and she gave a slight shake of her head. It seemed no one had told Richard that Darcy already proposed to Elizabeth once.

His aunt's eyes narrowed dangerously. "You wish to marry Miss Bennet even after she believed scandalous falsehoods about you? Don't you see the folly in that? You want a wife who will be loyal to you, not a stupid chit who believes every rumor that comes by her."

Darcy struggled with the anger that rose in him, seeking calm, but finding little.

"I wouldn't be loyal to him," Anne said. Her voice was small, but it carried in the stillness left by Lady Catherine's words.

Lady Catherine whipped her head toward her daughter. Richard grimaced. Giving Darcy a parting slap on the shoulder, he returned to his seat.

"Be quiet," Lady Catherine snapped at Anne. "Can't you see I have your best interests at heart?"

"No, I cannot. I don't think you know what my best interests even are," Anne said.

Seated beside Anne on the settee, Mrs. Jenkinson was managing to make herself impressively inconspicuous, her eyes on a needlepoint ring she wasn't truly employing. Darcy had long since noticed her engagement in such activities, while in the red and gold parlor, was a ruse. There wasn't enough light for needlepoint.

"I know better than you do." Lady Catherine glared at Anne. "What do you know of the world? Who but Darcy would marry you for any reason other than your money?"

Angered for Anne this time, Darcy felt his composure ebbing. "There are plenty of men who would love Anne."

"See?" Lady Catherine looked from Darcy to Anne, her expression smug enough to try Darcy's slipping patience. "He must love you to defend you so promptly."

"He loves me as a cousin," Anne said, but her tone was meek.

"I do," Darcy affirmed before his aunt could speak. He drew in a

38

slow breath. Few could so readily find chinks in his cool facade the way Lady Catherine did.

"As do I," said Richard. He leaned forward, his strong features arranged in an earnest expression. "I think that Anne would—"

"No one cares what you think," Lady Catherine snapped, not even looking at Richard. "Darcy, if you and Anne don't marry by the end of the month, I will publicize that Georgiana is compromised. She nearly eloped with the son of your father's steward. Do you think the ton will take such lewd behavior lightly? She will never make a good match, even with her connections."

Darcy had expected he would need to feign shock, but he didn't. He realized, in spite of Anne's report of her mother's ultimatum, he'd not truly believed Lady Catherine would have so little regard for Georgiana. He searched his aunt's face for some hint it was an idle threat, but found none. Lady Catherine, he was sure, would carry through on it.

"Aunt Catherine," Richard barked, his voice that of the colonel he was, not the easy-going gentleman he usually portrayed while in Rosings, who was an asset to any drawing room. "How can you even threaten such a thing? And Darcy, how could you let her know about it?"

Darcy resisted the urge to scowl, composing himself into an easy stance as he turned to Richard. "I did not tell our aunt about Georgiana. The information was contained in the letter Aunt Catherine appropriated from my desk."

"Which was intended for Miss Bennet?" Richard asked, his frown deepening. "What purpose could possibly drive you to share such sensitive knowledge? Obviously you care for the girl, but that hardly explains it."

Darcy grimaced, finding the condemnation in Richard's tone fair. Not wishing to share Georgiana's secret had been one of his main quibbles with the letter, one of the reasons he'd gone for a walk instead of sealing it. Taking in Richard's hard look, Darcy realized he would have to divulge his humiliation to his cousin. "Today wasn't the first time I proposed to Miss Bennet. I did yesterday as well, and was rejected."

Surprise registered on Richard's face.

"While she was declining, it came to light that Mr. Wickham had poisoned her mind against me with his lies," Darcy continued. He swallowed, still feeling the sting of her rejection and the mixture of anger and pain it evoked. "It was my feeling Miss Bennet should know the truth about him. I was confident she would keep it confidential." He swung back to glare at Lady Catherine. "I did not imagine my own aunt would come into my room, read a letter I wrote, and threaten to tell the world of it."

"I see. That makes things a sight clearer." Richard drummed his fingers on the dark wood of his chair arm. He turned to their aunt. "Aunt Catherine, if the information about Georgiana and Mr. Wickham comes out through you, I will never visit you again. I am co-guardian with Darcy and equally responsible for her. I will never forgive you if you take such a pointless, vindictive action."

Darcy took in the slight widening of his aunt's eyes. He could see Richard's threat carried weight. Richard was closer with their aunt than Darcy was. He visited more often and made himself more amiable to Lady Catherine's conversation, adding liveliness to a home sorely in need of it. She would miss Richard if he never returned.

"Furthermore, Darcy has already made the proposal," Richard said. "He is honor bound to await Miss Bennet's answer. Would you like him to sully the Darcy name by backing out now?"

Lady Catherine pursed her lips, glaring at Darcy. It amused Darcy to note that, while his aunt didn't care about dragging Georgiana's name through the mud, she did care about the Darcy name. He wondered which the distinction spoke worse of, his aunt for making it, or the society they lived in for treating young women like commodities to be traded.

"Mother." Anne's voice was nearly a whisper. "You must come to terms with this. Darcy will be marrying Miss Bennet, not me."

"That remains to be seen," Lady Catherine snapped, finding her voice. "Darcy, Miss Bennet is unworthy of you. I can prove it to you."

"What good will that do?" Richard asked. "If she accepts him, he is honor bound to marry her."

"She refused him once, witless minx. If he shows he no longer loves her, she will refuse him again."

"I do love her," Darcy said. "And you would do well to keep that in mind and modulate how you speak of the woman who will be my wife."

"You are blinded by her dubious charms." Lady Catherine gave no indication she'd heard his reprimand. "Once you see her in a greater variety of situations, you would see how beneath you she is. I will help you get to know her better, for in knowing someone as low as she, you must come to disdain her."

Darcy took a moment to compose his answer, removing the heat from it. "If you wish to assist me in coming to know Miss Bennet better, I welcome your help, Aunt."

"Of course you do. I shall begin at once."

"Thank you," Darcy said. He executed a stiff bow. "If you will all excuse me? I believe we have concluded this discussion."

Not waiting for their adieus, or his aunt's inevitable disapproval of his hasty departure, Darcy strode from the stuffy room. Long strides carried him through opulent halls to his quarters. He closed the door quietly behind him and dismissed his valet. He needed a moment alone to bring his anger under control. His aunt's unreasonableness, vindictiveness and continued insults of Elizabeth had eaten away at his typical calm.

As his mind settled, Darcy could appreciate that things had gone well. His aunt hadn't said as much, but she seemed to have dropped her threat of exposing Georgiana's secret, at least while he was bound by his proposal to Elizabeth. She'd also agreed to help him come to know Elizabeth better, something Darcy hadn't anticipated and was pleased with. Even though he was sure his aunt's attempts to sabotage his relationship with Elizabeth weren't spent, for now things appeared to be moving in his favor. Darcy smiled, relaxing. Though she may think it a ruse, he was going to enjoy courting Elizabeth.

4

Elizabeth added another careful annotation to the recipe card she was writing out. She, Charlotte and Maria were seated in the austere, yet sunny, parsonage parlor. Maria Lucas was curled into a chair in the corner reading, while Elizabeth and Charlotte sat at a table carefully transcribing recipes that were in danger of fading into complete illegibility. It was an activity that occupied both mind and hands, permitting little conversation.

This pleased Elizabeth, for she was still trying to sort through the turmoil of recent events. The ordering of her thoughts was not helped by her nerves. The warm afternoon light streaming in through the windows assured her that Mr. Darcy and Miss de Bourgh must have returned to Rosings long since. Elizabeth expected an irate Lady Catherine to storm into the parlor at any moment.

At the sound of rapid footfalls without, Elizabeth drew in a steadying breath and carefully set aside her pen. She turned toward the door, composing herself. She'd agreed to a sham of a courtship with Mr. Darcy. She would face the wrath it was sure to bring. Across from her, Charlotte too set aside her work. In the corner behind Charlotte, Maria lowered her book, peering over the top.

Instead of a red-faced Lady Catherine, a beaming Mr. Collins hurried into the room. "We have been invited to dinner again at Rosings," he cried, gesticulating widely. "Cousin Elizabeth, isn't it wonderful that you have the opportunity to see Lady Catherine again? You must have pleased her in some way for her to extend so generous an invitation. I am very glad I thought to have you here, to delight her."

"Yes, it was most well-done of you to provide your patroness with such agreeable entertainment as myself," Elizabeth said.

Under the cover of the table, Charlotte kicked Elizabeth's shin. Maria's faint giggle drifted across the room.

Elizabeth didn't have to pretend not to notice giggle or reprimand. Her mind was too full to linger on them. She'd expected to be banned from Rosings, at the very least, or at the worst, that Lady Catherine would demand Mr. and Mrs. Collins send her away. It was impossible Lady Catherine could find Elizabeth's courtship by Mr. Darcy acceptable. Had he and Miss de Bourgh not informed her yet? Or, perhaps, they had changed their minds and intended to marry after all.

Elizabeth frowned at the idea. She still worried over agreeing to involve herself in Miss de Bourgh's scheme. She was also still uncomfortable with all that had passed between her and Mr. Darcy. She'd been mildly interested, however, to experience what it was like to be courted by him.

"I said, Cousin Elizabeth, how long will you require to ready yourself?"

Elizabeth looked up, realizing Mr. Collins had been speaking. "I beg your pardon?"

"Woolgathering, Elizabeth?" Charlotte asked, her eyes twinkling with mischief.

Maria giggled again, louder this time.

It was on Elizabeth's tongue to deny it, but in a way she had been and, if the plot was still afoot, it might be best to perpetuate the notion. "Perhaps."

Charlotte's eyebrows shot up.

"Of course you were not," Mr. Collins said. "For that to be the case, you would need to have someone to woolgather over, which you cannot."

"I'm sure you are correct, Mr. Collins," Charlotte replied, her tone placating but her expression thoughtful. "On both points. Elizabeth ought to go to her room and ensure she has all the time she needs to ready herself to see Lady Catherine."

"I did not mean she should go this moment," Mr. Collins said. He turned to Elizabeth. "First, we must review your every interaction with Lady Catherine. It is best we discover what you have done to please her, Cousin, so you may endeavor to repeat it. I, myself, find she enjoys an attentive listener who can offer affirmation of her wisdom as she reveals it. I can instruct you in how best to do this."

Elizabeth stood, having no intention of subjecting herself to any of her cousin's propositions. "I am sorry, Mr. Collins. I'm afraid you were more correct than you knew when you suggested I needed time to ready myself. My walk this morning was revitalizing, but I'm afraid I still suffer some lingering effects from yesterday's malady. I must close my eyes in rest for a short time in order to be at my best for Lady Catherine."

"Yes, yes, well, if you think that is more important than learning how best to please her ladyship--"

"Indeed, I do." Elizabeth mustered a smile. "I promise, as I repose, I shall think on what I must have done to garner her attention."

"Well, then, I suppose--"

Casting a smile at Charlotte and Maria, Elizabeth made her escape, intending to catch up on her correspondences before readying for dinner. Instead, she found herself rereading Mr. Darcy's letter. She pondered it, his proposal, and their meeting that morning. This not only distracted her from writing her own letters, but ended with her losing track of time and being almost late coming down to leave for dinner.

The four of them walked to Rosings, Elizabeth enjoying both the exercise and the cool evening air. When they arrived, she was surprised to see carriages standing before the grand home. It appeared the gathering would not be so intimate as they were accustomed to. Elizabeth wondered what, if anything, adding more people to dinner could have to do with Mr. Darcy's supposed pursuit of her. She concluded it might be in their favor, hoping the additional guests would ease the awkwardness she worried would flourish between them.

They were greeted by a footman, who led them in a slightly different direction than usual. As always when visiting Rosings, Elizabeth was both impressed by the grandeur and amused by what she considered an overstated ostentatiousness of décor, which followed fads of twenty years ago rather than aiming at timeless beauty. The home itself was attractive, yet she couldn't agree with what could only be Lady Catherine's taste. Elizabeth wondered, if Miss de Bourgh did bar her mother, would the decorations change?

The parlor they arrived at was larger than the one Lady Catherine customarily received them in, and Elizabeth immediately preferred it. The room had oversized, airy windows, though the deep blue curtains were nearly closed. In spite of what, at a glance, appeared to be six additional guests over the usual gathering of Mr. Darcy, Colonel Fitzwilliam, Miss de Bourgh, Mrs. Jenkinson and Lady Catherine, there seemed to be more space than in the stuffy red parlor Lady Catherine preferred. Here, the theme was a subdued blue and cream, the colors more soothing, though the furnishings didn't appear any less fine.

The footman stepping aside. Mr. Collins took point and led their little party to a halt before Lady Catherine. He bowed. Elizabeth, Charlotte and Maria curtsied, Maria doing a much more practiced job than when they'd first reached Kent.

"Lady Catherine," Mr. Collins said. "May I say what a tremendous honor you do us by inviting us to dine with you. We are, as always, made better by being permitted to bask in your presence, your knowledge and the loveliness of your home. I think I can speak for . . ."

Elizabeth, rising from her curtsy, stopped attending to her cousin's speech. It was the same one he used each time, with small modifications she knew he labored over more than his Sunday sermons. Not needing to hear it again, she sought out Mr. Darcy with a look, wanting to assure herself their mock courtship was still on.

The moment she fixed her eyes on his, she was reassured. He gazed at her so warmly, in fact, she felt her skin heat. His mouth curved into a smile and he nodded in silent acknowledgement.

Elizabeth returned the greeting, feeling slightly breathless. Now she had an inkling of what it was like to be properly courted by Mr. Darcy. Even knowing his feelings about her family, that he'd wronged Jane, and that his courtship was a ruse, Elizabeth felt her blush heighten under his gaze.

"Of course it is your honor, Mr. Collins, Mrs. Collins, Miss Lucas." Lady Catherine's haughty tones brought Elizabeth's attention back. She realized her cousin's first speech of the evening was concluded. Lady Catherine fixed narrowed eyes on her. "It is to your credit you understand your place and how to conduct yourself among your betters."

Elizabeth suppressed her amusement as the rest of the greetings and introductions were exchanged. Lady Catherine took every opportunity to slight her, something Mr. Collins was obviously noticing. Her cousin began to sweat, casting frequent worried glances her way. Colonel Fitzwilliam and Miss de Bourgh, on the other hand, were courteous and warm. Elizabeth couldn't help but notice which of those in the room were truly displaying good breeding.

Of the six new people, four were women, and most took their cue from their hostess. Elizabeth didn't mind, not feeling the need to befriend Lady Catherine's followers. Their cold shoulders merely afforded her a greater opportunity to speak with the always affable Colonel, as well as with Miss de Bourgh and Mr. Darcy.

When dinner was announced they all made their way into Lady Catherine's formal dining room. The long table sparkled with enough additional silverware and crystal to make Maria's eyes go wide with worry. Elizabeth would have sat near her, to help her avoid mistakes, but this evening the table also boasted place cards. Due to the surplus of women, the cards didn't alternate between male and female guests. When Elizabeth found hers, she was between Miss de Bourgh and one of the two gentlemen Lady Catherine had invited, a younger man of about thirty. He seemed overly charming to Elizabeth, reminding her slightly of Mr. Wickham. Predictably, Elizabeth was seated almost as far from Mr. Darcy as the table permitted.

Miss de Bourgh reached the table as Elizabeth did. Frowning, she plucked Elizabeth's name card from the expensive linen. "I believe I am supposed to sit there," Miss de Bourgh said, switching her card with Elizabeth's. She cast Elizabeth a quick smile, then permitted a footman to pull out her chair.

As they were all seated, Elizabeth found herself moved nearer to Mr. Darcy. She now had Miss de Bourgh on her left and the other gentleman Lady Catherine had invited to her right. He was a pleasant enough looking fellow, somewhere on the north side of forty.

Lady Catherine finished fluffing her skirts and raised her gaze to survey the table. "Miss Bennet, what are you doing there? Can you not read, girl? You are in the wrong seat."

"I beg your pardon, Lady Catherine." Elizabeth kept her tone even, wondering why Miss de Bourgh had switched their cards. Being one seat nearer to Mr. Darcy wasn't worth having Lady Catherine label her as illiterate before the other guests. With a slight shrug, she picked up her card and displayed it to the man seated next to her, who'd been introduced to her earlier as Mr. Veitch.

"I can't see how it makes any difference, Aunt Catherine," Colonel Fitzwilliam said. "We aren't hosting members of parliament."

Lady Catherine scowled. "It is not where I want her to sit."

The younger man, now seated beside Miss de Bourgh, leaned forward to look around her at Elizabeth. He eyed her up and down in a way she decidedly didn't care for, looking eager. "I see, so you're the one--"

"Silence, you idiot," Lady Catherine snapped.

"The one, what?" Mr. Darcy asked, his voice cold.

The man swallowed and sank back in his chair.

"One nothing," Lady Catherine said. She glared about the room. "He's babbling nonsense. I'm of half a mind to expel him from our meal. This is not appropriate dinner discourse. What is the matter with the lot of you? Do you possess no manners whatsoever?"

There was a long silence. Elizabeth was actually relieved when Mr. Collins launched into one of his sycophantic speeches, freeing the rest of the room to talk. She was also relieved the party was large enough so that there were individual conversations. Unfortunately, she was too far from Mr. Darcy or Colonel Fitzwilliam to engage either of them. The good fortune of that arrangement was that it also put her too far from Lady Catherine to be expected to either speak to or listen to her.

Striking up a polite conversation with Mr. Veitch, Elizabeth soon suspected he would become boring after a week's acquaintance, but for a single meal, he had much to say. He was the magistrate for the district and brought up some interesting cases. She noticed he was careful not to talk about anything that had happened in the last few years, but sometimes a twelve-year-old case could be interesting.

She enjoyed their conversation enough that she wasn't paying attention to the servants. She was peripherally aware of footmen coming and going, and rather stunned when one spilled half a glass of red wine down her shoulder. Elizabeth could feel it quickly soak through her dress both front and back, but mostly across her chest. Tamping down an exclamation, she began applying her napkin in an effort to contain the damage.

"Have a care there, man," Mr. Veitch said, his gaze looking over Elizabeth's shoulder to the footman.

"I'm sorry, miss," the young man mumbled, backing away.

"What do you think you're doing?" Lady Catherine screeched.

Elizabeth looked up, finding their hostess glaring at her, not the footman. "Excuse me?"

"I embroidered that napkin," Lady Catherine said, all hauteur. "How dare you ruin it to save your paltry dress."

Elizabeth looked at the napkin, momentarily remorseful. She frowned. It was hemmed, of course, but there was no embellishment.

"I don't observe any embroidery, Lady Catherine," Mr. Veitch said, peering at the napkin Elizabeth held.

"Don't worry, Mother," Miss de Bourgh called from where she sat on Elizabeth's other side. "It seems I have the embroidered napkin, though why one is out when the rest of the set are not, I can't imagine."

Where he sat near Lady Catherine, Colonel Fitzwilliam covered his mouth, coughing. On her other side, Mr. Darcy smiled slightly. Lady Catherine scowled at her daughter.

Miss de Bourgh twisted in her chair, looking over Elizabeth's shoulder. "John, I have a shawl on the chair in my room. Please send one of the maids to bring it so Miss Bennet can use it."

"John, stay. The wine will ruin the shawl," Lady Catherine said. "I'll not have all of our fine things ruined by Miss Bennet."

Elizabeth couldn't see the wine-spilling footman where he stood somewhere behind her, but there were no footsteps to indicate his departure. Lady Catherine continued to glare at her daughter. Miss de Bourgh shrank into her chair, looking down.

"It won't ruin the shawl," Miss de Bourgh whispered, but neither tone nor posture held any defiance.

Elizabeth could see Miss de Bourgh's courage was failing.

"Yes, it will," Lady Catherine snapped, causing Miss de Bourgh to wince. "Besides, Miss Bennet should wear the mark of her vulgar ways as punishment. She deliberately caused John to spill the wine, to call attention to herself. Don't you agree, Mr. Collins?"

"Certainly. I am sorry my cousin is behaving so inappropriately," Mr. Collins said. "Cousin Elizabeth, we will speak on this later, at length."

It took all of Elizabeth's manners not to grimace, for that was a threat more dire than Lady Catherine's outrage. At least outrage spurred stimulating discourse. Mr. Collins in the mood to lecture would slay Elizabeth with boredom and absurdity.

"But Miss Bennet was speaking with me," Mr. Veitch said. "She couldn't have seen the footman. He was behind her."

"I saw the entire incident," said the woman across from Elizabeth. She cast a simpering glance toward Lady Catherine. "Miss Bennet was entirely at fault."

"I disagree," Mr. Veitch said, but he said it without force.

Elizabeth looked quickly about. Mr. Darcy's expression was darkening. Charlotte looked uncomfortable and Maria almost scared. Mr. Collins' face was growing more pale by the moment, and Colonel

Fitzwilliam's more red. Not wishing to prolong everyone's suffering, Elizabeth put on her most pleasant smile. "I'm sure, though the details may be obscure, in some way I was the responsible party."

"You see?" Lady Catherine directed this at Mr. Darcy. "She admits as much."

"I also believe that, if you are correct, Lady Catherine, the most fitting punishment is for everyone to return to their conversations. After all, did you not postulate my motive is attention?" Elizabeth kept her smile aimed at her hostess.

Colonel Fitzwilliam seemed to be taken with another of his coughing fits, this time raising his napkin to his face, muffling the sound and hiding his mouth. The corners of Mr. Darcy's lips twitched, the anger in his eyes fading to amusement. About the table, people exchanged glances. Lady Catherine scowled, but didn't intervene as conversation resumed.

Elizabeth dabbed at her dress again, sopping up the wine.

"I can send for a shawl," Miss de Bourgh whispered.

Not looking at her, something sure to catch Lady Catherine's attention, Elizabeth whispered back, "It's nearly dry. Thank you for taking the place set for me."

Miss de Bourgh didn't reply. Elizabeth resumed her discussion with Mr. Veitch, whom she felt even more kindly disposed toward than before. She decided his stories weren't as dry as she'd first imagined. Anyone willing to stand up to Lady Catherine for her certainly wasn't boring.

Much later, as the evening drew to a close and farewells were made, Mr. Darcy approached with a low bow. "Miss Elizabeth."

They weren't standing far from Lady Catherine. Elizabeth could all but see her ears turning toward their conversation. "Mr. Darcy. It's been an educational evening."

"I'm sorry we did not have the opportunity to hear you play tonight."

"You flatter me with your continued assertion I play well, sir."

He gave a slight shake of his head. "While I would flatter you in any way warranted, there is no flattery in my statement. You do play well, and I delight in listening."

Elizabeth smiled, hardly able to contain a laugh. How strange it was to hear such words leave Mr. Darcy's mouth. A quick glance showed Lady Catherine appeared quite livid.

"Will you walk tomorrow?" Mr. Darcy asked, favoring her with that warm look again.

Unaccountably, Elizabeth felt her pulse quicken. "I will. I've been enjoying seeing how much the park has changed since I've come here. I will walk directly following breakfast."

Mr. Darcy bowed again. "I bid you a pleasant evening, then."

"And I you," Elizabeth said, curtsying.

He moved away and the farewells continued. When they concluded and Elizabeth's party left, her final impression of Lady Catherine was of fury. She couldn't dwell on that, however, her mind taken up by the warmth in Mr. Darcy's eyes.

5

Elizabeth woke the next morning with a lightness in her heart. The bedroom was sunnier than the morning before, the decor somehow prettier. She smiled, recalling Lady Catherine's almost childish attempts to drive her off. Or had she intended for Elizabeth to have a strong reaction which would somehow show she was ill bred? It didn't matter, as it would take more than spilled wine and hollow accusations to cow her.

Recalling the spilled wine drew Elizabeth's eyes to her dress, which hung near the window. She and Charlotte had made a valiant attempt to remove the stains, all the while enduring Mr. Collins' lecturing, but the bodice would have to be reworked with new fabric. Elizabeth still had little intention of accepting the money Miss de Bourgh had offered, but thought she might ask for enough to buy fabric to repair her dress.

Bustling about the cozy room, Elizabeth readied for the day. Soon she was in the parlor, finding Charlotte and Maria there, but not Mr. Collins. It seemed the morning was only getting better.

"Good morning," Elizabeth said, heading for the sideboard. "Is Mr. Collins not yet about?"

"Good morning," Charlotte replied. She frowned slightly. "You must have missed him by moments in the hall. He's already breakfasted. He said he was wanted with all haste at Rosings."

"I think he didn't want to see Elizabeth," Maria said. "We heard the door to your room close and he went running from the parsonage."

"Maria, don't spread rumors." Charlotte's frown deepened as she turned it on her sister. "I'm sure he simply didn't want to get caught up in pleasantries when he knew he was meant to be at Rosings."

"But it seemed that he was listening for Elizabeth," Maria said.

"Maria."

Elizabeth used selecting her breakfast as an excuse to present her back, hiding her smile. Charlotte sounded exactly like Lady Lucas when she was angry. "Whatever his reasons, I'm pleased to breakfast with both of you."

In spite of her words, which she'd meant, Elizabeth found herself hurrying through her meal. She was looking forward to speaking candidly with Mr. Darcy on the previous evening's events. She wondered if she would have the courage to ask him what he suspected the young man she'd originally been meant to sit beside had been ordered to do. She had her suspicions, and none of them were appropriate avenues for conversation, pretend courtship or not.

As soon as she could without seeming rude, Elizabeth excused herself. Mr. Collins still hadn't returned, so she counted her morning triply blessed. She'd spent time with Charlotte, hadn't been made to endure her cousin, and would now meet Mr. Darcy.

Making her way outside, Elizabeth found the air was already warm enough she was glad she had worn short sleeves. She set a brisk pace across the parsonage lawn, turning down her favorite lane, where Mr. Darcy would be sure to find her. Her skirt swished against the taller grass alongside the road. All about her, the trees reaching out to offer dappled shade were alive with songbirds. Elizabeth couldn't imagine a lovelier day.

The sound of carriage wheels grew behind her, but Elizabeth didn't look back. It was uncommon for a horse drawn conveyance of one type or another to pass that way so early, but not unheard of. She moved deeper into the tall grass along the path to ensure she wasn't obstructing the road.

It wasn't until the vehicle slowed beside her that she realized it might be Mr. Darcy. She turned, smiling, and stopped. It was Lady Catherine's carriage, and it stopped as well. The curtain was pulled back and Lady Catherine peered out. Elizabeth's smile disappeared.

"You, Miss Bennet, get in."

Elizabeth raised her eyebrows at the harsh tone. "No, thank you," she said, and resumed walking.

The carriage creaked forward, keeping pace.

"I said, get in, you insolent hoyden."

Elizabeth shook her head, not looking or halting. If Lady Catherine had asked politely to begin with, she may have accepted. She was not going to obey such rude, impertinent commands, though. The angry tone, combined with Lady Catherine's attempts to humiliate her the evening before, made Elizabeth too distrustful to get into the carriage.

"I will not be disobeyed. Especially not by the likes of you."

Elizabeth continued to ignore her. She was coming up on a smaller path. If Lady Catherine wouldn't drive on, Elizabeth would take another trail. The carriage wouldn't be able to follow her down so narrow a passage, and she doubted the lady would get out and walk. Hopefully Mr. Darcy would still be able to find her, as it wouldn't be her usual route.

"Your previous impertinence forewarned me you would behave in this insolent fashion," Lady Catherine declared, her tone strident. "James, John, as I ordered."

Elizabeth glanced toward the carriage in time to see the two footmen standing on the back jump down. She halted, momentarily too incredulous to believe they were coming toward her. Her shock lasted only an instant. She turned and started running.

Elizabeth put forth her best effort, but her skirts encumbered her. Still, it took the footmen, James and John, several yards to catch her. One grabbed her about the shoulders. She struggled and writhed, calling out for help, but his arms encircled her like iron bands around a barrel.

The second tried to grab her legs, presumably to hoist her off the ground. Elizabeth kicked as hard as she could, scoring at least one good hit to his face and another to his chest. Eventually, though, he caught her up. They suspended her between them, lumbering back toward the carriage, which she could hear rolling nearer. The one who had her feet, who she thought might be John the wine-spiller from the evening before, was sweating and sported a reddened eye.

Elizabeth writhed in their grasp, still calling out. Something loomed to the side. She twisted to see the carriage. Muttering oaths, the footman holding her about the shoulders pulled open the door. Unceremoniously, they stuffed her in. She launched herself toward freedom, grabbing for the handle, but found the door wouldn't budge. She pounded on it, yelling for help. The carriage dipped, likely the footmen climbing back up, and then set off at a rapidly increasing pace. Gasping to catch her breath, Elizabeth fell silent.

"Have the sense to get off the floor, girl." Lady Catherine glared at her, holding her skirts away from Elizabeth as if they might be contaminated by touching her. "And don't bother with the doors. Even if you get one open, jumping at this speed would break your neck."

Elizabeth was still breathing hard. Unclenching her fists, she pushed her hair, most of it pulled loose, from her face. She glared up at her abductor. "You kidnapped me." She couldn't believe Lady Catherine would sink so low.

"No, you got in willingly, as my footmen and driver will tell anyone."

Elizabeth pulled herself into the seat across from Lady Catherine and slid over to the window. She didn't try the door again, for she could tell they were moving quite quickly. She did pull back the curtain, though, fixing her eyes on her surroundings. Unlike when she'd ridden with Miss de Bourgh, this time Elizabeth would make sure she knew where she was taken.

While she watched trees speed by, she worked to master her breath. She was more frightened than she would like to admit. Kidnapping was a serious offense, showing a terrifying desperation on Lady Catherine's part. She was obviously willing to risk persecution to be rid of Elizabeth. If she would kidnap, what other laws was she willing to break?

Elizabeth clenched her teeth over fear and anger. Lady Catherine wouldn't be worried about facing the repercussions of her actions. She would know no one would take Elizabeth's word over hers and her servants. There was no reason to imagine she planned anything worse. The woman wasn't mad. At least, Elizabeth hoped she wasn't.

"Why have you kidnapped me?" Elizabeth didn't take her eyes from the window.

"As I said, you got in willingly."

Elizabeth resisted the urge to shout at the infuriating woman.

"You will give up Darcy," Lady Catherine said, her tone as imperious as ever. "You will tell him you can never marry him. This time, be firm. It's obvious you made a mess of turning him down the first time."

Elizabeth gave a short bark of laughter. Maybe the woman was insane after all. "Even if I give him up, that does not mean he will marry Miss de Bourgh. Your daughter and I are not his only choices."

"I will attend to Darcy." Elizabeth could hear a rustle of fabric as Lady Catherine shifted in her seat. "Look at me when I speak to you, girl."

"I'm noting the way. You kidnapped me. I won't be abandoned in some remote location, unable to find my way back."

"Don't be a fool. I'm not going to leave you somewhere and have you try to lay blame on me for whatever ills befall you. Especially not when anything befalling you will be deserved, and the result of your own stupidity."

"I see your manners haven't deserted you," Elizabeth snapped, her voice sharp with sarcasm.

"You will not speak to me in that impertinent tone, girl."

"I will speak to you any way I please." Elizabeth pulled her eyes from the window to cast Lady Catherine a quick, baleful glare, but returned them to the landscape outside the carriage almost immediately. "You are the one who shed civility."

There was huffing from the other seat, but Elizabeth ignored it. She kept her eyes on their course. The carriage wasn't showing any sign of slowing down.

"If you must know, I am taking you to the Bird in Hand Inn. You will get on the stage there and go to London. When you get to London, my agent will meet the stage and give you money for cab fare to go to your relatives, along with fifty pounds to make it worth your while never to speak to Darcy again."

"You intend for me to go to London? Has it not occurred to you that I'll be missed?" Elizabeth decided not to dignify the offer of fifty pounds by acknowledging it.

"Later today, when you're too far away for him to follow, I will tell Darcy you realized you can never love him. You were so eager to go, you came to me and begged for a ride. Mr. Collins will inform his wife of the entire incident upon my return. She and her sister will have your things packed before you reach London. I'll see they're sent on to your relatives."

"I see you have every detail accounted for." Elizabeth pursed her lips, her mind churning. Knowing Lady Catherine's plan, she no longer felt much fear, but she was still deeply angered. She would not let Lady Catherine have her way.

"Of course I have everything figured out," Lady Catherine snapped. "I'm not a fool, and don't even think of walking back. It's nine miles."

Elizabeth didn't reply, for walking back was exactly what she was considering. Knowing the distance didn't deter her. Nine miles wasn't that far. She was strong. She could walk it in three hours.

"Well, girl?"

She ignored that. The carriage slowed, soon reaching a speed where Elizabeth might be able to jump without harming herself, assuming she could get the doors open. From her attempt earlier, she guessed the footmen had wedged them closed in some way. Without knowing what they'd done and having no tools, there seemed little sense in wasting energy trying to escape. It appeared, for the moment, Elizabeth was trapped.

She was not thwarted, however, though she still worried to what lengths Lady Catherine was prepared to go. Pondering the situation, Elizabeth realized her biggest obstacle was to appear to acquiesce so Lady Catherine would leave her alone. Left unobserved, she could embark on the journey back.

"I asked you a question."

"Not really," Elizabeth muttered, not considering 'well girl' to be much of a question.

"Speak up, girl."

"How do I know, once I'm in London, your agent will be there?" Elizabeth hoped questions would convince Lady Catherine she'd won. "Or that he'll turn over the money instead of keeping it?"

"He wouldn't dare defy me."

Elizabeth could hear the satisfaction in Lady Catherine's voice and cast her a quick glance. "Why can't your agent simply drive me to my relatives?"

"Stupid girl. He handles my money. He's not a coachman, but he'll be there. I sent him an express this morning, since he needed time to get the money. I knew it would only take a little pressure to persuade you to give up Darcy."

Elizabeth concentrated on memorizing the route still, but she lowered her shoulders, slouching back in the seat. She wanted to portray someone who'd given up. It was too bad Lady Catherine's agent would probably tell whatever story Lady Catherine told him to. Still, it might not hurt to find out more about him, in case she ever needed to find him. "How will I know him? I'm not approaching random men waiting at the coach stand in London. What's his name? What does he look like?"

After naming and describing her agent, Lady Catherine launched into a tirade, her voice so smug Elizabeth wanted to throw something at her. The subject was Elizabeth and her failings. Lady Catherine went on at length about how insignificant Elizabeth was, and how unworthy of Mr. Darcy. At some points, Elizabeth recognized an embellished version of Darcy's letter as Lady Catherine dredged up some of the complaints about her family. Most of the rant, however, concentrated on Elizabeth's unladylike behavior in taking long walks alone with either Darcy or Colonel Fitzwilliam.

Try as she might, Elizabeth had to hear most of what was said to her. She didn't respond, working to give no reaction at all and to appear utterly defeated. For a time, she was able to distract herself with daydreams about setting the authorities on Lady Catherine for kidnapping, but knew there was little help for her there. Not when it was her word against Lady Catherine's.

Finally, they slowed to a walk, entering a small town. The carriage pulled up before the Bird in Hand Inn. It bounced as at least one of the footmen got down. Elizabeth could hear something being done to the doors. Lady Catherine stuck her head out her window, ordering someone off her side. Elizabeth's door was yanked open. The footman she thought was John stood there, his wounded face a mask, his eyes straight ahead.

"Get out," Lady Catherine snapped.

Elizabeth did, not surprised the footman didn't offer any assistance, and not wishing him to. As soon as she took a step away, the door shut behind her. The footman scrambled up. Elizabeth didn't turn around when the carriage rattled away, stirring up a cloud of dust. It settled about her, clinging to her already dirty skirt. She blinked dust from her eyes.

A small man came down the inn steps toward her. "Miss, I am so sorry for the dust. You'll probably be more comfortable in the taproom. The sun getting hot and you don't have a hat."

Elizabeth hadn't realized her hat was lost until that moment. Thinking about it, she realized it must have come off during her struggle with the footmen, before she got into the carriage. She reached up, touching her hair. It felt a mess. She could only imagine how she looked, or how people in the taproom would view her. "I'm not comfortable going into the taproom," she said, meaning it. "I'll find a place in the shade."

The man squinted up at the sun. "But the stage isn't due for an hour and a half. It's sometimes early, but I'm not standing about out here for that long." He twined his hands together, looking nervously after Lady Catherine's fast dwindling carriage. "I'm to give your ticket to the driver when you board."

"Why don't you go to the taproom?" Elizabeth gave him a reassuring smile, taking in the small town with a quick glance. She made a vague gesture toward a grove of trees. "I'll be happier out here." Much happier. By the time the stage arrived, she hoped to be halfway back to the parsonage. Realizing he might look for her, she added, "I might look into sitting in the church or just walking around the town." Or I might not, she amended to herself.

"I suppose that will do well enough," he said, looking back toward the inn longingly. "You should be able to see the stage from anywhere on the main street, so keep to it. You'll have the time it takes for them to change the horses to get back here, but they are very quick."

"I'll keep that in mind." She headed toward the trees, which were in the same direction as the road she wished to take. Clouds were gathering, but they weren't thick enough to hide the location of the sun, and there was plenty of time to make the journey. She glanced back to see the man entering the tavern. Squaring her shoulders, Elizabeth lengthened her stride.

6

Darcy didn't join the others in the parlor for breakfast, not wishing to ruin a perfectly fine morning by listening to his aunt. He had his valet bring him up a light meal. Sipping his coffee, he dressed with greater care than usual. At one point, he realized he was humming and stopped, hoping none of the servants had taken note. A Darcy did not go about humming. He must be careful or the next thing he knew, he'd descend into something so vulgar as whistling.

After one last look in the mirror, something else he hoped wasn't noted, he quit his room and then, the house. Employing a lively pace, he soon found himself on Elizabeth's favorite trail. Giving in to the humming, for he was alone, he set out to find her. Anticipation built at each turn, only to go unrewarded. By the time he reached the end of where she usually walked, Darcy's mood darkened to one of concern.

Unsure how he could have missed her, he headed back. His eyes scanning the forests, fields and hedges, he returned not to Rosings, but to the parsonage. Still, he saw no sign of Elizabeth.

A knock on the parsonage door was rewarded by a maid. "Is Miss Bennet in?" Darcy asked. The girl cringed slightly, taking a step back, and Darcy realized his tone was overly harsh. "Or Mrs. Collins."

"I'll inquire, sir." The girl scurried away.

She hadn't asked him in, but she hadn't shut the door, so Darcy stepped into the foyer. A moment later, Mrs. Collins hurried down the hall toward him. Darcy sketched a quick bow.

"Mr. Darcy," Mrs. Collins exclaimed, her expression not reassuring him. "I'm told you're looking for Elizabeth. She isn't here. She went for a walk hours ago. If I may be so bold, I wasn't worried because I assumed she was with you."

"No. I have not seen her." Darcy was growing truly worried now. He'd hoped something had delayed Elizabeth at the parsonage, or their times had gotten crossed. He hadn't expected to find her missing.

"Mr. Collins was summoned to Rosings a short time ago. It's the second time he's been there this morning." Mrs. Collins imparted the information in a low voice, casting a quick glance over her shoulder, as if to ensure no one was in the hall behind her.

Darcy frowned. He wasn't sure what that could have to do with Elizabeth, but he shared Mrs. Collins' obvious concern. "I will go to Rosings now."

"Thank you. Please let us know as soon as you find her."

Darcy nodded, bowed again, and left. His long strides made quick work of the walk to Rosings. His aunt's carriage passed him on his way up the drive. As the curtains were open, it was easy to pick out Mr. Collins inside. Darcy waved, hoping the man would stop and speak with him, but Mr. Collins quickly looked away. His frown returned, Darcy hurried inside.

The footmen he questioned indicated Lady Catherine did not wish to be disturbed and that Anne was indisposed. Darcy found Richard in a small, sun-filled parlor at the back of the house. It was one Darcy knew their aunt never visited. Likely, she'd all but forgotten the cozy little room was there. Richard lowered his paper as Darcy came in.

"Good morning, if it is still," Richard said. He glanced over his shoulder, out a lace enshrouded window, as if trying to assess the time of day. "I trust you had a pleasant walk this morning, Darcy?"

"I did not."

Richard raised his eyebrows. "Your courtship does not fare well?"

"My courtship does not fare at all. I couldn't find Miss Bennet, though we were to meet. Mrs. Collins says Elizabeth has been away for hours. I'm beginning to worry." He kept his tone level, but knew he was understating. His worry already went beyond mere beginnings.

"Perhaps she did not take the path you believe?" Richard set aside his paper and stood. "I'll help you search."

"Thank you."

Mounted now, Darcy and Richard divvied up the various trails. They set out, agreeing they would return Elizabeth to the parsonage once they found her. Darcy covered his ground quickly, his concern growing with each mile. Finding nothing, he headed back, hoping Richard had better luck.

Darcy didn't see Richard's horse when he reached the Hunsford Parsonage, which gave him some hope. If Richard had discovered Elizabeth, they would be walking back, leading the horse. Feeling a bit less grim, he knocked. Another hope was that Elizabeth may already have returned, somehow missed by both him and Richard. To Darcy's surprise, Mr. Collins himself opened the door, stepping out.

"Mr. Collins." Darcy issued a nod of greeting. "Has Elizabeth returned yet?"

Mr. Collins looked over his shoulder, appearing nervous, but the face he turned to Darcy was composed into sanctimonious lines. "No, she hasn't returned, but you shouldn't be concerned about her. She is my cousin and my wife's guest. Instead of seeking out my cousin, you should turn your attentions to Miss de Bourgh. I can see to Miss Bennet's welfare. In my humble capacity as a clergyman I attend to many of my parishioners' needs, so you should not have any concern about my ability to take care of—"

Darcy didn't trouble himself to reply. He simply turned on his heels and walked back to his horse. He could hear the clergymen sputtering with indignation behind him, but didn't care. He would rather ride out to meet Richard than endure Mr. Collins' company.

He hadn't gone far when he spotted Elizabeth ahead on the lane, walking toward him. His first feeling was relief, quickly followed by joy. That happy emotion was chased away by a surge of annoyance for the grief she'd caused him.

This, too, did not last for long. As he urged his horse forward he discerned that she was hatless, her dress was dirty, her hair in disarray and her step slow. For a moment, Darcy's thoughts froze. Then all manner of terrible explanations ran through his head, leaving a blazing trail of anger in their wake. Not directed toward Elizabeth, but at whoever had put her in this state.

Reaching her side, he had one leg over his horse and was out of the saddle before the roan had even stopped. "Miss Bennet, what happened?"

She looked up at him, her eyes flashing with anger. Having feared a host of other emotions, Darcy felt he'd never seen so lovely a sight.

"Lady Catherine will deny it, but her footmen took hold of me and heaved me into her carriage." Her tone was as furious as her eyes. "I did my best to get free, but they were too strong. I got in a couple good kicks on one of them, though, at least once to the face. I think it was James or John. She took me to the Bird in Hand, and arranged for me to go to London. I decided not to."

Darcy took her hands in his, squeezing them tightly. He was aware of his heart's harsh pounding, in time with the drumming of livid anger churning in his breast. "She did what?" His voice came out very low as he struggled for calm.

"She abducted me and tried to force me to go to London."

Darcy shook his head, hardly able to believe it. Standing close now, he could see the red marks on Elizabeth's arms, looking like they would soon be bruises. If he got his hands on those footmen . . . but, no, that wasn't cutting off the head of the serpent, only the tail. "I see."

"I should like to go to the parsonage, to gather my things," Elizabeth said. "I no longer feel safe here."

"Yes, of course." Though it took some effort, Darcy relinquished her hands. Not for long, though. Once he retrieved his horse's reins, he offered her his free arm.

Elizabeth accepted it, leaning on it as if for actual support, not mere show. Darcy looked about, wondering who had dropped her there and why they hadn't taken her to the parsonage door. Was it someone who feared his aunt? He would like to thank them, and see if they would offer testimony, for he fully intended to confront Lady Catherine. He would not let her behavior go unanswered.

"Who brought you here?" he asked.

"No one. I walked." Elizabeth's voice was a mixture of amusement and weariness.

"You walked?" Darcy cast her a startled glance. "Are you sure it was the Bird in Hand? That's just over nine miles away."

"Yes, I'm sure and yes, Lady Catherine informed me of the distance. She seemed to think it enough of a deterrent. I did not agree."

Darcy's respect for Elizabeth increased. She could have gone to London and written him, instead of walking nine miles, alone.

"I must admit, I don't know what I would have done had I gotten lost. There were a few times I was worried I had. I kept a careful eye on our route, but distances covered by carriage can be deceiving."

If Darcy hadn't been leading his horse, he would have covered the hand on his arm with his. The thought of Elizabeth wandering about the countryside, lost, was not to be borne. They turned off the lane toward the parsonage.

The front door opened and Mr. and Mrs. Collins hurried out, along with Miss Maria Lucas. Mrs. Collins and her sister brimmed with relief and happiness, but Mr. Collins paled. Mrs. Collins hurried toward them, pulling Elizabeth away from Darcy to hug her. Her husband trailed behind, his face folded into a grimace. Maria Lucas looked on with uncertain eyes.

"Elizabeth, I'm so glad Mr. Darcy found you. I was so worried." Mrs. Collins released Elizabeth, only to take hold of her shoulders and look her up and down. "Whatever happened? Mr. Collins returned from the parsonage earlier and made Maria and I pack your things. He said Lady Catherine informed him you'd left, but I knew that couldn't be right. You're a mess. Please assure me everything is well."

"No real harm was done me," Elizabeth answered, with more charity than Darcy was feeling. "Lady Catherine wished me to leave and attempted to help me on my way. I thought it wrong to do so without saying goodbye or having an escort, so I walked back from where she left me."

"If Lady Catherine wishes you to leave, you should leave," Mr. Collins said. "You are no longer welcome here. I shan't permit anyone who's offended Lady Catherine to reside under my roof." He glared at the eyes turned toward him, but his gaze skittered away when it reached Darcy's. "Cousin Elizabeth, you must go."

Darcy's hand balled into a fist, his anger over Elizabeth's abduction finding new focus. He took a step forward, meaning to wipe Mr. Collins' attempt at an assertive look from his face.

A touch on his arm drew Darcy's attention to Elizabeth's slim hand resting there. She looked up at him, meeting his eyes with a mildly amused, though tired, gaze. She gave a slight shake of her head.

Pleasure pushed back some of his anger. The intimacy of that subtle communication, coupled with the fact she'd been aware of his intention, made Darcy smile. These things bespoke of a woman who was not disinclined, or even indifferent, but of one who cared for him. Darcy shot Mr. Collins a dark glare, but forced his fist to relax.

"Mrs. Collins," Darcy said, turning from her odious husband. "Miss Bennet needs a bath, a meal, and possibly a chance to rest."

"She can't stay here if Lady Catherine disapproves," Mr. Collins protested, all but hopping from foot to foot with worry.

"What about your assertion that you would see to the welfare of your cousin?" Darcy asked, his anger reigniting. He let the question hang for a long moment, unanswered, before turning to Elizabeth. "You said you would like to leave Kent. Would you like to go to London today? I can arrange it."

"Yes, thank you." To Darcy's ear, she sounded relieved.

"How long do you need to get ready?"

"One or two hours," Mrs. Collins said firmly, answering for Elizabeth. "Can you take my sister as well? She is a little young to travel alone. She was meant to return to Hertfordshire with Elizabeth."

Darcy suspected, from the look on Mrs. Collins' face each time she glanced at her husband, that Maria Lucas was also being sent away from what might, for a time, be a rather unhappy home. It served his purpose as well, for Elizabeth would need a companion. "Your sister will be quite welcome." He cast the girl, still standing nervously off to the side, a reassuring smile.

"But she can't rest here," Mr. Collins said, casting worried looks in the direction of Rosings. "Lady Catherine--"

"Elizabeth will be leaving soon enough to suit your Lady Catherine, I'm sure," Mrs. Collins said firmly. "Come inside, Elizabeth. I'll order you a bath. We'll have to unpack some of your things. You can't wear that dress. I hope it isn't ruined." She put an arm about Elizabeth, leading her away. "Come along, Maria. We must pack your things now, too."

Mr. Collins' gaze followed his wife as she shepherded her two charges inside. Elizabeth cast a smile over her shoulder at Darcy, drawing an answering one from him in return. Beside him, Mr. Collins mumbled and moaned, almost as a man possessed.

As soon as the parsonage door closed behind the women, Darcy turned to Mr. Collins. "Do not think I will forget this."

Mr. Collins gave a little squeak, jumped, and ran off across the lawn, in the direction of Rosings.

Darcy mounted, directing his roan back up the lane. He knew Collins was off to report to Lady Catherine, but didn't care. She could have ten fabrications waiting by the time he reached Rosings. He wouldn't believe a one. If possible, he didn't even intend to listen to them.

Richard was coming down the lane, obviously on his way to the parsonage. His face was creased in concern and he was carrying a hat that Darcy recognized as belonging to Elizabeth. Richard urged his horse into a quicker pace when he saw Darcy, meeting him in the center of the lane.

"Miss Bennet is in the parsonage, unharmed," Darcy said, though he didn't quite consider that to be the case. "Where did you find the hat?"

Richard's expression lightened with relief. "That's good to hear." He held up the hat, angling it so Darcy could see some of Elizabeth's hair still pinned to it. "It's obvious this was ripped off her head. I found it not far down her usual path. I don't mind telling you, I feared the worst."

"When I was looking for her earlier, I walked that way, and back. I never saw it." Darcy was glad he hadn't. He could only imagine how frantic finding it would have made him.

"It was in tall grass. I wouldn't have seen it on foot." Richard proffered the hat, which Darcy accepted. "You found her at the parsonage, then? What happened?"

"I found her coming down the lane. What happened is that Aunt Catherine abducted her this morning and took her to the Bird in Hand. She was trying to force Elizabeth to leave Kent." Darcy couldn't speak of it without anger adding a harsh edge to his tone.

"I beg your pardon?" Richard cast him a startled look. "Darcy, that seems a bit much, even for Aunt Catherine."

"She'll deny it, of course. She had two footmen with her." Darcy had to speak around clenched teeth. "They'll likely deny it as well, but Elizabeth said she kicked one in the face when they picked her up to shove her into the carriage. She thinks it was either John or James, so there might be evidence."

Richard still looked incredulous, but he nodded. "I'll look into that." He cast Darcy an assessing glance. "I don't know that I'd trust you with questioning them just now."

"You're probably right. I need to speak to my coachman. I'm leaving Rosings and taking Elizabeth and Miss Lucas with me. Shall we?" He gestured up the lane, toward Rosings.

Richard nodded, turning his horse. They rode in silence, Darcy in no mood for idle banter. When they reached the stable, he handed over his roan and went to find his coachman, to make arrangements for the journey to London. Richard slipped off in a different direction.

Darcy didn't seek out his aunt when he reached Rosings, but also made no move to enter with any stealth. His mood was too dark for subtlety. He was headed toward his room, to inform his valet they were leaving, when he heard his name called. Stopping, Darcy turned, his posture ridged.

"Have you heard what that ungrateful hoyden you've shackled yourself to has done now?" Lady Catherine cried, trundling down the hall toward him. "Why, she came to me this morning and demanded I see she reached London immediately. Then, after accepting my assistance, the fickle creature changed her mind and walked back from where we met the coach."

"Is that so?" Darcy's voice was cold enough to chill champagne.

"Of course it is so. Did I not just say it's so? My driver and footmen will all bear witness." She stopped before Darcy, breathing a bit hard from her exertions. She glared at him with an icy disdain to rival his own. "Obviously, the girl is unfit. You cannot see her again."

Darcy stared at is aunt, trying to master his emotions. "There is certainly someone in Kent I do not care to see again, but it is not Miss Bennet. Nor do I believe your tale."

"You must. I have my word and that of two servants. Miss Bennet, I'm sure, has only her own, and all know a little country hoyden like her will say anything to land a wealthy husband."

"Do not press me, Aunt Catherine."

She glowered at him, not backing down. Footsteps sounded behind her and Darcy looked up to see Richard coming toward them. Lady Catherine whirled to face him, her hauteur not dimming.

"I've spoken with the footmen, James and John," Richard said as he reached them.

"And they have informed you I am telling the truth." Lady Catherine's voice was triumphant.

"They did indeed," Richard said.

"For which I'm sure you've paid them well," Darcy added.

His aunt cast him a smug look.

"One of them, John, is sporting the beginnings of a truly spectacular black eye." Richard delivered this information in grim tones. "Aunt Catherine, I'm ashamed of you."

"What does a footman's black eye have to do with any of this?" she snapped. "Don't be absurd, Richard."

"Elizabeth said she kicked John in the eye when he picked her up to put her, against her will, into your carriage," Darcy said.

"I'm sure the fiendish woman simply noticed his eye at dinner and has taken it upon herself to invent further tales."

Darcy ignored that, for there were many witnesses, including himself, to attest to the footman's lack of a black eye at dinner the night before. They'd all gotten a good look at him, after all, standing behind Elizabeth, his face suffused with guilt and a half empty glass in his hand. "How does this footman explain his injury?" he asked Richard.

"He said he was kicked by a mule."

"You see?" Lady Catherine said.

"A mule?" Darcy didn't know if he should take that as further insult to Elizabeth, or be amused.

"Yes. When I asked the other, James, if he could confirm as much, he said he could." Richard gave Darcy a hard grin. "He also laughed and said it was the smallest mule he'd ever seen. Couldn't have been even nine stones."

"I see." Darcy turned to his aunt. "Aunt Catherine, I am leaving Rosings. You will be pleased to know I am taking Miss Bennet with me, so you will not need to suffer her presence again. I do not know if I shall return, ever. I wish you to know, no matter what happens between Miss Bennet and myself, I shall never, ever marry Anne."

"You think your plan to leave is news to me, you fool of a boy?" Lady Catherine screeched. "I already know of your plans. I have loyal servants, if not a loyal nephew." Lady Catherine's eyes bulged with anger. "And as for your little trip, see how your Miss Bennet feels about traveling with you unescorted, for the Lucas brat isn't going. I've spoken to Mr. Collins in no uncertain terms this time. Elizabeth Bennet shall not ruin Mrs. Collins' visit with her sister on a whim. She'll wish she'd gone on to London this morning. If you take her there in your carriage, her reputation will be in tatters. Marrying her will make you the laughing stock of the ton."

Darcy stared at her for a long moment. Her overstuffed, wrinkled bosom heaved with anger. He was amazed she hadn't showered spittle about the hall with the vehemence of her speech. Richard shook his head, looking disgusted.

"I will be leaving within two hours," Darcy said, his calm finally back in place. He gave his aunt a polite bow, then nodded to Richard. Turning, Darcy walked to his room without hurry. He could hear Lady Catherine's harsh breathing behind him as he walked down the hall.

"Aunt Catherine," Richard murmured in a sad, disappointed voice.

Darcy turned the corner and continued on to his room. He informed his valet of their impending departure. He wasn't sure if his aunt's threat about Maria Lucas had substance, but knew he'd find someone else, if needed. One way or another, he and Elizabeth were leaving Kent. He truly didn't care if either of them ever returned.

7

Bathed and wearing a dress that hid the marks on her arms, Elizabeth waited alone in the parlor for Mr. Darcy to appear. She didn't wish to be alone, for it would have been pleasant to spend her final moments in Kent with her friend Charlotte, but Charlotte had taken to her room. Earlier, when Mr. Collins returned from Rosings, he'd informed Charlotte that Maria was not to go with Elizabeth. He'd accompanied that with a rant about violating wedding vows and the consequences that could bring down on a woman. That led to a terrific argument between the two, loud enough for the entire household to hear.

Mr. Collins had prevailed, emboldened by what Elizabeth could only guess was an extreme fear of Lady Catherine's wrath should he fail. Charlotte, after a quick and tearful goodbye to Elizabeth, had retreated to her room. Elizabeth hadn't seen Maria, and assumed the poor girl was hiding.

Elizabeth supposed she might have been worried. After all, without Maria Lucas, who would chaperone her? Under the circumstances, it was conceivable Mr. Darcy might go back on his offer to take her to London. Or, if she permitted herself to be truly fanciful, that he would take her without a chaperone, thus forcing her to marry him. However, if he could procure an open carriage, their ride would at least have a semblance of propriety. She tried to imagine herself riding next to the coachman. She would become dusty again, but at least she wouldn't be walking.

Better yet, she might ride next to Mr. Darcy. She permitted herself to picture it, him smiling again, the anger he'd shown on her behalf smoothed away by a cheerful journey. They would speak on all the things they normally did, as they ought to have done that morning on their walk. The image of Mr. Darcy made it easier for her to avoid dwelling on the fear and anger she'd felt when the footmen forced her into Lady Catherine's carriage.

Elizabeth shook her head. No. She would not think about that. She would think positive and cheerful thoughts. Mr. Darcy was a man of his word. He would arrive in good time and with a proper escort for her. She realized this showed a change from her previously unflattering opinions of him, but she couldn't help herself from believing it.

True to her belief, after what she estimated was slightly over two hours from when last she'd seen him, Elizabeth sighted two carriages through the parlor curtains. The smaller, she assumed, held Mr. Darcy's servants. The larger was splendid, gleaming with paint and lacquer in the afternoon light, and promised a singularly comfortable ride to London.

Elizabeth stood, heading to the hall where her trunk already waited. A maid reached the door before her and opened it, stepping back with a curtsy. Servants came forward and hefted Elizabeth's trunk. She followed them to the carriage, where a well-dressed footman opened the door and offered her a hand up.

Elizabeth smiled as her eyes found Mr. Darcy. Nor was he alone. Colonel Fitzwilliam shared the long seat, and Miss de Bourgh sat opposite the colonel. Elizabeth took the space beside her, offering greetings, which were warmly returned.

The door was closed behind Elizabeth, but light spilled in the open windows. In moments, they were rumbling forward, leaving the Hunsford Parsonage behind. Elizabeth settled against the comfortably upholstered seat, aware Mr. Darcy's was the finest carriage she'd ever ridden in. "Miss de Bourgh, I am surprised, but very pleased, to see you here."

"As am I to be here." Miss de Bourgh smiled, her eyes livelier than Elizabeth had before seen them.

"I did not expect Mr. Darcy to secure me so exalted a chaperone, if I may presume to refer to you as such," Elizabeth said.

"You may, for I am," Miss de Bourgh replied. "From Darcy's point of view, I am here to keep your reputation safe."

"And from your own?" Elizabeth asked, not missing the distinction.

Miss de Bourgh's eyes sparkled with amusement. "From mine, I'm escaping my mother."

"Shall I keep a watch out the window for her carriage attempting to overtake us?"

Miss de Bourgh looked slightly startled at that, then laughed. "You are correct in your assumption that my mother refused me permission to go, but I reasoned with her."

Elizabeth managed not to comment on the likelihood of reason prevailing with Lady Catherine, but her face must have given away her incredulousness, for Miss de Bourgh's smile grew. Across from them, Mr. Darcy and Colonel Fitzwilliam were watching the exchange with amusement.

"Reasoned?" Elizabeth finally prodded, giving in to her curiosity over what role logical thought had played in dealing with Lady Catherine. In Elizabeth's experience, reason carried little weight with the woman.

"I told her that if she let you and Darcy go alone, he would be forced to marry you. She returned that he wouldn't, because he would be looked down on for such a marriage." She gave Elizabeth an apologetic shrug. "I reiterated that he would, and then the thing would be done and over with. She offered to send one of our maids with you. I replied that if I went, Darcy would be forced to spend time with me and see to my comforts. Once she heard that, she couldn't get me packed quickly enough."

Elizabeth raised her eyebrows. She shot a quick glance at Mr. Darcy, who still looked amused. It surprised Elizabeth how troubling it was to her that Miss de Bourgh should even hint that she might pursue Mr. Darcy.

Following Elizabeth's gaze, Miss de Bourgh shook her head. "I have no interest in marrying Darcy." She cast him an apologetic look. "That said, I don't mind forcing him to see to my comfort." She turned back to Elizabeth. "I truly was hoping to stay with you, though, to further our friendship. I'm assuming your aunt and uncle will have enough space for me, since they were planning to house Miss Lucas?"

"We will have to share," Elizabeth said. "But yes, they have room, and when the circumstances are explained, they will welcome you."

"Then it will be an adventure," Miss de Bourgh said, appearing pleased.

"Miss Bennet has already had an adventure," Colonel Fitzwilliam said. "From which I hope you have fully recovered?"

"I have, thank you. Really, no harm was done." Elizabeth caught Mr. Darcy's frown, but he didn't speak.

"What sort of adventure?" Miss de Bourgh asked. "I know

something happened, but couldn't learn what. Mother said you attempted to go to London and failed, which seemed quite odd."

"It was more along the lines of your mother attempting to persuade me to go to London, but failing," Elizabeth said, feeling that to say more would be impolite. Lady Catherine was still Miss de Bourgh's mother, no matter how monstrously she behaved.

Miss de Bourgh's eyes narrowed. She looked to Colonel Fitzwilliam, across from her. "I heard rumors one of the footmen was injured, somehow. How could Miss Bennet going to London or not result in that?"

"It seems one of the footmen was kicked during the incident," the colonel said.

Beside him, Elizabeth could see Mr. Darcy's temper worsening. She realized he was angry. Fortunately, for she wouldn't want him to do anything rash on her behalf, they were driving away from those who were the likely targets of the emotion. Even though that was the case, she couldn't help but feel a small thrill that his temper should be roused on her behalf.

"Kicked?" Miss de Bourgh's eyes were bright with interest.

"Yes, and I confirmed the injury. Miss Bennet rightly recalled the recipient of the blow was named John or James. Armed with that knowledge, it wasn't difficult to find one with a mark from Miss Bennet's kick."

"That was clever of you to remember their names," Miss de Bourgh said, turning to Elizabeth. "I don't know the circumstances of the kick, but I can't imagine I'd keep such a clear head."

"I was only able to recall because both names began with the same letter," Elizabeth demurred. "And because it was a similar name to the footman who spilled wine on me at dinner. In truth, I believe it to be the same man."

"If there was reason to kick him, is there reason to press some form of charges?" Miss de Bourgh asked, her tone tentative now.

Elizabeth shook her head. "I don't believe there is enough evidence for me to call on, and I don't wish to, at any rate. I'm unharmed."

Mr. Darcy turned to look out the window, but not before Elizabeth saw his glower.

"I was hoping to find sufficient evidence," Colonel Fitzwilliam said. "I fully planned to threaten charges, at the least, for Lady

Catherine shouldn't be permitted to feel no repercussions for abducting Miss Elizabeth and trying to force her to go to London, unescorted. Unfortunately, the footman told me he was kicked by a mule, and the other one confirmed that story."

"My mother did what?" Miss de Bourgh looked startled. "That was quite low, even for her, and the footmen are firm in their denial of the business? Have they no shame?"

"Actually, the one who was injured seemed fairly miserable," Colonel Fitzwilliam said. "Whether it was guilt, fear or embarrassment, I can't say."

"A mule?" Elizabeth reiterated with mock indignation, attempting to lighten the mood, for now Miss de Bourgh was as grim as Mr. Darcy.

"I believe they claimed it was a very small mule," the colonel replied with a straight face.

Elizabeth laughed, amused by the added insult. "Really, it's all quite ridiculous, and there's nothing to be done."

"No, I suppose not," Miss de Bourgh said. Her tone was angry, but thoughtful. "I shall not forget this, though. It will help me to stand up to my mother."

LONDON

"Miss Bennet's a sweet girl, who deserves a good husband. Just not me."

8

Once he got over reliving his anger at his aunt's treatment of Elizabeth, Darcy never remembered enjoying a journey more. Richard was his usual charming self. In spite of her ordeal, Elizabeth was cheerful and enchanting. Anne started out grim after learning what her mother had done, but soon began to contribute to the conversation.

Drawn into the comradery within the carriage, Darcy relaxed and enjoyed the company. It wasn't until Elizabeth was required to give directions to the coachman that he started to worry. Was he taking Anne somewhere that would be inappropriate? What would he do if he decided his cousin couldn't stay with Elizabeth's relatives?

Darcy looked across at Elizabeth. Her face not only showed no anxiety, but seemed to warm with anticipation. How could she be so eager to go to a part of town populated by tradesmen? More, how could she appear so enthusiastic to see her mother's relatives? Her mother and the one aunt that Darcy had met weren't people to inspire such enthusiasm. The nearer they drew to their destination, the tenser Darcy found himself.

Richard pulled the curtain farther back, peering out. "What do you suggest we tell your aunt and uncle about why you've arrived so early, and with us, Miss Bennet?"

"The truth," Elizabeth said. "It will go better if we let them in on it. They and my sister Jane can keep a secret." Darcy didn't miss the way she looked at him when she said her sister's name, some of the friendliness leaving her eyes. "We'll have to say something about Georgiana. May we reveal Lady Catherine is threatening to expose a secret about her? We can tell them it truly isn't bad, only something that would be embarrassing to her. My family will not pry."

"I think so," Darcy said. "Richard?"

"Agreed. The worst that can get out is that there is a secret."

"Anne?" Darcy asked.

"Shouldn't we prepare a false secret, in case someone does press us?" Anne asked.

Darcy realized his cousin was afraid she would give in, if questioned. While he would like to believe Elizabeth about her aunt and uncle, and did believe her about her sister, if the rumor that there was a secret got out, he could picture someone else questioning Anne. Still, it seemed wrong to compound an error with falsehood. "I don't care to lie."

"Nor do I." Anne sounded slightly offended. "I mean only to plan for contingencies."

"If someone troubles you about Georgiana, come straight to me," Richard said. "I will trouble them back."

Richard said it easily, almost as if he joked. Indeed, there was a smile on his face. Darcy could see the glint in his cousin's eyes, though. He knew Richard's general attitude of amiability, when not acting in his capacity as a colonel, fooled people into thinking him benign. Richard was anything but. He'd simply mastered an air of affability that had always eluded Darcy.

The carriage pulled to a stop and they disembarked. Darcy's mood darkened, though he saw nothing untoward about the compact, neat-looking building before him. Not outwardly, at least. He hoped Elizabeth's uncle and aunt would prove tolerable, that both Elizabeth and Anne would be welcome and that the household was acceptable. The sun hadn't set, but it was low in the sky. If he had to make other arrangements for Anne, it would have to be done promptly.

Gliding past Richard and Anne, Elizabeth headed confidently for the door. Darcy waved over one of his men, making arrangements for the smaller carriage to head to Darcy House as soon as Elizabeth's and Anne's luggage was unloaded. The larger carriage he bid wait. He resisted the urge to order a room made up for Anne, or to have a hunt put on for a proper chaperone to meet her at Darcy House, wanting to give Elizabeth's relatives a chance to prove suitable. His mind fleetingly went to his cousin, Lady Agatha, but her house was too noisy and chaotic for Anne. He turned back to see Elizabeth's knock answered almost immediately, the thick wooden door swinging open to reveal a maid. Surprise registered on the young woman's face.

"Miss Elizabeth." The maid's eyes moved past Elizabeth to Richard, Anne, Darcy and then the carriages.

"Hello Sarah," Elizabeth said. "Is my aunt at home? Or my

uncle?"

To her credit, the young woman hardly hesitated. She stepped back with a nod, dropped a curtsy, and rearranging her features into polite disinterest. "I will inquire. If you'll follow me, miss?"

"Thank you," Elizabeth said.

They were led down a clean, tastefully decorated hall and shown into an equally tasteful parlor. It wasn't a large room, but it was sensibly, gracefully and comfortably decorated. Darcy couldn't help but note how much more pleasant it seemed than most of his aunt's parlors. With another curtsy, the maid left them.

Darcy turned to Elizabeth, waiting for her to sit, signaling they all should. He could see Anne and Richard looking about them, but couldn't detect whether they were assessing the home for suitability for Anne to stay in or simply curious. Elizabeth moved toward a plush blue sofa.

Footsteps in the hall brought her back around. Darcy turned as well. A stylishly dressed woman entered. She was not young, but he could easily pick out the traces of youthful beauty in her face. A kind smile added to the impression of calm intelligence she projected.

"Elizabeth, how lovely to see you," she said, coming forward and embracing Elizabeth, who returned the gesture with obvious warmth. The woman, whom Darcy could only assume was Mrs. Gardiner, stepped back, looking about her. "And with guests."

Her pleasant demeanor didn't change as she remarked on the three strangers in her parlor. Again, Darcy couldn't help but compare this with his aunt. Lady Catherine would have railed against the intrusion of uninvited callers. Smiling, Elizabeth introduced them.

"It's a pleasure to meet you all," Mrs. Gardiner said amongst the obligatory murmurs of greeting. "Please, sit. Would you care for refreshments? You must tell me why you have arrived early. I sent Sarah for Jane. She's upstairs in the school room, assisting the children with their lessons."

"Refreshments would be lovely," Elizabeth said. "That is, so long as they don't endanger your plans for dinner. We've been on the road all afternoon."

Elizabeth sat, the others following suit, while Mrs. Gardiner sent word to the kitchen.

"Is Uncle Gardiner home?" Elizabeth asked.

"He will be shortly."

Miss Bennet hurried into the room, stopping to look about. "Elizabeth," she said, smiling, before turning to him. "Mr. Darcy," she added, obviously surprised to see him.

Miss Bennet dropped a curtsy, but not before Darcy observed a certain lackluster he hadn't seen in her before, along with a heightened paleness. She also appeared thinner, though the change didn't detract from her beauty.

Darcy and Richard stood, and more introductions were exchanged. During them, Mr. Gardiner entered and refreshments were served. Mr. Gardiner, Darcy was pleasantly pleased to note, was crisp in both dress and deportment, well-spoken, and comported himself like a gentleman. That he was a brother to Mrs. Bennet and Mrs. Phillips, Darcy could hardly credit. He could see why Elizabeth had looked forward to visiting the Gardiners with such obvious pleasure.

"Now, let us come down to it," Mr. Gardiner said, once all were served and settled. "I am always pleased to see you, dear Elizabeth, and honored to make the acquaintances of you all, but I sense a tale here."

Elizabeth looked to him. Darcy raised his eyebrows. Was it not more Elizabeth's tale? Richard cleared his throat, leaning forward in his chair.

"I believe we may start with mention of Darcy's and my mutual aunt, Miss de Bourgh's mother, Lady Catherine de Bourgh. She is, shall I say, a lady of superior resolve and admirable singlemindedness and self-assurance."

From there, Richard proceeded with a discreet and truncated version of events. He made no mention of Darcy's first proposal or the letter which had spurred Lady Catherine's initial ultimatum and threat. He also did not divulge any details of Georgiana's scandal, saying only that it was a harmless matter, but embarrassing for a young girl.

There was no avoiding mention of Darcy's, to their view, pretend courtship of Elizabeth, embarked on in order to counter Lady Catherine's threat until Anne's birthday, but Richard's brisk style of reporting permitted Darcy to sit through the recounting without embarrassment. He did catch Mrs. Gardiner's keen eyes on him at one point. He attempted a look of indifference, hoping she didn't see behind the façade of the proposal to his hopes he might still win Elizabeth.

Though Richard employed the same understated and efficient manner when he reached the incident which had spurred them to leave

Kent, namely Elizabeth's abduction, Darcy's mood darkened. He could sense a similar antagonism in both Gardiners. Miss Bennet, for her part, turned wide eyes on Elizabeth, reaching over to take her hand.

"So, here we are, humbly seeking succor," Richard concluded.

"As you can see, I am completely well," Elizabeth added, her smile reassuring.

"Oh, but Lizzy, how awful," Miss Bennet said, tears in her eyes.

Darcy realized Miss Bennet was, indeed, a gentle soul. If she had loved Bingley, which seemed more likely in view of the state they found her in upon their arrival, he hoped she would soon be over it. Though he considered Bingley a close friend, Darcy didn't think a man whose affections were as transient as Bingley's deserving of the heart of such a woman.

"Truly, I am well," Elizabeth repeated. "I do have a boon to ask, though." She looked to her aunt and uncle. "Can you spare room for Miss de Bourgh and myself?"

"Yes, of course we can," Mrs. Gardiner said. "You are always welcome here, Elizabeth, and we'd be honored for Miss de Bourgh to be our guest." She turned her warm expression on Darcy, then Richard. "And we would also be honored if you would both stay for dinner."

Dinner was accepted and arrangements made for the ladies' luggage and room, and for Darcy's carriage. Mr. Gardiner suggested the gentlemen retire to his study. Mrs. Gardiner excused herself to see to the children, who would be eating before the adults. Elizabeth followed her aunt, saying her cousins would be upset if she didn't greet them. Anne turned to Miss Bennet and expressed an interest in seeing the children as well. Darcy watched his cousin follow Miss Bennet out with some surprise. He couldn't remember Anne ever spending any time with children.

As they dispersed, Darcy realized he no longer had any qualms about leaving Anne with the Gardiners. Yes, she would have to share a room, something she'd never had to do before. They may not have a home as grand as Anne or he were accustomed to, but the Gardiners seemed intelligent, kind and well-mannered. Remaining would be a bit of an adventure for his cousin, but Darcy rather thought it might do Anne some good.

No, there was no reason to quibble over the arrangements for Anne. Nor was there anything disagreeable about adjourning to Mr.

Gardiner's office with him and Richard, the two of whom struck up a conversation on fishing even as they headed down the hall. Glancing back, Darcy caught a glimpse of Elizabeth's skirt as she went around a corner, following Mrs. Gardiner. The only disagreeable thing was that, for the first time since entering the carriage earlier that day, he was being parted from the woman he was courting.

9

After a few minutes with the Gardiner children, where Miss de Bourgh stayed in the background, Elizabeth, Jane and Miss de Bourgh retired to the room they were to share. It would be cramped, with three, but Elizabeth's aunt and uncle didn't have an excessively large home. Elizabeth watched Miss de Bourgh's reaction carefully as they stepped inside. She caught the surprise, but Miss de Bourgh was thoughtful enough to quickly cloak it in a smile.

"What a lovely room," she said.

In truth, it was. It was a bigger room than the one Elizabeth shared with Jane at Longbourn. It also had two beds. It was airy and done in light colors, without any garish or heavy-handed decorations to antagonize sensibilities.

As they unpacked, it soon became clear the wardrobe was a snug fit, though they were already dressed and left out what they would wear to dinner. Elizabeth carefully kept some of her things back, leaving them inside her trunk. As they worked, they agreed Miss de Bourgh would take the bed away from the window, while Elizabeth and Jane would share the other, which was larger. By how clumsily she went about it, it was readily apparent Miss de Bourgh had never unpacked for herself before.

Once everything was settled and they turned to readying for dinner, it became apparent she also hadn't ever dressed without a maid. Taking pains to alleviate Miss de Bourgh's obvious awkwardness, Elizabeth assisted her with her dress. Jane offered to do both Elizabeth's and Miss de Bourgh's hair, and both sister's made a point of helping each other with many small things, to convey what a natural state of affairs it was. Elizabeth couldn't help but feel charitable toward Miss de Bourgh, who'd lost her own sister and been encased alone in a house with Lady Catherine.

Dinner was a pleasant affair. Mr. Darcy actually spoke, seeming genuinely at ease with her aunt, uncle and Jane. Miss de Bourgh was as quiet as usual, but she took in everything with wide eyes. Colonel Fitzwilliam, seated beside Jane, was at his most charming. Elizabeth had the impression her sister was in no small amount responsible for that, but Jane seemed oblivious to the compliment.

As the evening progressed, Elizabeth realized she enjoyed having Mr. Darcy and his cousins meet those members of her family whose manners didn't cause her to blush. Though his frankness still rankled, she couldn't help but acknowledge the truth in much of what Mr. Darcy had said about her mother and younger sisters. The thought came without bitterness, and she realized she'd forgiven that portion of his letter. When the evening drew to a close and the time came for Mr. Darcy and Colonel Fitzwilliam to leave, Elizabeth was sorry. She couldn't recall a more amiable evening.

After the gentlemen departed, Miss de Bourgh stirred. "I do not mean to end a lovely occasion, but I must admit to being terribly tired."

"It's no wonder, of course, after the day you've had," Elizabeth's aunt said, her expression kind.

Miss de Bourgh looked between Elizabeth and Jane, her face questioning.

"I'm tired as well," Jane said, standing. "Miss de Bourgh, if you'll be so kind as to help me with my pins and ties, I'd be happy to help you."

"Thank you." Miss de Bourgh looked relieved.

Elizabeth realized she'd been embarrassed, not wanting to ask for help in front of everyone. She watched the two leave the room, glad Jane had understood so quickly. Then, Jane was always sensitive to the happiness of others.

"I'm off to peek in on the children and then to bed," Elizabeth's aunt said. "Do you require anything, Lizzy?"

"No, thank you." Elizabeth looked to her uncle. "There was a small matter I hoped to discuss with Uncle Gardiner, if I may?"

"Of course." Her aunt crossed the room, dropping a motherly kiss on Elizabeth's brow. "Don't argue philosophy into the night. Mr. Gardiner always rises early."

"We won't, Aunt."

As Elizabeth's aunt quit the room, her uncle turned to her, his expression questioning.

Elizabeth looked about, noting servants moving nearby. "May we speak in your office?"

"Certainly, my dear," Mr. Gardiner said. He led the way there, taking up a seat behind his desk.

Uncle Gardiner's desk wasn't as large or imposing as her father's, but it wasn't as strewn with books and papers either. The room was smaller as well, with fewer volumes. Nonetheless, it was almost soothing for Elizabeth to take a seat across from her uncle. He was one of the few people in her life she truly looked up to, and it was comforting to be able to place her troubles before him for his advice. He smiled patiently, the brow under his greying hair lined, but not creased with worry, and waited for her to speak.

"There is something Colonel Fitzwilliam left out of his recounting, likely a thing he doesn't even know, that concerns me directly," Elizabeth said.

Her uncle's eyebrows went up, but his calm didn't waver.

"To entice me to play the part of being courted by Mr. Darcy, Miss de Bourgh offered me five thousand pounds."

Her Uncle Gardiner's eyebrows inched higher and, this time, his whole face registered surprise. "That's a huge amount of money for what you are doing."

"I know, which is why I declined. Mr. Darcy encouraged me not to make my refusal official, however. It's on his recommendation that I'm seeking your advice on the matter."

"Is it?" Her uncle appeared thoughtful. "Then, my advice is that you must accept."

"I beg your pardon?" Elizabeth hadn't expected that answer.

He nodded. "Yes, you should definitely accept, but don't be surprised if she ends up not paying."

Now it was Elizabeth's turn to be incredulous. "Miss de Bourgh seemed quite sincere in the offer. Vehement, almost."

"That was in the moment, I should think." Her uncle regarded her skepticism with amusement. "You do realize that while she may be legally allowed to give you the money, she may not be. We aren't privy to the stipulations on her inheritance, which will likely change on the upcoming birthday of hers that Colonel Fitzwilliam spoke of, and will change again if she marries. A husband likely won't encourage her to keep her word to you. No one who has her interests at heart would encourage her to do so, in spite of whatever she promised you. Even if she put it in writing."

"She didn't." Although Elizabeth hadn't been inclined to accept the money, it disturbed her to think Miss de Bourgh's offer might not have been made in good faith.

"As she didn't put it in writing, you likely won't have a decision to make," Mr. Gardiner said. "If she does reissue the offer, you must carefully consider that five thousand pounds is enough to make a huge difference to you." He fell silent, contemplating her across the polished wood of his desk. Finally, he nodded, as if making up his mind about something. He leaned forward, his hands resting on the smooth wood between them. "It pains me to speak of it, but your father is not the most careful when it comes to his finances, and my sister is impossible in that regard. I worry for you and your sisters. As long as I am alive and reasonably solvent, you will not starve, but you are likely to outlive me."

Elizabeth was surprised to see an apologetic look overtake her uncle's face. Her instinct was to reassure him, but she didn't know the source of the emotion.

"You must understand, dear Lizzy, that my first priority must be to my wife and my own children."

"Of course it must," Elizabeth assured him, both surprised and touched his guilt stemmed from feeling the need to make that declaration. "We won't be completely destitute, though. We have the money settled on my mother. Surely, we'll make do without me compromising my integrity by accepting Miss de Bourgh's money." She was aware her voice had taken on a firm edge.

Her uncle shook his head. "Your mother's money won't be enough. If you, your sisters, and your mother live on the interest of five thousand pounds, you will feel the lack of money every day. You will be living mainly on porridge and the occasional cheap cut of meat. In the winter, you will wear many layers of clothes, because sufficient firewood will be beyond your reach. Every garment you own will have at least a dozen mends and your shoes will have holes in them. You will end up selling your father's books to feed yourselves. You'll lose that connection to him, and your minds will suffer." His tone had become almost pleading. "Very rarely, you'll get to read something borrowed from a friend. Even then, your reading must be by daylight, as you won't be able to afford enough candles. There will be no more pianoforte or needlepoint, and no carriage. You won't be able to pay to send letters, nor afford the paper and ink to write them."

Elizabeth stared at him, shocked at the picture he painted.

"Worse than all of this, what will happen if your mother and sisters learn their impoverished state could have been alleviated by the simple acceptance of money offered? If that were to happen, they would be rightfully angry with you."

"I hadn't considered that," she murmured, still dazed by her uncle's description of what it would be to be so poor. Elizabeth knew her family's wealth wasn't on par with Miss de Bourgh's or Mr. Darcy's, but she'd hadn't realized how low they could sink, especially once Mr. Collins took Longbourn from them. She'd always pictured them moving into a sunny little cottage, perhaps being forced to garden more and raise more of their own livestock. In her imaginings it was a beatific life; simple, but happy. It was never lacking in books or music, much less firewood and candles.

"I can see I have shocked you. I do not mean to." Her uncle leaned back, the intensity leaving him. "I only mean to make you aware of the realities of your situation. I had the feeling neither of your parents ever would have."

"Mother rants often enough about us becoming impoverished," Elizabeth admitted. "I took it no more seriously than her dozen other sufferings."

"Nor, likely, does she, but doubling the income could make a huge difference."

Elizabeth sat for a moment in silence, working her way around the idea. It was difficult to dispel the bleak future her uncle painted for her. She added to it the disdain of those she loved when, eventually, guilt drove her to admit she could have saved them, on more than one occasion. "Mr. Darcy proposed to me."

"Yes, so Colonel Fitzwilliam said."

She shook her head. "No, the day before. He proposed to me and I declined. He then wrote me a rather long letter, explaining away many of my reasons for not accepting him. It was that letter that spurred Lady Catherine's ultimatum. She got a hold of it and read it. It's also what gave her knowledge of Miss Darcy's scandal, to use against Mr. Darcy and Miss de Bourgh."

"I see," her uncle said. He drummed his fingers on the desk. "That explains some things that puzzled me."

"What?"

"Why the four of you thought Lady Catherine would believe Mr.

Darcy would propose. His courtship must have been noticed by everyone."

Not by me, Elizabeth thought, but she nodded. She knew Charlotte had seen it, so perhaps others had as well. "What else?"

"Why he was willing to propose to you. If you accepted and he didn't want to marry you, he would have been in a difficult situation." Her uncle smiled. "It would appear he is still interested in marrying you."

"I refused him in such a manner that he can't possibly still care." She couldn't keep a note of consternation from creeping into her voice.

"Lizzy, I can't believe you would do that unless you were extremely provoked. Why, may I ask, did you decline?"

"He proposed in so insulting a manner." Elizabeth looked down at her hands, folded in her lap. "He said he loved me against his judgement. He said I have no connections, and that my family is vulgar and would embarrass him as relations. I was also angry with him because I'd come to possess the knowledge that he helped separate Jane from Mr. Bingley, thinking Jane didn't truly love him." A quick glance showed the surprise on her uncle's face, which would have given her some vindication, if not for what she needed to impart next. "Added to that, I thought he'd gravely wronged Mr. Wickham, for whom I once held affection."

"I see," her uncle repeated. His hand had stilled during her monologue. "And his letter explained away all of this?"

"Some. It certainly set me right on Mr. Wickham, who is every sort of cad." Elizabeth sighed, feeling her next words were to be, in a way, nearly a betrayal, but she would speak the truth. "His letter did not address his words about our family. I was very angry over them. If I am being forthright, though, I think we both know there is truth in them. Mr. Darcy asked me if I would wish, instead of honesty, that he'd pretended to rejoice in them."

"Would you?"

"I cannot prefer falsehood over honesty, however harshly spoken."

"And Jane and Mr. Bingley? I have observed how unhappy she is. I would say she did love him, and very well may still."

"I cannot agree with his separating them because he felt Jane showed a lack of affection," Elizabeth said, but none of the old anger rose in her. "He also felt, it seems, that Mr. Bingley's affections were fleeting. I believe he may be correct in this. While Jane's winning nature may have spurred true affection in him had their association not been interrupted, he clearly didn't love her as he ought. Otherwise, he should have tried to see her long ere now." Elizabeth shrugged. "While I do not like to see Jane so sad, I also wouldn't care to see her wed to someone who wouldn't love her as she would love him."

"Here I think we come to the crux of this proposal of Mr. Darcy's, for all else would give way before it. Do you love him?"

"I didn't. I couldn't. It would be impossible while believing so ill of him."

Her uncle went back to his silent contemplation.

Elizabeth's mind returned to the picture of poverty he'd painted. "Should I have accepted Mr. Darcy's proposal?"

To her relief, her uncle shook his head. "At the time, you thought him a dishonorable man. You were justified in refusing him."

"But now I see more clearly what my rejection could do to my mother and sisters."

Her uncle grimaced. "I made too great an impression, I see." He leaned forward in his seat again, his expression earnest. "You were right to decline Mr. Darcy. A husband has a great deal of control over his wife, and an unpleasant husband can make his wife's life miserable. It would have been wrong of you to sacrifice the rest of your life for your family. You should sacrifice your delicate feelings for them, though."

Elizabeth nodded. "I understand. If Miss de Bourgh offers me the money again, I shall accept. I don't believe I can bring myself to demand it, though."

"A fair compromise." Her uncle's expression relaxed into a smile. "And one I will have to take as my answer."

"In truth, now that we're here, I can't see why we would need to carry on with her plan. Lady Catherine isn't here to witness whether or not Mr. Darcy courts me."

"I can readily come up with two reasons."

Elizabeth looked at him attentively.

"One is that what you do here will get back to Lady Catherine, one way or another, and it seems Miss Darcy's reputation is still at stake. The other is that Miss de Bourgh's offer still stands."

"The second seems a poor reason, like making someone pay for new curtains they commissioned weeks ago, before their house burnt down and they no longer need them."

"Be that as it may, for the sake of you and your sisters, you must endeavor to earn the money Miss de Bourgh offered. Is permitting Mr. Darcy to court you so terrible?"

She shook her head. "No. I can't say he's done much in the way of courting so far, but he's been more pleasant than I would have credited him capable of."

"Promise me, then, that you will try to pull off Miss de Bourgh's scheme as well as you're reasonably able. Don't give her an excuse not to give you the money."

Elizabeth nodded again. "I promise."

"Good."

Elizabeth smiled. "Thank you, uncle."

"I am always here to share your concerns, Lizzy, but before you go, I would like you to clarify one thing."

"If I am able, of course I will."

"You were going to be put on the stage and sent to London. How were you supposed to make your way to our home?"

Elizabeth realized she hadn't told anyone that part of the tale. For a moment, she wondered how Mr. Darcy hadn't thought to ask, but then a vision of his face, suffused with anger on her behalf, rose in her mind. She realized he was too angry over what his aunt had done to be as logical as her uncle was being. "Lady Catherine's agent was to meet me and give me money to hire a cab."

"How would he have known you were coming?"

"She sent an express," Elizabeth replied.

"You mean, she had a rider with her, ready to go?"

"No. She sent it before she kidnapped me." Elizabeth suppressed a shiver, not liking to be reminded of how meticulous, and ruthless, Lady Catherine could be.

Her Uncle Gardiner leaned back in his chair and smiled. "We may have confirmation of your kidnapping. There would be no reason to send such a message if you were going willingly. She could simply have handed you the money. If we discover who the rider was, we should be able to find her agent. He might confirm she planned it."

Elizabeth rattled off the name of the agent and his description. Her uncle pulled out pen and paper and wrote it down. "In itself, this won't prove anything, but it might be useful. I'll look into it. I'll write your Mr. Darcy if I find anything."

Her Mr. Darcy? He wasn't her Mr. Darcy, was he? "Thank you, Uncle."

"Is that everything you wished to discuss, my dear?"

"I can think of nothing more."

"Then I believe we both ought to retire, for dinner went later than usual and your aunt is correct about my habit of rising early."

Elizabeth smiled, nodding. She stood and moved around the desk, kissing him on the forehead as she would have her father, and bid him good night. She made her way to the room she was sharing, finding Jane and Miss de Bourgh nearly asleep. Soon, all three were abed and Elizabeth drifted off, her mind at rest over Miss de Bourgh's offer.

It was not at rest over other things, it seemed, for Elizabeth dreamed of hands thrusting her into a carriage. Lady Catherine wasn't inside and the space was dark and smelled of must. Not only the doors but the windows wouldn't work, the latter painted black. She bounced around, unable to tell where she was being taken, the wooden seats bare of upholstery and painfully hard.

Elizabeth woke up sweating and frightened. She lay awake for a long time, not wanting to wake Jane or Anne, but not wanting to revisit the dream, either. She was proud of how calm she'd remained while Lady Catherine's abduction took place, and all the rest of the day. Now, though, in the dark of night, the world no longer seemed as safe as it had before. Elizabeth realized she had a doubly good reason for heeding her uncle's advice. She resolved to try to earn the money Miss de Bourgh had offered, not only for the good of her and her family, but because it would give her at least some security in an unsafe world.

10

Though she didn't recall falling back to sleep after her dream, Elizabeth awoke to the sound of Jane and Miss de Bourgh readying for breakfast. They seemed cheerful and refreshed. She attempted to mimic their attitude, not wanting to alarm them with talk of her dream. When all three were presentable, they made their way to the parlor for breakfast. Elizabeth's aunt was there, lingering over her tea. She looked up as they entered, smiling.

"Good morning, ladies. I trust you slept well?"

"Yes, Aunt," Jane said, crossing to drop a kiss on Aunt Gardiner's cheek.

"Thank you again for accommodating me," Miss de Bourgh said. "It's very kind of you."

"It's our pleasure. What are your plans today?" Mrs. Gardiner asked. "Jane, I know you promised the children you would help them with their lessons again, but I'm sure they'll understand if you beg off because Elizabeth is here. Really, they take terrible advantage of you. It isn't as if their governess can't teach them properly."

"I enjoy the children," Jane said.

"I only caught a brief glimpse of them yesterday," Miss de Bourgh said.

"They are delightful children," Elizabeth said.

"Would it be disruptive if I go see them again when we finish breakfast?" Miss de Bourgh asked.

"Not at all, but I'm sure you have other things to do in London. I believe Mr. Gardiner invited the gentlemen back for dinner this evening, but the day is free."

"I was wondering, as we don't have any other plans, if I could borrow your carriage after meeting the children, Mrs. Gardiner?" Miss de Bourgh asked. "I would like to take Elizabeth to buy a new dress. I feel it's the very least I can do."

"That's really not necessary," Elizabeth said, surprised Miss de Bourgh had thought of it, and suspicious. After what her uncle said the evening before, she wondered if Miss de Bourgh was trying to get out of the five thousand pounds by giving her a gift instead.

"Truly, it is," Miss de Bourgh said, her narrow face earnest. "Though it should be my mother purchasing it for you, in a just world."

The sincerity in Miss de Bourgh's face made Elizabeth regret her uncharitable thoughts. "Charlotte and I already cleaned the hem, and the tears are small. I can mend them well enough they'll never be seen."

Miss de Bourgh's face clouded with confusion. "Tears? The hem?"

"It was soiled from walking so far." Elizabeth elected not to elaborate on the small tears, created when she'd been carried, struggling, to the carriage. That would only make her and everyone else in the parlor uncomfortable.

"The dress you wore yesterday morning," Miss de Bourgh said, her expression shifting from confession to dismay. "I hadn't considered it. I meant the evening dress. The one John dumped wine on."

"Dumped wine on?" Elizabeth's aunt repeated. "What's this? Who is John?"

Elizabeth looked from Jane to her aunt. Colonel Fitzwilliam's recounting the day before had been in the nature of a summary. He hadn't dredged forth every detail of his aunt's bad behavior. Elizabeth had agreed with the strategy, for she was never one for gossip or spite. She gave a little shrug, adopting an air she hoped conveyed it was nothing important.

"John is one of my mother's footmen," Miss de Bourgh said, but then turned to Elizabeth, indicating she should continue.

"Lady Catherine, as best we can assess, ordered her footman to spill red wine on me at dinner. I believe it was to make me look bad in front of Mr. Darcy. She was attempting to convince him of my unworthiness." An image of the footman's face, twisted into a snarl as she kicked it, loomed in Elizabeth's mind. She looked down, pushing the food about on her plate and hoping someone else would speak.

"What a dreadful thing to do," Jane said, sounding more surprised than angry.

"Indeed." Aunt Gardiner's tone was much less charitable than Jane's.

"The wine will never come clean," Miss de Bourgh said. "You'll need a new bodice if you wish to save the skirt. Either way, I intend you should have a brand new dress."

"It does seem reasonable, dear," Elizabeth's aunt said. "We would be happy to lend you the carriage for such a worthwhile mission."

"Thank you," Miss de Bourgh replied.

"Will you join us, Aunt?" Jane asked.

"I would be delighted to."

That settled, breakfast was rapidly concluded. They spent an hour with the children, who Miss de Bourgh appeared to enjoy, and then went to the waiting carriage. Elizabeth didn't recognize the directions Miss de Bourgh gave, to be passed on to the driver, but it was obvious her aunt did. Mrs. Gardiner's eyes widened ever so slightly and she took on a pleased air. Elizabeth watched the streets grow wider and more crowded as they rode. When they arrived, even she could tell the shop was quite fashionable.

"Surely, I don't need a dress this fine," she protested.

"You do," Miss de Bourgh said.

She used her authoritative tone, the one she seemed to have little trouble finding when around Elizabeth. Even in the less than optimal light inside the carriage, Elizabeth could read Miss de Bourgh's eyes, which held no confidence, belying the tone she'd used. Not wanting to crush the woman's budding attempts at asserting herself, Elizabeth let the matter drop. It wasn't, after all, as if Miss de Bourgh couldn't afford one dress, no matter how fancy the modiste.

Inside, the shop was even more elegant than Elizabeth had anticipated. Expensive looking fabrics were draped in graceful display, along with ribbons and an abundance of fine lace. Stylishly upholstered chairs stood at intervals about the showroom, in singles, pairs and groups. Small tables held fashion plates for browsing. Light and crystal glittered about the room.

A thin woman hurried from behind the counter to greet them, dropping a low curtsy. "My ladies, how may I assist you?"

"We've come for a dress for my friend," Miss de Bourgh said. She turned, gesturing to Elizabeth. "Miss Elizabeth."

"Yes, of course." The woman looked Elizabeth up and down, smiling. "And what sort of dress do you require, miss?"

Elizabeth glanced about, a bit daunted by the opulence before her. "An evening dress, of muslin. Something simple."

"Muslin?" Miss de Bourgh frowned. "Silk."

The shopkeeper looked from one to the other.

"Perhaps we should look at both?" Elizabeth's aunt suggested.

With a jingle of bells, the door opened behind them. Along with the others, Elizabeth turned to look.

The shopkeeper dropped another curtsy. "My lady," she said to the newcomer.

Elizabeth took in the warm look of recognition on Miss de Bourgh's face, mirrored on that of the impeccably clad woman standing just inside the doorway. She was slender, and tall for a woman, all but towering over Elizabeth. She looked to be in her middle thirties.

"Anne," the woman said, coming forward. "I didn't know you and Aunt Catherine were in town."

"My mother is still in Rosings," Miss de Bourgh said. She turned to Elizabeth's aunt. "I have the pleasure of staying with Mrs. and Mr. Gardiner, along with their nieces. This is Miss Jane Bennet and Miss Elizabeth Bennet. Mrs. Gardiner, Miss Bennets, this is my cousin, Lady Agatha Hurst."

"How do you do," Elizabeth's aunt said.

She, Elizabeth and Jane curtsied. Under the cover of the movement, Elizabeth cast a quick look Jane's way. As she'd worried, Jane had paled at the woman's name.

"Well, thank you," Lady Agatha said. "It's a pleasure to meet friends of my cousin's."

"Lady Agatha Hurst?" Aunt Gardiner repeated. "My niece Jane and I called on a Mrs. Hurst and Miss Bingley this past winter."

"That Mrs. Hurst is married to the younger brother of my late husband."

"Lady Agatha is the older sister of Colonel Fitzwilliam, whom you all know," Miss de Bourgh added.

"Is Richard in London as well, then?" Lady Agatha asked.

"He is, and staying with Darcy."

Miss de Bourgh smiled as she said it. Her obvious ease with Lady Agatha, coupled with the woman's warm manner, inclined Elizabeth to like her. She tried to gauge Jane's reaction, but her sister looked distracted, her color still poor.

"All three of you? So you have completely abandoned Aunt Catherine, have you?" Lady Agatha said. Her tone was curious, but touched by a barely perceptible hardness when she used her aunt's name.

"We have."

Even knowing the circumstances of their departure as intimately as she did, Elizabeth was surprised as the vehemence in Miss de Bourgh's voice.

Lady Agatha raised her eyebrows. "Well, you shall all come to my party tomorrow, Richard and Darcy as well. I would have sent invitations had I known you were in town. I expected the lot of you to be holed up in Rosings for another fortnight at least."

Miss de Bourgh turned to Elizabeth, but this time she didn't have an answer either. She looked to her aunt.

"We would be honored, Lady Agatha," Aunt Gardiner said, dropping another curtsy.

"Excellent. I shall send round the details." She paused while Elizabeth's aunt produced her card. "Do you have children, Mrs. Gardiner?"

"I do."

"Then they and their governess are invited as well. There will be many children in attendance. If I didn't make it clear, I would be happy to meet both of Anne's hosts, so Mr. Gardiner is invited as well." She awarded them all another smile. "I'll send another missive to Darcy House. Do be sure to pass along my invitation if you see Richard and Darcy, to be safe. You know how men can be with their correspondences."

Elizabeth thought Mr. Darcy was likely very orderly and punctual about his correspondences, but kept that to herself.

"We will tell them both," Miss de Bourgh said.

Lady Agatha turned to the patiently waiting modiste. "Please see to them. I'm merely here to have my new gown fitted. I'm sure your seamstress is up to the task."

"Yes, my lady."

The modiste hurried to the counter, pulling a silk cord. Somewhere in the back of the shop, beyond a curtained off doorway, a bell rang. With a parting smile, Lady Agatha moved in that direction.

"It is too bad you cannot have a dress by tomorrow," Miss de Bourgh said, turning to Elizabeth. "I should love to see you in something splendid for my cousin's party."

"I don't need anything splendid," Elizabeth said. "Simple will do nicely."

"Simple, but silk."

Elizabeth looked to her aunt for help, but she merely smiled. Jane, too, was no use. She was looking after Lady Agatha, her expression sorrowful.

"I beg your pardon, but did I hear you venture hope of a silk dress by tomorrow?"

Elizabeth turned to see the modiste hastening back toward them.

"Yes, but I realize it's impossible, no matter what I can pay," Miss de Bourgh said.

"If it would not insult Miss Elizabeth, we had a customer very like her in stature cancel a dress at the last moment. She had a death in the family and needed mourning. I think the dress would suit Miss Elizabeth well and require very little alteration. Also, the dress is silk."

A smile spread over Miss de Bourgh's face. "May we see it?"

"Yes, of course."

The modiste hurried away, returning shortly with a lovely light blue silk gown, resplendent with cream ribbons and matching lace. It was much finer than anything Elizabeth had ever owned. It did appear to be nearly complete, some of the stitching still loose where minor adjustments might be made during a final fitting.

"This is much too fine for me," Elizabeth protested.

"Oh, Lizzy, it's perfect," Jane exclaimed, appearing to have composed herself at last.

"We would need to fit miss now, of course," the modiste said. "Some of our girls would have to work late, finishing the dress."

"If it's a question of cost, do not worry over it." Miss de Bourgh shot Elizabeth a quelling look before she could form an objection. "I shall pay extra to have it finished for tomorrow."

"It's a lovely dress." Aunt Gardiner turned to the modiste, giving her a firm look. "Not to mention, you would be helping the shop, preventing them from taking a loss on the fabrics and workmanship."

Elizabeth hid her smile. Her aunt and uncle were in trade, after all, and it didn't hurt to bargain a little. Even if Miss de Bourgh didn't care about the money, Elizabeth didn't want to see her taken advantage of.

The modiste nodded, looking a touch disappointed. "Yes, you will be helping our shop. It is kind of you to consider the dress at all."

Elizabeth looked from face to face, feeling as if she had little choice but to accept.

"It really is the perfect gown for you," Jane said, her voice soft. "It's as if it was meant to be."

"Well, then, I suppose there's nothing for it but to try it on," Elizabeth decided.

This was met with happy exclamations. The dress was tried on and did, indeed, fit quite well, after some pins were put in to show where the alterations would be done. The modiste, Elizabeth thought, had a good eye. Everyone agreed Elizabeth looked splendid in it, including Lady Agatha, who was drawn by the commotion. She was being fitted into a stunning concoction of emerald fabric and black lace. Elizabeth was happy she loved her dress so very much, or she would have had a pang of envy for the widow, who was permitted to wear such daring colors.

After the modiste, Anne insisted on taking Elizabeth to a milliner, where a hat was selected to complement the dress. They returned and had tea with the children, which turned out to be a happy affair. Miss de Bourgh didn't seem at all put out to spend so much time with four children, the eldest an eight-year-old girl.

That evening at dinner, Elizabeth was prevailed upon to relate the day's activities. She did so as colorfully as she could without exaggeration. She also endeavored to make it clear she hadn't been behind the idea to purchase a dress. She didn't want Mr. Darcy and Colonel Fitzwilliam to think she was taking advantage of their cousin. The warmth of Mr. Darcy's regard as he sat through her telling, while apparent enough to force her to fight back a blush, assured Elizabeth he thought no ill of her for accepting the gift.

"Lady Agatha misjudged me," Mr. Darcy said once the telling was concluded. "I am quite up on my correspondences and well aware of the party."

"Don't permit him to fool you." Colonel Fitzwilliam pitched his voice low as if revealing a secret. "He wouldn't have had an eye out for the invitations my sister sent round if he hadn't known to look for them. Georgiana has already been invited and informed him as much this morning."

"Miss Darcy is in London?" Elizabeth asked, remembering that Lady Agatha had said she would send another invitation to Darcy House. The first, then, had not been deemed lost in a pile, but delivered.

"She is, and now I shall have the opportunity to introduce you,"

Mr. Darcy said, sounding pleased. "Her letter hadn't reached Rosings before we left. She cut short her visit to a friend's due to an ailment in their family."

"I hope nothing serious," Jane said.

Mr. Darcy shook his head.

Elizabeth looked down, not sure she was happy with the prospect of meeting Miss Darcy. It was one thing to pretend Mr. Darcy was courting her before cousins and strangers, but seemed a cruel trick to play on his sister. Not to mention, though she knew now what a liar Mr. Wickham was, she was still leery of meeting a young woman he'd painted as aloof. In view of how Mr. Darcy had conducted himself when he'd first come to Hertfordshire, Elizabeth was doubtful Miss Darcy would make any better of a first impression.

"You'll all be pleased you were invited to my sister's party," Colonel Fitzwilliam said. "Her parties are famous, but not for the usual reasons."

"We are already pleased, to be sure. To be invited, and to have the opportunity to meet Miss Darcy," Elizabeth said, realizing a response to Mr. Darcy's offer on an introduction was required.

"How are the parties different?" Jane asked, sounding a touch nervous.

Jane had eaten little, worrying Elizabeth. She regretted their day had set her sister to thinking overmuch about Mr. Bingley. Still, it was a very kind thing Miss de Bourgh had done in buying the dress, and seemed splendid Lady Agatha had invited them to the party. Elizabeth supposed they must take the good with the bad.

"All sorts of different things go on in different rooms. There will be dancing in one room, cards in another, and outdoor games, weather permitting. There will be serious whist and billiards, and people gathering in small groups, talking."

"Some people attend for the food alone," Miss de Bourgh said, the eyes she turned toward the colonel glinting with amusement.

"Yes. She has a buffet that is refilled regularly, full of delicacies," Colonel Fitzwilliam said with obvious anticipation. "Others, of course, come because you meet everyone there."

"As you know, she invites children. She provides entertainment for them," Miss de Bourgh added. "Sometimes, it's the most fun of all."

"Children," Mr. Darcy said. "I all but forgot. You'll have to begin your exploration of the event without me."

Everyone tuned to him in surprise.

"I promised Peter I would give him a fencing lesson next time I visited," Mr. Darcy clarified.

Elizabeth could only assume Peter was a child of Lady Agatha's.

"Surely, you can tell him it will wait until next time," Miss de Bourgh said. She shot a look at Elizabeth.

"No." Mr. Darcy's tone was firm. "I gave him my word. What would it teach him if I disregard it the moment it becomes inconvenient? I'm sure the rest of you will be well entertained, and it will not occupy me the entire time."

"It had best not." Miss de Bourgh's sounded oddly peevish. "Mother will hear of everything that happens there. While I expressly forbid you from asking me to dance, I expect you to dance at least two sets with Miss Elizabeth."

"Consider it a promise," Mr. Darcy said, glancing Elizabeth's way with a smile.

11

Elizabeth, slightly squeezed as she shared a bench with both Jane and Miss de Bourgh, peered out the window of Mr. Darcy's carriage. She was surprised they were traveling so far out of London, but as neither Mr. Darcy, Miss de Bourgh or Colonel Fitzwilliam seemed concerned, she could only conclude the coachman had his directions correct. Resisting the urge to stick her head out to make sure her aunt's and uncle's carriage still followed, Elizabeth sat back in her seat.

On the very outskirts of town, they turned down a long, tree-lined drive, and Elizabeth understood. While the area wasn't one of those central London locations sought after by the fashionable elite, the homes they'd been passing were quite large, and the grounds even larger. Lady Agatha's so-called London house was very nearly a country estate. Elizabeth could easily comprehend the appeal.

They queued up in the drive, the pace permitting plenty of time for conversation and admiration of the grounds visible through the carriage windows. Elizabeth found much to like about both, not minding the wait. When their turn to disembark came, she found that, at some point during the drive, other carriages had come between Mr. Darcy's and the Gardiner's. Elizabeth and Jane would have waited, but their aunt spotted them from her window and waved them ahead.

She and Jane followed Mr. Darcy, Colonel Fitzwilliam and Miss de Bourgh into a stunning foyer. The walls were clad in subtly shaded pattered silk. Ornate tables of fine, brightly polished wood stood at intervals, each boasting a vase of flowers, small statuary, or other adornment. A row of sparkling crystal chandeliers led the way forward.

Before they reached their hostess, Mr. Darcy dropped back to walk beside Elizabeth. "I must bid you adieu for now, Miss Elizabeth, but I beg you not to forget our promised dances."

Elizabeth nodded, amused by Mr. Darcy's attentiveness. "I shall look forward to your return, sir."

Miss de Bourgh looked back at them with a smile.

After greeting their hostess, Mr. Darcy hurried away. Colonel Fitzwilliam, now burdened with three single young ladies, turned to survey them. Elizabeth thought he looked as though he was sizing up the troops, until his eyes landed on Jane. Elizabeth couldn't be sure, but she felt there was a softening of the colonel's regard when he looked upon her sister.

Jane's dress was by no means the height of fashion, nor was it new. That mattered not at all, by Elizabeth's estimation. The pale green, touched modestly with ivory ribbons and lace, set off Jane's luminous complexion perfectly. No one could take in her shining curls, even features, perfect bow of a mouth and brilliant eyes without being moved.

Miss de Bourgh, for her part, looked fashionable. Jane had persuaded her to wear more ringlets about her face, muting the length and narrowness of her features. Miss de Bourgh's dress, a light yellow, made her hair look darker, instead of a middling brown. Her pearls were just right for her dress and not as gaudy as the jewelry her mother wore.

"I daresay we should attempt the buffet first." Colonel Fitzwilliam's voice broke into Elizabeth's thoughts. "The drive out was long enough to leave me famished."

Miss de Bourgh laughed. "You always wish to attempt the buffet."

The colonel offered her his arm. They headed in what Elizabeth could only assume was the direction of the buffet. As she and Jane followed, Elizabeth endeavored not to be too impressed with her surroundings. She didn't wish to gape like a miss fresh from the country. Especially not in her new dress, which made her look as modish and sophisticated as any Londoner.

The buffet room was sizeable, yet still crowded, for all its grandeur. Large statues were set along the walls, creating the semblance of alcoves. Between two, a lavish buffet was set. Even from a distance, the offerings appeared extravagant. The colonel led them toward one end, chatting amiable with Miss de Bourgh.

A third of the way across the room, Jane stopped. A gasp left her. Quiet as the sound was, Colonel Fitzwilliam must have sensed something amiss, for he turned back to face them with an alacrity that obviously startled Miss de Bourgh. Elizabeth registered the concern on his face and the pallor of Jane's. She followed her sister's gaze across the room.

Mr. Bingley stood in one of the mock alcoves the statuary formed. He was in what appeared to be intimate conversation with an attractive young woman in a deeply cut lavender gown, trimmed in grey. Their heads were bent close together, their low voices lost in the distance of the room. She placed a hand on Mr. Bingley's arm, smiling up at him with considerable warmth. Leaning down farther, he whispered something in her ear. When he straightened, she stood on tiptoe and whispered in his. Mr. Bingley tossed his head back, laughing.

Jane made a desperate sound, as if she couldn't breathe. Elizabeth's eyes flew back to her face, finding it drained of color. Miss de Bourgh, having obviously recovered from the colonel's abandonment, had turned to face Jane as well. Jane swayed, looking like she might faint. All three reached for her, but Colonel Fitzwilliam was quickest. He tucked her arm into his, steadying her. In so doing, he moved between her and the sight of Mr. Bingley.

Based on the quick look he cast over his shoulder, Elizabeth felt the colonel had ascertained the cause of Jane's distress. He turned to her, and Elizabeth could see understanding dawn. She realized he now knew Jane was the woman Mr. Darcy had separated Mr. Bingley from. Elizabeth wondered if he recalled the casual way he'd mentioned the act to her, on their walk. She knew, at the time, he'd meant it as a complement to Mr. Darcy.

"Miss Bennet, are you unwell?" Miss de Bourgh asked, her face pinched with concern as she regarded Jane.

"I suspect Miss Bennet would like to work up an appetite before eating," Colonel Fitzwilliam said. "There is dancing over there." He pointed in the opposite direction of Mr. Bingley. "Would you care to dance?"

Jane looked at him, but her eyes didn't hold much comprehension.

He smiled at her, placing his other hand atop hers, where it rested on his arm. "Come, let's leave this room, Miss Bennet. I'll show you where the dancing is being held."

"Yes." Jane gave a shaky nod. "I should like to leave this room."

With considerable care, giving the impression Jane was a fragile bloom, Colonel Fitzwilliam turned her about and led her out the door they'd entered through. Elizabeth would have followed, but Miss de Bourgh put a hand on her arm. Elizabeth hesitated before turning to her, worried for Jane, but her sister seemed to be in capable hands.

What good would she do, following them? The best thing for Jane likely would be to dance, and she wouldn't leave Elizabeth standing off to the side while she did it.

"I don't understand," Miss de Bourgh said. "Is your sister unwell? Is she prone to these fits?"

Now that the colonel was gone, Elizabeth could once again see Mr. Bingley. It was obvious, though they'd drawn some attention, that neither he nor his conversation partner had noticed. Miss de Bourgh craned her neck over her shoulder in the direction Elizabeth was looking.

"Oh," Miss de Bourgh exclaimed. She, unlike Colonel Fitzwilliam, had read Mr. Darcy's letter. "Mr. Bingley." She looked after Jane and her cousin, though they were no longer in view. "She truly did love him, didn't she?"

"And it seems she still does, or at least did until a moment ago. I've been worried that was the case, for she hasn't been herself." Elizabeth resisted the urge to look back and Mr. Bingley, whose laughter once again made its way across the room. "Who is she? The woman he's speaking with? I gather by her dress she's coming out of mourning. Is she a widow?" Elizabeth tried not to think about how Mr. Bingley shamelessly flirting with a widow in public might mean they were doing something even more shameful in private.

"Yes, another widow who shouldn't be a widow." Miss be Bourgh pursed her lips. "Although, I don't think she minds."

"I don't understand."

"Well, she does not seem to mind, does she?" Miss de Bourgh's tone held a noticeable amount of censure. "Nor does he. I believe they're both pleased she's a widow and afforded certain social liberties."

Elizabeth blushed. "I meant, I don't understand why she is another widow who shouldn't be one. I assume you mean, similarly to our hostess?"

"I apologize. I misunderstood the question." Miss de Bourgh did not blush. "Yes, like Lady Agatha, your Mr. Bingley's merry widow, Mrs. Kent, lost her husband too soon. My cousin Henry Fitzwilliam, the current Earl of Matlock and Lady Agatha and Colonel Fitzwilliam's older brother, runs with a wild crowd. They live on activity, and don't mind danger. They race carriages and horses. They hunt. Sometimes they fight duels over nothing. Lady Agatha's husband died trying to beat Henry's record on some stretch of road, I've forgotten which. Mrs. Kent's husband died trying to climb up a cliff."

"I take it the death wasn't recent," Elizabeth said, for the woman wore lavender, a mark of her status as a widow, not the black of mourning.

"About a year and a half ago. She married at sixteen and is now one and twenty. Though I think she's being a bit crass with Mr. Bingley, I must admit I envy her. Although most of Mr. Kent's money went to his children from his first marriage, she has complete control over her generous widow's portion. She's a fool if she remarries, although sometimes women are fools."

"What if she falls in love?" Elizabeth was surprised by both Miss de Bourgh's practicality and cynicism. Then, Miss de Bourgh had grown up with Lady Catherine, a mother who'd forced her to learn to bribe her own servants and taught her that if she showed too much affection for a man, she would be removed from him.

"I suspect love is a myth, especially for her, but who knows? I doubt I've exchanged a dozen words with her."

Possessed of Miss de Bourgh's revelations, Elizabeth took another look at the couple. They stood even closer together now, obviously not paying attention to anyone else in the room. She quickly turned back away, unable to help feeling disappointed in Mr. Bingley and resentful toward Mrs. Kent. As upsetting as it was to see a man she'd once hoped to call brother so engrossed in flirtation, Elizabeth was glad he didn't have the presence of mind to look about and see her.

"Why don't we seek other entertainment?" Miss de Bourgh asked. "I suspect you aren't really hungry."

"No, I'm not," Elizabeth said, more than happy to leave the room. She was aware of a mounting resentment toward Mr. Bingley, her thoughts lingering on Jane's distress. Logically, Elizabeth knew Mr. Bingley had every right to flirt with Mrs. Kent, but seeing the smiles he'd once bestowed on Jane being given to a fast widow made her angry. Half in jest, she added, "I think I would like to avoid the male sex altogether for a while."

"I know just the place."

To Elizabeth's surprise, Miss de Bourgh led her from the house. They crossed a short stretch of lawn to a row of hedges. At first, Elizabeth thought the hedges were part of a maze and wasn't sure she wished to go in, but she followed Miss de Bourgh around a corner to find the shrubberies simply screened a large area of lawn. The ample open space was outlined by more hedges, all taller than a tall man could reach.

There were chairs scattered around and Elizabeth spotted a number of women, some who looked like governesses and others who looked like mothers or older sisters. Some stood, but others were seated. Many watched the various groups of girls playing battledore and shuttlecock. Elizabeth smiled, instantly calmed. She too watched for a few minutes, observing the energy of the young women and girls using small paddles to try to keep the shuttlecock in the air. Looking around again, she realized some of the girls were old enough to be out, but most were younger.

"Lady Agatha has made it easy to get away from men," Miss de Bourgh said.

"This is splendid." Elizabeth couldn't help but feel renewed and invigorated. She hadn't expected something as fun as sports for girls at a party which included so much of the ton. She looked to Miss de Bourgh. "Would you care to play? Mr. Darcy is fencing, and Colonel Fitzwilliam and Jane dancing. We can't permit them to have more fun than we are."

"I can try." Miss de Bourgh led Elizabeth to one of the governesses, whom she introduced as Mrs. Annesley.

"May we join in?" Elizabeth asked once the introductions were done. She gestured toward the players.

"Of course you may." Mrs. Annesley produced two paddles, handing one to each of them. She pointed to a group. "You're just in time for a new round. We could use two in that group."

"Will you introduce us?" Elizabeth asked.

Mrs. Annesley smiled. "The Girls' Garden is deliberately kept informal. There will be time for introductions after the match, I'm sure."

Miss de Bourgh led Elizabeth out, but played for only a short while, tiring quickly and obviously inexperienced. Elizabeth hadn't played the game in years, but her previous skill partially returned and she enjoyed herself. Soon, most of the other women abandoned the game for chairs, leaving only children, Elizabeth and a tall young woman who was expensively dressed. She cooperated with Elizabeth in aiming the shuttlecock so that the younger girls had easy shots. Whenever the girls delighted in their success, the tall young woman would exchange a conspiratorial smile with Elizabeth.

Eventually, the game was reduced to four people, Elizabeth, the tall young woman, and two girls who were obviously sisters, aged about eleven and thirteen. Elizabeth had rarely enjoyed herself so much at a party, but she was beginning to wonder if she had the stamina to keep playing. She hadn't slept well yet again, and so didn't have her usual vigor. She didn't want to ruin the game for the others, but she was tired, starting to worry about Jane, and now truly had worked up an appetite.

She was contemplating bowing out when she noticed the two sisters seemed to be growing tired as well. Resolving it would be the final round, she lobbed an easy serve to the younger. They had a nice volley going when, a short time later, Lady Agatha appeared and announced that lemonade was served. She was followed by a line of tray-bearing maids, who were in turn followed by Elizabeth's cousins and their governess.

Though Lady Agatha hadn't specified what children were invited, Elizabeth's aunt had only permitted her daughters, girls of six and eight, to attend. She'd left her two young sons home with a nursemaid. The sisters Elizabeth was playing with quickly abandoned their game for the treat of lemonade, the tall young woman following them. Elizabeth waved to her cousins, but returned to Miss de Bourgh and Mrs. Annesley, rather than joining the chaos surrounding the treat.

"Don't you care for lemonade, Miss Bennet?" Mrs. Annesley asked.

"I do, but I shall wait for the crush to pass. It's quite popular, I see, and timely. I don't believe I could go on much longer, though I was having great fun."

"Lady Agatha's daughters were as well, I'm sure. It was kind of you to set up shots for them," Mrs. Annesley said.

"Is that who they are?" Elizabeth looked over at the two girls, standing with their mother as they drank their lemonade. Now that she saw them together, she could clearly observe the resemblance. "I didn't realize Lady Agatha had daughters."

"It's for them that she began this tradition," Miss de Bourgh said. "My cousin feels her daughters should be able to get away from the formality of the party."

The tall young woman started back toward them, carrying two lemonades. As she drew near, Elizabeth thought one might be for her.

To her surprise, however, the extra glass was passed to Mrs. Annesley.

"Thank you," Miss Annesley said.

The young woman looked from Miss de Bourgh to Elizabeth.

Miss de Bourgh offered her a warm smile. "This is Miss Elizabeth Bennet."

Elizabeth saw surprise on the young woman's face and, oddly, something that appeared to be recognition.

"Miss Bennet." Miss de Bourgh turned to Elizabeth. "It is my pleasure to introduce you to my cousin, Miss Darcy."

12

Darcy strode down the long hallway toward the fencing hall. He didn't want to teach Peter to fence. He wanted to dance with Elizabeth. The moment she'd appeared at the top of the steps, when he and Richard had collected the ladies from the Gardiner's home, Elizabeth had occupied nearly every one of Darcy's senses.

Seated across from her in the carriage, he'd availed himself of a marvelous opportunity to take in every lovely inch of her, displayed to perfection in her new gown. The blue suited her perfectly, her creamy skin seeming almost to glow. The musical sound of her voice and the soft brushing of silk each time she shifted had filled his ears. Even from across the crowded coach, her subtle perfume had reached him.

Darcy would have let that coach ride go on forever, except that every moment was a form of torture. His hands had longed to know if her skin was as soft as it looked, her tresses as silken. It was cruel to delight his other senses so, while denying touch.

He shook his head, endeavoring to clear it. If he carried on in this fashion, woolgathering like some young fool, he'd be a poor teacher. Peter deserved better. The lad was only nine and fatherless. It was Darcy's place as a male relative to step in where he could. He resolved that, for an hour or so, he would give his complete attention to Peter.

He found Peter waiting for him, already fitted out in his padding, his face eager. They exchanged a quick greeting while Darcy removed his coat and donned the gear set out for him. When he was done, he looked about for their masks, finally spotting several on a rack at the back of the room.

"Fetch us masks, will you, Peter," Darcy said. He began checking the available blades, selecting one to his liking.

"Masks?" Peter's tone was touched with derision.

Darcy turned to him, his face stern. "Yes, masks."

"Uncle Henry says masks are an insult to your opponent's skill."

Darcy frowned. That sounded like the sort of nonsense Lord Henry would say. "Even the most skillful opponent isn't perfect. When you fence with me, you will use a mask. If I ever find you fencing without one, I won't instruct you anymore." He waited, watching the turmoil on the boy's face. Darcy almost wanted Peter to refuse, giving him an excuse to walk away. Dancing with Elizabeth was bound to be more entertaining than teaching a sulky Peter.

"I'll get them," Peter said, sounding only a touch sulky. Leaving his foil, he jogged across the room.

In spite of wanting to dance with Elizabeth, Darcy was pleased. He took a certain amount of pride in his interactions with Peter, hoping he was molding him into a proper sort of man. The boy's willingness to get the masks spoke of a good character.

When Peter returned, Darcy began putting him through drills. They practiced lunges, focusing on the proper footwork. Darcy found himself repeating phrases his instructor had used, pertaining to the importance of a solid foundation. They then moved to parries, with Darcy delivering the appropriate attacks.

"But you are telling me how to parry with each attack," Peter complained. "Shouldn't I have to decide which one to use?"

"In time, yes, but the first step is to excel at each. If you cannot properly implement a parry, it does you no good to choose to employ it. Now, let's go back to parry quarte."

"But that's the first one you taught me. It's the easiest one."

"I still practice it, and so should you."

By this time, a number of people had drifted into the room. Several of the watching adults encouraged the young men with them to pay attention and learn. Peter seemed hardly to notice, intent on his lesson. Because drills were boring by nature, Darcy alternated them with brief bouts of fencing, allowing him to modify the drills to accommodate those areas where Peter showed weaknesses. Darcy felt the eyes of the watchers, but he was accustomed to being watched. Still, when his cousin, Lord Henry Fitzwilliam, the Earl of Matlock, came in, Darcy began to feel like he was on stage.

Fortunately, they'd already been at it for a little over an hour and Peter was wearying. Darcy deemed it legitimate to end the lesson. Peter had shown considerable poise for a nine-year old, but he would become clumsy and ill-tempered soon.

"I believe that is enough for today," Darcy said when Peter

finished the drill he was working through.

"Already?" Peter seemed almost to wilt in disappointment, though he was clearly tired.

"Next time I come here, I'll give you another lesson." Darcy didn't want to commit to a specific time, but he could promise that much. "Do you know how to stow your equipment?"

"I do." Peter puffed back up a bit, clearly proud of his competence. He pulled off his mask, revealing a smile. "Thank you for your assistance, Cousin Darcy."

"You are most welcome." Darcy was aware of Henry sauntering up behind him.

"Masks?" Henry said with contempt. "Are you afraid you can't defend yourself against a child or that you're so poor a fencer you will injure one?"

Suppressing a sigh, Darcy turned to his cousin and bowed. "Good afternoon, Henry. As I was telling Peter, masks are a sensible safety precaution." Darcy took his off.

"For a poor fencer."

Darcy didn't miss the belligerence in Henry's tone. To the uninitiated, it might seem that Henry was angry, even hateful, but Darcy knew better. The tone was all part of Henry's game. He would badger and push, goading his quarry into engaging in whatever amusement he'd set out to enjoy. Darcy became acutely aware that none of the onlookers had departed yet, and of Peter watching with wide eyes. "Or for a good fencer who doesn't want to risk anyone losing an eye."

"So you would wear a mask if you fenced with me?" Henry asked, still obstinate.

Darcy could guess where Henry was going, but saw no graceful way around it. With Henry, there rarely was. "Yes."

"You insult me. I should challenge you to a duel for that." Glee flashed in Henry's eyes.

Darcy suppressed a smile at that and altered his strategy. "I would pick pistols."

"You admit I'm a better fencer than you?" Henry cried, sounding both disappointed and surprised.

"No, but if you are not willing to don a mask, I won't face you."

Henry grimaced. He cast a look about them, taking in the steadily growing sea of faces. "Have it your way, Darcy. A mask it is."

Darcy answered that with a grin, shoving his back on. Teaching Peter hadn't been strenuous and Darcy wasn't tired, merely warmed up. Thought of the boy sobered him and when he saluted Henry, it was with calm focus. Darcy knew he had to beat his cousin for Peter's sake. He had to show the lad that a good fencer used a mask.

***

If Elizabeth was surprised to find her shuttlecock partner was Miss Darcy, Miss Darcy appeared equally surprised to learn hers was Elizabeth.

"My brother wrote me about you," Miss Darcy blurted, her tone as startled as her expression. "He said you are very clever." Snapping her mouth closed, she blushed.

"He must have caught me on those rare occasions when I say something clever. I'm due for another bout of wit sometime next January, I think."

Miss Darcy smiled, then looked down, obviously shy now that they were conversing, not playing. "I can see why he likes you," she mumbled.

Mrs. Annesley gave her a discrete nudge.

Miss Darcy looked up. She blushed again, but squared her shoulders. "But I have my own reasons to like you," she said in more audibly tones. "It was fun playing with someone as skilled and enthusiastic as you."

"While others are boasting of their skill at music or drawing, I will have to refer to you to tell how masterful I am at battledore and shuttlecock."

Miss Darcy pulled a face, glancing at Mrs. Annesley. "I've been informed I shan't have any skills if I don't apply myself better."

Elizabeth, recalling Mr. Darcy's recounting of his sister's accomplishments, doubted that was really a risk. "Well, I am pleased you took today away from your studies."

Miss Darcy's smile appeared a bit less timid this time. "I'm going back to them tomorrow, but Mrs. Annesley said I could enjoy myself today."

Behind her, Lady Agatha's daughters were calling about, angling to start a new game. They'd already found eager players in the two Gardiner girls, but wanted more matches going for a tournament of sorts. Elizabeth had enjoyed herself immensely, but she'd had her fill of the game for now. She cast Miss de Bourgh a questioning look.

Miss Darcy eyed her cousins. "Perhaps it would be nice to be with adults for a while." She glanced at her governess, who nodded.

"And I should like to look in on my aunt and uncle, if I can find them, and Jane," Elizabeth said.

Together, the four of them left the Girls' Garden. Elizabeth found her aunt and uncle seated at a small table with another couple. Separating from her companions, she approached and was introduced to what turned out to be old friends of the Gardiners. Her aunt and uncle appeared to have no desire to leave their current company, allowing Elizabeth to feel free to enjoy herself.

She spent a little time seeking Jane, but couldn't locate her. This troubled Elizabeth slightly, but not terribly. With the great mass of people seeming to fill every space both inside and out, Jane wasn't alone with Colonel Fitzwilliam, wherever they were. Not to mention that Elizabeth had come to know him with moderate familiarity. She trusted the colonel completely, both with Jane and to look after her.

Abandoning that search, she set out to rediscovered her companions from the Girls' Garden, soon finding them applying themselves to the buffet. A quick glance about the room showed that Mr. Bingley and the widow no longer occupied it, to Elizabeth's relief, so she joined them. Soon she, Miss de Bourgh, Miss Darcy, and Mrs. Annesley had all served themselves and set out looking for a table, finding an empty one in one of the shallow alcoves created by the grand statues set along the walls. The table had room for eight, allowing plenty of choice for seating. Elizabeth deliberately selected a place next to the wall, where she would be hidden by a statue. She didn't want to be seen by Mr. Bingley, should he return.

Elizabeth and her three companions chatted while they ate, Elizabeth answering Miss de Bourgh's polite inquiries about the Gardiners. Although Miss Darcy contributed the least to the conversation, she appeared comfortable enough with the current company. Miss de Bourgh was obviously so, apparently well accustomed to her cousin and Mrs. Annesley, and now easy in Elizabeth's presence as well. So much so, Elizabeth felt she often spoke over Miss Darcy's tentative attempts to converse. Elizabeth, in turn, gave Miss Darcy many conversational openings, subtly trying to make her comfortable talking. It didn't take her long to realize Mrs.

Annesley was doing the same thing. Miss de Bourgh, however, appeared to remain ignorant.

"Miss Darcy," a familiar voice exclaimed, suffused with false warmth.

Though the speaker was hidden from Elizabeth by the statue she sat near, she knew it was Miss Bingley. As all three of her tablemates had turned at the greeting, Elizabeth indulged herself in a grimace before schooling her features into polite indifference. Mr. Hurst strode into view, not looking at their table, and hurried off toward the buffet.

There was a swish of skirts and two sets of footsteps drew near. "It's so lovely to see you Miss Darcy, Miss de Bourgh," Miss Bingley said. "Good afternoon Mrs. Annesley, and who have we . . ."

Miss Bingley's voice trailed off as she rounded the statue and spotted Elizabeth. Mrs. Hurst followed, distaste flashing in her eyes when they landed upon the fourth occupant of the table. Well aware the sisters didn't like her, Elizabeth was unsurprised by the look, or the one of chagrin which overtook Miss Bingley's features.

"Miss Bingley, Mrs. Hurst," Elizabeth greeted with all the politeness and feigned pleasure she could stomach.

Miss Bingley turned to Miss Darcy. "Miss Darcy, how good of you to save us seats." She gestures to the empty chairs.

Miss Darcy said nothing, looking down. The sisters sat. Elizabeth hid a smile, wondering if the two seats they selected were meant to keep them near Miss Darcy and Miss de Bourgh, or far from Elizabeth. Likely, it was both.

After fluffing her skirts to her satisfaction, Miss Bingley turned a false smile on Elizabeth. "Miss Bennet, I am surprised to see you here." Her eyes shifted toward Miss Darcy and Miss de Bourgh.

"I wasn't expecting to see you here either," Elizabeth replied. She hoped the subtle difference in her statement would make it polite, not tit for tat. She hadn't missed Miss Bingley's glance, a not very subtle indication that part of her surprise was at finding Elizabeth seated with people of rank and fashion.

Miss Bingley's smile didn't waver, but she eyed Elizabeth like something she'd found stuck to her shoe. Something that would require the footwear not to be cleaned, but tossed out. "That is a lovely dress, Miss Bennet. I've never seen you wear anything so fashionable. It is so unlike what you usually wear."

Elizabeth raised her eyebrows. "Thank you." She made sure to keep her tone sweet, in spite of being certain the compliment was only given as an excuse for the insult. She suspected Miss Bingley would be upset to have her words taken kindly, which made her smile. It amused Elizabeth that Miss Bingley's dislike of her led her to say something inappropriate.

"Have you seen the house yet, Miss Bennet?" Mrs. Hurst asked. "You should take advantage of this chance."

Elizabeth permitted her smile to widen. First one sister insulted the clothing she usually wore, and then the other implied she didn't spend much time in such lofty company. It was amazing how much bad behavior her mere presence could inspire.

"I've already shown Elizabeth around," Miss de Bourgh said. "We arrived together."

Elizabeth hid her surprise at Miss de Bourgh's use of her given name, which implied a closeness anyone who knew Miss Bingley could guess would inspire jealousy.

"Together?" Miss Bingley said sharply, looking between them.

"Yes." Miss de Bourgh's chin angled up a notch, a defiant look coming into her eyes. "Lady Agatha invited Elizabeth and Elizabeth's aunt and uncle, with whom I'm staying. They never made it to the buffet, since they found some old friends and are catching up."

"You are staying with Miss Bennet's aunt and uncle? Aren't they in trade?" Miss Bingley gasped.

This time, Elizabeth nearly laughed. Miss Bingley spoke with such shock, she couldn't manage to maintain even the veneer of politeness. Mrs. Hurst frowned at her. Miss Darcy looked up, her wide, surprised eyes moving from face to face.

"I believe so." Miss de Bourgh's tone was, if anything, more aloof. "They are delightful people and offered me a refuge when I felt the need for space from my mother."

"But, to stay with them?" Miss Bingley gave her sister a pleading look.

"You should come stay with us," Mrs. Hurst said.

"You'll be much happier," Miss Bingley said. "We've plenty of room, and we can come to know each other better."

Elizabeth didn't think the offer would be accepted, but wasn't certain. Miss de Bourgh didn't appear to care for Miss Bingley and Mrs. Hurst, but it was difficult to tell how much that signified to a woman who'd lived with Lady Catherine for nearly twenty-five years. She turned to Miss de Bourgh, curious to find out which she valued more, a cheerful household, or her own room and a proper bevvy of servants.

13

Darcy won. Henry beat him on the third bout, but insisted they still fence the fifth after Darcy took the match by winning the fourth. Henry claimed he rarely had the opportunity to fence with someone who was better than he was, and said it was worth it to be beaten during the fifth round just for the experience.

Though he kept his focus on his opponent throughout, for Henry was no slouch, Darcy was aware that Peter watched with avid attention, as did the ever-increasing crowd they'd drawn. When the final match was over, Peter was sent on his way ecstatic over the display of swordsmanship and suitably impressed with Darcy as a fencing instructor. Darcy could only hope the end result would be that Peter would always wear a mask.

Darcy and Henry divested themselves of their masks and padding, shrugging back into their coats. The crowd began to thin, various people stopping to congratulate Darcy and praise the match. Henry took his defeat with grace, which was typical of his sporting nature.

"Well done, Darcy," Bingley's familiar voice called as Darcy was still easing himself into his coat.

Darcy used the excuse of his sleeves to give him a moment to compose his expression. If Miss Bennet cared for Mr. Bingley as much as Elizabeth seemed to think, things could go badly if the two met. Worse, where Bingley was, Miss Bingley was sure to follow. Darcy would have less patience than ever for her slights to Elizabeth. He gave one final tug to his sleeve and turned to his friend. "Bingley. I didn't know you were here."

"I only made the final bout, but I came as soon as I heard there was an exhibition of fencing between you and Matlock." He turned to Henry and bowed. "My lord."

"Bingley," Henry acknowledged with a nod. "I'm afraid I didn't give a very good show fencing." He turned to Darcy, a flash of challenge in his eyes. "I may have lost today, but bet that on my grey I could beat you on any horse of yours, Darcy."

"Certainly," Darcy said. "We'll race from London to Greenwich."

Bingley chuckled.

"But that's nine or ten miles," Henry said. "That's not a race. It's a mail run."

"That's the sort of stable Darcy keeps," Bingley said.

"I'm not interested in racing," Darcy said, almost apologetically. He knew he would never really win against Henry. If he won, Henry would insist on a rematch. If he lost, well, he lost. Darcy was starting to regret permitting himself to be drawn into the fencing match, for his cousin didn't care to let go of a rivalry. "I want a horse that will take me where I want to go."

"You always were the practical one, Darcy." Henry shook his head in sham sorrow.

Darcy smiled but, looking at Henry carefully for the first time, he was momentarily taken aback. He hadn't had the presence of mind to note before they began fencing, but there were growing signs of age in his cousin's face. Henry was what, thirty-three? In spite of the five years' difference between them, Darcy had always considered Henry a contemporary, perhaps because he acted like a younger man.

Henry slapped Darcy on the arm. "Don't look so grim, Darcy. I won't force you to race me. Especially when I know it would be no contest."

Darcy shook his head at Henry's taunting tone.

"Are you going to stand there and take that, Darcy?" Bingley asked, his voice full of mock indignation.

"No." Darcy took in the anticipation on Henry's face, amused his cousin was taking the bait. "Instead, I'm going to leave. I'm longing for a glimpse of Lady Agatha's buffet."

That earned him another friendly clout and a chuckle from Henry. "At least you've come by your appetite well. I'm hungry myself. Bingley?"

Bingley nodded and the three set out for the buffet room. As they walked, stopping often to converse with acquaintances, Henry regaled them with broken bits of a story about a recent carriage race. The tale was entertaining, but harrowing as well. The more Darcy heard, the more surprised he was that Henry was still engaging in such foolishness. By the time the story was finished, Darcy had no regrets about not permitting himself to be drawn into more foolery.

The buffet room was as crowded as ever. Darcy didn't see Elizabeth, but he spotted Anne and his sister at a table along the wall, tucked in next to one of the statues. Unfortunately, Miss Bingley and Mr. and Mrs. Hurst also sat at the table. Also unfortunately, Miss Bingley spotted them before Darcy could compile a reason to turn away.

As they drew near, Darcy found Elizabeth was with his sister and cousin after all, having been obscured by the statuary. Richard, Elizabeth's aunt and uncle and, fortunately, Miss Bennet, were not in evidence. Darcy knew there was little chance of Miss Bennet never encountering Bingley again, but didn't feel the need to be a witness to the occasion, if he could avoid it.

They reached the table and everyone stood, exchanging greetings. That done, Mr. Hurst returned to his seat, applying himself to the heaping plate of food before him. Most of the ladies retook their seats as well, but the gentlemen, Elizabeth and Miss Bingley remained standing. Elizabeth had come around the table during the greetings, and now stood beside Darcy, just near enough for him to catch a hint of the light scent she wore.

Miss Bingley turned to her brother. "Charles, Louisa and I have been attempting to persuade Miss de Bourgh to come stay with us. You must throw your weight behind us."

"I'm staying with the Gardiners." Anne's tone was calm but firm, impressing Darcy. "It would be insulting to leave them while I'm still in London, and they have been nothing but kind and accommodating."

Elizabeth smiled.

"Well, it seems we must leave London, then," Bingley said, sounding proud of his solution. "An excellent idea, Caroline. We'll return to Hertfordshire. The country should be enjoyable at this time of year. You must join my sister and me at Netherfield Park, Miss de Bourgh."

Miss Bingley cast a look of distaste toward Elizabeth. "It's still too early to go north."

"You were just saying you would like to see Pemberley at this time of year," Mr. Hurst mumbled around a mouthful of food.

Elizabeth's smile widened. Darcy could imagine what she was thinking. Pemberley was even farther north than Netherfield Park. They all knew Miss Bingley would travel there at any time of year, in any weather.

"Well, I'm going," Bingley said. "I fancy some riding in the country, and this is the last party of the season that I had any plan to attend. You really must come with me, Caroline, as hostess." He looked at the Hursts. "I would enjoy having your company as well."

Darcy was surprised at Bingley's statement about parties, for he was generally quite social. Elizabeth, too, appeared skeptical. Considering she knew Bingley less well, her disbelief more likely stemmed from his declaration that he would enjoy the company of the Hursts.

"Love to," Mr. Hurst said, pausing in his eating. "You keep a good table. We have to delay a couple of days, I'm afraid, because I have an engagement. Miss Bingley can go earlier."

Bingley turned to Darcy. "Darcy, would you like to join us?"

He took in Miss Bingley's eager expression. It occurred to him the subject of his courtship of Elizabeth must not have come up. Had it, Miss Bingley would be as eager to keep him away from Hertfordshire as she was her brother. Did that mean Anne had given up the idea of his courting Elizabeth, or simply hadn't had time to intimate the rumor yet? It didn't matter, for Darcy intended to pursue Elizabeth either way. "If Anne goes, I should. I believe her leaving Rosings was contingent on my being, well, not quite with her, but available."

"I haven't said I'm going," Anne said, sounding a trifle annoyed. "And do you mean, Darcy, that you'd abandon Miss Elizabeth?" The look she gave him was meaningful.

"Why should Mr. Darcy consider Miss Bennet?" Miss Bingley's tone was sharp. "Let her relations see to her." Her smile turned sweet. "You simply must come with us, Miss de Bourgh."

"If you wish to go, Miss de Bourgh, there's no need to worry over me. I shall simply return home," Elizabeth said.

Anne turned from face to face. Darcy wondered if she didn't know what she wanted, or was so unaccustomed to making decisions she couldn't do it with ease. Henry, standing on the other side of Elizabeth, looked on with obvious amusement.

"Colonel Fitzwilliam is staying with Darcy. We can't all desert him," Anne said.

"He's invited too," Bingley said. "As is Miss Darcy."

Where she sat off to the side between Mrs. Annesley and Mrs. Hurst, Georgiana's head popped up. Her eyes were wide with something near to terror. She gave Darcy a barely discernable shake of her head.

"Georgiana must stay in London and attend her lessons," he said, granting her the reprieve he knew she wanted. A house full of people, one of them Miss Bingley, was akin to torture to Georgiana. She might also be aware, as he was, that Mr. Wickham was in Hertfordshire. Darcy wanted to encourage her to be more outgoing, and would like to see her spend time with Elizabeth, but he wouldn't make her suffer.

"Miss Bennet," Henry said, turning to Elizabeth. "It looks as if you and I are the only ones not going to the wilds of Hertfordshire. Fortunately, I shall have you here in London to entertain me."

Though Henry's tone was light, Darcy bristled at the flirtation. Maybe now was the time to let the world know he was courting Elizabeth. Shocked by his inclination to blurt out the news then and there, he made himself draw a calming breath.

"I am afraid you are mistaken, my lord," Elizabeth said to Henry. "When I said I should return home if Miss de Bourgh leaves London, I meant I, too, would journey to Hertfordshire. I live but three miles from Mr. Bingley. I assure you it is quite tame there, and truly is lovely at this time of year."

"Then I'm sorry to miss it, especially with an example of that loveliness before me."

Anger flickered in Darcy again, but he'd come to his senses now. Letting Henry know of his courtship of Elizabeth would likely be an error. Courtship, as Elizabeth had pointed out at the start, was not engagement. If Darcy showed too much pique, Henry might take winning Elizabeth from him as a challenge. Since Darcy was well aware she felt no great love for him, yet, he didn't know which of them would win such a contest. At least he could assure himself she wouldn't marry Henry simply for his money. Of course, Henry also had a title.

As if remembering as much herself, Miss Bingley turned covetous eyes on Henry. "Charles," she prompted.

"I beg your pardon, my lord," Bingley said. "I would like to extend you an invitation as well."

"Splendid," Henry said. "I'd be delighted, and I'm sure Richard will be too. What do you say, Anne? Shall we make a party of it?"

Anne shook her head, but she smiled. "Yes, I suppose we shall. It seems I am destined to visit the wilds of Hertfordshire."

"Excellent." Henry grinned around at them, his gaze lingering on

Elizabeth.

Darcy didn't think Henry going was excellent, but it would certainly be interesting.

***

The following day found Darcy alone in his office, seated behind his elegant mahogany desk, working through a heavy pile of correspondences. The stack made him feel a bit guilty. He realized he'd been, not quite neglecting, but delaying seeing to his interests for longer than he really liked.

He'd made his way through a solid half of the pile when a knock sounded. Checking the clock on the mantel, he found it wasn't yet time for tea, which could only mean a visitor. He considered the diminished pile, shrugged, and called, "Enter."

His butler stepped into the room. "Are you at home to Mr. Bingley, sir?"

"Yes." Darcy watched the man disappear, closing the door. He could do with a break. Bingley likely wanted to finalize their plans to travel to Hertfordshire. Doing so in person would preempt the need to add more correspondences to the pile.

While he waited, Darcy organized his papers into several neat stacks, stowing most of them in the desk. It wasn't in an effort to keep Bingley from his affairs. Bingley knew most of Darcy's ventures in detail, and wasn't one to pry, regardless. He simply preferred his desk in order.

Another knock was followed by the arrival of Bingley. As he entered, Darcy gestured to the seat across from him. "To what do I owe this pleasure?"

Bingley didn't sit, Darcy's first indication he was agitated. He stood in the middle of the room, a slight frown on his face. Darcy sat straighter, wondering what could be the matter. Had Bingley decided not to travel to Netherfield after all? Had it occurred to him it might be awkward to encounter Miss Bennet? Or, more likely, Mrs. Kent was holding Bingley's attention more firmly than Darcy would have imagined. The brief report Richard had made on the subject hadn't convinced Darcy there was anything serious, but Richard had also said he'd not stayed in the room for long and so observed little.

Abruptly, Bingley claimed the offered seat. "Darcy, why do you think we are friends?"

The question wasn't what Darcy was expecting to hear, but answering didn't take much thought. Everyone liked Bingley. Men liked him because he was an asset at a party, holding up his share of conversation when appropriate. He was generally up for riding, hunting, billiards or any other activity, and never stingy with his coin. Mothers and their daughters liked him because he was amiable, always willing to dance, and, on the marriage market, he was a good catch. So much so, Darcy had even considered him for Georgiana. He'd set aside the idea because of the complete indifference on both sides, but he would have welcomed it. On top of all that, Bingley genuinely liked almost everyone he met and showed it. "You are pleasant, have a good character, have--"

"I don't care why you're friends with me. Almost everyone who isn't a total snob wants to be my friend. I'm the harmless puppy all reasonable people like. Why am I friends with you?"

That flummoxed Darcy. He'd never given it any thought. "I don't know."

Bingley smiled slightly. "I hate to say it, but you are a proud one, aren't you? Most people would have wondered at it, at least once."

Darcy had nothing to say to that. Though he was taciturn, he was accustomed to people seeking his company. True, it was usually for his wealth and status, but it need only start that way. His and Bingley's friendship had moved well beyond that.

"Do you remember when I bought that showy bay gelding and you criticized it as all flash and no substance, which turned out to be true?"

Darcy nodded.

"Do you remember when I said my handwriting was bad because my thoughts came too quickly and you pointed out that I was actually bragging about how fast I thought and wrote?"

Darcy nodded again. Was Bingley about to break off their friendship? If Darcy being honest didn't suit Bingley, as difficult as it would be, ending their association was likely for the best.

"You are the only one who criticizes me."

"Your sisters--"

"My sisters never stop criticizing me."

Darcy stared at him, wondering if Bingley had been drinking, though the hour was early. "You aren't making sense."

Bingley frowned. "Do you remember that girl in Hertfordshire, the pretty one? Miss Elizabeth's sister."

"Miss Jane Bennet," Darcy supplied, not liking the turn in the conversation.

"Yes. I almost married her. You were right to stop me. That's the sort of criticism I'm speaking of."

"Your sisters also didn't want you to marry her." It was obvious Anne still hadn't let out that Darcy was courting Elizabeth. Of course, it was a subtle thing to impart such gossip. Likely, Anne didn't know how to go about it. Darcy certainly didn't. "How was my addition to your sisters' objections more meaningful?"

"Because you only offer caution where caution is due. My sisters disparage most any woman I meet. They'll only be happy with someone of great wealth and rank, and would prefer I marry your sister. Miss Bennet didn't embody a single quality they value."

"Miss Bennet is beautiful, kind and sweet tempered. She would make any man an excellent wife."

Bingley's brow creased. "You said she didn't love me and her family was intolerable."

"Her family was intolerable," Darcy agreed, though it was a point of which he didn't care to be reminded. "I didn't say she didn't love you. I said I thought she didn't love you. I may have been wrong. At the least, she liked you."

"It doesn't matter." Bingley shrugged.

Darcy was surprised at how much the careless motion aggravated him. Though he'd little to say about Mrs. Kent, Richard had supplied an extended description of how brokenhearted Miss Bennet was to see Bingley with another woman. Yet here was Bingley, shrugging off the broken heart of a gentle soul as if it meant nothing.

"Miss Bennet was wrong for me," Bingley continued, apparently oblivious to Darcy's uncharitable turn of temper. "Furthermore, you were right about her family. They're practically deranged, barring Miss Elizabeth and possibly the father. The younger daughters are uncontrolled, and may never marry. I would have ended up with the three of them and that atrocious mother living with me. Can you imagine?" Bingley grimaced.

"I can." Darcy kept his tone neutral. "I also imagine, though, that her family situation wouldn't really have matter to you, had you loved each other."

"Love?" Bingley chuckled, as if Darcy had made a joke. "She may have loved me and I will admit I thought I loved her, but I've thought that before, haven't I? I was certainly angry with you and my sisters for insisting we separate, but I only missed her for a week or two. Then I met this girl."

"Mrs. Kent?" How could anyone favor that gaudy widow over someone as sweet as Miss Bennet?

Bingley shook his head. "There was this girl in Scarborough. The details don't matter, but a day with her and I'd forgotten all about Miss Bennet."

"How long did that last?" Darcy wanted to add, and how long did getting over her take, but restrained himself.

"About a month, but that's not the point. The point is, I've realized why Miss Bennet was so wrong for me. At least, the reason that matters most. I need a wife who will disagree with me."

Darcy frowned. Bingley was speaking without reason again. "You despise argument."

"Not a wife who argues with me, but who is willing to disagree with me," Bingley said. "Miss Bennet never would have. She was too sweet tempered. I need someone who will keep me from doing foolish things."

"You want a wife who won't permit you to purchase a showy horse that doesn't have the stamina for a hunt, let alone a journey?"

"Exactly."

Darcy's eyes returned to the clock. He was finding Bingley's company less pleasant than usual, and he still had letters to see to. "Fascinating. I'm glad you came by to share your revelation."

Bingley chuckled again. "Right, you wish me to approach the point. I've decided it's time to be married."

"To Mrs. Kent?" Darcy suppressed a sigh. It was his duty to talk Bingley out of it, of course, but he wasn't looking forward to it. Perhaps the conversation would wait until they were in Hertfordshire. Once there, it may not even be necessary. Bingley was sure to forget about the widow the moment he set eyes on another pretty girl. Unfortunately, they already knew most of the pretty girls near Netherfield Park, and Bingley had already thrown over the most amiable one.

"Mrs. Kent? Of course not. I wouldn't mind marrying a widow, but she hasn't exactly kept to herself since she was widowed. Not to

129

mention the issue of an heir. If she could have children, she would have had one by now." Bingley leaned forward in his chair. "To be frank, she's been hinting about marriage. That's why I'm so eager to leave London. Actually, I'm setting out in a few hours. I'll leave it to the rest of you to catch up."

"If not Mrs. Kent, then who do you have in mind?" Was Bingley running from London or toward Hertfordshire? "Miss Bennet?"

"What? Were you not listening? Her family is horrid, and she's too biddable." Bingley's eyes narrowed. "Has Miss Elizabeth said something, then? Truly, I'm sorry if I raised Miss Bennet's expectations, but our acquaintance lasted less than two months. After so long an absence, she must realize I'm no longer interested. Surely she took the hint when I didn't call on her here in London."

"You knew she was in London?"

"Did you?" Bingley asked.

Darcy nodded.

"I'm surprised you didn't mention it, but it doesn't signify." Bingley shrugged again. "I didn't bring it up because I was content to let Caroline think she was keeping it from me. It calms her machinations if she thinks she's controlling me, and I didn't actually have any desire to see Miss Bennet. I didn't fancy calling and trying to make it clear I still liked her, but wasn't interested in her."

"That would be a difficult line to draw," Darcy admitted, surprised Bingley had fooled them all into thinking he'd been unaware of Miss Bennet's presence in town.

"I didn't want to botch it up and leave her with reignited hope. Miss Bennet's a sweet girl, who deserves a good husband. Just not me." Bingley shook his head. "No, I'm not remaining in London to marry Mrs. Kent, or returning to Hertfordshire to court Miss Bennet, but I know myself. I risk marrying the next attractive woman I stumble across. It could be a widow with the morals of a cat or a country miss who is studying to be a saint. Neither would really suit me."

A sudden suspicion of why Bingley was there filled Darcy. "I don't believe you would be a good husband for Georgiana."

Bingley waved that off with a gesture. "Don't worry, that's not why I'm here. Your sister wouldn't suit me. She wouldn't contradict me. Her dowry is attractive, she has the right connections and she's a nice girl, but that's all." Bingley sighed, leaning back in his chair. "They're all nice girls. Almost everyone I meet is nice, but I've been thinking about this a lot and I know what I want in a wife."

"What?" Darcy asked, though his eyes strayed to the clock again.

"She needn't be a beauty or accomplished. I don't care if my wife can draw. I can buy drawings. I can live without music, but if I couldn't, I would hire a musician. I can hire a housekeeper, too. What I can't live without are children. I also want someone acceptable to the friends I have. You, for example, and my sisters. I know they can be tiresome at times, but they're my family and my wife will have to associate with them. Her manners will have to be good. There is no reason for me to marry down. I've enough money to expect a wife to have something. I would like a country home, but living off the income from one is chancy. Agricultural prices are dropping."

"True," Darcy said. So much so, he was often glad he had a number of varied investments.

"That means if I buy an estate, I must keep enough capital to generate an income to live on. I should marry someone with at least ten thousand pounds. Twenty would be better."

"You'll have competition."

"I know that, but I'll still have many choices and a decent chance. I believe we've already established everyone finds me amiable, including women."

Darcy nodded.

"You should also know I've given my fidelity serious consideration. I think if I married someone, I would stay loyal. It's the knowledge there's no commitment that makes me so fickle, and their absence that makes me forget them. I wouldn't absent myself from my wife."

"Why are you telling me this?" Darcy asked, worried Bingley's earlier dismissal of Georgiana as an option had been a ruse.

"Because, when the time comes, I want your honest advice about my choice." Bingley eyed him for a long moment. "Also, I want you to know I'm serious about marrying now. It's occurred to me that my past inconsistency may, at some point, spur you to feel honor bound to separate me from a woman who actually is worthy of being my wife. I know how keen your honor is, and value that in you, but I don't want it to come between me and a good match."

Darcy contemplated that. He wouldn't have seen it if Bingley hadn't brought it up, but it was true. If Bingley had approached, say, Georgiana, Darcy would possibly have warned him off, worried his friend would break his sister's heart as he had Miss Bennet's. That, he realized, was Elizabeth's doing. She'd introduced him to the other side of Bingley's fickle affection. In the past, Darcy had only considered his friend's interests. How Bingley had sensed the change, Darcy didn't know, but Bingley was always intuitive. "I see," he finally said. "Your commitment to a wife and marriage is duly noted."

Bingley stood, nodding. "Thank you. I look forward to seeing you in Hertfordshire. Caroline and I will already be there, so arrive whenever you like."

"Have a safe journey."

Bingley nodded, his amiable smile back in place. With a bow, he departed, leaving Darcy in no mood for correspondence as he tried to wend his way back through their conversation. He'd always considered himself a fine judge of character, but lately it seemed that had only been a prideful delusion.

Bingley wasn't who Darcy had thought he was. Darcy had fallen for Bingley's amiability, not looking too deeply at the man beneath. Not that there seemed to be anything terrible about that man. He was just more practical and jaded than Darcy would have guessed. He'd also, based on Richard's recounting of her reaction to seeing Bingley with another woman, misjudged Miss Bennet. Even Anne was surprising Darcy, seeming capable of negotiating the social rounds without her mother, something he hadn't suspected was possible.

Then there was Elizabeth, whom he'd misjudged completely, and disastrously, when he'd assumed she would accept his offer of marriage. That, however, he would mend. By the time his two months were up, he would prove to her that her answer shouldn't be no.

HERTFORDSHIRE

"She is a sweet girl, and if weren't for her awful family, she should make a good marriage, to someone of her own class."

14

Elizabeth sat beside Jane in Mr. Darcy's carriage. He was across from her, with Miss de Bourgh. In a perfect position to watch him during the journey to Longbourn, Elizabeth couldn't help spend much of the trip admiring how well turned out he was. Of course, he always cut a dashing figure. His tailor was obviously very expensive.

She smiled as she contemplated the reactions her most recent letters home must have invoked. Making it out as a perfectly normal occurrence, she'd explained that she had left Kent in the company of Miss de Bourgh, Colonel Fitzwilliam and Mr. Darcy, adding that Miss de Bourgh was staying at the Gardiners with her and Jane. She'd written again after the party at Lady Agatha's, describing the event in great detail, while leaving out almost everything of relevance. Shortly thereafter, once the arrangements for the trip had been finalized, she'd been obliged to send a third letter from London. That one had informed her family Mr. Bingley had left London for Netherfield and she and Jane would be returning to Longbourn, brought thither by Mr. Darcy and in the company of Miss de Bourgh.

"There is something I wish to discuss before we reach your home," Miss de Bourgh said, breaking into the lull in conversation that had held the interior of the carriage in silence for the past several miles. "I realize it will be more difficult for you in Hertfordshire, Miss Elizabeth, but we must adhere to the plan of you permitting Mr. Darcy to court you. No place is safe from my mother's spies."

"It will not be difficult for me," Mr. Darcy said.

"Nor for me." Elizabeth considered bringing up the money, but she felt it was crass. She also hadn't spoken about it to Jane, and didn't care to.

"Then we are agreed." Miss de Bourgh looked pleased.

"I do worry we still haven't found a good solution, though," Elizabeth said. "I know you will have control of Rosings soon, and that we've bought time with our subterfuge, but Lady Catherine still holds her card. She can still ruin Miss Darcy."

"How could anyone think to ruin that sweet child?" Jane said, shaking her head.

Elizabeth glanced at her. When Jane and Georgiana had met, late in the day at Lady Agatha's party, her sister had seemed too distraught to take any real note. "You have not had the pleasure of making Lady Catherine's acquaintance. She is formidable."

Jane shook her head again, her expression full of sorrow for the inexplicable unfairness in the world.

"As I said, once I possess Rosings, I will threaten my mother with expulsion if she attempts to defame Georgiana."

Elizabeth nodded, deciding to let the matter drop, but she wasn't sure in their plan. Miss Darcy's reputation wouldn't be safe until either Miss de Bourgh or Mr. Darcy married, forever ending the possibility of their union. That cause wouldn't be furthered by them journeying to Hertfordshire, she realized. Who would either find to marry there?

The conversation lulled again and Elizabeth turned to the window. She peered out, her smile returning as she took in the familiarity of the passing fields. They were almost to Longbourn. She'd been away for two months, admittedly only half as long as Jane, yet still she was anxious for the familiar and to see her family. Even her mother.

"You're eager to be home, Miss Elizabeth?" Mr. Darcy's rich voice reached out to her from across the carriage.

"I am. I enjoyed Kent, for the most part, and have no dislike of London, but I find I miss the country air."

"And Mama and Papa," Jane said, giving Elizabeth a reprimanding look.

"Of course. I miss all of those with whom I've a lifetime of daily familiarity, right down to the staff, the hounds and even Papa's prize sow."

"Lizzy, you aren't comparing our family and the servants to a pig?"

"Of course not. There can be no similarity between lovely people like Mrs. Hill or Father and livestock." She deliberately didn't include her mother and younger sisters in her rejoinder.

Jane shook her head, laughing. "Oh Lizzy. Your sharp tongue will someday get the better of you."

Elizabeth contained a grimace, thinking perhaps it already had, when she'd belittled Mr. Darcy following his proposal.

"You have three other sisters, I believe I recall?" Miss de Bourgh asked, looking from Elizabeth to Jane.

"We have one sister and two hoydens who reside in our home," Elizabeth said.

"Lizzy." Jane's tone was pleading.

"But perhaps they have learned better manners in our absence," Elizabeth added, to mollify Jane.

"I shall be delighted to meet them." Miss de Bourgh turned to address Mr. Darcy, seated beside her. "I'm sure being related to Miss Bennet and Miss Elizabeth, they can be nothing but lovely and kind?"

Elizabeth could have laughed. She turned a broad smile on Mr. Darcy, awaiting his answer.

"The younger two are quite pretty, especially the very youngest, and very friendly. The middle daughter is exceedingly diligent in honing her accomplishments," he said.

Elizabeth raised her eyebrows, impressed.

"I see we've arrived." Mr. Darcy's tone was touched with relief.

Elizabeth realized the carriage was turning. Looking back out the window, she took in the familiar scenery lining the short drive leading from the road to Longbourn. "Will you come in? I'm sure they'd be pleased to see you."

"I'd rather not," Miss de Bourgh answered. "I would prefer to meet your family some other time than at the end of a long journey."

"Of course, and know you are always welcome." Elizabeth looked to Mr. Darcy, feeling oddly shy. "Both of you."

"Thank you again for bringing us home," Jane said. "It was most considerate of you. Please give my regards to your cousin, Colonel Fitzwilliam. He was exceedingly solicitous of me at Lady Agatha's party but I was, at the time, too . . ." She colored slightly, looking bereft.

"Indisposed," Elizabeth supplied.

"Yes, thank you." Jane nodded. "I was too indisposed to properly thank him, and I haven't seen him since that evening. I feel I owe him both thanks and an apology."

"I'm sure he will accept neither, and thank you for both," Miss be Bourgh said.

"Knowing the way Henry drives, I expect he and Richard are already at Netherfield, though they departed later than we did," Mr. Darcy said. "I'm also certain we'll all call on you soon."

The carriage drew to a halt and farewells were exchanged while Elizabeth and Jane disembarked. Their trunks were lowered from Mr. Darcy's smaller carriage and then the two carriages lumbered away. Elizabeth turned to find her mother and her sisters, Mary, Kitty and Lydia, piled into the doorway, watching. Mrs. Bennet hurried forward.

"Jane, Elizabeth, how pleasant to have you home." Their mother held her arms out wide, but made no actual attempt to embrace them. Nor did they go to her, knowing the gesture was for dramatic affect only. "Was that Mr. Darcy's carriage? Why did you not invite him in?"

Elizabeth, bemused, wondered at her mother's change of heart toward Mr. Darcy. Did a ride from London count for so much?

"What a splendid carriage," Lydia said.

"I prefer Mr. Bingley's," Kitty answered.

Making shooing noises, Mrs. Bennet turned, using her still outstretched arms to usher everyone inside and toward the parlor.

"We did invite him in, Mama," Jane said as they all made their way down the hall.

"Not convincingly enough, obviously." Mrs. Bennet sounded aggrieved.

Spotting her father seated in his favorite chair, Elizabeth hurried over to drop a kiss on his brow. "Papa."

"Lizzy, Jane, at last some semblance of reason has returned to our home."

"Mr. Bennet, you are the unreasonable one, and now Elizabeth and Jane have let Mr. Darcy get away."

"But you don't even like Mr. Darcy, Mama," Mary said.

"It isn't Mr. Darcy I want, of course, but I need him to pass along an invitation to Mr. Bingley, to dine here. Since you two let him get away, I must return to persuading your father to visit Mr. Bingley and issue the invitation."

"I have no intention of doing so. He knows where to find me, and my two eldest daughters deserve some attention, since they just arrived after months of absence."

"Jane was gone for more than four months, and I can understand you missing her," Mrs. Bennet said. "But Lizzy was not even gone two, so you didn't have time to miss her. It won't take you very long to visit Mr. Bingley. You will be able to spend plenty of time with Jane."

Elizabeth and her father exchanged an amused glance.

"I'm sure Mr. Darcy will return soon enough," Jane said, arching a brow at Elizabeth.

"Maybe Mr. Bingley will throw another ball." Lydia's voice was dreamy.

Elizabeth looked about the parlor, finding it felt slightly odd to be home after so long away. Everything was as she'd left it, including the people. She didn't know why she'd thought two months would change anything in Longbourn, except that she was different now. She hadn't realized how much so until she stood among them again.

"Why should Mr. Darcy return here?" Kitty wrinkled her nose. "No one likes him."

"Jane, tell your father he must go invite Mr. Bingley to dinner," Mrs. Bennet cried.

"I am going to my room to wash up." Jane crossed to their father, gave him a kiss, and hurried away.

"Did she not hear me mention Mr. Bingley?" Mrs. Bennet said, looking after Jane.

"We all did, my dear. Even the neighbors," Mr. Bennet muttered, raising his paper before his face.

Elizabeth wondered if her home had always been so chaotic. Looking back, she thought it must be the case. She, however, was no longer accustomed to it.

"Don't you understand?" Mrs. Bennet wailed. "It isn't just Mr. Bingley. I've heard there's a large party with several eligible gentlemen. You must visit them."

"Oh, Lizzy, are there eligible gentleman? Do you know? Weren't you with them in London?" Lydia asked.

"She said as much in her letter," Mary said, her tone condescending. "You've no head on your shoulders, Lydia."

"I do so, and a very pretty one," Lydia tossed her curls, "unlike some people."

"Miss de Bourgh was with us in London," Elizabeth temporized. "Her cousins, Mr. Darcy and Colonel Fitzwilliam, dined with us at the Gardiners. We also attended her cousin Lady Agatha's party in their company, as you already know from my letter. It was while there we encountered another of their cousins, the Earl of Matlock, and Mr. Bingley, Miss Bingley and the Hursts, inspiring a return to Hertfordshire."

"Which must mean Mr. Bingley intends to offer for Jane at last." Mrs. Bennet sounded pleased.

"A colonel," Lydia said. She whispered something in Kitty's ear. Both girls giggled.

"I wouldn't put too much hope in Mr. Bingley, Mother." Elizabeth said it out of a duty to Jane. She knew her mouther wouldn't listen.

"And an earl, of all things," Mrs. Bennet said. She looked at each of her daughters speculatively, finally settling her gaze on Lydia. "Yes, an earl."

"Why would an earl come to Hertfordshire?" Mary asked.

"He is a cousin to Miss de Bourgh and Mr. Darcy, and brother to Colonel Fitzwilliam." Elizabeth shrugged. "Why wouldn't he accompany them?"

"Did he dance with you at the party, Elizabeth?" Mrs. Bennet asked.

"Once, as did Colonel Fitzwilliam."

"And Mr. Bingley?"

"No." Elizabeth hadn't made any mention of Mr. Bingley's merry widow in her letter.

"I bet Mr. Darcy didn't dance with anyone." Lydia accompanied her statement with a grimace.

"Did he dance with anyone, Elizabeth?" Mary asked.

"He danced with me, and with Jane. All three gentlemen were very attentive and danced with both of us and Miss de Bourgh." Elizabeth was beginning to wish she'd included more such details in her letter, for it might have resulted in fewer question now.

"Of course they danced with Miss de Bourgh. She's an heiress," Mrs. Bennet said. "And now she has a houseful of eligible men all to herself, as if an heiress needs any luck finding a husband."

"Miss Bingley is also at Netherfield," Elizabeth reminded her.

"Why didn't Mr. Bingley dance with any of you if he was at the party?" Lydia asked. "That hardly seems like him."

"He departed before we began dancing." At least, before Elizabeth and Miss de Bourgh had moved to the room where the dancing took place. Jane and Colonel Fitzwilliam were already there.

"Left? A party?" Mrs. Bennet frowned. "Was he unwell?"

"I did not ask." Elizabeth endeavored to sound indifferent, though she was anything but. She was very suspicious of Mr. Bingley's motives. He'd disappeared with his widow, then reappeared to invite them all to leave London, and then quit the party. If Elizabeth were being uncharitable in her thoughts, she'd suspect he'd availed himself of what he was angling for from Mrs. Kent and then proceeded to cut her acquaintance.

"Imagine, though, Jane and Lizzy danced with a colonel and an earl." Lydia's voice was dreamy again.

"It means nothing if we cannot persuade them to call here." Mrs. Bennet cast a glare at Mr. Bennet, who ignored her.

"I'm sure they will visit us," Elizabeth said. Her mother's eyes on her, Elizabeth sought to reassure without admitting to Mr. Darcy's pretend courtship. She was too fatigued from her journey to endure the histrionics it would invoke. "Miss de Bourgh stayed with the Gardiners and will surely want to visit us here."

"Who cares if Miss de Bourgh visits? What is she to us? We don't need an heiress attracting all the eligible men."

Her mother carried on in that theme for some time, until she drove both Elizabeth and her father from the parlor. As she hurried away, seeking the quiet of the room she and Jane shared, Elizabeth smiled. It was nice to be home, even if her mother's rant about Miss de Bourgh having all of the money and access to all of the available gentlemen followed her down the hall.

The next day, the four gentlemen in question did call, the attractions of Miss de Bourgh apparently not enough to keep them at Netherfield Park. A carriage brought Mr. Darcy, Mr. Bingley, Colonel Fitzwilliam and the Earl of Matlock to Longbourn. With four eligible men in the house, Elizabeth watched with amusement as her mother attempted to sort out which one she should work the hardest to please, although clearly Mr. Darcy was last on the list.

Jane met Mr. Bingley with calm courtesy. Elizabeth was proud of her sister. Jane's greeting didn't show any anger over his desertion, nor did she act in any way like she was trying to attract him. She welcomed him as one would an old friend, but not as someone she was in love with.

Mr. Darcy sat next to Elizabeth, as if by chance. They exchanged a few words while her mother sent for refreshments, but soon fell silent. It amused Elizabeth to note Mr. Darcy appeared as interesting in watching the others as she was.

The seating had broken the party into small groups, there being far too many people for one conversation. Lydia and Kitty vied for Colonel Fitzwilliam's attention, though Elizabeth noticed his eyes straying to Jane at regular intervals. With a little maneuvering on Mrs.

Bennet's part, Mr. Bingley ended up sitting between Jane and Mary. Jane spoke to him pleasantly, but diligently drew Mary into the conversation.

The Earl of Matlock, somewhat to Elizabeth's surprise, took the seat beside her father. Their conversation appeared engaging, and she caught bits letting her know it centered around the doings of parliament. Even so, the earl glanced more than once at his younger brother. Her mother's attention flitted from group to group. She routinely poked her nose into other people's conversations, obviously believing she was assisting her daughters. Elizabeth was relieved her dislike of Mr. Darcy kept her away from him.

Once tea and sweets had been served and the others were occupied in their own conversations, Mr. Darcy turned to Elizabeth. "I'm relieved. After Richard's description of what occurred at Lady Agatha's, I didn't know how your sister would behave when confronted with Bingley again." His voice was pitched low.

Elizabeth replied in similar tones. "I'm impressed by her. At the party, and later at my aunt's and uncle's, she was a wreck, though your cousin did much to soothe her. He was very gallant." She wondered if Mr. Darcy sensed anything between the two. She didn't think Jane did yet, but would wager Colonel Fitzwilliam was already considering the idea. Elizabeth hoped he wouldn't pursue it without good intentions. She recalled him telling her he hadn't enough money to marry where he would, which ought to rule out Jane. Her sister should not be made to suffer another false courtship.

"She is very convincing," Mr. Darcy said. "If I didn't know to look, I wouldn't see that she keeps her hands clasped, for when she separates them you can see that they tremble, and hasn't touched a morsel of food."

Elizabeth turned to him in surprise. She had only noticed one of those things, but then she still hadn't managed a full night's sleep since the incident in Kent. The lack was likely dulling her wits. She was pleased, however, to learn Mr. Darcy was endeavoring to be more observant of people. "I am impressed by you as well."

He smiled. "Thank you. It's recently come to my attention that I am too quick to judge people and seek too little information before I do so. I'm attempting to remedy that."

"One must, of course, always pursue self-improvement."

"Indeed. Even me."

Elizabeth laughed. She hadn't thought Mr. Darcy would joke at his own expense. Obviously, she was guilty of judging too quickly as well.

"I'm pleased we called today." His voice was even lower than before. "I missed conversing with you."

"We conversed yesterday in the carriage, the whole way from London."

"Was it only yesterday? When I cannot be with you, time marches a cruel, slow pace."

She laughed again. "Did you read that somewhere? It's a bit dreadful. I don't think anyone can hear us, you know. You needn't say such silly things."

"I enjoy saying them, though I obviously require practice." He shrugged. "I'm not accustomed to courting. I'm fortunate you've given me time. I hope now that we're in Hertfordshire, I may employ it better."

"Better?" Elizabeth repeated, confused.

He held up a hand, ticking off on his fingers. "We rode together from Kent, in company. Richard and I dined with you at the Gardiner's. We didn't dine together at Lady Agatha's, but did dance twice, and had another full carriage ride here. Unfortunately, in between the party and the journey here I was forced to see to my interests, having somewhat neglected them."

He'd counted their dances on one finger. Elizabeth would have given each its own count, for Mr. Darcy was a splendid partner. Dancing with him, in that fine gown, had made her feel like a princess. "It seems to me we've seen a great deal of each other."

"We were in London. Were I at all practiced, I should have taken you to the theater, or for a ride in the park, or some such thing."

"Well, we're in Hertfordshire now, so you may take me for a ride here, providing you have an open carriage. It would certainly cause appropriate gossip."

"For a ride with you, I would commission one," Mr. Darcy said, the smile he gave her warm. "Fortunately I don't have to, since I've arranged for my curricle to be brought here. It should arrive later today."

Elizabeth answered his smile with one of her own, but inside she was shaken for it had, in that moment, occurred to her that Mr. Darcy's courtship might not be pretend at all. Lydia's laughter rang across the room, louder even than usual. Elizabeth, relieved, took the excuse to turn away from Mr. Darcy's penetrating gaze. She shook her head. "My hope for better manners seems to have gone unanswered."

"She is young," Mr. Darcy said, diplomatic once more.

Elizabeth couldn't help but be amused by his new tactic. It appeared he meant to speak only the truth, just as before. He seemed to have decided, however, that he needn't put forth every bit of it that came to his mind.

They talked a while longer, Elizabeth keeping the conversation to incidental things. It was no hardship, for Mr. Darcy was now an easy person for her to converse with, but she was still shaken by her suspicion about his courtship. Soon, too, she would have to field questions concerning it, for people would notice and word would get out, as it always did.

When, after the correct half an hour, the gentlemen left, Elizabeth was sorry to see Mr. Darcy go, but also relieved. She required time to think. If he was serious in his intentions, she must be prepared for the moment he would ask for her hand again. The trouble was, she was no longer sure which answer she wished to make ready. Her uncertainty confused her.

"Jane, how can you expect to attract Mr. Bingley if you keep bringing Mary into the conversation?" Mrs. Bennet's querulous tone broke into Elizabeth's musing. "And Mary, you should stay out of any conversation between Jane and Mr. Bingley."

Mr. Bennet stood, leaving the room. Elizabeth cast a look across at Jane. She could tell from Jane's face she wished she could escape as easily as their father. Elizabeth could sympathize, for she wished to avoid their mother's inevitable dissection of the gentlemen's call as well. Or, if there was no escape, she wished they could at least stuff their ears. In moments, Mrs. Bennet's voice filled the parlor.

15

Darcy followed Bingley into the airy parlor they all seemed to favor, Henry and Richard behind them. Miss Bingley and Anne were there already, the former occupied at the corner desk and the latter with a book. Both set aside these diversions as the group of men entered, exchanging greetings. Soon, they were all seated on the loose circle of couches and chairs.

"How was your first visit to Longbourn, my lord?" Miss Bingley asked, focusing her attention on Henry, as she had been since they arrived. The arrangement suited Darcy. He was happy to let someone else fend off Bingley's avaricious sister for once. "I see you survived your first encounter with Mrs. Bennet and those hoydens she's raised." She gave a dramatic shudder.

"Hoydens?" Henry chuckled. "They are a lively bunch, I'll give you that, and what a bevy of beauties! Bingley, how did you tear yourself away from Hertfordshire?"

"It wasn't easy." Bingley appeared troubled. Darcy wondered if he was falling back in love with Miss Bennet after all. "I almost proposed to Miss Bennet."

Henry nodded, as if he'd expected as much. "Even with so brief a meeting, I can see she is a nonpareil in both appearance and manners. Is she as sweet as she seems?"

"I thought so, but I'm not so sure now." Bingley frowned, his brow creased in thought. "I thought she was in love with me when I left. She only had eyes for me then, but now . . . I don't know, she was friendly, but she acted as if she didn't care anymore. I didn't think she was so shallow. I'm wondering if I completely misjudged her."

"Mr. Bingley, excuse me for saying it, but you're a fool." Anne's voice was sharp with anger.

Darcy turned to regard her in surprise, as did everyone else.

"I beg your pardon, Miss de Bourgh?" Bingley was clearly taken aback.

"Miss Bennet saw you at Lady Agatha's party, with Mrs. Kent. She was devastated. The poor creature nearly fainted. You hurt her deeply. If you had seen her then, your ego would be satisfied that you broke her heart. You should be grateful she's recovered enough to behave appropriately in company. In her place, I would be throwing things at you."

Darcy rather thought Anne looked and sounded as if she might throw things at Bingley now, for Miss Bennet's sake. He had noted Anne's increased confidence around Elizabeth and Miss Bennet, and she'd presented herself well with the Gardiners. It wasn't until this moment, though, that he realized her self-assurance extended to males she was not related to. It was good to see. Now, if only she could manage to stand up to her mother.

"Throwing things?" Bingley echoed, looking a bit dumbstruck.

Anne threw up her hands. "Richard?"

"I was with Miss Bennet at the time as well," Richard said. "I removed her from the room out of sheer pity, although it is not a burden to comfort a sweet and beautiful woman."

"So she was hurt?" Bingley asked.

"She was devastated. Does that make you happy?" Anne's tone spoke clearly of what Bingley's answer had best be.

Darcy took in the book in Anne's lap. Her hands now rested atop it. He wondered, if Bingley said yes, if Anne really would throw it. He almost hoped Bingley would botch his answer. Anne throwing things would be diverting.

"No. I didn't mean to hurt her." Bingley looked around the room. Following is gaze, Darcy saw skeptical faces. "Really. I did seriously consider marrying her, but I had a right to change my mind. I never proposed. I never told her I loved her."

"You most certainly had the right to change your mind," Miss Bingley said. "It was a harmless flirtation. Even if one went so far as to label it a courtship, that, too, isn't binding." She shot a resentful look toward Darcy. "Courtships may be broken off, after all. They aren't engagements." She glared at him a moment more before turning back to her brother. "If Miss Bennet took your attentions too seriously, that is too bad, but it isn't your fault. She is a sweet girl, and if weren't for her awful family, she should make a good marriage, to someone of her own class." She cast a glare over all four gentlemen, as if to remind them she spoke of all five Bennet daughters.

Silence descended on the room. Miss Bingley raised her chin a notch, her narrowed eyes once again on Darcy. It was clear Anne had begun spreading the rumor he was courting Elizabeth. She must have mentioned it to Miss Bingley while Darcy and the others were visiting Longbourn.

Darcy met Miss Bingley's censuring with a calm façade, echoed by unruffled thoughts. He was already well acquainted with her opinion of the Bennets. Once, he'd shared it, but no longer. Regardless, he'd also decided the individual woman mattered more than her family and wealth. A lifetime of happiness was more important than catering to the expectations of the ton.

"Darcy, Bingley, who's up for a game of billiards? Richard?" Henry stood as he spoke, prompting the others to as well. "Ladies?" He drew the word out.

"Definitely not," Anne said. "I'm sure a billiards room is no place for us."

Darcy took in the conflict on Miss Bingley's face, amused. A billiards room was indeed no place for a lady. Miss Bingley was obviously torn between wishing to further her acquaintance with Henry and upholding the values she was always spouting.

"Thank you for the invitation, my lord, but I must return to my correspondences." Miss Bingley made a vague gesture toward the writing desk.

"Until later, then," Henry said, bowing.

Darcy, Bingley and Richard followed suit. With long strides, Henry lead them from the parlor and toward the billiards room. Darcy wasn't sure if they were retreating or regrouping, but he was pleased to leave Miss Bingley and her acid tongue behind.

Netherfield Park offered only one table, so they agreed to take turns playing the winner. The arrangement was least fair to Bingley, as he played the poorest, but he didn't seem to mind. He and Richard elected to go first, leaving Darcy and Henry standing off to one side.

"I received an odd letter from Aunt Catherine," Henry said as they watched Bingley miss another shot.

"Oh?"

"She claims you're breaking off your engagement to Anne to pursue, in her words, a low country chit of no moral fiber. I assume she means Miss Elizabeth? Richard said you're courting her, which you might have mentioned. I wouldn't have flirted with her at Agatha's had I known. I'm not a poacher, Darcy."

Darcy smiled slightly, not sure he entirely believed Henry. Henry didn't have a reputation for purloining other men's women, but it was only a courtship. Henry loved a challenge and Elizabeth was certainly that. "I was never engaged to Anne, as you well know. Furthermore, I don't want to marry her and she doesn't want to marry me."

"Yes, I do well know. I think Aunt Catherine's assured herself of the engagement so often, she's come to believe it. I'm glad Anne's escaped from her for a time. Seems to be doing her good to see how the rest of the world lives. Lady Catherine is a little too certain her rank allows her to act as she pleases."

Bingley looked up from another botched shot. "I should think you, of all people, would think that rank has real meaning."

"It does. Several real meanings." Henry said. "One of them is that when I beat someone at fencing, I'm never quite sure if I really won."

"You don't need to wonder on those rare occasions when you beat me," Richard said, sighting up his next shot.

Henry nodded. "Right. Unless Darcy or Richard is fencing with me. They wouldn't even let me win out of pity."

Bingley raised his eyebrows, appearing almost insulted.

Henry shrugged. "I don't know you well enough to know if you'd let me win."

"I don't really know myself," Bingley admitted, grimacing as Richard made his shot. "I'm not competitive like the three of you are. I'm more concerned with trying to please people. It's not just those of rank. It's nearly everyone. Besides, I'm a terrible fencer."

"He is," Darcy confirmed. "He's as likely to beat you as I am to marry Anne."

Bingley chuckled. "True enough. I'll leave the fencing to you and you can leave the marrying to me."

"Of Anne?" Henry asked.

Bingley shook his head. "Would that I could set my sights so high."

"Be my guest," Henry said, offering a bow.

A small gasp sounded in the doorway. Turning, Darcy found Miss Bingley standing there, a letter held in one hand. She had a look of shock on her face, which quickly gave way to a façade of calm. "We've received an invitation to a party at Lucas Lodge tomorrow. Would you like to attend?"

"Yes, send our acceptance," Bingley said after a quick glance to ascertain Darcy's and his cousins' opinions. "Make sure they know the size of our party."

"This isn't my first répondez, s'il vous plait," Miss Bingley said. "I believe you can trust me to handle it properly, Charles."

"Of course."

She cast a speculative look about the room, her expression reminiscent of Lady Catherine's when selecting tea cakes from a tray. She settled on Henry, offering a smile. "Until later, then, gentlemen."

They all bowed as she walked away. Darcy wondered how much Miss Bingley had overheard, and what form of trouble it would bring. He shook his head, returning his attention to the game.

Later, they rejoined the ladies for a generous tea. The Hursts were expected to arrive late, so dinner had been moved back accordingly. After eating their fill, they all returned to the parlor.

"What about a game of whist?" Miss Bingley said brightly.

"No, thank you," Anne said. "I should like to finish my book."

"I'd enjoy it," Henry said, crossing to the table Miss Bingley was setting out the deck on. "Richard? Darcy?"

"Why not," Richard said, following his brother.

"I was thinking of finishing the paper." Having to share the paper with Bingley, Henry and Richard, Darcy hadn't had as much time with it as he liked.

"I'll be your fourth, Caroline," Bingley said with a cheerful smile.

Miss Bingley frowned. "That won't do, Charles. You're the host. You must sit with Miss de Bourgh and see to her amusement. She's been reading that dreary book all day. You must lighten her mood."

"Really, you needn't trouble yourself, Mr. Bingley," Anne said, looking up from her book.

"He must." Even though it wasn't turned on him, Miss Bingley's smile grated on Darcy's nerves. "Don't permit him to become a terrible host."

"Quite right," Bingley said, all amiability. He took a seat on the opposite end of the sofa on which Anne perched. "Darcy, you'll have to be the fourth."

"Of course he must. Mr. Darcy would never be so rude as to deny us a proper game of whist." Now Miss Bingley's false smile was aimed his way.

Darcy manfully suppressed a sigh, setting aside the paper. "No, I would not." He left the comfortable armchair he'd claimed and joined the party gathering around the table. He pulled out a chair.

"Not there, Mr. Darcy." Miss Bingley pointed to the space on her left. "Here. We can't permit brothers to be partners. They would decimate us. I'll partner you, my lord." She batted her eyes at Henry. "If it's not too distressing to you to have a female as a partner. I'm sure I shan't be as practiced in the nuances of the game as you fine gentlemen."

"Somehow, I suspect you're an accomplished player, Miss Bingley." Henry took his place across from her.

Miss Bingley kept the game going for a considerable while, giving Bingley plenty of time to converse with Anne. Though he would have preferred to read the paper, Darcy took Miss Bingley's obvious maneuvering in stride. It was to be expected. In truth, he was surprised she hadn't thought of matching her brother with Anne sooner. Anne was a better catch for Bingley than Georgiana. Though both had essentially the same connections, Anne was by far the greater prize from a financial standpoint. Miss Bingley valued money almost, but not quite, as much as she did rank. Besides, if she'd set her sights on Henry, she no longer needed her brother to marry Georgiana in order to assist her pursuit of Darcy.

As the game went on, Henry's prediction showed itself to be true. The teams were quite evenly matched, making for more entertainment than Darcy had anticipated. There was also the added enjoyment of watching Henry deflect Miss Bingley's advances. Henry, of course, was accustomed to such treatment from women, and not one to take offence. It only made sense for Miss Bingley to attempt attracting the highest ranked man there. Besides, Darcy had resisted her charms for more than a year. Henry, for all Miss Bingley knew, could be tempted.

Mr. and Mrs. Hurst's arrival released everyone to ready for dinner. When the augmented party assembled for their meal, Mrs. Hurst quickly joined her sister in maneuvering to get Bingley and Anne together, and further Miss Bingley's cause with Henry. Darcy could tell Bingley was aware of what his sisters were doing, and making no effort to combat it. Likely, Bingley saw the opportunities presented by Darcy's cousins in the same light as his siblings. Darcy decided to leave them to it.

The following morning, Darcy had his open carriage readied. He'd promised Elizabeth a drive. It was a beautiful morning and he was looking forward to keeping his word.

Richard met him outside, his look inquiring. "Off to see Miss Elizabeth?"

"I am. I promised to take her for a drive."

"Mind if I impose on you for a ride? I thought I might walk with Miss Bennet. I didn't have much of an opportunity to speak with her yesterday."

"Be my guest."

Richard climbed up and they set out for Longbourn. They conversed pleasantly on the journey, Richard filling Darcy in on the news he'd still not found time to read in the paper. They were turning down the drive when hooves rang out behind them. Darcy turned to see Henry charging up on his grey.

They all came to a halt at the Bennets' front door. A manservant hurried out to take the reins of the carriage horses. Darcy and Richard climbed down as Henry swung out of his saddle, striding over to meet them.

"Thought you could visit the bevy of beauties without me, did you?" Henry wore a wolfish grin.

"If I'd known you were interested, I would have waited for you." Even as Darcy said it, he wondered if it was the truth. Henry had that look, the one he got just before he proposed a race.

"Would you have?" He looked from Darcy to Richard. "I thought I might ask one of the fine Bennet girls to walk with me this morning."

"Miss Elizabeth already agreed to ride with me," Darcy said quickly.

"And I am here to ask Miss Bennet on a walk." Richard was regarding his older brother through narrowed eyes.

Henry chuckled. "I must be here to walk with the others, then." He swung around, leading the way to the door.

Darcy and Elizabeth had their ride, the open carriage offering the perfect combination of privacy and decency. He did his best to be charming, and she seemed effortlessly witty. On occasion, he would glance her way and find a speculative look on her face, which would always bloom into a smile when his gaze was noticed. Darcy could only hope he was what she speculated on.

Eventually, knowing they'd been driving for some time and his horses would require a rest soon, Darcy was forced to return her. They reached to Longbourn to find Miss Bennet and Richard speaking together in the yard, standing near the Bennet home, though Henry's grey was absent. Darcy felt a moment's guilt, realizing he'd all but forgotten he'd given his cousin a ride over. Far from put out, Richard wore a smile as he changed places with Elizabeth. The sisters lingered in the yard as they left, waving goodbye.

"I apologize for stranding you. I lost track of time."

"Stranding?" Richard repeated. "We'd only just returned."

"Did you walk to Netherfield and back?" Darcy asked, amused.

"I've little idea where we walked. I permitted Miss Bennet to select the path."

"Did Henry tire of the younger Bennet girls?" Darcy's team wasn't setting as slow a pace as he'd expected. They must have guessed they were on their way back to their feed.

"I don't believe so. We caught sight of him leading his grey, Miss Lydia atop it. She seemed to be enjoying herself. Miss Kitty was watching from nearby. We didn't join them, so I can't be certain they didn't return before we did. Miss Bennet said she'd rather walk on."

"I didn't think Miss Lydia was dressed for riding." Not to mention, Henry's grey hadn't been saddled for a woman to ride.

"I'd say she was not. She was astride and showing a shocking amount of leg."

"I hope Henry was taking care," Darcy said. Trust Henry to turn a peaceful walk into a way for a young woman to risk both her limbs and her reputation. He hoped his cousin realized Miss Lydia couldn't be relied on to make intelligent choices. Darcy had a terrible vision of the two spurring each other into greater acts of foolishness.

When Richard didn't reply, Darcy glanced his way, seeking his opinion. His cousin wore an abstract expression, his gaze on nothing. Richard had obviously lost track of the conversation. Darcy returned his attention to the road, hiding a smile.

16

Though she was a bit tired, still not sleeping well, Elizabeth was looking forward to the party at Lucas Lodge that evening. She'd already seen Mr. Darcy once that day, when he'd taken her on an exceedingly pleasant carriage ride, but found she was pleased she would have more time in his company. She readied with care, electing to wear the dress Miss de Bourgh had purchased for her. It seemed too fine for Hertfordshire, but she loved it and flattered herself to think she looked nice in it. With an earl in the neighborhood, there were sure to be many parties, but Sir William Lucas's would be the most lavish, making it the most suitable for the dress.

She'd already shown it to her sisters, and endured Lydia's lamentations that Elizabeth should bring home so fine a dress when she was so terribly short, it could never be made to fit anyone else. They had not seen it on Elizabeth, though, with the exception of Jane. She was suitably gratified by their reaction. Her mother all but swooned with delight, declaring that in the dress, even Elizabeth had a chance to secure the interest of the earl. Her father, Elizabeth thought, looked misty eyed.

Elizabeth was aware of many heads turning her way when she and her family arrived at Lucas Lodge. Even Sir William, who had known her from a babe, bowed lower to her than he ever had before. She noted these things, but paid them little mind. Her searching eyes quickly picked Mr. Darcy from the crowd, already making his way across the room toward her.

Elizabeth went to meet him, aware of her mother shepherding her sisters about and her father disappearing in the opposite direction. They reached the center of the room simultaneously. Elizabeth made a curtsy she knew was rendered more graceful by the silk she wore. Mr. Darcy, clad to elegant perfection as usual, answered with a bow.

"Miss Elizabeth, may I say you look lovely this evening?"

"I believe you may, Mr. Darcy, as rumor has it you are courting me."

"Rumor only?" He arched a brow. "That is the gown you wore to Lady Agatha's party."

"It is. I suppose I am wearing it again too soon." Elizabeth hadn't considered that, for the gown begged to be worn and few in Hertfordshire had seen her in it before. "To behave as a woman being courted, I ought to have worn something you've not seen before."

"I'm pleased you wore it. It suits you perfectly, and conjures up happy memories of when we danced together. Memories I hope to add to tonight."

"Mr. Darcy, are you asking me to dance?"

"I hope I am. I must secure my sets before you're monopolized by the other men here."

She smiled. "I am not interesting to them. Most of them have danced with me many times before."

"Not in that dress."

His appreciative gaze left Elizabeth feeling oddly flustered. Then he frowned. For a moment, her heart fell, but she quickly ascertained it was something over her shoulder that had caught his attention. Mr. Darcy gave a curt nod. Elizabeth looked behind her in time to see Mr. Wickham's return nod from where he stood near the door. He turned and made his way to a different part of the room. Elizabeth thought he'd do better to turn around and walk back out, but then most of the people there didn't know the truth of him.

Soon, to no one's surprise, Mary moved to the piano to play music for dancing. Mr. Darcy offered his hand to Elizabeth, a smile replacing the harsh look he'd aimed at Mr. Wickham. Placing her gloved fingers in his, Elizabeth let Mr. Darcy lead her out to dance.

As they made their way through the steps, she caught sight of other members of both of their parties. Unsurprisingly, her sister Lydia was dancing with Mr. Wickham. Equally expected, Colonel Fitzwilliam partnered Jane. Lord Henry was dancing with Miss Bingley, though Elizabeth uncharitably suspected the latter to have maneuvered that. She also assumed Miss Bingley was somehow responsible for her brother partnering Miss de Bourgh.

Elizabeth tried to keep her mind on Mr. Darcy, where she would like it to be, but was troubled by Mr. Wickham. Now that she knew so much about him, she was taken aback that he dared mingle so easily in polite company. She especially didn't care for Mr. Wickham dancing with Lydia. She pursed her lips. It wouldn't do. She ought to warn him off.

"You seem troubled," Mr. Darcy said, his voice low.

Elizabeth returned her attention to him, feeling a bit guilty. "It's Mr. Wickham."

Mr. Darcy cast a look about the room. Elizabeth knew the moment he sighted Mr. Wickham. Mr. Darcy's eyes went flat.

"If he asks me, I think I should agree to dance with him," Elizabeth said.

"Why?" The whispered word was harsh.

"Because it will give me a chance to chide him on some of his lies. He should not feel he can get away with spreading lies about you or Miss Darcy." She could read the disapproval in Mr. Darcy's face. "I will only allude to the money paid for the living and his claim that your sister was proud. It would be a natural thing for me to do and it will make him think harder before dancing with my sisters."

"As you wish," Mr. Darcy said, but Elizabeth could tell he still did not care for the idea.

She turned the topic to happier things, determined to enjoy her much looked forward to dance with Mr. Darcy. He was an excellent partner, especially now that he spoke to her with ease. In short order, she momentarily forgot about Mr. Wickham, Lydia, and the rest of the room.

Then their first set of the evening was over and Colonel Fitzwilliam asked her to dance, while Lord Henry partnered Jane. Elizabeth observed with amusement that the colonel kept a close eye on his brother and her sister, though he was attentive enough and a fine partner. Somewhat to her surprise, Mr. Bingley asked her to dance next, putting to rest Elizabeth's lingering worry he'd stay aloof from her and her sisters. During both dances, she was displeased to see Mr. Darcy standing off to the side. Much as she didn't want him to give too much notice to any other woman, she also couldn't like his rudeness in sitting out when there were so many hoping to dance.

Mr. Wickham appeared after Elizabeth's dance with Mr. Bingley. "Miss Elizabeth, may I have the pleasure?" He accompanied the question with an elegant bow.

Elizabeth nodded, offering her hand. Mr. Wickham led her out to the set in which Miss de Bourgh already stood. She exchanged smiles with Miss de Bourgh, who was dancing with the oldest Lucas boy, but she could not bring herself to smile at Mr. Wickham. The music took back up, the dance beginning.

"I met Miss Darcy in town," Elizabeth said, moving through the first turn.

"Oh?" Mr. Wickham responded cautiously.

"Yes, and she wasn't proud at all, only shy," she said when next the steps brought them together. "I found her delightful. I was surprised you misjudged her so, knowing her as well as I feel you must, since you told me you'd devoted many hours to her entertainment." She swung away, minding her place in the dance for a moment, then came back.

"I'm glad to hear she was sociable," Mr. Wickham said. "Perhaps she has grown up and realizes her pride is not winning her friends. Assuming shyness would hide the fact that she really doesn't know how to behave in society without offending people."

"How so?" Elizabeth couldn't believe the temerity of the man, elaborating on his falsehood instead of retracting it. She regretted they were drawn apart again, giving him more time to formulate his answer.

"By staying in the background and saying nothing, so no one will notice how proud she is," Mr. Wickham said.

Again, the steps took him away. Miss Darcy hadn't been proud, Elizabeth thought, but Mr. Wickham appeared to be, of his lies. Moments later, he rejoined Elizabeth.

"She undoubtedly adopted a quiet, ladylike poise to cover her pride," Mr. Wickham continued. "It is an easy pose to maintain. All she has to do is always be silent and never do anything that isn't ladylike."

"Well, she went about it in a very odd way, then. She played battledore and shuttlecock with some of the younger girls. I would think the governesses watching would gossip about her activity and enthusiasm."

Mr. Wickham frowned. They stepped apart.

"I'm glad to say it sounds as if she's improved," he said when they came together once more, his composure recovered. "People do change."

"Really?" Elizabeth made her tone sweet. "Do people change their minds about being a clergyman and think that law might be a better choice, for example? Especially if they have financial support?"

"How did you . . ." He looked about the room through narrowed eyes. "I mean, rather, what gave you that idea? I can't imagine Darcy saying anything like that."

"I thought Miss Elizabeth should know," Miss de Bourgh said.

Elizabeth cast her a surprised look. She'd thought they were speaking in low enough tones not to be overheard by the other dancers. She turned back to see Mr. Wickham regarding Miss de Bourgh with annoyance. Catching Elizabeth watching he blinked, bowing to her. Elizabeth realized the dance was ending.

"That's a particularly lovely gown, Miss Elizabeth," Mr. Wickham said. His eyes roamed about the room again, his expression speculative. "I don't recall seeing it before."

Although his words were polite, somehow he seemed to be intending them as an insult. Elizabeth frowned.

Miss de Bourgh stepped up beside her. "The gown was a gift."

"It was?" Mr. Wickham smirked, looking Elizabeth up and down.

"Yes. From me." Miss de Bourgh's tone was honeyed. "I purchased it for her to replace one ruined on my account."

"Oh." Mr. Wickham grimaced. "Ladies." With another bow, he turned on his heels and walked away, leaving a smiling Miss de Bourgh in his wake.

"Thank you," Elizabeth murmured to her.

"Miss Elizabeth?"

She turned to see the Earl of Matlock at her shoulder. She dropped a curtsy. "My lord."

"I understand you play."

"I do." She hadn't been expecting that. Elizabeth smiled, amused at herself. Simply because she'd put on a pretty frock didn't mean every gentleman must ask her to dance.

Lord Henry held out his arm. "Would you indulge me by taking a turn at the piano so I may dance with your sister?"

"Of course." Elizabeth placed her hand on his arm. "Pardon me, Miss de Bourgh."

"Anne," he said, nodding to his cousin before leading Elizabeth toward the piano.

Mary looked up as they drew near, her face showing she was surprised to see the earl there, and a touch daunted.

Lord Henry bowed. "Miss Mary, your sister is kind enough to allow me to dance with you. Will you do me the honor?"

Mary gaped at him. As discreetly as she could, Elizabeth poked her foot out from beneath her gown and nudged Mary on the shin. Her sister blinked rapidly, opened her mouth, closed it again, and nodded.

"Splendid," Lord Henry said, offering Mary his arm.

Elizabeth played for several dances, until Miss Bingley took over. As soon as Elizabeth left the piano, Lord Henry asked her to dance. He was an expert partner, and quite energetic. Elizabeth was impressed with both, especially the latter. As far as she could ascertain, he'd not stood out a single dance. This was in stark contrast to Mr. Darcy who had danced with her, Miss Bingley, Mrs. Hurst, and Miss de Bourgh, but no one else.

Another woman took over playing for Miss Bingley. Lord Henry immediately escorted Miss Bingley to the dance floor. As the evening progressed, he danced with every woman who played. At one point, looking over from her place on the dance floor, Elizabeth nearly laughed. At first, she'd imagined Lord Henry was trying to keep Mary from playing, but many of the other women were as unskilled as her sister. Whatever the earl's goal, it was amusing to see women flocking to the piano, begging for a turn.

"Miss Elizabeth," Mr. Darcy's rich baritone called as Elizabeth's dance with their host's eldest son ended.

Like Lord Henry, Elizabeth hadn't lacked for partners. Even so, she'd been waiting for Mr. Darcy to reappear. She turned to him with a smile.

"Will you dance with me?" he asked.

"Let me sit this one out with you." She led him to a quiet corner where they could watch the dancing. Once the dance was underway and people's attention focused there, she described her conversation with Mr. Wickham.

"I suspect he will avoid you," Mr. Darcy said, sounding satisfied.

"That is what I intended." She paused, choosing her next words with care. "There is something else I wanted to talk to you about. Do you remember when we first saw each other? It was at the assembly."

Mr. Darcy frowned. "The assembly, yes. I recall seeing you, but we never spoke."

Elizabeth gave him an amused smile. "No, but you spoke *about* me, which was more than enough. You said, and I believe I have this correct, 'She is tolerable, but not handsome enough to tempt me; I am in no humor at present to give consequence to young ladies who are slighted by other men.'"

His look of shock was comical. He quickly composed his features into contrition. "I am sorry you overheard that. I did not mean it, but that is no excuse for having said it. I was trying to put Bingley off. He was pressing me to dance."

"Yes. In retrospect, I realize that was the case. You were willing to insult me, and, if I may be so bold, to lie to one of your closest friends, simply to avoid dancing."

Mr. Darcy looked exceedingly uncomfortable. "I am sorry. I didn't mean it. You're beautiful."

Taking pity on him, she gave him a reassuring smile. "I'm not trying to solicit a compliment. Nor am I really concerned about the first part of your statement, but the second. When you give consequence to young ladies, does it take away from your value?"

He looked thoughtful, but shook his head. "Certainly not, but it does take away from my ability to give consequence. When I dance with you, you become more important in the eyes of everyone here."

"That is . . . interesting of you, but I am not in need of importance. I am sure enough in myself, with or without a man's regard. Many ladies are not, though. To them, not being danced with relegates them to dwell in a state of misery. Would it be so terrible if you gave import to more of them? You've already admitted it takes nothing from you."

"You're saying you would like me to dance with all of the ladies no one wishes to dance with?" Mr. Darcy asked, his tone colder than any he'd taken with her in some time.

"What would please me is for you to show me you know how to behave at a party." Elizabeth let some exasperation enter her voice. "This isn't a dance, not formally, so if you decide to go off and play cards, that will be fine, but if you're going to linger about the dance floor, you should not let people realize you think you are above their company."

He winced, frowning. He appeared quite chagrinned.

"I take special offence in view of how insulting your standards are to me," Elizabeth pressed.

"To you?"

He looked quite off balance now. Elizabeth was pleased she'd put a chink in his armor. "My sisters, Kitty and Lydia, had partners for every dance at the assembly I mentioned, and at most any dance we attend. I do not. By your standards, they have more consequence than

I. I realize tonight is different but, if I may be frank, that is not because you, or any man, danced with me. It's because of the dress Miss de Bourgh gave me."

He dropped his eyes to the dress. "Your sisters do always have partners," he said when he looked back up. His face was thoughtful. "I never thought of it that way."

"Your cousins are giving consequence to everyone here. I think in the long run, it adds to their significance."

"But I don't enjoy dancing." His eyes moved over her. "Except with you."

"Why then did you dance with Miss Bingley, Miss de Bourgh and Mrs. Hurst?"

"I am obligated. They are in my party." He shrugged. "I owe them a dance, or at least, I owe it to Bingley that I dance with them. He is my host in Hertfordshire."

"Maria Lucas is the daughter of your host at Lucas Lodge. Don't you owe her a dance, at least on behalf of her father?"

"Yes, I suppose I do, but she's as empty headed as he is."

Elizabeth sighed, glad she'd led him to a secluded corner. Had no one ever taken the time to teach Mr. Darcy manners? Likely not, as people seemed only to fawn over him and he to take it as his due. "That is unkind, even if it is true. Either don't talk to her while you dance or try to fill her head with something less silly. Or just be kind."

"Kind?"

Elizabeth set her lips in a firm line. "Talk to her about the weather, compliment her on her dress, ask her how she liked traveling to Rosings. Kind."

***

Darcy looked down at Elizabeth, marveling at her beauty. It was no wonder she'd had a partner for every dance. The dress Anne bought her fit her with precision, the light blue color emphasizing her luminous complexion. Not that she needed a fashionable dress to make her beautiful. Her loosely curled tresses gleamed. Her eyes, flashing with annoyance, beguiled. There was nothing about her that wasn't perfect. If she wished him to dance with Maria Lucas, if that was what would make her happy, then he would do it.

Darcy danced with Maria Lucas the next dance. They spoke little, making it not as much of a hardship as he'd feared. The smile Elizabeth rewarded him with was dazzling. He then selected a wallflower at random and danced with her. Elizabeth rewarded him with a second dance, her happiness making every moment spent with the two dull young ladies worthwhile. It wasn't proper to dance with Elizabeth a third time, but he danced with several more wallflowers, just to see her smile.

On the carriage ride back to Netherfield he and Richard, predictably, were maneuvered into riding with Mr. and Mrs. Hurst. The journey down the drive away from Lucas Lodge was slow, for they were in a line of carriages. Darcy felt no need to speak. He imagined Richard and Mr. Hurst felt the same. Mrs. Hurst, apparently oblivious to the late hour, kept up a critical monologue about the party. Darcy hoped no one outside their carriage was in a position to hear her.

He certainly wasn't hearing her, though he was trapped inside the carriage with her. He couldn't have focused on Mrs. Hurst's chatter if he'd tried. His mind roamed over Elizabeth's words. Was he selfish in wanting only to please the people he cared about or thought well of? Was there any purpose in pleasing people who meant nothing to him? Yet, he'd been attending a party in Sir William Lucas's home. He should try to please him and other members of his household. Maybe that even applied to other guests. Maybe Elizabeth was right.

He frowned, picturing her. He enjoyed remembering her smiles, but something troubled him. Not when she laughed or was happy, but in the brief moments of repose he'd glimpsed throughout the night. She seemed troubled, when she wasn't engaged, as if something unpleasant lingered in her thoughts. He resolved to find out what it was, and to fix it.

". . . same dress she wore to Lady Agatha's?" Mrs. Hurst said, breaking into Darcy's thoughts.

Mr. Hurst grunted, mumbling something in reply. Darcy was relatively sure he was asleep.

"I'm sure it was. She obviously doesn't realize how pathetic it makes her look to wear it again in front of all of the same people, mere days later. One would think she'd be embarrassed to be seen in it again so soon. It's dreadfully clear she has only the one suitable gown. Of course, she likely has nothing else even remotely stylish. Possibly she thought everyone would be too busy ogling her assets to realize it was the same dress." Her face took on a particularly nasty look. "Or maybe whoever bought it for her was there and she owed it to that person to wear it. We all know her father can't have paid for a dress like that."

"Anne bought it for her, to replace one Aunt Catherine's footman spilled wine on at dinner," Richard snapped.

Darcy looked over to see his cousin glaring at Mrs. Hurst.

"Really, Luisa," Mr. Hurst muttered.

"Well, I didn't know. How could I?" She sniffed. "It still doesn't excuse her wearing it to two events in a row."

Darcy turned his gaze out the window, pleased they were moving now. He wished he'd the right to buy Elizabeth dresses. If he could ever persuade her to become his wife, he would make sure she was dressed finer than Mrs. Hurst or Miss Bingley. Maybe he should suggest that Anne purchase Elizabeth another gown?

His mind, back on Elizabeth, wandered to something more she'd said; that she didn't need any man to dance with her to know her self-worth. He supposed it was true. That was part of her allure. She didn't need fancy dresses, either, but someday he would see she had them anyhow.

What, he wondered, must it be like for women who didn't have Elizabeth's confidence? Ones to whom it truly mattered what they wore, or who danced with them. What would it be like for a woman who wanted to dance but wasn't asked? He was aware of these women as being somehow less important and less liked than other women. Did they see themselves that way? Elizabeth had said they dwelled in a state of misery. He'd assumed she was exaggerating but, thinking about it, it seemed likely that every dance they sat out could be agonizingly embarrassing. Should a woman be judged by the fact that no available man understood her worth?

Darcy frowned, feeling uncertain in this new world of thought Elizabeth had thrust upon him. He didn't like being uncomfortable, and the knowledge she'd imparted made him so. Yet, oddly, it seemed necessary. Should he really go through life with so imperfect an understanding of half the people around him?

It occurred to him he'd been wiser than he'd realized when he'd fallen in love with Elizabeth. She had the characteristic Bingley most valued. She would criticize Darcy when he needed to be criticized.

17

To Elizabeth's amusement, everyone in the neighborhood who had an eligible daughter and a pianoforte began to hold parties, which somehow always turned into impromptu dances. The daughter of the house would play, sometimes exhibiting very little skill, and be rewarded by a dance with the Earl of Matlock. Elizabeth enjoyed the events for more than their comedic value, for she danced with Mr. Darcy twice at each party. For his part, Mr. Darcy seemed to have taken her words to heart, dancing most every dance, usually with women who had trouble finding partners.

The only one not pleased with the abundance of parties was Mrs. Bennet. Elizabeth would have added that to her list of absurdities, but she couldn't find it as amusing as she would like. This was mostly due to the ongoing complaints to be endured. By the time the parties had been going on for weeks, Mrs. Bennet's complaints would begin at breakfast, extend the length of the day, and carry on into the night.

"What is Mr. Bingley doing?" Mrs. Bennet said from where she reclined on a sofa in the parlor, one arm draped over her eyes. "He dances with Jane, but he also dances with Elizabeth and sometimes Lydia, Kitty, and even Mary. Why can't he make up his mind? Maybe he's deferring to the Earl of Matlock. Perhaps he wants Jane. He's unwed, after all, and Jane is the one everyone should want to marry."

"I don't believe that's the case, Mama," Jane murmured.

Jane was winding a ball of yard, the loose end of which Elizabeth held wrapped about her extended hands. Kitty and Lydia were at the table, making a pretense of playing cards. Their father sat in his favorite chair, a small stack of letters at his elbow, one held firmly before his face, deterring conversing with him. Mary, nearby, mimicked him with a book.

"Why is that not the case, I ask you? Each time Colonel Fitzwilliam comes to walk with you, Lord Henry comes as well. You've

163

no right to say you won't attract an earl. It's your duty to your family to do so."

"I daresay the earl is simply looking for amusements," Elizabeth offered. "He's always about the neighborhood, from what I hear."

"He has the most amazing stallion," Lydia said.

Kitty giggled.

"What could that possibly have to do with his liking Jane?" Mary asked, looking over the top of her book.

"Nothing. I just like the earl's stallion." Lydia tossed her curls at Mary. "Sometimes he lets me ride it."

Kitty let out another giggle, then devolved into coughing.

"Don't cough, Kitty, it's unbecoming," Mrs. Bennet said. "I don't know what these gentlemen are thinking. None of them will settle. They dance with every miss at every party. Even Mr. Darcy, and twice always with Lizzy. Mrs. Phillips tells me rumor has it he's courting you, Lizzy, but I know that for the foolishness it is. We all know he doesn't even find you pretty. Not that he seems to have any judgement in that regard. Why, he even danced with Mrs. Long's nieces. Hideous little things."

"Mama." Jane's tone was sharp with reprimand.

"What? They can't hear me. They aren't here. Not that they shouldn't know it. It would do them good to understand they're nothing to look at. Look how it helps Mary. She knows she must read and play and philosophize to attempt to attract a man, because she surly won't with her looks."

"Mama," Elizabeth and Jane cried in unison.

"Mr. Darcy, Colonel Fitzwilliam and Lord Henry all often partner Mary," Jane added. "She is perfectly lovely."

"I don't think it is much of a distinction to dance with any of the three. Even Lord Henry," Mary said. "He danced with a governess who tried to refuse him and with Mrs. Long, who usually doesn't dance at all."

"And you can see why," Mrs. Bennet said. "She was a great oaf. I shouldn't embarrass myself like that, no matter if an earl asked me. Dancing indeed. At her age."

"I don't care who the earl dances with, just so long as he stays here," Lydia said. "We've never had so much dancing. I wish the regiment wasn't leaving so soon. Although, Matlock is as fun to dance with as any officer. You wouldn't think someone that old would be that good a dancer. And he's an earl. I've never danced with an earl before."

"Yes, it is certainly a distinction to dance with an earl," Mrs. Bennet said. She peered under her arm to glare at Mary. "A distinction someone of your looks is due, Lydia. I just wish that Miss de Bourgh wasn't at Netherfield. No one can compete with an heiress. I don't know that I care for her one bit."

"If you don't care for Miss de Bourgh, it's a shame she's written," Mr. Bennet said behind his letter.

Mrs. Bennet sat up abruptly, dropping her arm to her side. "What? Who has she written? When? Mr. Bennet, why do you keep these things from me?" Mrs. Bennet cried. She fell back onto the couch again. "Have you no consideration for my nerves?"

"Who has she written to, Papa?" Elizabeth asked.

"She has written to Jane, whose hands are quite busy, so I had not yet remarked on it."

Elizabeth was a bit disappointed Miss de Bourgh hadn't written to her, but it was most correct to write Jane, as eldest, and no one was to know Elizabeth and Miss de Bourgh had a special relationship. Jane looked at Elizabeth, who nodded. Setting the wound ball of yarn on the table, Jane crossed to their father. He lowered his letter, selected one from the pile, and handed it to her.

"Thank you, Papa," she said, before returning to her seat.

"Well, what does it say? What does she want?" Mrs. Bennet cried.

"I don't know yet, Mama." Jane's tone was patient. She opened the letter. "It seems Lizzy and I are invited to Netherfield Park tomorrow morning."

"Not me?" Lydia said, her face forming into a pout. "Why just you and Lizzy? You're both so boring."

"I'm sure they'll invite you next time," Jane temporized. "What do you suppose they plan? It's too early for luncheon."

Elizabeth shrugged. "I suspect we'll find out tomorrow."

***

When she and Jane arrived at Netherfield Park the following morning, Elizabeth was surprised to find only Miss de Bourgh, Miss Bingley and the Hursts. Miss de Bourgh greeted them warmly, and the other two women greeted them with their typical false smiles. Mr. Hurst seemed happy enough to see them, but excused himself immediately, muttering that he was not attending.

"Attending?" Elizabeth repeated as Mr. Hurst ambled from the room. She resisted the urge to rub her forehead. Although she sometimes had a good night's sleep, the previous night she hadn't slept well, again assailed by terrible dreams about being shoved into carriages, and wasn't sure she was game for dealing with Miss Bingley and Mrs. Hurst.

"My cousins and Mr. Bingley have arranged a race," Miss de Bourgh explained. "They would like an audience."

"Mr. Hurst doesn't wish to attend?" Jane asked.

"Mr. Hurst is above racing," Mrs. Hurst said with a sniff. "As am I."

"Well, I am not." Elizabeth smiled. "How are we to go? We have our carriage."

"I've already sent for ours," Miss Bingley said. "I'm sure your horses wish to rest."

"Of course." Elizabeth was certain Miss Bingley simply feared the Bennets' carriage wasn't fine enough for her, since the horses would hardly need rest after a mere three miles.

Mrs. Hurst bid them farewell and they all filed out into the courtyard. Elizabeth had to admit, but only to herself, that the lovely open carriage waiting for them would be a preferable way to travel. It seated the four of them easily, providing a smooth and enjoyable ride to where the gentlemen waited.

The gentlemen hurried over to help them down from the carriage and more greetings were exchanged. Elizabeth was amused to see how eager the Earl of Matlock looked, and even Mr. Darcy wore an anticipatory smile. She looked up and down the curved stretch of country road they'd arrived at. It was tree lined and didn't strike her as auspicious for racing. "Where will you run?"

"Down this road," Mr. Bingley replied. "Darcy pointed out at this time of year, we can't ride across fields without hurting the crops."

"As if a few plants matter," Miss Bingley said.

"Well, Darcy said they do, so we found this lane instead." Mr. Bingley didn't look at his sister. "It's little used, and we have servants posted to keep carts off."

"Mr. Darcy again?" Elizabeth guessed.

"Me, I'm afraid," Colonel Fitzwilliam said. "But Darcy sent out his coachman to find out who usually used the road and paid them a small amount to stay off it."

"A very sensible idea," Jane said. "It wouldn't do to cause an accident or keep farmers from their work." She looked nervous.

Though Jane hadn't said anything about it, Elizabeth suspected her sister didn't actually approve of racing.

"Richard and Darcy worry like old women," the earl said.

Miss Bingley laughed, giving every appearance she found the statement exceedingly funny.

"Will you all fit on the lane? Where does it go?" Miss de Bourgh asked, peering one way and then the other.

"The road curves around and meets another lane." Mr. Bingley's tone was bright with enthusiasm. "It's perfect. We'll basically be going in a circle. We'll have the driver pull the carriage off to the side there." He pointed to a place where the trees were farther from the road, where the gentlemen's horses were being minded by a groom. "We'll start off that way, and come back around here. You'll be at both the start and finish line."

Elizabeth shook her head. "I agree with Miss de Bourgh. The lane isn't wide enough."

"We're going in pairs," Lord Henry said.

"Colonel Fitzwilliam and I are first, then Darcy and Lord Henry," Mr. Bingley elaborated.

"Then I'll face the winner of the first race," Lord Henry said, shooting Mr. Darcy a challenging grin.

"We'll see," Mr. Darcy answered.

"Come, let's begin. Enough dawdling." With that, the earl crossed to the carriage and started giving orders to the driver.

They quickly arranged themselves, the ladies piling back in the carriage, now moved off the road. The elevation gave them a splendid view as Mr. Bingley and Colonel Fitzwilliam lined up. When they left, their horses were neck in neck, but by the time they returned, Colonel Fitzwilliam was several lengths ahead, for which Mr. Bingley was forced to endure amiable ribbing.

Mr. Darcy and Lord Henry lined up next. Mr. Darcy's roan, a sleek animal with an even temper, struck Elizabeth as the better horseflesh. Lord Henry's grey, however, was a very high strung beast. As the route the gentlemen had selected seemed short, she feared the earl would win.

Her fear was realized, though it was a near thing. Lord Henry rounded the turn ahead of Mr. Darcy, but the earl's grey, sides heaving, was obviously nearly spent. The grey's burst of speed behind him, Mr. Darcy gained ground, but not quickly enough. They crossed the finish line with the earl ahead by half a horse length. Miss Bingley cheered, rushing over to congratulate the winner. Elizabeth helped Mr. Darcy walk his roan.

"In a longer race, I would have had him," Mr. Darcy said.

"I agree. Who picked the length of the track?"

Mr. Darcy chucked. "Henry did. Well noted. I'll remember his trick for next time."

"Are you finished dawdling, Henry?" Colonel Fitzwilliam called. "I think it's time for us to race."

"Can't you see I'm dutifully entertaining a lovely young miss here, Richard?" Lord Henry said, nodding to Miss Bingley.

"No, but I can see you're resting your mount for as long as you can get away with."

Colonel Fitzwilliam's comment elicited a round of laughter. Soon, under the taunts of the other gentlemen, Lord Henry bowed to Miss Bingley and returned to the roadway saying, "My horse can rest when it's crossed the finish line and waiting for you."

Elizabeth stood beside Mr. Darcy for the final race, giving up her seat in the carriage to Mr. Bingley, who sat beside Miss de Bourgh. There was an abundance of good natured teasing as Colonel Fitzwilliam and Lord Henry lined up. Elizabeth watched, greatly amused, and wondered if she was seeing an example of what life would have been like with brothers.

"Darcy, ten pounds says Matlock wins," Mr. Bingley called from the carriage.

"I like my money where it is."

"Colonel? I've got ten pounds against you."

Colonel Fitzwilliam laughed. "Beating Henry is all the reward I'll need."

"Ten? You'd take it if you really thought you could beat me. Twenty pounds says I win, Bingley," Lord Henry offered.

"No thank you, my lord. Not against you and that grey."

"Give the word, Richard," Lord Henry said, grinning at his brother.

Colonel Fitzwilliam gave the count and the two set out amid a shower of cheers. Both men leaned low over their horses' backs, their faces intent. Mr. Bingley kept up his badgering about wagers after they left, but even he fell silent when they didn't reappear in the expected time.

"Darcy?" Mr. Bingley's tone was tense. He jumped down from the carriage.

Mr. Darcy nodded. "We'd best go check. If you'll excuse me," he added, bowing to Elizabeth.

"East or west?" Mr. Bingley asked, mounting.

"I'll go east."

Jane, her cheeks pale, climbed down from the carriage, looking up and down the road.

Elizabeth went to her. "I shouldn't worry yet," Elizabeth murmured.

"Worry? Of course not," Miss Bingley snapped, but her face was pinched with concern.

Mr. Darcy turned his mount east, Mr. Bingley west. They'd just set off when Colonel Fitzwilliam and Lord Henry walked into view. Lord Henry was riding Colonel Fitzwilliam's horse and the colonel was leading the earl's grey.

Jane sagged with relief. Elizabeth was very happy to see the two men unharmed as well, and intrigued at the strength of her sister's reaction. Jane and Colonel Fitzwilliam had been walking together often, but Elizabeth hadn't realized how taken her sister was with him. She hoped, and suspected, he felt the same.

"My horse fell," Lord Henry said as they drew near. "He's too lame to carry weight. Richard, like the old woman he is, insisted I ride back. I tried to pull rank on him, but that didn't work." He slid off Colonel Fitzwilliam's horse cautiously.

Elizabeth wasn't certain if he was hurt or not. He seemed to be putting weight on both legs. Aside from the damage to his clothing, there didn't appear to be anything amiss.

"Oh, Lord Henry," Miss Bingley cried, hopping down from her perch and hurrying to his side. "Are you certain you're unharmed? You'd best ride back in the carriage. I'm sure one of the Miss Bennets will give up their place for you. They adore walking about the countryside."

"A carriage?" He grimaced, though in pain over the idea or because he was injured, it was difficult to ascertain. "I will if I may have a beautiful lady to accompany me."

"But of course you shall." Miss Bingley smiled up at him. "I'll accompany you. It's my duty as hostess to see to your comforts."

Lord Henry looked about. "Don't let me spoil the morning for the rest of you. Except you, Bingley. As undisputed loser, you get to walk my horse to Netherfield."

"That sounds fair to me," Colonel Fitzwilliam said, looking at Jane. "Someone needs to take your grey straight back, and I was planning a longer route."

Elizabeth caught Jane's slight blush and suppressed a smile. It was good to see her sister happy again.

"Charles," Miss Bingley said. She darted her eyes toward the carriage, where Miss de Bourgh sat. "Weren't you going to join the three of us in the carriage, to take Lord Henry back? You are his host. Perhaps a groom—"

"Actually, I would like to walk, but not too far," Miss de Bourgh said, standing. "If Mr. Bingley must go straight back, I shall have someone to walk with."

"It would be my pleasure," Mr. Bingley said. He hurried forward to help her down from the carriage.

"Perfect," Lord Henry said. "It is a lovely day for a carriage ride with a beautiful woman." Miss Bingley hovering at his side, he got into the carriage without any difficulty or hesitancy, though he didn't offer to help her up.

Elizabeth understood why Colonel Fitzwilliam had insisted his brother ride back. As Lord Henry lounged back in the seat across from Miss Bingley, it was impossible to tell if his easy manner was due to being perfectly hale, or born of bravado. It was obviously best to error on the side of caution.

Soon, Miss Bingley and Lord Henry departed in the carriage, Mr. Darcy's and Colonel Fitzwilliam's horses tied to the back. Mr. Bingley turned his horse over to the lone groom, who was ordered to inform the servants waiting to turn back traffic that the races were over. Miss de Bourgh and Mr. Bingley set out, the latter leading Lord Henry's grey.

After a brief discussion, the remaining four broke into two groups. Jane and the colonel headed east, so she wouldn't have to witness the spot where Lord Henry fell. Elizabeth and Mr. Darcy, though Elizabeth had no real desire to see the location either, set out the other way. As it wound about, it would eventually meet the road Jane and

Colonel Fitzwilliam had taken, but not too soon.

"Lord Henry took his fall in good spirits," Elizabeth said. "I suppose it will be Colonel Fitzwilliam's duty, later, to point out to his brother that he forfeited, meaning Colonel Fitzwilliam won."

Mr. Darcy smiled. "If Richard hadn't been so distracted by your sister, he would already have thought of it."

"He does seem to find her rather distracting." Elizabeth looked down the sun dappled lane, relishing the beauty of the day, and the pleasure of the company. "If Lord Henry's horse wasn't obviously lame, I'd suspect he organized his fall to allow the party to break up."

"Henry would never throw a race. Richard is a good rider, and Henry tries very hard to win. I suspect he took dangerous chances."

"I haven't known him long, but that does seem like something he would do. Still, I'm impressed by how easy he was with the outcome. I wouldn't have guessed he was such a good-spirited loser."

"Henry spends his life in an endless series of challenges. He doesn't find sport in it if his opponents don't have a chance to beat him. He wins more than he loses, but he's lost too many times to count. I don't believe there's much he takes seriously, to be honest."

Elizabeth nodded.

Mr. Darcy paused, glancing up and down the empty roadway, bringing her to a halt as well. She looked up at him, curious why they'd stopped, and he dropped is gaze to study her face. A thrill of anticipation went through her, though she hardly knew for what. Did Mr. Darcy mean to kiss her? Had their relationship come to that place, where he should attempt it? The thought made her nervous, but at the same time she was rather sure she would let him.

"I know it is not my place to comment on it, nor likely good practice while courting someone, but I can't help but notice you seemed not quite yourself of late," he said.

Elizabeth blinked, disappointed. It seemed he had no thought of kissing her at all. "Well, as no one is here to listen in, I don't suppose you must act the proper suiter. Will you clarify what you mean?"

He reached out, running a thumb across her cheek, hardly touching her. She suppressed a shiver, confused. Maybe he did mean to kiss her?

"It's something in your eyes." Mr. Darcy's tone was kind. "A shadow. It's lingered there since we were in London."

She dropped her gaze from his searching look. "It's . . . I haven't been sleeping well, nothing more."

"Nothing more?"

"I dream about being thrown into a carriage, and not being able to get free. I'm sure, soon, it will stop."

With gentle fingers under her chin, he tilted her face up. "I see." His expression was flat. "You can't sleep because of what Lady Catherine did."

"I'm sure it will improve. No actual harm was done to me."

He stared at her, obviously wanting to say or do something more. She could read the indecision and frustration on his face. He placed a hand on her cheek again, and Elizabeth leaned into it, comforted.

"What can I do?" Mr. Darcy asked.

"Behave as normal, so that I may regain normalcy."

He nodded. With a sigh, he dropped his hand, offering his arm. She took it and they resumed their walk. Silence spread out about them. Elizabeth was surprised by the comfort she'd found in his touch, but knew no good could come from the two of them behaving in such an intimate way. They were friends now, of that she was sure. Whether or not they were more, she didn't yet know. She felt she would like them to be.

Deliberately, she launched into conversation, turning it to an ongoing discussion they'd been visiting over the viability of agriculture as an investment in their changing times. Soon, they were at ease once more. Elizabeth pressed all thoughts of Lady Catherine and nightmare carriages from her mind. She'd much rather learn more of Mr. Darcy's views, even those pertaining to fields and livestock, than dwell on such things. They walked back to Netherfield Park very indirectly, making what could have been a journey of a quarter hour into one that took nearly two.

18

Darcy and Richard were engaged in a game of billiards in the elegant, but old fashioned, room where the table was kept, Henry and Bingley observing, when Bingley's butler entered. They all turned, knowing the man wouldn't be there if not for something pressing. The butler, well trained, focused on Bingley, waiting for a nod of acknowledgement which was readily supplied.

"A Mr. Wickham is here, asking to see Mr. Darcy in private, sir."

"Wickham, here?" Bingley turned to Darcy. "What could he want?"

"I've no idea." Darcy frowned. "Knowing Wickham, it's likely trouble."

"If I may be so bold, sir?" the butler asked Bingley.

Bingley nodded. "What is it?"

"Mr. Wickham does appear rather harried."

Bingley turned back to Darcy. "Do you wish to see him?"

Darcy nodded. "Put him in the library, please."

"Of course, sir." The butler strode away.

"You aren't going in there alone," Henry said.

"I agree." Richard set aside his cue stick. "I'm going with you."

"This is my house. I should be there, in case of trouble," Bingley said.

"Wickham is trouble," Henry said with unaccustomed grimness. "I'll join you as well."

Darcy wasn't sure he wanted a full audience, but he didn't protest. Returning his cue stick to the rack, he led the way to the library. When they arrived, Henry hung back, lounging in the doorway. Darcy wondered if Henry was ensuring none of the servants would listen in, or that Wickham couldn't make a run for it.

As they crossed the library toward him, Wickham grimaced, looking around at the four of them. True to what the butler had intimated, Wickham's clothing was rumpled and he appeared not to have shaved. His usual attitude of insolent confidence was missing, as well. If Darcy had to guess at what was in Wickham's face, he would say fear.

His mouth pressed into a thin line, Wickham acknowledged them with a nod. "I take it this is as private a meeting as I'm to be allotted?"

"It is," Henry said from the doorway.

Shrugging, Wickham pulled a folded piece of paper from his coat. "I'm putting my cards on the table, gentlemen. I wish I could withhold something, but I can't. Read this."

Darcy took the proffered note, recognizing Lady Catherine's stationery. A quick glance showed no signature, but he recognized his aunt's handwriting. "It's in Aunt Catherine's writing, and on her stationary, though it isn't signed."

Henry cast a glance up and down the hall. "Read it."

Richard was already doing so, over Darcy's shoulder. Darcy read aloud for the benefit of Henry and Bingley. "Dear Mr. Wickham. It has come to my attention that my nephew, Mr. Darcy, has been spending time with Elizabeth Bennet. She is beneath him in every way; breeding, manners, wealth and appearance. Nevertheless, I am concerned she will use her arts and allurements to lead him away from my daughter."

"She'll never let it rest, will she?" Richard muttered.

Darcy read on. "If you use your charm or any other means to keep Elizabeth Bennet away from my nephew, I will be grateful. If you marry her, I will give you three thousand pounds. If you do something else that separates them, whatever it is, I will give you one thousand pounds."

Henry let out a low whistle. Bingley's expression was shocked.

"As you undoubtedly know, I am not to be trifled with," Darcy continued. "If you refuse to do as I ask, I will be very angry with you and you will feel the full force of my wrath. I know your regiment is scheduled to leave Hertfordshire soon. That is no excuse for avoiding doing my bidding. I will find you, for your reward or just due, wherever you go. You know who I am and what I can do."

Darcy resisted the urge to crumple the note and toss it on the fire. Silence reigned in the library as he exchanged grim looks with his cousins. This time, Lady Catherine had gone too far.

"How was this delivered?" Richard asked.

"It came in a coach bearing Lady Catherine's crest. If I recall right,

I remember the driver as working for her from, oh, about ten years ago, but I can't be sure, and there was a man with him, in her livery, who I didn't know. I doubt she generally loans her vehicle to servants for long country drives, so they undoubtedly came here at her request."

"Did anyone else see this coach?" Richard was as grim as Darcy had ever seen him.

Wickham shook his head. "They approached me when I was alone. No one else saw it delivered."

"Ensuring you knew who sent it without giving you any means to confirm it," Richard said.

"You can't think she means . . ." Bingley's voice trailed off. "That is to say, it sounds like a very grim request."

"Aunt Catherine has always been petty and vindictive, but now she's crossed the line," Henry said, his tone harsh.

"I don't have an out." Wickham said. "What is she asking me to do, murder Miss Elizabeth? I don't think Lady Catherine would have me harmed, but she's quite likely able to pressure someone high up in the militia to let me go. They don't pay well, but I'm making a living. I don't have many other options."

Darcy nodded, still unable to set aside enough anger to speak. Wickham spoke the truth about himself. He didn't have any skills to recommend him. He lacked the fiber to apply himself to anything remotely arduous. At least he wasn't so low as to carry out Lady Catherine's request.

"I neither know nor care if you are going to marry Miss Elizabeth, Darcy, but she wouldn't marry me under any circumstance, ever. I may have done a few things in my life that are unethical, but anything I could do to intervene in this case would be a hanging offense."

"So you came to me." Darcy was aware his tone was grating, but it was difficult to speak past the fury burning in his chest.

Wickham shrugged. "Where else would I go? Look, if you aren't planning to marry Miss Elizabeth Bennet, please tell your aunt so we can put this behind us. Better yet, let me tell her and collect my thousand pounds. If you are going to marry the girl, well, if you are, I would like . . ." Wickham's voice trailed off.

"You would like protection from her," Henry supplied.

"You know we have no control over her," Richard said.

"You're refusing to help me?" Wickham said. It was almost a statement rather than a question.

"Yes," Richard said as Darcy simultaneously said, "No."

The others looked at Darcy in surprise. Wickham's expression became hopeful.

"Frankly, I want you out of England," Darcy said, hoping the stern look he leveled on Wickham would warn him not to ask why. Darcy saw no need for Henry and Bingley to know Georgiana's secret.

Greed replaced the fear in Wickham's eyes. "I'm happy to go to Ireland, but paying my passage won't be enough."

"I'll pay more than your passage, but you're going to Canada," Darcy said. "Ireland is too close."

"From what I hear, Canada is practically a block of ice. I want passage to the United States, and two thousand pounds."

Henry let out a bark of laughter.

"We're at war with the United States," Richard protested.

"Darcy will make it work." Wickham shrugged again, appearing at ease for the first time since they'd entered the library. "At least, he will if he wants me to go farther away than Ireland."

"If they profit from it, I'm sure there are bankers who will accommodate me in spite of the war," Darcy said. He eyed Wickham, knowing the offer had to be generous. Wickham was well acquainted with how much Darcy was worth. "I'll pay your passage to Canada. You can make arrangements to go to the United States. I'll give you a hundred pounds to do that and to get you started. You will go to a large bank. They will arrange the details of your annuity with my bank in England."

There ensued a brief argument about amounts, but Darcy argued mostly for show, knowing Wickham would ask for more if he realized he could get it. In the end, the annuity they agreed upon would give Wickham a life, but he would be forced to find some form of employment if he wished to keep himself like a gentleman. Darcy thought the sum was well worth it to get Wickham out of the country. He proffered his hand, meaning the gesture both as concluding their negotiation and as good bye.

Wickham shook it. He then bowed to the room at large, a jaunty grin on his face. "Gentlemen, my lord. It's been a pleasure." He strolled past Henry and out of the library.

"Good riddance," Richard muttered.

Henry stayed where he was, looking in the direction of Wickham's fading footfalls. Once they were out of hearing, he closed the door and crossed to where Darcy, Richard and Bingley still stood. Gesturing for them to join him, he took a seat in the far corner. Darcy dropped his aunt's note on the low table they sat around.

"Well, that's half of our problem," Henry said.

Richard nodded. "Lady Catherine has obviously become convinced her rank allows her to do anything. She won't give up."

"Why don't you just make it plain you aren't going to marry Miss de Bourgh?" Bingley asked. "Or is that still a possibility?"

"I thought I made it plain," Darcy said.

"Make it more plain."

Darcy looked at Richard, wondering how much they should reveal.

Richard grimaced. "The details aren't precisely mine to tell, but Darcy did make it quite clear he has no intention of marrying Anne. Frankly, she was just as clear on her lack of enthusiasm for the match. All that did was elicit an ultimatum from Aunt Catherine." He cast a quick glance at Darcy, who nodded for him to continue. "Darcy proposed to Miss Elizabeth, giving her two months to make up her mind. We'd hoped that courtship would put Aunt Catherine off long enough for Anne to gain control of Rosings, which she will on her birthday. Anne then plans to use the threat of eviction to keep Aunt Catherine in line. Miss Elizabeth is fully acquainted with the plan."

Henry raised his eyebrows. "And here I've been keeping my distance from that delectable creature, thinking your courtship was sincere."

"It is," Darcy said. "The only reason I agreed to the courtship scheme was because I intended to court Miss Elizabeth in truth, not just as a subterfuge."

"So you really do want to marry Miss Elizabeth?" Bingley asked, his tone touched with surprise. He blinked several times. "Does she know that?"

"I don't know, and it gets worse." Darcy grimaced. "When we were all still in Kent, Lady Catherine abducted Miss Elizabeth. She had two of her footmen pick her up and force her into a carriage, where she waited. She then drove Miss Elizabeth to an inn about nine miles from Rosings and arranged for her passage on the stage to London. Instead, Miss Elizabeth walked back."

Bingley was staring at Darcy in shock once more. "Your aunt kidnapped Miss Elizabeth rather than permit you to court her? Is she mad?"

"I don't know how crazy Lady Catherine has become, but I think I'll have to make it my business to find out soon," Henry said in the same harsh tone he'd used earlier. He frowned at Darcy and Richard. "As for the two of you, you must realize the threat of eviction, or even casting her out, won't stop Aunt Catherine. You have put Miss Elizabeth in a dangerous situation. A woman alone on the stage to London could easily be harmed. If Wickham was a violent man instead of simply a dishonest one, Miss Elizabeth's body might have been found in a ditch long ere now. The next person Lady Catherine approaches might strike without warning. You've been lucky up to now, but a man can't live on luck."

"There's no way to know she hasn't already approached someone else." Richard's expression was grim. "Or ten people, for that matter. She sent her coachman and a footman. They may have carried more letters than one."

Darcy stared at him, horrified by the thought. "She wouldn't know anyone else here."

"Are you sure? Would that even stop her? Her coachman could hire someone she doesn't know," Richard said. "We have to do something."

"I realize that," Darcy growled. "If we hadn't made the courtship so public, I could tell Aunt Catherine it's off and stay away for a time." He knew staying away wouldn't be easy, but it would certainly be preferable to Elizabeth being hurt. "As things stand, calling it off would impinge my honor and, worse, humiliate Elizabeth."

"You could ask her to decline you," Henry said.

"Or marry you now," Bingley added.

"Were I sure I could persuade her, I would marry Elizabeth now." Darcy ignored the suggestion Elizabeth should refuse him again, though he resolved he would ask her to if he thought it was necessary to keep her safe. "Even Aunt Catherine would have to see she can't make me marry Anne once I am wed."

Henry and Richard both shook their heads.

"Won't work," Henry said.

"If she's willing to do Miss Elizabeth harm to stop a courtship, why should she draw the line at removing her once you're wed?"

Darcy frowned at them. He couldn't wrap his mind around the idea that Lady Catherine would have Elizabeth killed, even after the abduction she'd staged and the letter. It was all such madness. Mad or no, though, he would prevent it. So long as he was breathing, no harm would come to Elizabeth.

"Obviously, the only real solution is for Miss de Bourgh to marry," Bingley said.

Darcy turned to look at him.

"It's an easy thing for a gentleman to remarry, but once Miss de Bourgh is wed and the union consummated . . ." He coughed, looking embarrassed. "Not, of course, that widows can't remarry, but marriage is a different sort of thing for a woman than a man, and Lady Catharine surely sees that. Even if she doesn't, it's a much greater crime to have a gentleman of means murdered than a country girl residing on the edge of polite society, begging your pardon, Darcy. I doubt even Lady Catherine would dare attempt to remove Miss de Bourgh's husband if he's a gentleman."

Silence filled the library. Darcy contemplated Bingley's words, realizing he was correct. From their faces, Henry and Richard were doing the same.

"So, we find Anne a gentleman," Henry said, glancing at Richard.

Richard's eyes widened in surprise. "Not me."

"Well, I won't do it," Henry said. "When I marry, it will be to someone who enjoys the kind of life I'm living. I don't need Rosings or more money. Anne is a pleasant woman, but there's no reason I should shackle myself to her to free up Darcy."

Darcy raised an eyebrow. This was the first time he'd ever heard Harry suggest he might marry someday. Darcy generally thought of him as the young man who never grew up.

Bingley cleared his throat. "A possible solution is that I marry her, assuming she would have me. She's wealthier than I have a right to expect, but I would try to be a good husband to her."

Silence descended again as Darcy and his cousins turned to study Bingley. Richard looked thoughtful. Henry seemed vaguely amused, much of his good humor finally restored.

Darcy found himself nodding. Bingley would be a good husband to someone, so why not Anne? True, Darcy wouldn't have given Bingley permission to court Georgiana, not after his friend's revelations about himself, but Anne was different. Out from under her mother's thumb, she was stronger. Definitely strong enough to deal with Bingley. After all, she'd put him in his place when he'd lamented Miss Bennet's lack of misery upon seeing him again. "She may not want you."

"I can ask." Bingley turned to Henry.

"Be my guest," Henry said, much as he'd done in jest in the billiards room.

Richard nodded.

"Right, then." Bingley stood. "No time like the present, is there? Especially not if your aunt is to be speedily put off." He marched from the room.

They all watched him go, then Henry turned to Richard. "And what about your situation, Richard?"

"My situation?"

"Are you going to offer for Miss Bennet? You're clearly in love with her."

"I've thought about it." Richard's expression was glum. "I don't feel I can. You know how little I have beyond my pay. She deserves more. She's used to more."

"Perhaps," Darcy said. Remembering how he'd erroneously assumed Elizabeth's answer the first time he proposed to her, he added, "But she deserves the right to decide for herself. Explain the situation to her. There's no point in going through life wondering whether she would have agreed to marry you."

Henry leaned forward in his chair, frowning. "That's excellent advice, and all well and good, but the more I think on it, the more I feel we haven't resolved the original issue."

Darcy turned to his cousin questioningly.

"Even assuming Anne accepts your friend Bingley's offer, Miss Elizabeth will be in danger until Aunt Catherine recognizes the marriage. If she has already recruited others, Miss Elizabeth may be in danger even after that. There may be no way to retract offers already made."

All of the tension Darcy had shed in the past few moments returned. "You're right. Elizabeth isn't safe. I'll have to speak with her father." Though what he would say to Mr. Bennet, Darcy didn't know.

19

Darcy wished they didn't have a party to attend that evening, or that they'd spent less time conversing in the library. As it was, he had no opportunity to ride to Longbourn before the festivities, or even to speak privately with Bingley to ascertain if he'd indeed asked for Anne's hand. Darcy found having so much uncertainty in his life was trying to his patience. At least, he reasoned, he'd be able to keep watch over Elizabeth while they were together. He also he doubted she was in danger inside her home. All he needed to do was contrive for her to be either in Longbourn or with him at all times.

The carriage he and Richard shared with the Hursts was quiet on the journey over. Darcy kept most of his attention out the window, looking for anything suspicious. He didn't believe he'd see anything, but it couldn't hurt to keep an eye out. As they took their place in the long line of vehicles meandering up their host's drive, he idly marveled at the level of collusion in the community. It was obvious the locals were conspiring not to have conflicting events, even though someone held a gathering nearly every night.

His party reached the front and disembarked. As they made their way inside, Darcy was unsurprised to hear music. Though not billed as such, each gathering inevitably included a dance. He smiled slightly, realizing he didn't feel his once typical dread for the idea. By following Elizabeth's advice and dancing with more different ladies, he'd become better practiced at engaging them. He hadn't shed his taciturn nature, for to do so would be dishonest, but they seemed to accept that he seldom spoke. Now, when he asked a woman he'd danced with at a different event to dance again, he was met with genuine smiles. He was surprised how little effort it took to please.

Seeing Elizabeth already had a partner for the set about to begin, Darcy followed his now customary pattern, asking the first wallflower he saw to join him. It took him only a few moments to realize how difficult it was going to be to safeguard Elizabeth while he partnered anyone but her. Even though logic said she wasn't at risk in the middle of a party, his heart took up a frantic beat each time the steps drew her from view. Halfway through the set, he was strongly considering bowing out, frantically searching his mind for a plausible excuse.

It was then that he noticed Henry withdrawing from the floor, apologizing to his partner profusely. Darcy wasn't very near, but he caught snippets of Henry complaining about his leg. His cousin took a seat with an excellent view of the dancers, chatting away amiable with the girl he'd been partnering.

"Is everything well, Mr. Darcy?" the young woman Darcy was dancing with asked when the steps next allowed.

"Yes." Darcy added a pleasant smile to that syllable.

She followed his gaze. "You must be worried about your cousin. We all heard of his fall."

Fortunately, the steps drew Darcy away, alleviating the need to respond, for Henry was not who he was worried for.

From that point on, Darcy observed that Henry, though always carrying on in lively conversation, sat in such a way as to have a good view of wherever Elizabeth was. Darcy was unsure if his cousin's leg truly pained him or not, but he was sure Henry was helping him keep an eye on Elizabeth. He soon realized Richard was using his soldier's eyes, not so much to look at Elizabeth, but to sweep the area around her. Their efforts lent him some assurance, permitting him more calm.

The daughter of their host, a better player than many they'd come across thus far in Hertfordshire, took her turn at the piano and didn't bother leaving for some time, which also added to the enjoyment of the evening. Normally, if a girl lingered behind the keys for more than a few sets, a flustered mama would intervene. Darcy observed sardonically that, without an earl offering to dance with each young lady who played, switching out performers had become unimportant.

As the evening moved on, much to Darcy's surprise, Miss Lydia danced far less than usual. She seemed to prefer Henry's stories instead. Darcy, considering himself a good judge of husband seeking misses, felt most of the women who clustered around the earl listening to his tales of hunting, racing and general trouble making, did so with false curiosity. Miss Lydia, on the other hand, displayed genuine interest.

". . . of you not to invite me to the race," Miss Lydia was saying, her tone pouting, as the steps of a dance drew Darcy near where Henry sat. "I should have loved to see you beat Mr. Darcy. I would have cheered and cheered."

"Next time, pet," Henry said. "You shan't be disappointed. I often beat Darcy."

Miss Lydia laughed.

Darcy shook his head, not slowing his steps. He had no doubt Henry had seen him passing.

It was with something akin to relief that Darcy finally managed to wend his way to Elizabeth. With the plethora of women thrown in his way and her complete lack of shortage for partners, he'd begun to suspect a conspiracy to keep them apart. By the time he found himself standing up with her, he'd already danced with two of her sisters, Miss Bingley, Mrs. Hurst, more than a few wallflowers, and Anne. He'd missed having Elizabeth on his arm. Once he finally did, she smiled up at him.

"If I'd realized taking your advice would mean I wouldn't be able to partner you, I should have remained aloof," he said.

Her smiled turned into a laugh. "But how can you not understand that seeing you create so much happiness makes me desire my turn so much more?"

"Does their pleasure come from my rank and wealth?" he asked, knowing it didn't stem from his conversation. "Or perhaps more accurately, my eligibility?"

"In very small part. Everyone knows you're courting me, after all."

Darcy tried to smooth his frown, but he couldn't be pleased with her unknowing reminder that he'd put her in danger.

"It's more to do with you being an exceedingly well favored gentleman," she said when next the steps brought them near. "You are also an excellent dancer."

"I was well taught. It has nothing to do with me." He realized he sounded curt and reminded himself his anger was neither directed at Elizabeth nor known to her.

She tipped her head to the side, studying him. "You have a natural grace, and I'm sure you've cultivated it. Also, I believe you are learning how to be amiable to your partners."

He smiled slightly, realizing she sensed his mood and sought to cheer him. "I doubt I am amiable to any but you."

"Not so." She shook her head, making the loose curls framing her face dance. "Their expressions tell me they're happy, and the gossip that makes its way back to me confirms it. My mother is annoyed at it, because it makes her doubt you are a serious suitor."

Darcy turned that over in his mind, wondering if he could use it to his advantage. Should he flirt with other women? Would that make Elizabeth safe? What if, as his cousin suggested, nothing would make her safe? Not in Hertfordshire, at least. Surely, were she removed, she would be infinitely more secure. The sort of men who would do Lady Catherine's bidding weren't likely to have the means to track Elizabeth down if she changed vicinities.

"Mr. Darcy?" she asked.

He looked down to see her frowning up at him. "I beg your pardon."

"Are you well?" Her eyes held touching concern.

Casting a quick look about the room, Darcy made a decision. Elizabeth should know of her own peril. "I must speak to you in private. It's important." He kept his voice low.

She raised her eyebrows.

"Exceedingly important," he said, permitting some of the desperation he felt for her safety to color his tone. Would them leaving together be noted? He didn't want to cause her embarrassment, but he was resolved to keep her safe. "A few minutes after this dance, I will leave by the front door and circle around to the terrace. Give me a moment to get there, then walk out on the terrace and head for the garden."

She regarded him for a long moment, during which he worried she would refuse. Finally, she nodded.

They finished the dance without speaking again. Elizabeth appeared intrigued, perhaps even hopeful, but permitted him his silence. After bowing to her with a smile he hoped didn't look as strained as it felt, Darcy made his way to Richard.

"A word," he said, cutting his cousin off before he could approach another partner.

"Of course."

He led Richard to the foyer.

"Is something amiss?" Richard asked, his tone quiet.

"No. I'm going to talk to Elizabeth in the garden. She should know she's in danger."

"In the garden?"

"I can't tell her in there." He gestured back toward the assemblage. "Someone might overhear, or she may not be able to master her reaction to the news." Darcy didn't think Elizabeth was the sort to panic, but it wasn't every day you were told someone had been asked to murder you.

"I see. Not to mention, if you happen to get caught, her mother would insist that you marry her."

"That is not my goal."

"No, of course not."

Darcy shot him a scowl. "I know you and Henry are keeping an eye on her. Thank you for that. Can you let him know she's going to be with me? I don't need either of you to follow her into the garden."

"I'll let him know."

"Thank you."

Darcy slipped out of the house and made his way to the terrace. It was a warm night, and their host had every door and window thrown wide to let in the air. A few others lingered outside, standing in the rectangles of candlelight spilling out and speaking in small groups. The moon was very bright, but low on the horizon. It cast slanting shadows across an already dark ground.

Elizabeth walked out onto the terrace and moved away from the groups of people. When her scanning eyes alighted on him, she wandered his way casually, as if merely trying to escape the heat.

He held himself in the shadows until she reached him, then offered her his arm. She placed her white-gloved hand atop it, using the other to hold her skirt up from the gravel walk. In silence, they headed down a path. Darcy couldn't help but glance at her every few seconds. In the moonlight, she was luminous, seeming to cast a glow of her own. She appeared hardly real.

When they reached a spot where they could still see the brightly lit rooms twinkling between interlacing branches, but it was unlikely they could be seen, even with the moonlight, she let go of his arm, stepping away. "Mr. Darcy, I hope you have a good reason for asking me here. This is quite scandalous and goes against all good breeding and sense. I'd like to think I haven't thrown off years of propriety for anything insignificant." Her voice was low, but he heard the amusement lurking in her tone.

Darcy resisted the urge to close the distance between them, for she'd put it there. When he'd asked to speak in private, he hadn't been prepared for the intimacy of the experience. To have Elizabeth alone in the dark garden, bathed in moonlight, struck a longing in him he wasn't sure he could withstand. "I'm afraid it is serious. Alarmingly so."

"Oh dear, you do sound dire."

"Mr. Wickham came to meet with me today."

"Mr. Wickham?" The moonlight revealed confusion on her face.

"Lady Catherine wrote to him." He couldn't keep the harshness from his tone. "This isn't going to be easy for you to hear."

"Mr. Darcy, you're worrying me."

"Then we are both worried, as are Henry, Richard and Bingley, for they were with me for the meeting. Lady Catherine asked Wickham to marry you." Elizabeth gasped, but Darcy pressed on. "She offered him three thousand pounds to do so."

Her eyes were wide with surprise. "That's quite the sum, but he must know I will never marry him."

"He does know, which is why he came to me." He moved closer to her, unable to help himself. Somehow, it made him feel he was offering her protection from his next words. "She also intimated she would pay him for removing you in any other way he saw fit, and threatened dire retribution should he fail to do so."

She went still. "In any way? Meaning what?"

"We aren't certain. He wasn't, either. He came to me asking for help. I've bought him passage to Canada."

Elizabeth sagged, her expression relieved. Darcy reached toward her, but she didn't faint. He let his arm fall back to his side.

"So I am safe." She smiled up at him. "Thank you. I'm sure, knowing Mr. Wickham, you were forced to provide him funds as well."

He nodded. "I was, but we are not sure you are safe. Lady Catherine sent two of her servants and her coach. We have no way to know if they attempted to hire any other miscreants, or if they succeeded."

Elizabeth went still. "Two servants and her coach?" she repeated in a small voice.

Even by moonlight he could see her face had lost all color. She swayed. Darcy closed the remaining distance between them, wrapping her in his arms. He didn't mean to do it. As soon as he did, he remembered he ought not, but as soon as he did, he knew there was no way he could let go.

"What must we do?" she murmured, her cheek pressed to his

chest. "Does this mean you shall stop courting me? Do you wish for me to decline your offer of marriage?"

Did he imagine the sorrow in her voice? "We don't know that would help." As he spoke, he was acutely aware of the light scent she wore wreaking havoc on his wits. "If she's hired ruffians, she likely has no means of calling them off. Bingley is going to ask Miss de Bourgh to marry him, or perhaps already has. If she says yes, once Lady Catherine acknowledges the union, things should get better. She won't have any reason to come after you again." He hoped. His aunt was so vindictive and seemed so crazy in her actions, he worried she might lash out at Elizabeth in some demented attempt at revenge.

Darcy pushed that thought aside. There would be time to worry over vengeance from Lady Catherine later. They would likely have warning. His aunt wasn't one to conceal her ire. He held Elizabeth tight, wishing he could do more to comfort her.

"So we shall do nothing? I will live my days knowing someone may be out there, watching me and plotting who knows what?" She pushed him away enough to look up at him. "I will not be thrown into another carriage. I won't."

Darcy's heart lurched at the terror underlying her tone. He tilted his head down and covered her lips with his, taking them in a long, lingering kiss to drive her fear away. When he lifted his head she was swaying, or perhaps he was, so he held her tighter. He drew in a ragged breath, steadying himself. He would never be able to let her go. He would make her his, and he would keep her from harm. "No, we won't do nothing. Come to Pemberley with me. Let me keep you safe."

"To Pemberley?" she breathed, leaning her head back to look up at him again, her eyes wide.

"Yes. Be my wife, Elizabeth. I love you. I won't stop loving you. Ever."

She searched his face with her gaze. He worked to still his nerves. She couldn't say no this time, could she? Was he that poor a judge of her? She seemed so amiable, so pleasant, and happy to be around him. When they kissed, he'd felt the hesitancy of inexperience, but her lips were soft and pliable under his. How could—

"Yes. I will marry you. I love you."

All thought fled as he once again took her lips under his. It wasn't until his hand, seeking to burry itself in her hair, encountered the resistance of pins that Darcy came back to himself. Slowly, agonizingly, he forced himself to draw away. He placed his hands on her shoulders, once again unsure which of them needed steadying more.

Elizabeth blinked up at him, looking dazed. As her expression cleared, mischief flittered across it. "That was definitely, by far, the most fun I've ever had at a party."

Darcy suppressed a bark of laughter, knowing they weren't far enough from the house that it wouldn't be heard. "I should hope so."

"Will you speak to my father soon?" She blushed.

"I will, but we dare not announce our engagement until Anne takes control of Rosings or is married. Who knows what acts of madness us becoming engaged would drive my deranged relative to." Some of the harshness returned to his tone as he spoke.

Elizabeth nodded. "Let's not speak of that now. I mean for this to be a happy occasion, and you are frowning." She reached up, tracing the curve of his mouth with a light touch. A devilish smile formed on her face. "One more kiss, and then we'll go in."

20

The carriage ride back to Netherfield was as silent as the one away from it had been. Once again, Darcy didn't mind. He felt quite unable to converse. In spite of his fears for Elizabeth's safety, he had to concentrate to keep a grin from his face.

Reaching Netherfield Park, both carriages emptied of passengers. Darcy, along with the others, made his way into their favorite evening parlor, filled with plush sofas and broad-armed chairs. He selected a seat away from the fire, feeling no need for additional warmth.

"It was a lovely evening," Anne said from the doorway. "I bid you all goodnight." She turned and glided away.

Darcy eyed her retreating back for the brief moment it remained in view. She hadn't so much as looked at Bingley. It was her custom to retire immediately following a party, but Darcy had expected . . . something. He glanced at Bingley, but couldn't read his face. Perhaps he hadn't found the opportunity to pose his question to Anne yet.

"I'm headed to bed as well," Henry said from where he stood near the fire.

"So early, my lord?" Miss Bingley asked. She pursed her lips in a pout.

"There are times even I tire. Good night all." Henry left to a chorus of well wishes.

Darcy looked to Richard, wondering if Henry truly had injured himself in the race. Normally, the earl was indefatigable. Richard, however, had stretched out on the sofa, his eyes closed. Darcy didn't think he truly slept, but was beginning to suspect a collusion.

To further the cause, which he assumed was to politely rid themselves of Miss Bingley and the Hursts, he picked up a nearby book and proceeded to read. He often read before he retired, so his behavior wasn't all that unusual. Bingley seated himself near his sisters and Mr. Hurst, engaging them in dull conversation. It wasn't long before Mr.

Hurst began to doze.

"Well, I can see the lot of you aren't going to be of any more entertainment this evening." Mrs. Hurst glanced about the room. "Finally danced yourselves to boredom, I see. It was inevitable. There's only so much one can take of partnering common country girls. They were bound to sink you into a state of ennui eventually."

Darcy lowered his book to see her stand, and politely mimicked the movement, one finger marking his place. With her foot, Mrs. Hurst nudged her husband.

Mr. Hurst grunted, blinking up at her. "What is it, Louisa?"

"It's time to retire. Caroline, Charles, Mr. Darcy." She nodded to each of them in turn. When she reached Richard in his pretend slumber, she frowned. Shrugging, she turned and sailed from the room.

Mr. Hurst pulled himself from his chair to follow. "Night all."

Before Darcy retook his seat, Miss Bingley rose, looking about the room in annoyance. "Louisa is right." She said her farewells and left.

Silence descended on the room as her footsteps faded down the hall. Bingley leaned back in his chair, grinning at Darcy. Richard opened one eye, peered about, and sat up.

"Do you think she's really gone?" Bingley whispered.

Richard held up a hand. On silent feet, he moved to the door and out. He returned a moment later, taking a seat near Bingley. "She went to her room. I doubt she'll come back out tonight."

Darcy set his book on the table, joining them. "I have news."

"As do I," Bingley said, looking smug.

"A moment." Richard held up his hand again. "Henry should return soon."

"Should I send for him?" Bingley asked.

"No need." Henry strode through the doorway. "I was waiting until I heard enough doors close to account for unwanted ears." He seated himself in a chair near Richard. "Did you all have interesting evenings, then?"

"I asked Elizabeth to marry me and she accepted." Darcy said it as casually as he could, belying the joy in his heart.

There was an unsurprised, but sincere, round of congratulations.

"I took the plunge as well." Richard's face split into a grin. "I don't want to make it general news until I talk with Mr. Bennet, but I asked Jane to marry me. She said yes."

"Congratulations," Darcy said. "She's a lovely woman."

"I'm sure you will be very happy." Bingley's approval appeared genuine.

"Indeed, congratulations, little brother," Henry said. "I assume this means Miss Bennet reacted well when you expressed your concern about possible hardships?"

"She said it would be the greater hardship by far to be without me than to be poor with me." Richard's expression would have been comically besotted, if Darcy didn't feel much the same about his own evening. "She is an angel."

"Her father won't be able to give her much, if anything," Bingley warned.

"Jane told me as much. She said she almost felt wrong accepting my offer because I should have a wife with a large dowry. Someone like Anne."

"Too late. Anne is going to marry me," Bingley said smugly.

"Well, congratulations to you as well, Bingley," Henry said.

"I'm sure you'll make Anne a fine husband," Richard added.

Darcy offered his congratulations, doing his best to school his tone into happiness, not relief. Now, hopefully, they would be able to make Lady Catherine realize there was no hope for him and Anne marrying. Once she acknowledged Bingley was Anne's husband, Elizabeth would be safe.

Darcy couldn't help but contrast his and Richard's happiness with the self-satisfied look on Bingley's face, but marrying for love wasn't for everyone. Bingley had been in love many times, so Darcy assumed he knew what he was giving up. Darcy had been in love only once, and intended it should remain that way. Life without Elizabeth had become unimaginable.

"I didn't say anything earlier because Anne put a number of conditions on the marriage. First and foremost, she said I may not tell anyone but the three of you until within a day of the wedding. Even though she's old enough to wed if she wishes, she seems to think Lady Catherine will swoop in and prevent it." He chuckled, but his laughter died as he took in their face.

Darcy didn't find Anne's fear unreasonable. Nor, it appeared, did Henry and Richard.

"Ah, she also wants to marry immediately," Bingley continued soberly. "I'll have to get an attorney to write up a contract for the rest, as it pertains mostly to Rosings and future offspring. She wrote it all down for me." He patted his pocket. "Do any of you have a way to get a special license? I can foot the bill."

"I do." Henry said. "Give me Anne's requirements. I'll see to that as well. Discretely," he added when Richard opened his mouth to speak.

Bingley handed over the paper.

Not unfolding it, Henry tucked it away. "I'll go to London in the morning, if Darcy will lone me his roan." He turned to Darcy. "My horse is lame and you've bragged about how that roan does for distance."

Darcy nodded. "Certainly." He hoped his favorite riding horse would return sound.

"Perfect." Bingley smiled. "We can be married tomorrow."

"Tomorrow?" Henry raised his eyebrows. "Even I can't make it to London and back before noon. You do know you have to get married in the morning, don't you?"

"Yes, of course I do." Bingley grimaced, obviously embarrassed. "Though it's a ridiculous law."

Henry shrugged. "So get someone to change it. You'll be wealthy as sin soon."

Bingley grinned.

***

The following morning, Darcy and Richard called at Longbourn, as had become their habit. Darcy knew Miss Kitty and Miss Lydia would be disappointed Henry didn't accompany them, but he didn't always do so, so it wouldn't be suspicious. Besides, as soon as Richard and Miss Bennet made their news known, the family would momentarily forget about the Earl of Matlock.

Instead of asking if Elizabeth and Miss Bennet could walk with them, Darcy and Richard went in. After greetings were exchanged, Darcy took a seat in the parlor. He could guess from Mrs. Bennet's bright eyes and the way she was looking between Richard and Miss Bennet that she had a suspicion as to the cause of their alteration in routine.

"Mr. Bennet." Richard forwent sitting. "May I speak with you in private, sir?"

Mrs. Bennet let out a squeal of delight. Seated beside Darcy,

Elizabeth grimaced at the sound, but cast a smile toward her sister.

Mr. Bennet nodded. "Right this way."

"Oh Jane," Mrs. Bennet cried as Mr. Bennet and Richard left the room. "Oh my dear, sweet, beautiful Jane. You're finally to be married."

"Mama." Miss Bennet looked down, blushing.

"Well, you are, aren't you? What else could Colonel Fitzwilliam wish to speak with your father about, in private?"

"I wanted Jane to marry Mr. Bingley," Miss Lydia said, her face folding into a pout. "Mr. Bingley is rich, and he throws parties."

"But Colonel Fitzwilliam is an officer." Miss Kitty nodded along to her own words. "Just think, Jane will be married to an officer."

Miss Bennet's color deepened, but Darcy could catch the edges of a smile on her downturned face. Elizabeth looked at him, offering an expression somewhere between amused and exasperated. Darcy gave her a look he hoped conveyed he'd made his peace with her mother's and sisters' behavior.

"What matters is if they suit," Miss Mary said. "It seems to me they do."

"No, Lydia is correct, of course." Mrs. Bennet let out a sad sigh. "It would have been better for Jane to marry Mr. Bingley. When your father leaves us, poor man, we'll be destitute, and there's nothing Colonel Fitzwilliam will be able to do to aid us. Oh, if only Jane had brought Mr. Bingley up to scratch." She slumped in the chair in which she sat, draping an arm across her forehead.

"Well, I like Colonel Fitzwilliam," Miss Kitty said.

"I like him well enough." Miss Lydia tossed her curls. "I simply like Mr. Bingley's money more."

"Lydia," Miss Bennet said, her tone sharp.

"Well, I do. Is it more wrong to say it than to lie about how I feel?"

"It would be best to remain silent, if how you feel is offensive," Miss Mary said.

"My poor Jane, destined to be destitute," Mrs. Bennet wailed.

"Mother." Elizabeth's tone held exasperation. "Jane loves Colonel Fitzwilliam, and she will be well looked after. Most importantly, she'll be happy. I'm certain of it. He's a wonderful gentleman, and he's not destitute. Even if he only had his salary as a colonel, he wouldn't be destitute, and I believe he has more."

Miss Bennet cast Elizabeth a grateful smile.

Footsteps sounded in the hall and they all turned. Richard and Mr. Bennet marched back into the parlor. Mr. Bennet looked about the room, a sea of expectant faces. Behind him, Richard smiled.

"Jane and Colonel Fitzwilliam are to be married." Mr. Bennet winced at the shrieks this evoked.

Everyone stood from their seats and began hugging Miss Bennet and congratulating both parties. Under the cover of the crush, Darcy made his way to Mr. Bennet. He gestured for them to step to the side of the press of people.

"Mr. Darcy?" Mr. Bennet's expression was one of curiosity.

"Mr. Bennet." Darcy kept his voice low. "I'm afraid I must speak to you on a serious matter, one which may not paint me in an entirely favorable light and which must be kept absolutely secret, even from your household."

Mr. Bennet's eyes flickered to where Elizabeth stood beside Miss Bennet. "Am I going to require a second for this meeting?"

Darcy blinked. "No. No, of course not. It's . . ." He shook his head slightly. "No, I have not done anything to harm your daughter." He couldn't count last night's kisses as harm. "It's a complicated matter, involving some of my relations, in which I've foolishly entangled Miss Elizabeth."

Mr. Bennet answered this with a frown.

"I'm going to ask Miss Elizabeth to walk with me. Can you contrive to meet us without arousing suspicion? Is there a location you think would suit?"

After a strained silence, Mr. Bennet nodded. He provided a location Darcy knew. It would be private and was a quarter of an hour walk for him and Elizabeth, but easily accessible by a nearby road. "I shall see you there, sir, and expect a convincing explanation," Mr. Bennet added.

Darcy nodded, hoping he could give one.

As the fuss surrounding Miss Bennet and Richard died down, Darcy suggested he and Elizabeth take their usual walk. Richard asked to do the same with Miss Bennet, causing a brief disruption to Darcy's plan as he maneuvered the other couple into taking a route that would keep them away from the meeting with Mr. Bennet. As he and Elizabeth walked, arm in arm, he explained that he'd asked her father to meet them.

"You could have spoken to him in his library," she said, looking slightly amused.

Darcy shook his head. "I was too worried someone might overhear, or that your mother would assume, rightly so, we spoke of my marrying you. Even if your father denied it, she could quite possibly spread the news."

"You are correct, of course." Elizabeth sighed. "Has Mr. Bingley asked Miss de Bourgh yet? Do you think she will accept? I should like to put the threat of Lady Catherine behind us."

"You've been taking care not to journey out alone?" he asked, worry coursing through him.

"Yes. As I said, I have no desire to be shoved into a coach again." Her tone was hard.

Darcy drew in a steadying breath. Each time he thought of Elizabeth under duress, his mind clogged with fear, and anger. "Bingley asked, and Anne accepted. They're to be married tomorrow morning. Anne gave me permission to tell you, Miss Bennet, and your father, but you must keep it secret from anyone else, at least for a few more hours. Richard and I should like to bring you and Miss Bennet, if I can secure your father's permission."

"That's wonderful news." Elizabeth smiled up at him, making the world about them brighter.

"It is, but I still worry. I would prefer to remove you to Pemberley. As I said, I fear my aunt may have unleashed agents she can't call back, or may release others before acknowledging the union. Even more, I worry she might be pushed deeper into madness by the news and lash out. I'll feel much better if you're safe in my home."

"Your home." Her eyes took on a dreamy quality. "Tell me of Pemberley. You always speak of it with such devotion."

As they walked, Darcy described the grounds to her. He did his utmost to do them justice, for he knew Elizabeth would love Pemberley as he did. He longed for when he could walk her down the paths he could only speak of now.

They found Mr. Bennet waiting for them at his chosen location. They were far enough from the main road their voices wouldn't easily reach it, and screened from it by a low hill and a grove. Mr. Bennet eyed them as they approached, his gaze lingering on their interlocked arms.

"Sir," Darcy greeted, pulling away from Elizabeth to bow to her

195

father.

"Mr. Darcy, what's this all about?"

Elizabeth stepped forward. "Papa, Mr. Darcy has asked me to marry him, and I have accepted."

Mr. Bennet gave him a considering look. He turned back to Elizabeth. "Which Mr. Darcy? The one who wouldn't dance with one of the prettiest girls in Hertfordshire or the one who will kindly make sure no one is a wallflower?"

"Papa," Elizabeth exclaimed. She cast Darcy an apologetic look.

Darcy grimaced. It was a well-aimed barb. "As your daughter is responsible for the change, I hope to be a reasonable compromise between the two."

Mr. Bennet was still looking at Elizabeth. "And if Mr. Darcy reverts back to his original ways after you are wed?"

"I will have married a good and honorable man, who doesn't please others at large parties." Elizabeth reached out and clasped Darcy's hand. "What's more, I will have married a man I love."

Darcy couldn't help but smile at her.

"You are both being very circumspect in going about this. It's not odd for a man who the whole of Hertfordshire knows is courting you to ask for your hand. I assume more is going on here that I'm not aware of."

"Yes, sir, and that's the part I'm not proud of." Darcy proceeded to explain about his aunt's delusion that he and Anne were engaged, her ultimatum, and her threat to defame his sister. He didn't mention what had spurred the ultimatum, or the form the defamation might have taken, nor did Mr. Bennet ask.

He then related how he and Elizabeth had agreed to go along with Anne's plan to put her mother off until she gained control of Rosings, and thus a means of restraining her mother as well. Casting a quick glance at Elizabeth, Darcy admitted he'd gone along with the plan because it provided him the opportunity to court her. Mr. Bennet shook his head at this, but didn't interrupt.

Lastly, Darcy told of his aunt's abduction of Elizabeth, their removal to London, and of Mr. Wickham's part in the tale. Mr. Bennet's expression became grim. Darcy felt his face heat slightly, aware he and Anne had put Elizabeth in danger. He despised himself for that, and felt obligated to say, "I will understand if, in view of these events, you feel disinclined to grant me permission to marry your daughter." Darcy had to press the words out through wooden lips, his whole body protesting them.

"There was no way to know Lady Catherine would become so deranged," Elizabeth said, squeezing the hand she still held.

Mr. Bennet looked down at that hand. "I assume you are taking steps to secure my daughter's safety?"

"We are doing what we can. Mr. Wickham has been removed to Canada. Mr. Bingley is to marry Miss de Bourgh tomorrow. Lady Catherine will be informed immediately."

"Papa," Elizabeth interrupted. "Jane and I would like to attend the wedding. We'll both be cousins to Miss de Bourgh soon. I think it is appropriate, and she'll have so few people in attendance, it would be kind as well."

Mr. Bennet frowned at her. "Yes, I suppose you may, so long as you stay with Colonel Fitzwilliam and Mr. Darcy." He waved a hand dismissively, turning his angry visage back to Darcy. "I'm less concerned about weddings than Elizabeth's safety. How do you know Mr. Wickham is the only person Lady Catherine has solicited to harm my daughter?"

"We do not, sir," Darcy admitted. "However, it is my feeling the type of men Lady Catherine may have recruited will lose interest if their path becomes difficult or too much time passes. Knowing my aunt, she issued constraints of time and result, as she did with Mr. Wickham. Until a long enough interval passes, and word of Anne's and Mr. Bingley's union spreads, I should like to remove Elizabeth to Pemberley. She will be safe there."

"And if your aunt recruits there?"

"She will have no reason to. Anne and Mr. Bingley will send word Anne is wed. Lady Catherine's chance to have Anne marry me will be ended."

"I will require time to think on all of this." Mr. Bennet turned to Elizabeth. "I can see how that, were you and Mr. Darcy engaged, it would need to be a secret. You can't risk word of your impending marriage reaching Lady Catherine before she accepts Miss de Bourgh's and Mr. Bingley's union. In view of that, and the tale I have heard today, I cannot yet grant you permission to marry Mr. Darcy."

The words ran through Darcy like a sword thrust.

"But, Papa, I--" Elizabeth cried.

"No. No but anything." Mr. Bennet's tone was harder than Darcy had ever heard it, or assumed it could be. "Mr. Darcy and Miss de Bourgh have put you in danger, perhaps mortally so. Mr. Darcy cannot, at this time, publicize his intentions to the world at large. I will not consent until he can prove his proposal is sincere by announcing it, and proves he is deserving of you by rectifying the situation he helped place you in. I am not happy with you, either, miss, for agreeing to this scheme of Miss de Bourgh's in the first place."

"Yes, papa." Elizabeth's face was pale, but her expression firm. "I will accept your delay because I know Mr. Darcy does love me, and longs to tell the world. I also know he will ensure my wellbeing."

Darcy felt the pain of Mr. Bennet's words dim, swept away by Elizabeth's faith in him. "Sir, even in light of your refusal, I ask you to allow me to take Miss Elizabeth to Pemberley, for her safety."

"Permit you to take my unwed daughter, whom you've professed to admire, to your home?" Mr. Bennet still appeared quite angry. "All else aside, what possible reason would I put out?"

Darcy frowned. Mr. Bennet had every right to be dismayed. Darcy wasn't pleased either. The man was becoming illogical, however. What did the story they put out matter? They spoke of Elizabeth's safety, and any harm to her reputation would be repaired when he married her.

Elizabeth looked back and forth between them. "Please, both of you, don't become unreasonable. It's simple enough. Jane can be married at Pemberley. Mr. Darcy will offer to host the wedding, as he wishes to gift Jane and Colonel Fitzwilliam with a lavish celebration and we cannot house all of their relatives at Longbourn." Her eyes took on a mischievous gleam. "And you, Papa, will in turn add whatever you would have spent on the affair to Jane's dowry."

Darcy looked down at her, impressed by the idea. "It could be plausible."

Mr. Bennet sighed. "In spite of all I've learned today, and in spite of my anger, I agree you would be safer anywhere than here, Elizabeth. I could send you back to London, but I can't imagine you being more secure in town than in Mr. Darcy's ancestral holdings. If Jane and Colonel Fitzwilliam agree, it seems as if we shall all be going to Pemberley."

"Thank you, sir," Darcy said. "If you could speak to Miss Bennet, I'll apprise Richard of the plan."

"I'm putting my trust in you, Mr. Darcy. Elizabeth and Jane are the two most important people in my life. Their wellbeing and happiness matter more to me even than my own. Do not fail me."

Darcy released Elizabeth's hand to bow to her father. "I won't."

21

There was, inevitably, a party that evening, during which Darcy struggled to appear normal. Richard's and Jane Bennet's engagement and news of the impending journey to Pemberley were welcome distractions, enlivening the community and turning eyes from Darcy and Elizabeth. For their part, Bingley and Anne appeared to suffer no difficulty in hiding the change in their relationship. This was even though Bingley had ridden out that afternoon and made circumspect arrangements for them to be married in a small, unfrequented church he'd located nearby.

Darcy had feared they would have to play up Henry's injury to excuse his absence, adding another layer of lies and convolution to the mess they'd embroiled themselves in, but the earl arrived at the party before it became necessary. Darcy, standing nearby, heard Henry apologize to their host, saying he'd been attending to business concerns. Henry then strode over to him.

"Your horse will be brought back by one of my grooms tomorrow, in easy stages," he informed Darcy in a low voice. "Don't worry. He's fine."

"I shouldn't have expected anything less."

"No, but I could tell you did."

With a grin, Henry strolled away. The next Darcy saw of him, he was dancing.

Later that night, once they'd all returned to Netherfield Park, Darcy, Henry, Richard and Bingley once again shed the company of Miss Bingley and the Hursts. Miss Bingley was particularly tart over another curtailed evening, but there were matters too pressing for excessive civility. Darcy reflected that it would work out better for all if Miss Bingley routinely retreated to her room early and Anne stayed up, but some things couldn't be changed.

Once they were sure the others had retired, Darcy turned to

Richard. "I assume from the talk this evening that Miss Bennet agreed to be wed at Pemberley?"

"I heard the talk too," Bingley said. He reclined on a plush sofa with his feet resting on the arm, smugness still lingering in his features. "How did that come about?"

Darcy had explained the plan to Richard on the ride back from Longbourn, but hadn't yet found the opportunity to enlighten Bingley or Henry. "Mr. Bennet wouldn't permit me to remove Elizabeth to Pemberley without a reason the community will accept, wishing to safeguard her reputation. With Miss Bennet's wedding taking place there, it is only reasonable for me to invite the entire family."

"Even the mother?" Bingley said with a sly smile.

Darcy chose to ignore that comment.

"Isn't your engagement enough to safeguard her reputation?" Henry asked. "I assume you spoke to Mr. Bennet."

"Darcy wouldn't be able to announce the engagement yet," Richard put in quickly, shooting Darcy a sympathetic look. "Not until enough time passes to ensure Aunt Catherine knows Anne is wed."

Darcy appreciated Richard's effort on his behalf, but there was no point in denying Mr. Bennet's answer. "Mr. Bennet did not give me permission to marry Elizabeth." Darcy felt again the bitter disappointment experienced with Mr. Bennet's answer.

Henry's brows shot up.

Bingley let out a low whistle. "Sorry to hear it."

"He didn't reject the union out of hand," Darcy hastened to assure them. "He said I must first be in a position to announce the engagement and that I must also put an end to any threat against his daughter, as we are attempting to do."

"As we will do." Henry's tone was firm.

"Speaking to that, Anne has made a request." Bingley swung himself into a sitting position, turning to Darcy. "She is reluctant to return to Rosings until after her birthday, or until we have confirmation Lady Catherine has accepted our union. I'll send my attorney to Rosings to inform Lady Catherine of our marriage and obtain her written acknowledgement, but in the meantime, Anne's not felt safe here since I told her about Mr. Wickham. With all of the talk tonight about Pemberley at the party, she's asked if we may join you there. I feel Anne's being a bit dramatic about it all, but I'd be happy to indulge her if you're willing, Darcy."

"It's difficult to say if Anne's being overly cautious. Lady Catherine can be quite the force when she's of a mind." Darcy shrugged. "We'd be happy to have you, of course."

"And Caroline and the Hursts? I can't very well leave them here and Mr. Hurst closed his house in London before joining us here."

Darcy nodded, containing a grimace.

"It's decided, then," Henry said. "After the wedding in the morning, we're all off to Pemberley." He shot Darcy a quick grin, obviously aware he hadn't specifically been invited.

Darcy shrugged again. His cousin knew he was always welcome in Pemberley.

Henry turned to Bingley. "Bingley, the documents Anne requested will arrive first thing tomorrow, though I pity whoever they send out early enough to get them here in time."

"I'm sure he'll be well paid. Thank you for seeing it done."

"Also, you should know I made arrangements for Agatha to come to your wedding tomorrow, and bring Georgiana along." Henry stood while he talked, stretching. "Aggie's willing to come without knowing why. She said she'd bring Georgiana and her companion."

"That was thoughtful of you," Bingley said. "Anne will be pleased."

"I'm a thoughtful sort of fellow." Henry looked about the room. "Now, who's up for some billiards?"

***

The following morning, Darcy rose early and made ready for the day, enjoying a quiet breakfast in his room. Leaving as soon as he was finished, he went to knock on Mr. Hurst's door. It was opened by Hurst's valet, who issued a bow.

"Is Mr. Hurst available?"

"Who the blazes is it?" Mr. Hurst's groggy voice said inside the room.

The valet half turned toward the room. "Mr. Darcy, sir."

"What the devil does he want at this hour?"

Hurst's valet turned back to Darcy. "May I enquire what this pertains to, sir?"

Darcy resisted the urge to push past the valet. The man was only doing his job. "Please tell Mr. Hurst that Mr. Bingley is leaving to marry Miss de Bourgh. I am also departing now, to collect other guests. The Earl of Matlock will be leaving here in one hour. If Mr. Hurst, Mrs. Hurst, or Miss Bingley wish to attend the ceremony, they should be ready to leave with him. I'm tasking your master with letting the ladies know in a timely fashion."

"I will convey that to him, sir." The valet bowed.

"Thank you," Darcy said.

"Did he say Bingley's getting married?" Mr. Hurst's surprised voice reached Darcy's ears as the door closed. He lengthened his stride, not wanting to be available to detain. Perhaps it was better he'd told the valet after all. Servants didn't argue.

Richard was waiting for him by the front door. "Good morning, Darcy."

"Richard," Darcy acknowledged with a nod. "Carriage ready?"

"It is."

They walked outside and into the waiting carriage. In short order, they reached Longbourn and collected Elizabeth and Miss Bennet. Darcy and Richard didn't share one seat, leaving the other to the ladies. Instead, they'd taken opposite sides, ensuring each man could sit beside his fiancée, or in Darcy's case, the woman he hoped would soon be his fiancée. None of the four spoke of the change, though they did, perhaps, sit closer to the person they were sharing with than was necessary in the comfortably wide seats.

When they reached the church, it was to find they were the last to arrive. Darcy was pleased to greet his sister, Mrs. Annesley and Lady Agatha. Miss Bingley and Mrs. Hurst both glowed with so much happiness, one would have thought they were brides. Mr. Hurst stood off to the side, looking half asleep still.

Darcy was glad they'd all managed to make it. Relatives weren't needed to validate a wedding, but having her Fitzwilliam cousins in attendance would show Anne she was cared for. Perhaps it would mitigate the fact that her mother wasn't there to see her wed, though Darcy was unsure this troubled Anne.

He didn't know how much Henry had told Lady Agatha, and assumed Georgiana knew little of the circumstances leading up to the nuptials, but trusted no one who knew Lady Catherine would be surprised by her lack of attendance. If anyone other than Anne actually regretted her not being there, Darcy would be amazed.

Finishing his greetings, he left Elizabeth, Richard and Miss Bennet with the throng of people, strolling to the front of the church where Anne, Henry and Bingley stood looking over some papers. Anne greeted him with a smile. Henry with a nod. A priest stood quietly off to the side.

Bingley looked relieved when he spotted Darcy. He proffered the papers. "Darcy, I've been waiting for you. I was hoping you would read over the contract for me before I sign. I've read it, but I want to see if you think it says what I think it says."

"I told you what it says." Henry sounded slightly annoyed.

Darcy lowered his eyes to the page, beginning to read. Blank spaces had been left for names of people and property. Those, and sums, were filled in Henry's hand.

"If you don't mind me saying, as Anne is your cousin, I feel you have a conflict of interests. You may behave impartially, or you may weigh things more heavily toward her best interests." A slight smile flickered over Bingley's face. "I don't know you well enough to know if you'd let her take advantage of my lack of legal aplomb."

Henry laughed. "If I thought you'd pose any challenge, I'd take offence and demand a duel."

Darcy glanced up from the page. "Bingley's a terrible fencer, but he's a crack shot."

"Darcy, don't encourage Henry to shoot my soon to be husband," Anne said. "Just read the document so you can assure Charles everything is in order."

Darcy did. It was straightforward. Bingley would not inherit Rosings, but any children of the marriage would. If there were no children, it would go to a niece of Anne's father. Bingley would have the right to half of the income from Rosings for his lifetime and Anne would have the right to the other half. If Bingley died prior to Anne, his half would revert to her. If she died first, though he wouldn't inherit, he would keep his income. "It appears correct to me." Darcy nodded to Henry. "I'm impressed you were able to get it written and here so quickly."

"I had no difficulty being motivating." Henry grinned. "After all, I was spending Bingley's money."

Anne and Bingley both signed the contract, with Henry and Darcy as witnesses. They waved the clergyman over. Darcy stayed beside Bingley, and Anne asked Miss Bingley to stand with her. As the vicar wended his way through the marriage ceremony in a reedy voice, Darcy was amused he didn't receive a single covetous glance from Miss Bingley. When her eyes did stray from the ceremony, they went immediately to Henry.

The ceremony was concluded with a chaste kiss. Bingley and Anne, arm in arm, walked down the aisle amid a shower of congratulations. Georgiana and Miss Bennet both looked misty eyed. Elizabeth appeared glad for the couple. Miss Bingley and Mrs. Hurst wore matching expressions of triumph.

They all filed out after the newlyweds, returning to Netherfield Park in a veritable fleet of carriages. The wedding breakfast was a happy affair, full of laughter and cousinly teasing. Darcy's spirits were lighter than they'd been in days. In addition to the fact that Lady Catherine would now be forced to give up her quest to marry him to Anne, it was pleasant to have Bingley as part of his family.

As the meal wound down, Darcy let his mind wander over the arrangements he must make. He'd have to ride ahead to Pemberley to ensure all was ready for the influx of guests. He realized he may as well invite Lady Agatha as well, and encourage Georgiana to join them. With the entire Bennet family, the Hursts, Miss Bingley, Mr. and Mrs. Bingley, Richard, Henry and Agatha, Pemberley would be fuller than it had been in years. There was more than enough room, of course, but it would be odd to have his home so enlivened. Georgiana would likely be horrified. For his part, Darcy found he was actually looking forward to it.

PEMBERLEY

"I once thought Mr. Wickham was an honorable man and your brother wasn't."

22

The day following Miss de Bourgh's wedding found Elizabeth ready to leave for Pemberley. She'd packed all of her possessions, sure she wouldn't be returning. Mr. Darcy would soon meet her father's requirements for consent to the marriage, and Pemberley would be her new home. Jane had packed similarly, for she and Colonel Fitzwilliam wouldn't return to Hertfordshire after Pemberley, but rather planned to travel to his residence in London.

Elizabeth stood in the middle of the room she and Jane had shared for so many years. It was empty of all that had made it theirs. All, that was, except the memories. Unstoppable tears slid down her cheeks, but they mingled sorrow with joy, for she and Jane were both leaving to be with men they loved. She heard Jane call her from below and dried her eyes.

She and Jane took their place in the procession of carriages in a coach containing Colonel Fitzwilliam and Miss Darcy. Miss Darcy's companion, Mrs. Annesley, was journeying back to London with Lady Agatha. There, they would collect Lady Agatha's and Georgiana's things before heading to join the others in Pemberley.

Elizabeth was pleased for the opportunity to get to know Miss Darcy better, but sad she couldn't know the same joy Jane did. Her sister and Colonel Fitzwilliam were quite clearly in love, and took no pains to hide how happy they were to travel together. Elizabeth, instead, must content herself with them and Miss Darcy. Fair travel companions indeed, but they didn't quite dull the ache she felt at Mr. Darcy's absence. She put a smile on her face, however, and told herself she was being silly. He'd left only the day before, to make his home ready for them, and she would be reunited with him before long.

More diverting than her travel companions were Lord Henry's antics. The earl had elected to drive his own open carriage. Each time they stopped to change horses, he invited a different unattached lady to ride with him. Miss Darcy declined to ride with her cousin, but Miss Bingley was elated to be invited, though Elizabeth heard her complain more than once about the inevitable dust. To her amusement, the bits of Mary's conversations with the earl that Elizabeth overheard seemed to contain earnest observation about the enhanced view. Kitty coughed so much that Lord Henry put her in with Mr. and Mrs. Bingley before they even reached the next scheduled stop. He never asked Elizabeth, which she hoped no one took note of. He did ask her mother once. To Elizabeth's surprise, Mrs. Bennet accepted. When they reached the next change of horses, her mother complained vehemently about the dust, but Elizabeth knew she would relish recounting every detail of her ride with an earl. In the end, Lord Henry's passenger alternated between Miss Bingley, Mary, and Lydia.

By the time they neared Pemberley, Miss Darcy had reemerged from her shell, once again relaxed as she'd been in the Girls' Garden at Lady Agatha's party. All four of them had agreed they should henceforth address each other on more intimate terms, as Richard was soon to be Elizabeth's brother and Georgiana was now fast friends with both sisters.

Elizabeth had worried Pemberley would be ornate, imposing and ostentatious, as she'd found Rosings. Instead, the carriage approached the most elegantly situated manor she'd ever thought to see. Mr. Darcy's home was placed in perfect accord with nature. The grounds they passed through evidenced the lightest, most desirable enforcements of man's will, leaving natural beauty unaltered. Elizabeth caught her breath, unable to believe this would be her home.

When they reached the end of the stately drive, they found Mr. Darcy waiting for them. Among the seeming hoard of people arriving, it took all of Elizabeth's will not to rush to his side. It seemed she must have forgotten how very handsome he was, or he'd somehow grown more so in little over a day. The smile he turned on her was warm, the sight of it making her blush with memories of their last kiss, stolen on the walk back from meeting with her father.

There would be no secret kisses among the throng of people descending from arriving carriages, though. There was only a polite greeting. Among the babble of voices, most prominent Mrs. Bennet's and Lydia's, Elizabeth looked over and took in Georgiana's dazed expression.

Giving up on finding a moment alone with Mr. Darcy for the time being, Elizabeth went to Georgiana's side, aware Jane excused herself from Richard to follow. "Georgiana, I know it's your duty as hostess to see to all of your guests, but Jane and I are hoping vehemently you could show us the best place to stroll the grounds. We've been so long seated in the carriage, our legs are in need of a stretch."

Georgiana turned to Elizabeth with grateful eyes. "Do you think it would be acceptable for me to show you? I should help see everyone situated. There are so many people, and someone needs to see to them." Her voice trailed off as she turned from Elizabeth back to the throng of guests, something near to fear widening her eyes.

"Jane and I are country sorts with no manners at all," Elizabeth assured her. "We've no idea it's impolite to take you away from your other guests by asking to see the grounds. You, however, are possessed of fine manners. Too fine to correct us in our request."

"And I think your brother and housekeeper have them in hand," Jane added, the smile she gave Georgiana gentle.

Georgiana glanced about quickly. "This way," she whispered.

That was the first of many walks the three of them took about the grounds in the following week. Everyone seemed to settle into Pemberley well, the large manor providing sufficient room for all. To Elizabeth's surprise, and relief, her mother was so awed by the grandeur of Pemberley and the company of Lady Agatha, who arrived the day after they had, she became subdued. She spent large quantities of time sitting in a room with Mrs. Bingley, Mrs. Hurst, Mrs. Annesley and Lady Agatha, quietly taking in their conversations. Elizabeth's father, for his part, was entranced with Mr. Darcy's library to the point there was no other place one might hope to find him. Mr. Bingley and Mr. Hurst often could be seen fishing.

Mary spent a great deal of time in the library as well, trying to improve herself, though she also played with Georgiana. Georgiana, who had been exposed to the benefit of excellent tutors for most of her life, quietly gave Mary advice. To everyone's relief, this resulted in a conspicuous improvement in Mary's playing. Noting it, Elizabeth began to join them as well. She knew her playing, too, could do with improving.

Lydia and Kitty spent much of their days about the grounds in the company of Lord Henry. Miss Bingley made valiant attempts to join them. They never dissuaded her, but it was readily apparent she didn't enjoy the activities they selected. She soon became peevish, snapping at even Jane.

Jane and Richard were permitted to be alone with each other often, a luxury not yet afforded Elizabeth and Mr. Darcy. Elizabeth disliked being jealous of her older sister, but couldn't help it. In spite of their distraction, both of her parents somehow managed to see her better chaperoned than they'd ever done before, while Jane had every happiness. Elizabeth's jealousy was a small thing, though, and didn't dampen her joy for Jane the first week the banns were read.

Later that day, the gentlemen busy, Elizabeth, Jane and Georgiana went for a stroll. They'd invited Miss Bingley, to be kind, but she'd informed them she had better occupations for herself than spending time in the company of Bennet women. Mary had elected to read instead, and the married women and Lady Agatha to extend tea. Kitty and Lydia were nowhere to be found. Feeling their duty to the others well executed, the three, fast friends by now, made their way to a particularly lovely glade, where green-tinted sunlight slipped through the leaves of ancient elms to dapple the ground.

Reaching the glade, Georgiana threw her arms out, turning in a slow circle, her face lifted toward the treetops. She let out a long, happy sounding sigh. "It's a perfect afternoon, don't you feel?"

"You seem to be in more than fine spirits today," Elizabeth observed with a smile.

"I am. I'm happy the first week of waiting for the wedding is through, making it that much sooner that Jane will be my cousin, and my brother told me this morning that Mr. Wickham left England. Somehow that makes me feel lighter inside. I was always afraid I would see him one day, and I was afraid he would tell people . . ." She trailed off, dropping her gaze from the leaves above to the ground.

"About the fact that you briefly agreed to elope with a man who was trusted by your father, but then you thought better of it?" Jane's tone was gentle.

Georgiana's head popped up. "You know?" She looked from Jane to Elizabeth. "Both of you?"

"I do, but I've told no one," Elizabeth said, turning a questioning look on her sister.

"Richard told me, and said you already knew, Elizabeth." Jane smiled at Georgiana. "You did make a mistake, but you corrected it before any harm was done."

"If people knew, they would look down on me." Georgiana's

voice was small.

"Jane and I know, and we don't look down on you," Elizabeth said.

"But I was wrong to agree to the elopement," Georgiana said. "How can I expect my brother to respect me after that?"

"Yes, you were wrong, but it's understandable and excusable." It was Elizabeth's turn to be embarrassed. "I once thought Mr. Wickham was an honorable man and your brother wasn't," she admitted. "Your brother has forgiven me for that. I doubt he was ever angry with you."

"He should have been, and disappointed as well," Georgiana said.

"I believe he was too livid with Mr. Wickham for there to be room in his heart for anything but relief toward you."

Georgiana's face looked glum. "That makes it worse. The blame wasn't entirely on Mr. Wickham. I should share it."

Elizabeth shook her head. "Don't you trust your brother?"

"Of course."

"Then you may trust his judgment in this. If he feels the blame belongs on Mr. Wickham, it does."

Georgiana's face became thoughtful. After a time, she shrugged. "I do trust my brother, and I realize I should trust his judgment about what happened. I just think he should have been angry with me."

"He didn't need to be," Elizabeth said. "You were sufficiently angry with yourself."

Georgiana sighed, then her face brightened. "Elizabeth, thank you for not telling anyone my secret, and you for not speaking of me behind my back, Jane."

"I would never have told," Elizabeth assured her. "I came to know it through . . . convoluted circumstance, but it was clearly not my secret to pass around. I wouldn't do that to you."

"Did you even know me when you found out? I know it must have been Fitzwilliam or Richard. They're the only ones who know."

"I didn't know you, but that didn't matter. It would have been wrong to tell." She gave Jane an apologetic look. "Even to Jane."

"Yes, Elizabeth is brilliant at keeping secrets, even from me." Jane's tone was amused, but Elizabeth narrowed her eyes, wondering at the statement.

"Well, I am lucky to have two such friends in my life, one of them soon to be my cousin." Georgiana turned a shy smile on Elizabeth. "And I can only hope the other will someday be my sister."

Elizabeth flushed, but she couldn't keep from smiling. "I hope the same."

Georgiana opened her mouth to say more, but Jane held up her hand. Elizabeth turned to her sister questioningly. A moment later, she heard the rumble of male voices. They soon clarified themselves into those of Mr. Darcy and Richard. A smile bloomed on Jane's face.

". . . sure they went this way?" Richard said.

"There is a glade just up here which Georgiana prefers excessively," Mr. Darcy replied. "I expect we shall find them there."

Elizabeth exchanged a smile with Georgiana. "I expect you shall indeed," she called.

Mr. Darcy and Richard came around a bend in the trail, marked by a large and ancient elm. Elizabeth looked on in envy as Jane hurried to Richard, taking his hands in hers. Mr. Darcy crossed to her and Georgiana, but all Elizabeth was allotted was a bow.

"Mr. Darcy, Richard, how nice to see you," Elizabeth said.

Mr. Darcy looked at his sister. "Mrs. Annesley wished for me to remind you that you're due for a lesson with your drawing master shortly."

Georgiana's eyes went wide. "Is it so late?" She looked from Elizabeth to Jane. "I have to return. Please don't let that spoil your walks." She dropped a curtsy and hurried away.

Mr. Darcy watched until she disappeared into the trees. He turned a smile on Elizabeth. "You and Georgiana seem to be getting along well."

"We are. So well, in fact, she let us in on her secret. I'm happy she did, because she still feels guilt and I welcome the opportunity to help her overcome it."

"Her secret?" Mr. Darcy asked, his smile disappearing.

"Her near elopement. She found out today that Jane and I both knew, but I didn't know Jane knew. I think it brought us closer in more ways than one. She was very happy to learn neither of us had shared that we knew her secret."

Mr. Darcy frowned. "Is that a reprimand to me?"

Elizabeth shook her head. "No. You were right to tell me. I needed to learn the truth about Mr. Wickham, and it was your secret as well. You were a part of it."

He nodded. "For a moment, I feared she had another secret." He still sounded worried, his eyes on the path his sister had disappeared down.

"If she does, she's not telling, but I doubt she does." Elizabeth glanced over her shoulder at Jane and Richard, only to find them already meandering off down one of the paths leaving the glade. She turned back to Mr. Darcy with narrowed eyes. He and Richard had obviously planned to meet them and send Georgiana away. She wondered if it was even time for Georgiana's drawing lesson.

She turned back to find Mr. Darcy offering his arm. "Come. There is a spot on the grounds I should like to show you, one I'm sure Georgiana has not."

Elizabeth took the proffered arm. The fabric of his sleeve was soft under her palm, for she hadn't donned gloves to walk the grounds with Jane and Georgiana. "I believe, sir, you have connived to rid me of my chaperones."

"What if I have?" he asked, leading her in the opposite direction Richard and Jane had gone.

"Then I applaud you."

"I'm looking forward to the day I don't have to do any conniving to get you alone," he said as they walked down a narrow path. "I've never had so many secret meetings as since I first proposed to you."

"Secret meetings? Oh, like Anne's wedding?" Elizabeth asked.

"I hadn't counted that one, but the first was the one Anne arranged and brought you to. I was unhappy when I saw you, but looking back, I'm delighted she did it. Henry, Richard, Bingley, and I even had secret meetings in Netherfield Park. We had them so often, it became routine."

"Secret from Miss Bingley and the Hursts?" she asked.

"Yes. Now all we need is privacy, not secrecy."

Elizabeth pressed nearer to Mr. Darcy on the narrow trail, rather than walking in file. She wasn't sure it was a truly meant for humans. It looked more like one left by deer. Mr. Darcy was correct that Georgiana had never suggested that path. Elizabeth hadn't even noticed it before, though it touched the edge of the glade.

The narrow track turned, circling a stand of soft pines, but Mr. Darcy didn't follow it. He stopped, pushing back the thick branches to reveal another glade, one encircled by dense conifers. A statue of Artemis stood in the middle, bathed in the lone beam of sunlight in the center of the clearing. She had her bow raised, the look she leveled across the space at once penetrating and thoughtful. The ground about her was thick with soft moss, mute testament to the solidity of the pines. Mr. Darcy ducked inside, pulling Elizabeth along with him.

"She's beautiful," Elizabeth said, walking in a slow circle about the statue, admiring the perfection achieved in every drape of cloth. "This place is lovely, but why is she here, closed in, with only a deer trail leading to her?"

Mr. Darcy was watching her walk. "She's been forgotten. In my grandfather's time, the trees were small. She stood above them. There was a trail of white stone. We have a painting of it in the green parlor."

"Yet, the trees obviously grew. No one thought to hinder them? How did you find her?" She'd come full circle now, and stopped before him.

"I used the painting. Rather, the painting inspired me to hunt for her." His gaze swept over the space before coming to rest once more on Elizabeth. "I don't know why she was forgotten, but I used to come here, to think."

Elizabeth searched his face. There was so much warmth there. Yes, it was austere, his fine features only adding to the image of the aloof aristocrat. Yet, his eyes were full of emotion. She'd seen the color of them stormy or light, as the mood took him. His mouth, too, told the tale of his inner feelings. Its perfect lines could be pulled taut with anger, or turned down in annoyance. Right now, though, his eyes were bright and his lips appeared inviting, turned up slightly at the corners.

"Thank you for bringing me here," she murmured, reaching up to lightly trace his smile. "She's extraordinary."

"You're extraordinary." He took her into his arms, and showed her just how expressive his lips could be.

***

The moment Darcy and Elizabeth returned to Pemberley, a footman met him and informed him that Mr. and Mrs. Bingley awaited him in his study. Darcy frowned, sure that must mean trouble, but turned to Elizabeth with a smile. The happiness shining in her eyes was enough to drive away all worry for Bingley and Anne. Not caring that they stood in the hall, he brought one of her hands to his lips. "I shall see you at dinner."

"I should hope so. I also hope nothing is too amiss with Mr. and Mrs. Bingley."

Reluctantly, Darcy released her. He nodded his agreement and left to find out. From the silence behind him, he knew Elizabeth watched him go. Moments later, as he drew near his study, he could hear someone speaking.

". . . done to Miss Bingley?" Richard's voice reached him through the open door. "Jane said she's been particularly venomous today."

Darcy paused, wondering if he'd misheard his footman about who awaited him, or where.

"I made her see I will not be marrying her," Henry said. "I took Miss Lydia and Miss Kitty fishing. Miss Bingley attempted to participate, comically so. She was obviously revolted. Miss Kitty was as well, actually, but she tried to do it."

"Miss Bingley isn't one to give up an earldom over baiting a hook and netting a few fish," Richard said.

Darcy grinned, picturing Miss Bingley trying to bait a hook while maintaining her all-important dignity.

"While we were at the stream, I also expounded on what I'm looking for in a wife." Henry's voice was amused. "I told them I expect to have a wife who hunts, climbs mountains with me and rides, or at least attempts to learn those things. I said I want someone who prefers to spend their summers outdoors. I also said I'd had more fun in Hertfordshire and here in Pemberley than I could dream of having in London. After I made that little speech, Miss Bingley left in a huff."

"What did Miss Lydia say?"

"She said she'd be happy to learn to do anything I enjoy doing."

Darcy could hear the delight in Henry's voice. Someone guffawed, but he wasn't sure which of his cousins it was.

"She said what?" Richard's words were garbled with laughter.

"How, I ask you, is any man to pass up an offer like that?" Henry said.

"Will you two grow up? Richard, send another footman to look for Darcy." Anne's tone was flat.

Darcy started forward, feeling a bit guilty. He hadn't meant to eavesdrop. He'd just been caught up in Henry's story. Long strides carried him rapidly into the room.

Richard, who was standing, sat back down, nodding in greeting. A glance showed he and Henry seated on either end of the long leather couch. Anne had taken one of the plush armchairs before Darcy's desk, and both were turned to face into the room. Bingley sat in the other,

217

several pages clutched in his hand and a scowl on his face. A man Darcy didn't know was off to the side, on the sofa across from Henry and Richard.

"There you are," Anne said. "Where have you been? No one could locate you."

Darcy took in the hard look on her face and the anger on Bingley's. He'd never seen either of them wear the expressions they wore now. "What's wrong?"

"Darcy, this is my attorney, Mr. Grey," Bingley said, standing.

Mr. Grey also stood, bowing. "Mr. Darcy."

"He came from Rosings," Bingley continued, before Darcy could speak. "They kicked him out. Two footmen grabbed his arms and forced him out."

Darcy rocked back on his heels. "Did they say why they were ejecting you? Please, sit."

Mr. Grey looked to Bingley, who nodded, before reseating himself. Darcy walked past Bingley and Anne, taking his place behind his desk. Bingley turned Anne's chair and his own, and everyone resettled.

Mr. Grey cleared his throat. "It was on Lady Catherine's orders, sir. She had, um, several areas of contention." He lifted a case and took out some papers, shuffling through them. "Her first statement is that her daughter's marriage is not legal." Mr. Grey glanced up quickly. "That is nonsense, of course." He looked back down at the papers. "Lady Catherine's second is that, if the marriage is legal, then it was not authorized by her, which she claims means Mrs. Bingley cannot inherit. I've seen a copy of Sir Lewis de Bourgh's will. That is also nonsense. Mrs. Bingley will gain full control of Rosings on her birthday."

Mr. Grey wiped his brow and shuffled through the papers again. "Lady Catherine also claims that even if the marriage didn't violate the terms of the will by taking place, the will states that Mrs. Bingley is not permitted to reside at Rosings if her husband has another residence. That is also not true. The existence of another residence has no bearing on Mrs. Bingley's rights to Rosings." More papers moved under his fidgeting fingers. "Lastly, Lady Catherine says her late husband's will states that so long as Mrs. Bingley resides at Rosings, Lady Catherine must also be permitted to live there." He looked up at them. "There is absolutely nothing in Sir Lewis's will that says that." He cleared his throat again. "As she informed me of these things, Lady Catherine didn't refer to Mrs. Bingley as Mrs. Bingley, but as Miss de Bourgh."

Darcy looked between Anne and Bingley. "What will you do?"

"What can we do?" Anne shook her head. "She's being completely unreasonable. My birthday is in two days." She raised her chin, her jaw set. "I think we must evict her."

Darcy held her gaze for a moment, trying to ascertain if she meant it enough to go through with it. If they began to remove Lady Catherine from Rosings but then relented, there would be no living with her. Seeing the resolve in his cousin's eyes, he turned to Mr. Grey. "Does Mr. Bingley have a legal right to evict Lady Catherine?"

"Yes, beginning two days from now, he does. Only, he'd better bring someone who can handle her footmen."

They all looked about the room at each other. Darcy took in the grim expressions, knowing one was mirrored on his face. If they did this thing, their aunt would never forgive them. Her anger would be unfathomable. With relief, though, a small part of him noted it wouldn't be aimed at Elizabeth any longer.

"Are you up to evicting her?" Henry asked Bingley, breaking the silence.

Bingley looked at Anne. "Are you certain that is what you want?"

"Yes," she said.

"Then I am up to it," Bingley said.

Darcy reached into his desk and pulled out several clean sheets of paper. "Anne, I think you'll need to make a list of the servants you wish to keep. With your permission, I'll write and have Lady Catherine's new residence made ready."

"Hand me over a page as well, Darcy," Henry said, standing to cross to the desk. "I'll write the magistrate."

"I think I must write a letter too," Richard said. "I have an idea. Does anyone recall the name of Aunt Catherine's doctor?"

"I do," Anne replied.

After handing over the requested sheets, Darcy set out several before himself. "Before we left London, Mr. Gardiner asked me if I knew where Lady Catherine's London agent lived or worked. He said he might be able to get some confirmation of Elizabeth's kidnapping. That could be helpful."

Feeling grim, Darcy offered pens and ink, and they set to writing.

KENT

Lady Catherine has been a thorn in the side of this community for too long.

23

They had to cancel the plans for Anne's birthday, for she insisted they set out the next morning to begin making arrangements to take hold of Rosings, and those arrangements would take several days. She and Bingley were to go first to Netherfield Park to gather any servants who were willing to move, then on to London to collect the others they would need. Before they left, to be followed shortly by Darcy, Richard and Henry, Bingley assured them he had a gift for Anne and would make her birthday special, no matter where they were.

Henry went to Kent to enlist the aid of the magistrate. It didn't surprise Darcy that Henry expected to meet Mr. Veitch without anyone noticing him. Henry's only concession to his safety and rank was to have his long-suffering valet go with him. Two riders, only packing what could be conveniently carried on their horses, wouldn't attract any attention.

Darcy and Richard headed to London where, with Mr. Gardiner's help, they began investigating Lady Catherine's agent there. They shortly received a letter from Henry informing them where to meet him and Mr. Veitch. He also enlightened them on his conversation with Lady Catherine's doctor, following up on Richard's letter to the man. Darcy and his cousin completed their investigation, a corroboration of Mr. Gardiner's findings coupled with a fruitless attempt to discover more, and headed to Kent. Before leaving London, they passed along their findings and Henry's information to Bingley and Anne, selecting a time to meet near Rosings.

When Darcy and Richard arrived at the magistrates, they found him and Henry waiting. "Henry, Mr. Veitch," Darcy acknowledged as the two settled themselves in his carriage. He directed his gaze to the magistrate, who'd taken the place across from him, beside Richard. "I hope you're firm in your resolve to aid us?" Darcy knocked on the roof, signaling they were ready to continue on to where they expected to find Anne and Bingley, and their caravan of carriages and wagons.

"I am." Mr. Veitch tugged at his cravat, but his expression was resolute. "Lady Catherine has been a thorn in the side of this community for too long." The magistrate looked about the carriage, appearing quite worried. He cleared his throat. "You should know, one of Lady Catherine's tenants came to me saying his twelve-year old son saw two footmen force a woman into Lady Catherine's carriage. The woman fought vigorously. From the description, it sounded like Miss Bennet. One of Mr. Collins servants said Miss Bennet arrived at the parsonage a few hours after this incident with fingermarks on her arms, and with a dirty and torn dress. I didn't have enough information to act, but I was wondering if you know anything about it?"

"I do," Darcy said. He detailed Elizabeth's abduction, trying to keep his voice calm. Mr. Veitch listened with mounting grimness. "We also have proof Lady Catherine sent a note to her agent in London to expect Miss Bennet to arrive there, hours before the kidnapping."

Henry nodded, looking satisfied by the news.

"I see. Miss Bennet's testimony and the agent's collaboration add considerably more information than I had." He nodded several times, looking thoughtful. "I would be willing to consider prosecution."

"So would we," Henry said, though Richard looked uncertain.

"I don't think we should make a decision on that yet," Darcy said.

It didn't take them long to reach Rosings, and they had only a short wait before Anne and Bingley appeared, staff in tow. Darcy's carriage led the caravan up the long drive. Reaching the imposing front façade, Darcy, Henry, Richard and Mr. Veitch got out. Anne and Bingley disembarked a moment later. Henry walked down the line of vehicles, waving a group of footmen out of one and gesturing for them to follow.

Darcy half-feared they would have to knock the door down, but it swung open as they neared. Ignoring the rest of them, Lady Catherine's butler fixed his eyes on Anne. "Welcome back, Miss de Bourgh."

"She is Mrs. Bingley," Bingley said.

"You've just lost your job," Henry said. "I suggest you pack your things."

"You can't--"

Henry pushed his way past the butler, the man's offended voice stuttering to a halt. The butler pressed himself against the wall as Darcy, Richard, Mr. Veitch and the Bingleys followed Henry into the ornate foyer. Four of the footmen they'd brought came in behind them. The butler, his eyes wide, turned and scurried away. Darcy hoped he wasn't going for reinforcements.

Henry stomped his way across the marble inlayed entryway and stopped. He looked back over his shoulder at Richard. "Which way?"

Richard moved to the front of the line, leading the way to Lady Catherine's favorite parlor. Idly, Darcy hoped Anne would toss out every bit of furniture in the room. None of it was comfortable, and all of it was ostentatious. Of course, Anne might prefer it. It was difficult to say what her tastes were, since she'd never been permitted to express them.

They all followed Richard into the crimson and gold themed room, forming a line of defiance between Lady Catherine and the door. She sat in her usual place, her skirts arranged about her in a grand billow of dark silk. To one side of her stood her steward, appearing almost like a guard beside a throne. Mrs. Jenkinson sat on her other side, looking pale.

Anne stepped forward, her spine ridged. "Mother, I have come to take my rightful place as mistress of Rosings. In view of your reaction to my marriage, I am requiring you to move to out. Have Dawson pack your possessions."

"No, you insolent, ungrateful child. This is my home. I am not leaving."

Bingley stepped up beside Anne. "I'm sorry, Lady Catherine, but you're wrong."

Lady Catherine didn't look at him, keeping her eyes on Anne. "Furthermore, I am ordering these cretins, these treacherous nephews of mine and other riffraff you've permitted to accompany you into my home, to depart immediately."

"No, Mother. This is my home and I have invited them here."

"This is not your home. You stupid, stupid girl. Can't you see your cousins have tricked you?" Lady Catherine surged to her feet. "They've married you off to some fool who will take Rosings from you, along with everything else you have. Then he'll cast you aside for that Bennet girl he was ogling last winter. Don't think that just because I don't gallivant about London that I don't know the truth. It was the talk of the season. How can you be so foolish as to think that man loves you? Look at you. No one will ever love you."

Bingley put a hand on Anne's shoulder. "You are wrong. I cannot imagine how you haven't noticed how wonderful your daughter is. I love her."

Anne looked at her husband in pleased surprise, but quickly turned back to her mother. She raised her chin. "That is enough, Mother. You are leaving."

"Mr. Veitch, tell these fools Rosings is mine," Lady Catherine cried, turning to the magistrate.

Mr. Veitch shook his head.

"You would take their side?" Lady Catherine screeched, and Darcy noticed he wasn't the only one who winced at her tone. "You imbecile. I will ruin you for this. I will see you hang."

"That's enough." Henry strolled forward. "I would order the footmen to do this, but it gives me great pleasure to see to it myself. Richard, Darcy."

Darcy and Richard moved toward Lady Catherine, following Henry.

She glared at them, her lips pulled back in a snarl. "You wouldn't dare."

"In fact, I would." Henry grabbed one of her arms.

Darcy took the other. Bodily, they lifted her off her chair. When she let her feet drag rather than walk, they carried her from the room. Richard went ahead, waving the footmen to follow, and ensured no one attempted to stop them. Lady Catherine fought and screamed all the way to Darcy's carriage.

Darcy and Henry put her inside and climbed in after. They went about it as gently as they could, though Darcy could still vividly recall the marks on Elizabeth's arms after her carriage ride with his aunt. Henry took a seat beside Lady Catherine, preventing her from attempting to get out. Richard joined them a moment later. The house Lady Catherine owned was just a mile away. She didn't stop belittling and berating them once during the drive.

When they arrived, Lady Catherine refused to disembark, forcing them to carry her inside. The home's caretaker was waiting, looking frightened and distraught. Darcy and Henry placed Lady Catherine in the first chair they saw, in the front parlor. The caretaker hurried forward with a glass of wine. She took it and threw it at him, staining his clothing and the carpet. Richard pulled the man into the hall and spoke to him too low for Darcy to hear, coming back a moment later alone.

Darcy, Henry and Richard took up seats about the room. Lady Catherine didn't attempt to leave, launching into a new series of rants against them and what they'd done, with particular emphasis on her view of their intelligence, or lack thereof. Rosings' servants began arriving, their possessions in tow. Darcy knew Anne planned to let most of them go, with a quarter's wages. Then a wagon came, loaded with Lady Catherine's possessions, including the furniture from her suite of rooms and her favorite parlor.

Those weren't the last rants Darcy and his cousins endured over the next few hours. They stayed with Lady Catherine, half to ensure she remained and half out of concern for her. Darcy weighted his feelings as such, at least. He was relatively sure Henry stayed only to keep their aunt from causing trouble, and that Richard was the most sympathetic toward her of the three of them. Enough food was brought over from Rosings to last Lady Catherine and her servants for a week. Darcy hadn't thought of that and appreciated Anne attending to it. When Lady Catherine seemed to have calmed somewhat, he sent a message to Bingley.

Bingley marched into the parlor, his stern look at odds with his pleasant face. He came to a halt before their aunt and bowed. "Lady Catherine."

Lady Catherine stared straight ahead, ignoring him.

Bingley's expression darkened. "Lady Catherine, do you still refuse to recognize Anne's and my marriage?"

"Do not refer to my daughter in that vulgarly familiar manner. She is not your wife. If you have touched her, I shall have you brought up on charges of assault."

"Really, Aunt Catherine," Richard said. "Try to be reasonable. Anne is twenty-five. She is legally permitted to make her own choices and fully able to do so. You're only making yourself miserable with this."

"Traitor," Lady Catherine spat out, glaring at Richard.

He sighed, shaking his head.

"I will take that as a yes," Bingley said. "In view of your refusal, I've come to inform you that you will not be permitted access to Rosings until you publicly acknowledge our union and Anne's change in status."

"Never," Lady Catherine said.

"Furthermore, several of the servants you were sent have agreed to keep us informed of your activities. Of course, we can't tell you which ones," Bingley said.

"What? That is intolerable. I'll let them all go and start over again."

"That is your choice," Bingley said. "We've thought of that possibility and will recruit new informants from anyone you hire."

"I'll keep them all here," Lady Catherine said. "No one will be allowed to leave."

"We've also talked to your doctor about declaring you of questionable mental stability," Henry said. "That might involve appointing a trustee to oversee your household."

"I suppose you bribed him," Lady Catherine snapped.

"Oddly enough, no," Henry said with a smile.

Darcy understood the smile. Henry hadn't offered the doctor money, but he was also bluffing. He'd included his full conversation with the doctor in the note he'd sent to London. The man had said he wasn't going to declare Lady Catherine insane. He'd gone on to make it clear he wasn't any more willing to do so than he was willing to declare Anne incompetent and added that he wished wealthy and titled people would stop trying to use him to solve their problems.

"Another thing," Bingley said, his tone hard. "Your coachman said he would testify against you concerning the abduction of Miss Bennet. Mrs. Bingley is keeping him on."

"Two people against three, and one of them a lady," Lady Catherine said with contempt.

"Three against three. There was a witness. We also have proof you sent a note to your agent in London to expect Miss Bennet to arrive there, hours before you abducted her."

Darcy smiled grimly.

"Elizabeth Bennet deserved it, the conniving hussy. It is your treatment of me that should be considered mad." Her eyes swept the room.

"You had her thrown in a carriage," Darcy said.

"The lot of you threw me into one. Me. Your own aunt."

"At least we didn't attempt to pack you off to London, alone, uncertain as to whether you would have cab money," Darcy said.

"What do you mean uncertain? I told her it would be attended to. She would have been well enough. Her sort knows how to handle themselves around all manner of low creatures."

Darcy had heard enough. "Her sort?" he repeated, his voice

coming out a low rumble of anger.

"Still entranced with the hoyden?" Lady Catherine asked. "Lift her skirts for you, did she?"

Darcy surged to his feet before he could stop himself. He clenched his fists at the smug smile on his aunt's face, wishing he hadn't let her know how well she was goading him.

"I see." Lady Catherine's tone was snide. "The real question is, how many came before you, and how many will there be after."

"Darcy," Henry said, putting out an arm.

Darcy looked down, realizing he'd taken a step forward. He shook his head. There was no reason to move any closer to his aged relation. He couldn't attack a woman, and he wouldn't sink to raising his voice. She would derive too much satisfaction from his loss of control. "If you'll excuse me," he said. He bowed to the room and stepped outside.

He didn't go anywhere, merely leaning against the wall beside the doorframe, just out of sight. He took several deep breaths, trying to regain his composure.

"Really, Aunt Catherine." It was Richard's voice. "That was uncalled for."

"He wouldn't react with such force if he didn't think it true. I'm helping Darcy out, making sure he faces up to what kind of woman she is before he does something irreparable."

"The kind of woman she is, Aunt Catherine, is kind, intelligent and good natured, and you'd do well to remember that."

Lady Catherine answered that by launching into another screaming rant.

"You've done all you can for the time being, Bingley," Richard said, his voice pitched loud enough to carry over Lady Catherine's. "In fact, I think we all have. You two can go to Rosings, or Pemberley, or where have you. Darcy too. Give me a moment with Aunt Catherine."

There was some shuffling inside the room. Henry and Bingley came out.

Seeing Darcy leaning against the wall, Henry gestured for him and Bingley to stay. "I want to wait a moment to make sure Richard can handle her." Henry's whispered voice barely reached Darcy's ears through Lady Catherine's screeching.

Darcy nodded, sharing Henry's concern. Lady Catherine wasn't a frail woman. If she became violent, Richard would have a time restraining her alone without harming her, something he wouldn't do.

Darcy had no desire to see is aunt harmed. They'd already won. She wouldn't have another opportunity to do injury. The scheme with Wickham had involved stealth. With so many eyes on her, it was unlikely she would be able to clandestinely recruit someone to attack any of them.

Still gesturing for them to remain, Henry walked to the front door and opened it. Closing it rather forcibly, he returned on silent feet, taking up a position alongside them. The moment Henry slammed the door, Lady Catherine's tirade broke off. Darcy realized she no longer had her intended audience. The yelling wasn't for her benefit, but to torment them. Richard had been correct to send them away. Then, he'd always been closest to her, if anyone could be considered close to their cantankerous aunt.

"I have every right to run Rosings." Lady Catherine's tone was peevish now. "I've run it well since Sir Lewis died. I ran it before he died."

"If he wanted you to have it, he would have willed it to you," Richard replied evenly. "You married Sir Lewis de Bourgh, not Rosings. You were left very well off. You know I've looked at the books. You've lived well at Rosings expense for years."

"I haven't cheated anyone. I paid for my own purchases and my personal maid."

"You've invited the guests you wanted, not the ones Anne wanted."

"Anne could have--"

"No, she couldn't have. Don't make me remind you how you've treated her." There was a long silence. "Anne corresponds regularly with Agatha, you realize," Richard continued. "All else aside, my sister knows you've never invited a single eligible man to Rosings. Not one who wouldn't repulse Anne, at least. Agatha has been very angry with you for that."

"Anne was supposed to marry Darcy," Lady Catherine muttered. "I didn't want to distract her."

"So you invited the sort of men who accidentally touch their dinner partners, and hired that idiot clergyman Collins, whom you knew would not support Anne and would not be interesting to her."

"He was my choice."

Darcy raised his eyebrows. He hadn't heard about the groping dinner companions, or realized his aunt had hired a clergyman Anne would never fall in love with. Lady Catherine, and Richard, were both more cunning than he'd realized.

"You had a right to make the choice, but you should have consulted Anne."

Again, silence filled the room. Darcy resisted the urge to look around the doorframe.

"Aunt Catherine, we're being as kind about this as we can," Richard said. "It could be much worse. Don't you see you've done things that are illegal? We had to stop you before you went too far. Even a lady can hang."

"Hang? Don't be absurd, Richard. I haven't done anything illegal, let alone to hang for."

"Forcing Miss Elizabeth into a carriage was kidnapping." Richard's voice was soft.

"You forced me to leave Rosings."

"I seem to remember you sent people to evict one of your tenants, what was it? Three or four years ago?"

"They hadn't paid their rent."

"Meaning they had no right to stay. You had no right to stay at Rosings."

"Rosings is mine," she snapped.

"No. It isn't, and hiring someone to kill Miss Elizabeth will not make it yours, and is a hanging offence."

Lady Catherine gasped. "I did no such thing."

"I read the letter you wrote to Mr. Wickham. He fled the country because he knew Miss Elizabeth wouldn't marry him and didn't want to be a murderer. He was afraid of what you would do to him."

Lady Catherine started laughing. For his part, Darcy didn't find anything amusing in what Richard said. Beside him, Bingley shifted. Darcy looked over to see him frowning.

"Fled the country?" Lady Catherine chortled. "I was only going to write an angry letter to my cousin in the government. He would have been able to have Mr. Wickham dismissed from his post. He's no loss to the militia, I'm sure. I didn't ask him to murder her."

"You said he should separate her from Darcy by any means," Richard said in that same calm tone.

Darcy clenched his fists again, impressed with his cousin's forbearance. Obviously, it was the right way to handle Lady Catherine, as she was calming. Darcy wasn't sure he'd be able to manage it, though.

"I didn't mean murder."

"What did you mean?"

"He should compromise her. Seduce her, if necessary. Darcy wouldn't marry her then. She may be alluring to him, but he'd have no use for Wickham's used goods."

Darcy started to move forward in anger, but Henry reached past Bingley and caught his arm. Reluctantly, Darcy stepped back against the wall.

"And if she'd refused to be compromised or seduced? How did you expect him to accomplish that without some cooperation on her part? Even if you won't believe Miss Elizabeth loves Darcy, you can't imagine a woman who had him on the line would willingly find herself in Mr. Wickham's embrace."

This time, the silence stretched out long enough that Darcy began to wonder if they should leave.

"If you thought you were doing something acceptable, you would have signed the letter," Richard said.

A strange sound came from the room. Bingley turned questioning eyes on him. Darcy held up a hand, trying to identify the noise. After a moment he looked past Bingley to Henry, who appeared as stunned as Darcy felt. Lady Catherine was weeping.

"I'm going to be married soon," Richard said. "If you invite me, I'll come and stay with you. I may not be able to stay more than a short time, because I've heard they will be giving me a regiment to command. If you want my company, you've only to ask, but you must invite my wife as well, and she is Miss Bennet's sister. She is the kindest woman I've ever known. She is aware of what you've done, and tried to do, to her sister, but she will forgive you. If you let yourself, I'm sure you'll come to care for her."

A chair creaked against the backdrop of Lady Catherine's growing sobs. Footsteps crossed the room. Richard came out. He nodded to them, seeming unsurprised to see them there. With a gesture for them to follow, he led the way to the door.

Once they were outside, Bingley offered each of them his hand, in turn. "Thank you, gentlemen, my lord. I couldn't have done this without you. In spite of everything you three and Anne told me, I didn't realize Lady Catherine was so . . ." He trailed off, looking about helplessly.

"Formidable?" Richard supplied.

"Unyielding?" Darcy suggested.

"Stark raving mad?" Henry said, grinning.

Bingley chuckled. "Perhaps all three. Regardless, you have my thanks. Will you join us at Rosings? I'm sure Anne would be happy to have you."

Darcy didn't care to. He wouldn't admit it to his cousins or Bingley, but he missed Elizabeth. Waking up each morning knowing he wouldn't see her was bleeding his days of any trace of happiness. He glanced at Richard, who gave a slight shake of his head in the negative. Henry, Darcy noted, was grinning at the two of them.

"No, thank you," Darcy said, realizing he'd let the silence go on too long. "We have to return to help ready for Richard's wedding. We'll still see you and Anne for it?"

"We wouldn't miss it," Bingley said. "I'm sure we'll have things well enough in hand here by then. We nearly do. Mr. Veitch plans to watch Lady Catherine and made it very clear he wouldn't stand for her returning to Rosings. Also, we're finding more of the servants were loyal to Anne than we'd suspected, especially the maids and kitchen staff. She was kind to the maids and she ate the cook's food, not sending every dish back with a reprimand. It's more a few key positions we need to fill, and we can borrow from Netherfield while we sort it all out."

"Did you really tell the servants to spy on Lady Catherine?" Henry asked.

Bingley looked a bit embarrassed. "No. It was Anne's idea to say we were. She made the servants come in one at a time for their wages and she kept some a little longer. James and John were each kept for much longer. I'm sure someone will report it to Lady Catherine as suspicious."

That did seem too devious for Bingley, but Darcy found himself unsurprised that Anne had thought of it. "We'll expect you soon, then," Darcy said.

Bingley left and Darcy set about organizing their return to Pemberley, chaffing at every delay. By the time their property and servants were sorted and all the proper instructions given, his mood was one of impatience. He ushered Henry and Richard into the carriage and knocked on the roof to signal they could be on their way.

Darcy settled into his seat, letting his mind turn to Elizabeth. They were leaving late enough in the day that they might have to spend three nights on the road, so he would have to wait to tell her what had happened in Kent. He worried over what details he should gloss over, to spare her feelings, or if he should tell her all. He was eager to walk beside her again. To hear her voice and her soft laughter. Perhaps visit their glade. Maybe—

"A bit on edge, aren't you, Darcy?" Henry's voice intruded into Darcy's thoughts. "Keen to be reunited with a certain beguiling pair of eyes, among Miss Elizabeth's other assets?"

Darcy turned a repressive frown on Henry, but that only elicited a grin.

"I don't know about Darcy, but I'm keen on seeing Jane again. I can't say I haven't missed her," Richard said. "Now that Aunt Catherine's in hand, you shouldn't have any trouble getting Mr. Bennet's permission to marry Elizabeth, Darcy."

"Would you like me to put in a good word for you?" Henry asked.

"No." Darcy doubted he'd need help, or that anything Henry would say would be helpful.

"It's too bad he refused you before," Henry said. "You're a week behind Richard. Otherwise, you could have had a double wedding."

"You jest, but it would have made Jane happy." A look of guilt flashed across Richard's face. "I know Elizabeth hasn't told Jane about your most recent proposal and Mr. Bennet's refusal. I'm afraid I did. I can't seem to help myself. I tell her everything. She's so accepting, and she always places things in a pleasant light, leaving my world brighter than before we conversed." He shrugged. "The point is, she would have liked a double wedding."

"So put yours off," Henry said.

Richard's eyes widened. "I, that is, rather--"

Henry laughed, slapping his brother on the back. He reached into his coat and pulled out some papers. Opening one, he read it, refolded it and put it back. He handed one to Darcy and another to Richard. "I think I have a solution."

"What's this?" Darcy opened it as he asked. To his surprise, it was a special license for him and Elizabeth. He looked up at Henry. "How do you have this?"

"I got it at the same time as Anne's. If you're going to let an archbishop do you a favor, there's no reason to make it easy on him."

Darcy didn't try to hide his smile.

PEMBERLEY

In mere hours, Elizabeth would be his. Forever.

24

The day before their weddings, Elizabeth and Jane were listening to Mary and Georgiana practice the duets they planned to play for the celebration to be held on the marrow. Jane and Richard would have the luxury of leaving the day following the weddings, but Elizabeth and Mr. Darcy would remain in Pemberley, and their guests would as well, at least for a few days. Then, everyone would depart, including Georgiana, who would return to London with Lady Agatha and Mrs. Annesley.

Miss Bingley, who sat reading as far away from Elizabeth and Jane as the room permitted, would also be returning to London, along with the Hursts. She had a sour expression on her face. Elizabeth assumed she was only in the same room as they were because she was too proud to visibly mope. Looking at Miss Bingley's pinched face, Elizabeth tried not to be annoyed that she and Mr. Darcy must entertain guests on their wedding day. She supposed that was why people didn't normally host their own nuptials, or at least partially so.

Elizabeth turned her attention from Miss Bingley and back to the happier occupation of listening to Mary and Georgiana play. There was a rustle of fabric. Elizabeth turned to see her mother fly into the room, followed by the other married ladies. They were quite the parade. The group had regained Anne several days ago, and been augmented by Mrs. Gardiner when she and Uncle Gardiner arrived for the weddings. They'd been spending their afternoons in cheerful discussion in a sunny parlor on the west side of the manor.

Cheerful discussion had obviously given way to something more lively today. Mrs. Bennet's face was red and her breath ragged. Elizabeth stared at her in surprise, for she'd grown accustomed to her mother's of-late more decorous ways. Mary and Georgiana stopped playing. Both looked over with startled expressions.

"Where is Mr. Bennet?" Elizabeth's mother cried, waving a piece of paper.

Jane stood. "Mother, what's wrong? Is everyone well?"

Elizabeth scrutinized the array of women who'd followed her mother in. Mrs. Hurst looked annoyed, which would have been typical a month ago, but was an expression she'd worn much less often since Mr. Bingley's wedding. Mrs. Annesley's expression was neutral, Mrs. Gardiner's undecipherable. Anne and Lady Agatha both appeared amused. "He's not in the library?" Elizabeth suggested.

"How can my nerves be expected to take a shock like this?" Mrs. Bennet cried, collapsing onto a sofa.

Mrs. Gardiner glanced at her, then turned back to Elizabeth and Jane. "He is not. We looked there first."

"Weren't he and Uncle Gardiner speaking to Mr. Darcy about fishing today?" Mary said from where she and Georgiana still sat at the piano.

Mrs. Bennet let out a chortling cry. Jane hurried across the room to her.

Elizabeth followed, worried her mother had spilled over the edge into madness. Perhaps repressing her volatility these long weeks in Pemberley had done her mind harm. "Mother, what is the matter?"

Her mother waved the paper she held. Elizabeth wasn't sure if she was crying or laughing, and wondered if they should slap her. She decided to read the page first, and caught it after one failed attempt. It contained Lydia's handwriting. Elizabeth held it so Jane could read it with her.

"Lydia and the Earl of Matlock?" Elizabeth breathed, shocked.

"Your sister and Lord Henry?" Miss Bingley surged to her feet. "Why are they contained jointly in a letter?"

Elizabeth had all but forgotten Miss Bingley was there.

"They've eloped," Mrs. Bennet cried.

Elizabeth realized her mother really was laughing. Not sobbing, or in hysterics, but practically giggling with joy.

"They what?" Miss Bingley screeched. The book she was holding dropped to the floor with a thud.

"Not really eloped, Mama," Jane said, looking up from the letter. "It says they took Kitty with them as a chaperone for Lydia so it would all be proper before they married and that Papa gave his blessing."

"Gave it in writing, with witnesses signing as well," Elizabeth added. "Very thorough. It seems more of a marriage than an elopement, though they did run off this morning to do it."

"Married?" Miss Bingley's second screech, louder than the first, caused Elizabeth to wince. "The Earl of Matlock has married your sister?"

Elizabeth composed her face. "So the letter says." She looked around the room. "You've all seen it?"

The gathered women nodded.

Elizabeth turned to Miss Bingley. "If I understand properly, they should be back soon. They have a special license and left early this morning. It's not really an elopement, but it was unkind of Father not to tell us."

Miss Bingley let out a high-pitched wail. It echoed about the room as she ran forward, pushing the ladies arrayed across the end of the room aside to reach the door. The sound, uninterrupted, trailed back to them as Miss Bingley fled down the hall.

"Jane with a dashing colonel, Lizzy to one of the wealthiest men in England, and now Lydia to an earl. An earl," Mrs. Bennet reiterated.

Elizabeth grimaced, casting an embarrassed glance at the women still gathered to either side of the doorway. This was precisely the sort of carrying on she'd been pleased not to see from her mother in recent weeks. The others, though, merely looked amused.

"Yes, Mama, we all heard," Mary muttered.

Jane sighed. "Trust Lydia to run off and get married the day before our weddings."

"It's better than trying to steal attention from us during our weddings," Elizabeth said.

Mrs. Hurst had turned to face down the hall. "Caroline took that better than I expected."

Elizabeth wondered how Miss Bingley could have behaved worse, but decided she didn't wish to know.

"An earl," Mrs. Bennet murmured, chuckling.

Georgiana stood up, drawing everyone's eyes. She flushed. "I guess, that is, I mean, congratulations are in order. We should arrange something special for their return." She looked around. "Shouldn't we?"

Lady Agatha smiled at her. "Yes, dear, that would be lovely."

***

239

Darcy reclined on one of the sofa's in the library, a snifter held loosely in one hand. He and his cousins were enjoying a quiet drink. There had been many toasts at dinner, perhaps more than were wise. They'd Henry's marriage to celebrate, and Darcy's and Richard's upcoming weddings in the morning to raise their glasses to. Now, though, the celebrating was over for a time. It was quite late. Everyone else had retired. Darcy knew he should as well, but he was too comfortable to move.

Richard chuckled. "I can't believe you married that girl, Henry."

"Why's that? You're marrying a Bennet girl. Pretty things, most of them."

"She's half your age," Darcy felt compelled to mention.

"The good half."

Darcy wasn't quite sure what that meant, but he joined Richard and Henry in laughing.

"Be serious, though. Why did you run off and do it?" Richard asked.

"You're not making sense. Do you want to know why I married her or why we ran off?"

"Both," Darcy said.

Henry shrugged. "We ran off because Lydia thought it would be fun. She wanted to be the first to marry, and she thinks eloping is romantic. She also wants to lord over her two oldest sisters with her new rank. In the normal course of events, we would marry and then leave. Now she gets to do it and stay for their weddings."

"You eloped to encourage your wife's bad behavior?" Richard said incredulously.

"She'll get over it. She needs to do it somewhere. Her family doesn't respect her, so this won't change anything."

Darcy frowned, thinking that through. It seemed to make a great deal of sense, but he was aware he'd drank a bit more than usual. "Why her?"

"Describe her," Henry said.

"She's tall, she's fair, she's got--" Richard began.

"Not physically. Describe her character," Henry cut in.

"Headstrong. Energetic. Cheerful. Heedless of what others think. Not very bright," Darcy offered.

"Now describe me," Henry said.

Darcy saw his cousin's point, but he shook his head. "You're much more intelligent than she is and you care what others think."

"I was stupid when I was her age and didn't care what people thought. Now, I court good opinion when it's useful to me. It often is. I'll teach her the advantages of that."

Darcy muddled his way through that one. "Wait, if you court good opinion because it's useful, why were you courting it in Hertfordshire? What did it gain you?"

"I did it to help you."

"Now you're not making sense," Darcy said. "Not a lick of it."

"Darcy, barring Richard, you're the best friend I have."

"Why thank you, Henry. You always say that when you're drinking my liquor, though."

"I'm being serious here. Look, I know how you behave with people you think are beneath you, and we all know you offend them. I knew you liked Elizabeth, and I could see the look on her face when you were snobbish. At first, I considered behaving even worse than you, to make you seem reasonable by comparison. As an earl, I might have gotten away with it. I decided, though, that people would only end up hating us both. I opted instead to lead by example. I hoped seeing me treating the locals like peers would help you unbend a little. You exceeded my expectations."

"That does make a kind of sense," Richard said.

"Does it?" Darcy frowned. He hadn't changed because of Henry, but rather for Elizabeth. Henry had made it easier, though. His cousin didn't need to know he wasn't solely responsible. Darcy always liked to encourage Henry to do good deeds. "Thank you. In truth, once I got used to it, it became fun."

"It was fun," Henry agreed. "Sometimes it's nice to turn protocol on its head. Besides, you did me a favor at Agatha's party. I wanted to return it."

"A favor? All I recall from that day was trouncing you in fencing," Darcy said smugly.

"You did, and you put me in my place. I went home and asked myself what would happen if I put Peter's eye out or killed him. I think I would shoot myself."

"That's a bit dramatic," Richard said.

"It is?" Henry shrugged.

Darcy saluted his cousin with his glass. "Happy to have helped."

"Well, I can't give you all the credit," Henry said. "It was my horse falling that finally convinced me. My horse didn't fall because I was a bad rider or he a bad horse. I put him in a position he wasn't able to handle. He's rounded many sharp corners before, but this time he failed. What if Peter, or some other fencer, wasn't up to the challenge one day? Even with the button on the end, a foil could blind someone."

Darcy looked at him soberly.

"Do you mean to say you, Lord Henry, Earl of Matlock, are going to take up fencing in a mask?" Richard said.

Henry grimaced. "I hate to admit it, but I'm getting older. Someday, the failure could be mine. From now on, I'll wear a mask and encourage Peter to do so too."

"To Henry's horse," Darcy said, downing what remained in his glass. He rose unsteadily to his feet and crossed to the sideboard.

"Darcy."

He turned to find Henry and Richard standing as well. He raised an eyebrow inquiringly. "More?"

Richard nodded, crossing the room.

Henry shook his head, looking amused. "No, not for me. I have a girl half my age waiting for me upstairs, remember?"

"You realize it didn't go unnoticed that you and your wife disappeared for an hour or more this afternoon," Richard said.

"I still expect to go upstairs to my young wife," Henry replied smugly.

"Right. That's worth drinking to." Darcy turned back to the crystal laden shelf.

"Darcy," Henry repeated.

He turned back again. "Change your mind?"

"I didn't, but you have," Henry said. He turned to his brother, who was reaching for the crystal bottle. "Neither of you should have any more. My wedding was uncomplicated and only witnessed by a couple of people. Both of you will be upholding the Fitzwilliam name tomorrow. You can't do that with a hangover."

"The Darcy name," Darcy said.

"Your first name is Fitzwilliam," Richard said. "You have to uphold both first and last names."

Darcy found that funny, but realized he wouldn't have sober. For that matter, if Richard hadn't already had a few, he wouldn't have said it. Darcy put his glass down.

Richard looked at the glass in his hand and grimaced, setting it beside Darcy's. "We've already had too much."

"Do either of you need an escort to your rooms?" Henry asked.

Darcy exchanged a glance with Richard. "I think I can make it back to my room without being sidetracked by grapes." It was too silly a joke to make while sober.

"Until morning, then, gentlemen." Henry bowed. He turned away, strolling from the room with a jaunty stride.

Richard saluted and left. Darcy headed toward his room, unable to stop grinning. In mere hours, Elizabeth would be his. Forever. He started whistling.

25

Because Jane was the elder, they'd decided she should marry first, rather than alternate vows. Elizabeth stood in the pew with her mother, Mary and Kitty. Her mother silently took her hand, and tears welled up in Elizabeth's eyes. These were her last moments as her parents' daughter. Soon, she would be a man's wife. Not Elizabeth Bennet any longer, but Elizabeth Darcy.

Jane stood before the priest with Richard, smiling happily. Elizabeth was sure her sister was the most beautiful, luminous bride the world had ever known. From the besotted look on Richard's face, he felt the same.

Jane wedding was a change too. Elizabeth tried to quell her tears, not wanting to be puffy-eyed when she married Mr. Darcy, but it was impossible not to cry. Jane looked so quietly joyous, and Elizabeth was losing her best friend forever. Her mother squeezed her hand, dabbing at her own eyes.

Elizabeth cast a glance about the church, smiling through her tears. It turned out Lady Agatha and the married women hadn't been spending their days in idle chatter as Elizabeth had assumed. To her surprise and utter delight, they'd arranged a trousseau for her and for Jane. Jane's was a practical trousseau, with fabric for bed linens, table linens, and towels, and enough lengths of fabrics for several dresses.

Since Pemberley had no need of those things, Elizabeth's consisted of fine fabric and lace to be made up the way she wanted it. There was a glorious peignoir and one dress made from her measurements, but the choices of styles for the rest would be hers. Anne had paid for it all, and Elizabeth wondered, as she had at the last gift, if this was Anne's way of paying Elizabeth for her help without having to turn over five thousand pounds. Not that she would ever ask for it, or begrudge Anne it. Elizabeth hadn't helped Anne because she'd offered money, and she and Lydia could now both ensure their mother, Mary and Kitty were well looked after.

The colluding ladies had also likely emptied an entire hothouse of its content. Pemberley and the church overflowed with flowers. Likewise, a chandler had certainly been bought out, for Elizabeth had never seen so many candles lit at once. Their honeyed aroma wafted through the chamber, nebulous and sweet. It mingled with the scent of the flowers Elizabeth wore in her hair. She felt like royalty, and the chapel was a kingdom created by magic.

As the clergyman droned through the words of the ceremony in a plodding rhythm, Elizabeth stole a quick glance about the church at the guests. The morning sun and stained glass windows colluded to spread a rainbow of hues across them, adding to the illusion of magic created by the candles and flowers. Her heart filled with love for the smiling faces filling the chapel. Her mother and father, the Gardiners, her sisters, her soon to be new sister and cousins. So much happiness, and she and Jane were the center of it.

If Miss Bingley sat in the back, scowling, that didn't trouble Elizabeth today. Nor did Lydia's pout as she looked about at the magnificently decorated church. Nothing troubled Elizabeth today, for she was marrying Mr. Darcy.

She peered around her family at him, finding him looking back, the warmth in his eyes bringing a blush to her cheeks. How was it possible she was marrying such a handsome, kind, honorable man? She knew there'd been a time when she thought otherwise of him, but that seemed laughable now. A momentary descent into insanity. One fortunately well behind her.

Elizabeth turned back to watch Jane and Richard exchange their vows, her eyes dry again. Yes, parts of her life were ending, but the kindness and regard of the people sharing the church with her that morning never would. Her family wasn't becoming smaller, but growing.

Then Richard was placing a ring on Jane's finger, and their vows were coming to the conclusion. The clergyman led them through the traditional prayer. Smiling at them, he proclaimed them man and wife. Jane blushed as Richard placed a single kiss on her upturned lips. Taking her hand, he turned her toward the assemblage, his face wreathed in happiness. They walked down the aisle amidst congratulations and well wishes, to take their place, together, in the pew. Elizabeth felt tears build in her eyes once more, taking in how

Jane kept looking up at her new husband, her eyes shining.

Elizabeth's mother let go of her hand, urging her forward, and she realized it was her turn. She felt dizzy. She felt elated. She couldn't remember what they'd spoken of, how they'd planned she should traverse the change from onlooker to bride. It didn't matter, because Mr. Darcy was waiting for her at the end of the aisle. She went to him. Together, they took their place before the clergyman.

He began the ceremony again, but Elizabeth wasn't listening this time. She was watching Mr. Darcy's face, cherishing every detail. She knew the clergyman was speaking. She even managed to form the correct words at the right times. At least, she hoped they were correct. No one laughed or gasped, so she assumed they were. Her head seemed full of a joyful, murmuring buzz, the setting dreamlike and unreal. She felt almost as if she floated on a sea of happiness, not quite touching the ground.

Which would be good, she thought, craning her head back as she looked at Mr. Darcy. Floating would make her taller. "I will," she said in response to the priest's words.

Mr. Darcy's warm hands enveloped hers. He slid a ring onto her finger.

"Those whom God hath joined together let no man put asunder," the clergyman said. He began leading them through the final prayer. Again, Elizabeth said the words she knew she was to say, not needing to think about them. Not needing to do anything but look into Mr. Darcy's eyes.

Silence fell. Elizabeth blinked, realizing the ceremony was over. Slowly, a smile turned up her lips, mirrored on her husband's face. Then she was in his arms, and he was kissing her. It wasn't the chaste kiss Mr. Bingley had given Anne, or the tentatively sweet one they'd all seen Jane receive a short time ago. Mr. Darcy's kiss was fire, and light, and Elizabeth wasn't sure she was even breathing, but she was sure she didn't need to. Not if it meant ending their kiss.

Cheers and laughter blundered their way into Elizabeth's awareness. Mr. Darcy's mouth smiled against hers, a sweet ending to their first kiss as husband and wife. She tilted her head back to look into his eyes, finding them alive with amusement.

"I think we are putting on a show," he murmured.

"This troubles you?"

"Not in the least."

He covered her lips with his again. The clergyman cleared his throat. Mr. Darcy broke off their kiss, casting the man a sheepish look. Elizabeth blushed, having forgotten the clergyman stood beside them. Her husband offered his arm. Elizabeth took it, allowing him to escort her through a sea of smiling faces and from the church.

The wedding breakfast was magnificent, the entertainments of the day splendid. Still, Elizabeth had to work to enjoy them. She spent too many moments not attending to what went on about her, her eyes seeking out Mr. Darcy.

When the hour arrived and Elizabeth retired, it suddenly seemed as if the day had sped by. Minutes and hours that had dragged were gone, leaving only moments before her husband would open the door adjoining her new chamber to his. She sat at the unfamiliar dressing table, turning a brush in her hand, her hair hanging unbound about her shoulders. She was wearing the new nightgown the other married women and Lady Agatha had selected for her. It was lace and ribbons and soft, shear material, and she couldn't believe, and didn't like to consider, that the group of them had spent time selecting it.

There was a click. Elizabeth swiveled in her chair, watching the door to Mr. Darcy's room swing open. He stepped through, bereft of his shoes, jacket, waistcoat and cravat. He closed the door softly behind him, crossing to her. Elizabeth found herself hardly able to breath, let alone move. It was all she could do to tilt her head back, keeping her eyes on his. He looked down at her for a long moment, his gaze traveling over her nightgown while she blushed.

"Elizabeth," he murmured, holding out a hand.

She put the hairbrush down with a loud clatter. Her hand shaking, she placed it in his. He pulled her to her feet. Elizabeth drew in a deep breath, her trembling stilled by his nearness. His presence was reassuring, chasing away any fears she had of what was to come. This was Mr. Darcy, and he loved her.

"Mr. Darcy," she said, finally responding to his greeting.

"Now that we're in private, there's something I was hoping you would do." He took her in his arms.

"And what was that?" she asked, blushing again.

"Call me Darcy."

"Not Fitzwilliam?"

"Only my relatives ever call me that and you, thankfully, are not among them."

"Well, I am your wife. I thought we'd quite settled that."

"Oh, we have."

His lips descended on hers, and Elizabeth knew their joy would endure forever.

***

Three days after her wedding, Elizabeth finally found time for a quiet walk with her father. As happy as she was in her new home, she knew she would miss him terribly. While she loved all of her family, Jane and her father were dearest to her. Elizabeth knew from her trip to Kent that not having them in her daily life left a painful hole.

They strolled along a wooded path, keeping near the house. Not only were the farther reaching paths a domain for her and Darcy alone, Elizabeth knew her father tired more easily than he liked to let anyone see. She made sure to steer them away from paths that would require a long journey back.

Mr. Bennet walked at a slightly slower pace than Elizabeth would have otherwise, his hands clasped behind his back. "I like your Mr. Darcy. He's put up with us with considerable patience."

"Mr. Darcy has come to care for you all, though Lydia seems to be making a special effort to be a trial to everyone's patience," Elizabeth replied.

Her father nodded. "Mrs. Bennet enjoys her calling by her title, but I don't like Lydia insisting on it."

"When I call Lord Henry by his, he corrects me, insisting I call him Henry or Matlock. He's been calling me Elizabeth. Maybe Lydia will learn by his example."

Mr. Bennet shrugged. "That's his problem now."

"I hope all of our problems are as trivial."

"I hope so as well, my dear, but it seems to me you haven't any. Anyone can see your marriage is getting on well. You practically glow, and the two of you can't keep your eyes from each other, or your hands."

She blushed, vowing to try not to be as affectionate with her husband when other people were about. Then she smiled, unsure if she could keep her vow, especially if Darcy wouldn't join her in it. Her smile grew. Not that she'd ask him to.

"Jane and Richard seemed happy as well, but I'm not sure Jane has your glow," Mr. Bennet said, his tone thoughtful. "I hope their visiting Lady Catherine isn't a mistake."

"They can leave if it doesn't work out. As to the glow, I think they are both better at hiding their feelings than Mr. Darcy and I are."

They walked some more, conversing about trivial things. As they reached the final turn back toward the house, her father stopped. Elizabeth did as well, turning to him questioningly, wondering if anything was wrong.

"Before I leave tomorrow, I want to thank you for the money you and Darcy have settled on Jane, Mary, and Kitty."

Elizabeth shook her head. "Really, it isn't much. I wish I could do more."

"I must admit, I'm surprised Mrs. Bingley gave it to you. I agreed with your uncle, thinking she wouldn't honor the bargain you and she struck. I'm also pleased you did as your uncle advised and settled it on your sisters. Although you have a wealthy husband now, it still speaks well of you."

"I wouldn't have held it against Anne if she hadn't kept her word. I wasn't sure if we truly struck the bargain, and I feel guilty accepting money from her. I only did so because Uncle Gardiner persuaded me that it was my duty to accept it if it would do my sisters good. I don't need it now, and Lydia certainly doesn't."

"As I said, how you handled the money speaks well of you. It also speaks well of Mrs. Bingley that she kept her word."

Elizabeth smiled, happy to let him think so. She'd been surprised when, the day after her wedding, Mr. Bingley spoke to her about where to send the money. She hadn't expected Anne to remember their tentative bargain, or honor it. Especially not after the money she'd spent on Elizabeth's and Jane's trousseaus. Elizabeth had been both stunned and gratified.

It wasn't until later that evening, when she and Darcy were alone, that she'd learned the truth. Mr. Bingley, having become acquainted with the details of the original scheme, had told Anne she must honor her word. Anne, apparently, hadn't wanted to give Elizabeth the money. She'd told Mr. Bingley she hadn't signed anything. She'd gone on to argue that Elizabeth hadn't ended up doing much, had benefited from Darcy's courtship excessively, and didn't need the money.

Apparently, Mr. Bingley had responded that a person was only as good as their word and told Anne she was acting like her mother.

Elizabeth had gathered from Darcy's explanation, passed along from Mr. Bingley, that it had taken Anne some time to calm down after hearing that statement. Once she had, she'd agreed to give Elizabeth the money.

Elizabeth didn't tell her father any of that, though. It was pleasant to permit him to think her new cousin was a better person than, perhaps, she was. Who knew, with Mr. Bingley's influence, Anne might become more like him. Not that Mr. Bingley was perfect, but he was amiable and pleasant, and showed no sign of his affections wandering from his wife as they had from Jane. Of course, it hadn't been a month yet.

Elizabeth took her father's arm, missing him already, and headed back toward the house, where she knew Darcy awaited them. As they walked, she shook her head to dispel any lingering uncharitable thoughts. Let others fill the world with gloom and doubt. Elizabeth was determined to think everyone as happily married, and as happy in love, as she and Darcy were.

LONDON

[S]he almost regretted not thanking Lady Catherine.

Epilogue

Elizabeth walked with her daughter, Lizzy, to the Girls' Garden, followed by their nanny and her two-year-old son, William.

"But William isn't a girl," Lizzy complained, looking back over her shoulder at her squirming little brother.

"Boys are allowed if they're young enough," Elizabeth said.

"How young do they have to be?"

Elizabeth suppressed a smile. Her daughter always had more questions. "I'm not sure, but I think they are allowed if they are under six."

"I'm nearly six. Does that mean if I was a boy, I wouldn't be allowed soon?" Lizzy asked.

"I'm not sure precisely what Lady Agatha's rules are. When William is almost six, we'll have to ask her."

They rounded the hedge that screened the Girls' Garden from the bulk of the grounds. William squealed in delight, spotting a painted rocking horse. Elizabeth gave an encouraging nod to their nanny and she put the boy down. On sturdy legs, he started running toward the horse, dodging around older children as they played.

Lizzy let out her own squeal, no longer concerned about her questions as she recognized the Bingleys' daughter, who was her age. Elizabeth exchanged an amused look with the nanny and left to join the adults. She loved her children dearly, but this was her party too and she welcomed the chance to see her sister and cousins.

She crossed the lawn to where Jane and Anne sat together. The two had become good friends, a happy situation as Richard had inherited Lady Catherine's personal estate a few months ago. It bordered Rosings, putting their homes a little over a mile apart. "You see each other all the time," Elizabeth teased. "You should be mingling and engaging other people."

"I've been avoiding some of them," Anne said. She pulled a face.

"Especially your sister."

"Lydia?" Elizabeth asked. "Last time I saw her, it seemed as if she'd gotten over her snobbishness."

"She has," Jane said.

"I admit she has," Anne said.

"Some new quirk, then?" Elizabeth knew Lydia could be trying, but privately thought Anne had never given her little sister a fair chance.

"Not so much a quirk." Anne sighed. "I guess I just don't want to hear about the twenty mile hike she took with Matlock last week or her new hunter. I keep hoping she'll have children so she'll be forced to slow down at least a little."

Elizabeth held her peace, not pointing out that Lydia was nearly ten years Anne's junior.

"They both like it that way," Jane said, her tone soothing.

"Well, I suppose I should like it too," Anne said. "I would rather have your son inherit the title than a hypothetical one of Lydia's."

"Thanks to Lady Catherine, we have more than enough," Jane said. "I don't covet Henry's title for our Thomas."

Anne gave Jane a speculative look. "No, I suppose you don't. It's a shame I'm not more like you, Jane. I think I've too much of my mother in me. I'm ashamed to admit it, but I was angry when I learned she'd willed her holdings away from me, as if I need more when I have Rosings."

"Even though it was to Richard?" Jane appeared genuinely surprised, as close to reprimanding as Elizabeth knew her to get.

"Yes." Anne shook her head. "I should have realized that by refusing to reconcile with her, I gave my mother a reason to will her property elsewhere. It was her way of telling me how disappointed she is in me one final time, and I must never forget it, because the lands border mine and you live on them, giving me reason to visit."

"She did write in her will that she gave them to Richard because he was a hero at Waterloo," Jane said, her tone tentative.

"That's nonsense," Anne said. "She never cared about that kind of thing."

"Still, it may not have been against you. It may have been to be kind to Richard. They did share a certain closeness."

Elizabeth frowned. "I'm afraid I agree with Anne. I don't think it was a matter of giving it to Richard, but of not giving it to Anne."

Anne nodded, her face set. "I agree. Mother died a bitter, friendless woman. If she'd admitted she was wrong, I would have made my peace with her, but she insisted to the end that she was cheated out of Rosings. She always maintained dragging Elizabeth away in a carriage was right, but Darcy and Henry evicting her was criminal. She would tell that to anyone who would listen. Fortunately, it didn't take too long before people stopped listening, except Mr. Collins."

"I thought her estate was in a different parish," Elizabeth said, glancing to Jane for confirmation.

"It is," Anne replied. "But he remained loyal to her. He would visit her at least twice a week. He was her only company, because she couldn't bring herself to be friends with her servants."

"I wrote her every month," Jane said quietly.

Anne turned to her in surprise. "Why?"

"We stayed with her for about two weeks, just after we were married. I'm sure you recall. Richard felt sorry for her. Then he got his regiment. I wrote her a thank you letter, which she answered at length. It didn't seem right not to respond."

Elizabeth decided not to say anything about good manners being rewarded. She had the impression Jane already felt guilty about their inheritance. Elizabeth realized that was the true reason her sister wanted to make Lady Catherine's generosity about Richard, because Jane would feel she'd cheated Anne if Lady Catherine's kindness had been aimed at her. Yet, being Jane, she didn't want to take the easy way out, claiming the action as spiteful, because she didn't like to believe in spite. Elizabeth glanced at Anne, hoping her mind hadn't gone down the path of concluding subterfuge on Jane's part. Jane was incapable of subterfuge or plots of any kind.

Anne regarded Jane for a long moment. "I'm glad you inherited," she finally said. "You and Charlotte are my favorite neighbors, although I could do without Mr. Collins."

"Anne," came a stage whisper from the edge of the garden.

Elizabeth turned to see Darcy, Richard and Bingley standing at the very edge of the Girls' Garden, grinning like errant children. She laughed, standing. "I think we'd best go to them, before they incur Lady Agatha's wrath by coming in any farther."

A glance showed Lizzy and William well in hand, Lizzy under the watchful eyes of the Bingleys' nanny, playing with their daughter. That left Elizabeth's nanny with only William to look after, a still challenging task as he was a bundle of energy and trouble.

When Elizabeth reached the edge of the garden, Darcy offered his arm. Taking it, Elizabeth strolled alongside him, Bingley and Anne to one side, Jane and Richard to the other.

"How was the fencing?" Elizabeth asked.

"Peter beat Henry three out of five," Darcy said.

"Did Henry demand a rematch?" Anne asked.

"Yes, but not today."

Elizabeth caught Anne's smile at that and wondered if her cousin was hoping Lord Henry was finally slowing down. Elizabeth hoped not. Far from envying Henry and Lydia their energy, she thought they all benefited from it. Except when Lydia was being trying, their liveliness was contagious.

The six of them walked together for a time, conversing easily. They often saw others they knew, acknowledging friends and acquaintances with a wave. Elizabeth couldn't help but reflect on how happy her life had become.

Eventually, Bingley begged off to go dine, increasingly one of his favorite occupations. Anne accompanied him, as she generally did. She wasn't what Elizabeth would describe as a clinging wife, but she didn't like to let Bingley off on his own for too many hours at a time. Too, perhaps, Anne recalled another time in the buffet room, years ago, when Bingley had laughed with a flirtatious widow.

Soon after, Jane and Richard left the lawn to go dance. They both had wistful smiles on their faces as they departed. Neither danced as much as they used to, unlike Lydia and Henry, but when they did, it was usually with each other. She looked up at Darcy speculatively, hoping he would ask her to dance later.

He likely would, as Georgiana would be dancing with all of her beaus. Darcy liked to keep an eye on them. Sometimes, Elizabeth wished Georgiana would simply pick one and be done with it, but knew she was having too much fun as one of the most eligible catches in London to do so.

"Is that your aunt and uncle?" Darcy said, drawing Elizabeth's attention back to the garden.

"It is," Elizabeth agreed, smiling.

Without consulting each other, they both changed course to head in that direction. Elizabeth let go of his arm as they sat down to enjoy the Gardiner's company. She smiled, watching his genuine pleasure in conversing with her aunt and uncle. It amused her she'd once lamented his inability to socialize. Now, he was perfectly comfortable talking to her relatives in the midst of a large party.

Elizabeth let the three talk, her mind going back to her conversation with Jane and Anne. Reminded of Lady Catherine's death by their conversation, Elizabeth reflected that, without her ultimatum against Georgiana, Elizabeth might never have read Darcy's letter or permitted him to court her. If it hadn't been for Lady Catherine's tyrannical ways, they might not be married at all, and Elizabeth wouldn't be the happiest woman in England. Now that it was too late, she almost regretted not thanking Lady Catherine for her intervention. Almost.

~ The End ~

About the Authors

Renata McMann

Renata McMann is the pen name of Teresa McCullough, someone who likes to rewrite public domain works. She is fond of thinking "What if?" To learn more about Renata's work and collaborations, visit www.renatamcmann.com.

Summer Hanford

Summer Hanford is primarily a fantasy author, although she enjoys turning her pen to science fiction, Regency and adventure as well. In 2014, Hanford was given the opportunity to team up with McMann to contribute to Renata's passion for *Pride and Prejudice* fan fiction, and is loving every moment of it. To learn more about Summer's other work, visit www.summerhanford.com.

Printed in Poland
by Amazon Fulfillment
Poland Sp. z o.o., Wrocław